Edith Wharton

The upper stratum of New York society into which Edith Wharton was born in 1862 would provide her with an abundance of material as a novelist, but it did not encourage her growth as an artist. Educated by tutors and governesses, she was raised for only one career: marriage. But her marriage, in 1885, to Edward Wharton was an emotional disappointment, if not a disaster. She would suffer the first of a series of nervous breakdowns in 1894. In spite of the strain of her marriage, or perhaps because of it, she began to write fiction, and published her first story in 1889.

Her first published book was a guide to interior decorating, but this was followed by several novels and story collections. They were written while the Whartons lived at Newport and New York, traveled in Europe, and built their grand home, The Mount, in Lenox, Massachusetts. In Europe she met Henry James, who became her good friend, traveling companion, and the sternest but most careful critic of her fiction. *The House of Mirth* (1905) was both a resounding critical success and a best-seller, as was *Ethan Frome* (1911). In 1913 the Whartons were divorced, and Edith took up permanent residence in France. Her subject, however, remained America, especially the moneyed New York of her youth. Her great satiric novel, *The Custom of the Country,* was published in 1913, and *The Age of Innocence* won her the Pulitzer Prize in 1921.

In her later years, she enjoyed the admiration of a new generation of writers, including Sinclair Lewis and F. Scott Fitzgerald. In all, she wrote some thirty books, including an autobiography, *A Backward Glance* (1934). She died at her villa near Paris in 1937.

C·A BANTAM CLASSIC·A BANTAM CLASSIC·A BANTAM CLASSIC·A BANTAM CLASSIC·A BANTAM

Ethan Frome and Other Short Fiction

by Edith Wharton

With an Introduction by
Mary Gordon

BANTAM BOOKS

TORONTO • NEW YORK • LONDON • SYDNEY • AUCKLAND

ETHAN FROME AND OTHER SHORT FICTION
A Bantam Book

PRINTING HISTORY

Ethan Frome *was first published in 1911.*
The Touchstone *was first published in 1900.*
The Last Asset *was first published in 1904.*
Xingu *was first published in 1911.*
The Other Two *was first published in 1914.*

Bantam Classic edition / April 1987

*Cover painting, Maurice Cullen: Logging in Winter, Beaupré,
Courtesy of Art Gallery of Hamilton, Ontario, Canada*

ISBN 0-553-21255-9

Published simultaneously in the United States and Canada

Bantam Books are published by Bantam Books, Inc. Its trademark, consisting of the words "Bantam Books" and the portrayal of a rooster, is registered in U.S. Patent and Trademark Office and in other countries. Marca Registrada. Bantam Books, Inc., 666 Fifth Avenue, New York, New York 10103.

PRINTED IN THE UNITED STATES OF AMERICA

O 0 9 8 7 6 5 4 3 2 1

CONTENTS

Introduction	vii
Ethan Frome	1
The Touchstone	91
The Last Asset	159
Xingu	191
The Other Two	217

INTRODUCTION

Edith Wharton was a lady. Every aspect of her life, from her birth on Fifth Avenue to her death on the Riviera, was touched by the enlivening hand of privilege, a hand, which though sure and firm, could quite readily constrict. An astonishing number of critics, seemingly almost against their will, think of her in terms of her class and wealth; even the most admiring commentators seem to let the punitive tone in. An upper-class woman was an absurd figure as a writer, particularly a writer of fiction. The novel, we have been told, grew up with the middle class, and by and large its creators have come from that temperate zone. Few of the genuinely poor have written novels, nor have the unimaginably wealthy kept up their end. It takes a long time to write a novel; more than any other literary genre, it partakes of toil. The novelist as laborer is an idea that fulfills something important in the readerly imagination; to imagine a fashionable woman writing on a lapboard in her bed, as Edith Wharton did, offends our sense of what should be. Is it because we feel somewhat ashamed of devoting so much time to reading what has not happened and is not true? In any case, the novel has always had to defend itself against the charge that it is read by indolent ladies alternating pages with chocolates, killing time while waiting for their rakish lovers, or their fittings at the dressmaker's, or the shampooing of their little dogs.

Edith Wharton wrote in bed, her secretary sitting across the room patiently waiting to pick up the pages as they fell, like petals, to the floor. Wharton never wrote in a mean room, or an ugly one. The look of things, the rightness of them, was important to her. She could afford to make distinctions. She was the daughter of one of the oldest families of Old New York—the kind of family that resented the Astors and the Vanderbilts as parvenus. The love of beauty, but not only of "good things," seems to have been one of her earliest driving forces. She spent eight years of her childhood in Europe, and the return to New York shocked her: she would always, even in her most charitable moments, find New York to be a horror aesthetically. It seems odd to think of her as having been born during the Civil War, but 1862 was the year of her birth; and she lived to decry Mussolini. She came of age during that acutely felt and self-reflective historical time that was the transition to modernity.

But what was it a transition from? Our image of the nineteenth century as a time of solid and predictable probity is mere fantasy; Europe was regularly convulsed by political events, and by 1860 economic life was radically different from what it had been fifty years before. But the conventions of private life, it would seem, held. How they held and at what cost is the subject of most of the fiction we associate with Edith Wharton.

Her most successful and most fully realized novels, *The House of Mirth* and *The Age of Innocence*, concern themselves with the collision between the free spirit and the restraints of conventional society. But Edith Wharton was no simpleminded romantic; if she was aware of the price that society exacted, she was appalled by what would happen if society's props were pulled away. Her heart was with the sensitive, the impetuous, the sexually responsive, but her reason concluded it was better that they be sacrificed individually than bring down those who stood in their way. We find her caution sometimes hateful: why keep the structure up, we moderns ask ourselves, when it is only a shelter for rotting corpses, who steal oxygen from those who still draw breath?

But none of the great novelists was optimistic about the outcome if the human heart followed its course. Anna and Vronsky end up quarreling and disillusioned; Emma Bovary poisons herself, and not a day too soon. Oddly, for the texture of their fiction is so different, Wharton invites comparison with Hardy. For Hardy, the universe and its ambassador, Cruel Nature, are strong, implacable, ill-wishing forces. The weak human spirit has no chance. For Wharton, the universe is not natural but social; no less than the heaths or the unloving storms, the world of men waits to devour the responsive flesh. But unlike Hardy's natural forces, which destroy heedlessly and to no benefit, the society that Wharton presents feeds on its young for its survival. And the alternative is—what? An anarchy she shrank from and condemned. We do not go to Edith Wharton to find a problem solver. Her view of life is tragic, but her gods sit not on Olympus but on upholstered furniture in perfectly appointed rooms. And unlike the Greek gods, they have Reason and reations on their side, which they can summon by the silent raising of a gloved hand.

The biographical roots for Wharton's preoccupation with the sensitive, generous soul thwarted by society are obvious. She was the daughter of a stiff, judging mother and a kind but ineffectual and distant father. She had no reason to believe her parents understood her. They inhabited a world of social duty and social pleasure; her father's dilatory interest in his library—and in his daughter's increasingly frequent presence in it—was the closest anyone in the family came to an artistic or an intellectual life. Edith "scribbled"—poetry mostly—but no one took much notice of it. This, perhaps, was fortunate, for if they'd noticed they'd have discouraged it in no uncertain terms; ladies did not write. Edith came out, was proposed to, but the marriage was thwarted by the groom's mother, who resented the Whartons and their kind for having treated her with the cold indifference they reserved for the nouveaux riches. A man named Walter Berry then courted her but inexplicably failed to propose, although he became her lifelong friend.

These two rejections left her humiliated, and at twenty-four she married Teddy Wharton, a genial, simplehearted man who loved the outdoors and shared her affection for dogs. The dogs were almost all they had in common. Sexually, the marriage was a disaster, and after a short time there was no physical union between husband and wife. Nor did he understand her work. He seems not to have read her books, and once, while walking behind her, he remarked to a guest, "Look at that small waist. You'd never think she wrote a line of poetry."

When she was in her forties, her strong erotic nature was awakened by an affair with a journalist named Morton Fullerton. But as their relationship was reaching its maturity, Teddy Wharton had a kind of breakdown and revealed to his wife that he had squandered part (though by no means all) of her fortune and had kept a mistress in a Boston house—renting some of the house's other rooms to chorus girls. To Edith this must have seemed a grotesque, distorting mirror held up to her own life with Fullerton; their sexual relationship dissolved soon thereafter, though they remained always on good terms.

Long before the Fullerton affair, Edith Wharton had transformed herself from lady scribbler to *femme de lettres*. More than that: she had begun to earn money by her writing. It is impossible to trace this transformation; the pressure of some thrusting assurance—without which no one goes on writing—

must have inexorably made itself felt. She never gave up he interest in society, her position as a hostess, her luxurious an indefatigable traveling. But every morning she wrote, and he production is staggering: a score of novels and collections c stories, poems, and travel writing. Her great friends were Henr James and Bernard Berenson, but she was on easy terms with th nobility of several countries and entertained the artistic luminar ies who passed through or lived in Paris (although, notably, nc the circle whose center was Gertrude Stein). How odd, then, th she should write a book like *Ethan Frome*.

The source of the novel was a sledding accident that too place near Wharton's American home in Lenox, Massachusetts The incident resulted in the death of one eighteen-year-old gi and the maiming and permanent disfigurement of two others Wharton kept this incident in her mind for four years before sh began writing *Ethan Frome;* one can imagine it cropping up crowding out other more intellectual or fashionable images. Th preface that Wharton attached to *Ethan Frome* betrays her inse curity about her subject. She is almost defensive, as if assertin her right to cross the class boundaries she so fervently believe in. Yet, she assures us, in a sentence odd if only for its rathe humble straightforwardness: "It was the first subject I had eve approached with full confidence in its value, for my own pur pose, and a relative faith in my power to render at least part c what I saw in it."

What can she possibly have meant by this? That other sub jects, closer to her immediate experience, failed to grip her wit the immediate rightness of this one? Perhaps what took hold c her as a writer of fiction was the possibility of portraying a lif shaped almost exclusively by necessity. For, as Cynthia Ozic has pointed out, Wharton's life never felt the impress of neces sity. The double chance of her being free from any economi constraint and any familial emotional tie meant she could liv anywhere, see anyone, do anything. For Wharton and the peopl she chiefly wrote about, anguish came as a result of the soul' wrong choices. But the limits of Ethan Frome's life had thei roots in the physical. The poverty of the land and the ill health o his parents prematurely turned Ethan from a promising youn man studying engineering in Worcester—shyly taking pleasure i being referred to by his fellow students as "old Ethe" and "ol Stiff" and worrying about his awkwardness with local girls— into the embodiment of the Suffering Servant. Scarcity is character in the novel, the dark side of the Puritan austerity tha was part, Wharton felt, of the New England landscape itself. As the novel progresses, the grip of winter is more and more surely felt. Interestingly, the French translation of *Ethan Frome* is titled *Hiver*.

Ethan Frome is a masterpiece of evocation, and it is remarkable that in this tale about rural life written by a woman, some of the strongest images are not natural but mechanical and metallic, two categories that we associate with the urban male worker. Consider this description of a winter night:

> The night was perfectly still, and the air so dry and pure that it gave little sensation of cold. The effect produced on Frome was rather of a complete absence of atmosphere, as though nothing less tenuous than ether intervened between the white earth under his feet and the metallic dome overhead. "It's like being in an exhausted receiver," he thought. Four or five years earlier he had taken a year's course at a technological college at Worcester, and dabbled in the laboratory with a friendly professor of physics. (14)

And here is Edith Wharton describing the excluded Ethan looking in at the dance from which he must fetch Mattie:

> Seen thus, from the pure and frosty darkness in which he stood, it seemed to be seething in a mist of heat. The metal reflectors of the gas-jets sent crude waves of light against the whitewashed walls, and the iron flanks of the stove at the end of the hall looked as though they were heaving with volcanic fires. The floor was thronged with girls and young men. Down the side wall facing the window stood a row of kitchen chairs from which the older women had just risen. By this time the music had stopped, and the musicians—a fiddler, and the young lady who played the harmonium on Sundays—were hastily refreshing themselves at one corner of the supper table which aligned its devastated pie dishes and ice cream saucers at the end of the hall. The guests were preparing to leave, and the tide had already set toward the passage where coats and wraps were hung, when a young man with a sprightly foot and a shock of black hair shot into the middle of the floor and clapped his hands. (15)

These images are astonishing on several levels. Like meta
physical conceits, they bring together surprising combination
the winter night and an exhausted receiver; the country danc
and volcanic fires. In the case of both passages, some large
spiritual realm is suggested with a telegraphic spareness.
Ethan's mind there is room both for the whole world of scientifi
knowledge and for the sensual overrichness of hell. The youn
man with a shock of black hair is a diabolic figure; the pie dishe
are "devastated." In contrast to this, the emptiness of the winte
night in which all traces of the body have been eliminated seem
infinitely desirable. Yet these are the thoughts of a young man i
love with a young woman—and how appropriate. Ethan imag
ines that fate has destined that he will be forever the frozen chil
staring in at the warm room where his beloved stands before th
fire of ordinary happiness. What happens, of course, is incalcu
lably worse.

The second extraordinary aspect of these images is that the
were written by Edith Wharton. One of the problems for *Etha
Frome* is that, perhaps because of its length, perhaps because c
its emotional accessibility, it has become a standard high scho
text, and much of Wharton's extraordinary imaginative achieve
ment is lost to its first readers. But if all readers could be taug
before they are of voting age that it is possible for a writer t
write far outside the experiential range of his or her own lif
well, that could only be a good thing for the body politic. Th
reader should marvel—and I mean marvel literally, as in
response to a genuine mystery—at the fact that a woman wh
spent all her life among the rich and powerful knew to th
marrow of her writerly bones how a young man who had had on
year at a technical college felt when he was cold, and what
was like at a country dance for New England farmers. She coul
not possibly have attended one; she could not possibly even hav
looked, like Ethan, through the window: her self-regard woul
not have permitted it. Yet in a paragraph we know everythin
about those dances just as, in a few words, every unreal winte
night in our personal histories comes back to us, its inorgani
beauty heightened in our memories by the breathtaking power c
Wharton's language.

The power of the language—spare, passionate, and durable—
one of the factors that contributes to this highly dramatic story
utter lack of melodrama. Another factor is the story's relentles
insistence on the impossibility of happiness in the lives it de
scribes. Melodrama, really, is a palliative; it allows for release

even if the release is death. The death, in melodrama, is a beautiful one, eminently illustratable. The circle is inevitably closed; if the young mother dies, she has not failed her child; the lovers, if temporarily parted, will meet in eternity. Had Wharton allowed Ethan and Mattie to succeed in their original plan, she would have written melodrama. And she would have failed us, for what she has portrayed is far worse than the violent, untimely, self-willed death of two lovers. It is the horrible reversal of love that she shows us, the change of the beautiful love object into the disfigured, petty tormentor. *Ethan Frome* has elements of romance in it, but Wharton radically refuses the Romantic's romance with time. Time here is not the swift devastator—like the consumers of the pie and ice cream at the dance. It is rather the gradual, relentless poisoner; each day a bit more of life is soured, hardened, and the crust, unpalatable, must nevertheless be consumed.

The end of *Ethan Frome* is, in fact, the triumph of the realistic mode over the Romantic one. Our penultimate vision of Mattie is of an ardent young woman about to face her death for love. Our last encounter with her—we are spared the visual details of her impairment—is our hearing her complain about the insufficiency of Zeena's tending the fire. "It's on'y just been made up this very minute. Zeena fell asleep and slep' ever so long, and I thought I'd be frozen stiff before I could wake her up and get her to 'tend to it." (86)

The character of Zeena is a brilliant portrayal of the kind of woman whose métier is illness and whose strength comes from the kind of certainty invented by the invalid's unlimited free time and the innocence born of the truth that most wrongdoing requires a physical capacity the invalid lacks or chooses to stifle. Ethan married her because he was both grateful to her for nursing his mother and fearful of losing his mind, as his mother did, if he stayed by himself on the desolate farmstead. But marriage turns Zeena from nurse to invalid. She becomes expert at her own symptoms, a connoisseur of the latest medical knowledge as it applies to her own case. She makes trips to consult doctors—her last one is the occasion of Ethan and Mattie's only night alone together—and comes back "laden with expensive remedies . . . her last visit to Springfield had been commemorated by her paying twenty dollars for an electric battery of which she had never learned the use." (32) But in fact, Zeena does not travel only to consult a doctor; her trip's real purpose is both to get medical justification and to lay plans for Mattie's being replaced by a hired girl. The efficiency and speed with which she achieves her goal are thrilling to watch: she is the consummate destroyer, all the more horrifying because her destruction brings her no pleasure. Her only prosperity will accrue from nursing her symptoms, from her satisfaction at having destroyed the lives of two people whose capacity for happiness is greater than her own, and from the triumphs of having pressed the claims of her legitimacy and having kept her man.

But Fate is not even kind to the twisted desires of the legitimate wife. Zeena must nurse the woman who stole her husband from her; Mattie and Ethan's physical incapacity restores her strength. There is, though, the suggestion that however unbearable the conditions of Mattie and Zeena's life, Ethan's is worse. The women afford each other a kind of dreadful company, carping at each other with the freedom of equals. It is Ethan who has been utterly destroyed. The worst aspect of his survival is the Frome longevity. "Ethan'll likely touch a hundred," (4) says a Starkfield observer. We recall that the wife of one of the Ethan Fromes in the graveyard was named Endurance. Endurance is both the stone that crushes Ethan's life and the dark god in whose service he is raised up. Silent, maimed, he is heroic in his very bending to the Necessity that Edith Wharton lived her life so far from.

It is with a jolt that we turn from Starkfield to the world of Edith Wharton's short stories. The characters in these stories are typical of the people Wharton lived among, and if the stories lack the austere perfections of *Ethan Frome*—which Wharton referred to as her "granite outcroppings"—they provide a worldly massiveness that satisfies another kind of readerly desire. If *Ethan Frome* is a Shaker pie safe, these stories are a Louis XV armoire; if Scarcity is a character in *Ethan Frome*, then Artifice lives in the stories. Concealment is an important activity for people whose lives are radically divorced from the natural. Spontaneity is no virtue in a world whose center is the drawing room; under the gaze of ancestral portraits in heavy frames, one does not act directly from the heart. Or one does at one's peril and most probably to one's loss. Yet under all the well-tailored clothes are hearts and bodies whose demands press. These people must live their lives and move among their kind; their employment is the work of human relations, and the enforced constrictions of that field create demands and sorrows almost as impossible as the situation of Ethan and Mattie.

"The Other Two" is one of Wharton's most curiously modern stories. Alice Haskett Varick Waythorn is the survivor of two divorces; the story begins at the inception of her third marriage. It is told from the point of view of her latest husband, who looks upon the prospect of marriage with Alice with a comfortable and quiet optimism. Alice so embodies the domestic harmony he has always prized and so easily fits into his notions of private felicity that he congratulates himself on his liberality in not balking at her past failures. He understands that she has triumphed over her victimization with a quiet heroism of a particularly feminine kind. In the end, however, he discovers that what he thought was heroism was really a species of ambitiousness. She does possess strength, but it is the strength of being able to invent herself in the image of whatever man is the next step on her steadily upward climb. In a brilliantly realized scene, Waythorn takes tea in his library with the other two husbands and realizes that he will never genuinely possess his wife, because if there is an essentially true Alice, she will never give it to a man. Mysteriously, ineffably, this consummate wife will nourish the self that will present itself to no husband.

The theme of divorce recurs frequently in Wharton's fiction, and this is not surprising, either in biographical or in aesthetic terms. If marriage is the perfect metaphor for the conjunction of public and private life, divorce is the ideal one for that life's dissolution. Wharton must have often contemplated divorcing Teddy, but she shrank from the kind of implications of divorce that she suggests in "Autres Temps" (not included in this collection). This subtle, wistful story's theme is that "the success or failure of the deepest human experiences may hang on a matter of chronology." "Autres Temps" is the story of a Mrs. Lidcote, who left her husband and was divorced in an age when this meant being cast out by society. Her daughter, Leila, does the same thing at a time when it means only a new note in a hostess's engagement book.

Mrs. Lidcote has an admirer, Franklin Ide, who tries to reassure her that her belief that she is still being punished by society is only her paranoia. But it turns out that she is right. Leila must uneasily hide her mother upstairs—with protestations that she is merely securing her mother's rest—while she entertains an ambassador's wife below. It is understood that Mrs. Lidcote's presence at the table would scotch Leila's new husband's chances for a diplomatic post. Changes in mores have come too late for Mrs. Lidcote; she has lost everything, including her lover. "She had had to pay the last bitterest price of learning that love has a price: that it is worth so much and no more. She had known the anguish of watching the man she loved discover this first, and of reading the discovery in his eyes." She cannot accept the kind offer of Mr. Ide because she knows that for women like her there are no second chances.

It is interesting to compare the treatment of attractive, traditionally feminine women in the works of Edith Wharton and George Eliot. For Eliot, these women are destructive parasites, manipulative, acquisitive, a symptom of all that is harmful in human life. But Wharton grants these women their strengths; she sees that prettiness need not be a veneer covering up corruption, that underneath a charming facade there may be a valuable repository of virtue. This idea is treated comically in "Xingu," in which Mrs. Roby, the supposed flibbertigibbet, shows up the pseudointellectual women of the reading circle, thereby saving them from social disaster but being ostracized by them (it can only have been a relief) for her pains.

The question of female beauty and its powers forms the center of the novella "The Touchstone." "Genius is of small use to a woman who does not know how to do her hair," (100) Wharton tells us. But does she speak from the secure perspective of a woman who believes she does know how to do her hair, or the anxious one of the woman who fears that she does not? The matter of "The Touchstone" concerns the love of a distinguished woman writer, Mrs. Aubyn, for a young man, Glennard, who cannot reciprocate her passion because he does not find her beautiful. After Mrs. Aubyn's death, he falls in love with a young woman as poor as himself and as lovely as his dreams. In order to have enough money to marry her, he offers Mrs. Aubyn's love letters for publication. The book is a wild success—but Glennard is torn apart by self-revulsion. He deliberately arranges that his wife will find him out, and her response is the triumph of one of those Wharton women, cool, harmonious, seemingly impassive, who are the source and the embodiment—the "touchstone"—of the only genuine virtue in a world steeped in corruption, self-service, and self-deceit.

The great strength of these stories comes from the beautifully sculpted sentences that are the foundation of Wharton's formal genius. I mean *formal* in its two senses: pertaining to form, and the opposite of informal. Wharton, like her friend Henry James, writes always from a distance. The observer, never dispassionate, is at the aristocrat's remove. This position allows Wharton the opportunity for the grand, patrician generalization, impossible in a less wrought prose. It may no longer be open to writers in the new democracy of fictional language to write sentences like these: "The desire to propitiate a divinity is generally in inverse ratio to its responsiveness." ("Xingu," 200) "If man is at times indirectly flattered by the moral superiority of women, her mental ascendency is extenuated by no such oblique tribute to his powers." ("The Touchstone," 100) And it would be difficult to imagine a contemporary feeling free to describe Rome as Wharton does in another story, "Roman Fever" (not included here):

> The clear heaven overhead was emptied of all its gold. Dusk spread over it, abruptly darkening the Seven Hills. Here and there lights began to twinkle through the foliage at their feet. Steps were coming and going on the deserted terrace—waiters looking out of the doorway at the head of the stairs, then reappearing with trays and napkins and flasks of wine. Tables were moved, chairs straightened. A feeble string of electric lights flickered out. Some vases of faded flowers were carried away, and brought back replenished. A stout lady in a dust-coat suddenly appeared, asking in broken Italian if any one had seen the elastic band which held together her tattered Baedeker. She poked with her stick under the table at which she had lunched, the waiters assisting.

The genius, then, is formal, it is distant, but it is never cold. For all her sophistication, Wharton believed in innocence (Ethan is an innocent), and her sympathy is with the innocents who are shredded in the teeth of the machinery of the world. Perhaps the truest reflection of her sense of life occurs in her story "The Last Asset," which has at its center two innocents, Samuel and Hermione Newell, a father and daughter whose lives have been shaped and disfigured by the shrewd and desperate calculations of the woman who is wife to one, mother to the other. Newell offers his philosophy to a fellow American whom he meets in a Paris restaurant: "If you make up your mind not to be happy there's no reason why you shouldn't have a pretty good time." (162)

Newell has been estranged from his wife and daughter because his wife has, in some way that Wharton does not specify, emotionally assassinated him. But Mrs. Newell has made a brilliant match for her unpromising daughter, with a member of one of the oldest French families, and the marriage cannot take place unless Mr. Newell appears at the wedding. At first he refuses; he has asked only to be left in peace, to his life of small activities. But in the end the goodness and courage of Hermione triumph. "It was one more testimony to life's indefatigable renewals, to nature's secret of drawing fragrance from corruption; and as his eyes turned from the girl's illuminated presence to the resigned and stoical figure sunk in the adjoining chair, it occurred to him that he had perhaps worked better than he knew in placing them, if only for a moment, side by side." (189)

It is possible that only a woman born of privilege could have written those sentences; but what is necessary is that the woman who created them was first and most passionately from her birth a writer, and a writer with a heart.

MARY GORDON

ETHAN FROME

I had the story, bit by bit, from various people, and, as generally happens in such cases, each time it was a different story.

If you know Starkfield, Massachusetts, you know the post-office. If you know the post-office you must have seen Ethan Frome drive up to it, drop the reins on his hollow-backed bay and drag himself across the brick pavement to the white colonnade: and you must have asked who he was.

It was there that, several years ago, I saw him for the first time; and the sight pulled me up sharp. Even then he was the most striking figure in Starkfield, though he was but the ruin of a man. It was not so much his great height that marked him, for the "natives" were easily singled out by their lank longitude from the stockier foreign breed: it was the careless powerful look he had, in spite of a lameness checking each step like the jerk of a chain. There was something bleak and unapproachable in his face, and he was so stiffened and grizzled that I took him for an old man and was surprised to hear that he was not more than fifty-two. I had this from Harmon Gow, who had driven the stage from Bettsbridge to Starkfield in pre-trolley days and knew the chronicle of all the families on his line.

"He's looked that way ever since he had his smash-up; and that's twenty-four years ago come next February," Harmon threw out between reminiscent pauses.

The "smash-up" it was—I gathered from the same informant—which, besides drawing the red gash across Ethan Frome's forehead, had so shortened and warped his right side that it cost him a visible effort to take the few steps from his buggy to the post-office window. He used to drive in from his farm every day at about noon, and as that was my own hour for fetching my mail I often passed him in the porch or stood beside him while we waited on the motions of the distributing hand behind the grating. I noticed that, though he came so punctually, he seldom received anything but a copy of the *Bettsbridge Eagle,* which he put without a glance into his sagging pocket. At intervals, however, the post-master would hand him an envelope addressed to Mrs. Zenobia—or Mrs. Zeena—Frome, and usually bearing conspicuously in the upper left-hand corner the address of some manufacturer of patent medicine and the name of his specific. These documents my neighbour would also pocket without a glance, as if too much used to them to wonder at their number and variety, and would then turn away with a silent nod to the post-master.

Every one in Starkfield knew him and gave him a greeting tempered to his own grave mien; but his taciturnity was respected and it was only on rare occasions that one of the older men of the place detained him for a word. When this happened he would listen quietly, his blue eyes on the speaker's face, and answer in so low a tone that his words never reached me; then he would climb stiffly into his buggy, gather up the reins in his left hand and drive slowly away in the direction of his farm.

"It was a pretty bad smash-up?" I questioned Harmon, looking after Frome's retreating figure, and thinking how gallantly his lean brown head, with its shock of light hair, must have sat on his strong shoulders before they were bent out of shape.

"Wust kind," my informant assented. "More'n enough to kill most men. But the Fromes are tough. Ethan'll likely touch a hundred."

"Good God!" I exclaimed. At the moment Ethan Frome, after climbing to his seat, had leaned over to assure himself of the security of a wooden box—also with a druggist's label on it—which he had placed in the back of the buggy, and I saw his face as it probably looked when he thought himself alone. "*That* man touch a hundred? He looks as if he was dead and in hell now!"

Harmon drew a slab of tobacco from his pocket, cut off a wedge and pressed it into the leather pouch of his cheek. "Guess he's been in Starkfield too many winters. Most of the smart ones get away."

"Why didn't *he?*"

"Somebody had to stay and care for the folks. There warn't ever anybody but Ethan. Fust his father—then his mother—then his wife."

"And then the smash-up?"

Harmon chuckled sardonically. "That's so. He *had* to stay then."

"I see. And since then they've had to care for him?"

Harmon thoughtfully passed his tobacco to the other cheek. "Oh, as to that: I guess it's always Ethan done the caring."

Though Harmon Gow developed the tale as far as his mental and moral reach permitted there were perceptible gaps between his facts, and I had the sense that the deeper meaning of the story was in the gaps. But one phrase stuck in my memory and served as the nucleus about which I grouped my subsequent inferences: "Guess he's been in Starkfield too many winters."

Before my own time there was up I had learned to know what that meant. Yet I had come in the degenerate day of trolley, bicycle and rural delivery, when communication was easy between the scattered mountain villages, and the bigger towns in the valleys, such as Bettsbridge and Shadd's Falls, had libraries, theatres and Y. M. C. A. halls to which the youth of the hills could descend for recreation. But when winter shut down on Starkfield, and the village lay under a sheet of snow perpetually renewed from the pale skies, I began to see what life there—or rather its negation—must have been in Ethan Frome's young manhood.

I had been sent up by my employers on a job connected with the big power-house at Corbury Junction, and a long-drawn carpenters' strike had so delayed the work that I found myself anchored at Starkfield—the nearest habitable spot—for the best part of the winter. I chafed at first, and then, under the hypnotising effect of routine, gradually began to find a grim satisfaction in the life. During the early part of my stay I had been struck by the contrast between the vitality of the climate and the deadness of the community. Day by day, after the December snows were over, a blazing blue sky poured down torrents of light and air on the white landscape, which gave them back in an intenser glitter. One would have supposed that such an atmosphere must quicken the emotions as well as the blood; but it seemed to produce no change except that of retarding still more the sluggish pulse of Starkfield. When I had been there a little longer, and had seen this phase of crystal clearness followed by long stretches of sunless cold; when the storms of February had pitched their white tents about the devoted village and the wild cavalry of March winds had charged down to their support; I began to understand why Starkfield emerged from its six months' siege like a starved garrison capitulating without quarter. Twenty years earlier the means of resistance must have been far fewer, and the enemy in command of almost all the lines of access between the beleaguered villages; and, considering these things, I felt the sinister force of Harmon's phrase: "Most of the smart ones get away." But if that were the case, how could any combination of obstacles have hindered the flight of a man like Ethan Frome?

During my stay at Starkfield I lodged with a middle-aged widow colloquially known as Mrs. Ned Hale. Mrs. Hale's father had been the village lawyer of the previous generation, and "lawyer Varnum's house," where my landlady still lived with her mother, was the most considerable mansion in the village. It stood at one end of the main street, its classic portico and small-paned windows looking down a flagged path between Norway spruces to the slim white steeple of the Congregational church. It was clear that the Varnum fortunes were at the ebb, but the two women did what they could to preserve a decent dignity; and Mrs. Hale, in particular, had a certain wan refinement not out of keeping with her pale old-fashioned house.

In the "best parlour," with its black horse-hair and mahogany weakly illuminated by a gurgling Carcel lamp, I listened every evening to another and more delicately shaded version of the Starkfield chronicle. It was not that Mrs. Ned Hale felt, or affected, any social superiority to the people about her; it was only that the accident of a finer sensibility and a little more education had put just enough distance between herself and her neighbours to enable her to judge them with detachment. She was not unwilling to exercise this faculty, and I had great hopes of getting from her the missing facts of Ethan Frome's story, or rather such a key to his character as should co-ordinate the facts I knew. Her mind was a store-house of innocuous anecdote and any question about her acquaintances brought forth a volume of detail; but on the subject of Ethan Frome I found her unexpectedly reticent. There was no hint of disapproval in her reserve; I merely felt in her an insurmountable reluctance to speak of him or his affairs, a low "Yes, I knew them both . . . it was awful . . ." seeming to be the utmost concession that her distress could make to my curiosity.

So marked was the change in her manner, such depths of sad initiation did it imply, that, with some doubts as to my delicacy, I put the case anew to my village oracle, Harmon Gow; but got for my pains only an uncomprehending grunt.

"Ruth Varnum was always as nervous as a rat; and, come to think of it, she was the first one to see 'em after they was picked up. It happened right below lawyer Varnum's, down at the bend of the Corbury road, just round about the time that Ruth got engaged to Ned Hale. The young folks was all friends, and I guess she just can't bear to talk about it. She's had troubles enough of her own.''

All the dwellers in Starkfield, as in more notable communities, had had troubles enough of their own to make them comparatively indifferent to those of their neighbours; and though all conceded that Ethan Frome's had been beyond the common measure, no one gave me an explanation of the look in his face which, as I persisted in thinking, neither poverty nor physical suffering could have put there. Nevertheless, I might have contented myself with the story pieced together from these hints had it not been for the provocation of Mrs. Hale's silence, and—a little later—for the accident of personal contact with the man.

On my arrival at Starkfield, Denis Eady, the rich Irish grocer, who was the proprietor of Starkfield's nearest approach to a livery stable, had entered into an agreement to send me over daily to Corbury Flats, where I had to pick up my train for the Junction. But about the middle of the winter Eady's horses fell ill of a local epidemic. The illness spread to the other Starkfield stables and for a day or two I was put to it to find a means of transport. Then Harmon Gow suggested that Ethan Frome's bay was still on his legs and that his owner might be glad to drive me over.

I stared at the suggestion. ''Ethan Frome? But I've never even spoken to him. Why on earth should he put himself out for me?''

Harmon's answer surprised me still more. ''I don't know as he would; but I know he wouldn't be sorry to earn a dollar.''

I had been told that Frome was poor, and that the saw-mill and the arid acres of his farm yielded scarcely enough to keep his household through the winter; but I had not supposed him to be in such want as Harmon's words implied, and I expressed my wonder.

''Well, matters ain't gone any too well with him,'' Harmon said. ''When a man's been setting round like a hulk for twenty years or more, seeing things that want doing, it eats inter him, and he loses his grit. That Frome farm was always 'bout as bare's a milkpan when the cat's been round; and you know what one of them old water-mills is wuth nowadays. When Ethan could sweat over 'em both from sun-up to dark he kinder choked a living out of 'em; but his folks ate up most everything, even then, and I don't see how he makes out now. Fust his father got a kick, out haying, and went soft in the brain, and gave away money like Bible texts afore he died. Then his mother got queer and dragged along for years as weak as a baby; and his wife Zeena, she's always been the greatest hand at doctoring in the county. Sickness and trouble: that's what Ethan's had his plate full up with, ever since the very first helping."

The next morning, when I looked out, I saw the hollow-backed bay between the Varnum spruces, and Ethan Frome, throwing back his worn bearskin, made room for me in the sleigh at his side. After that, for a week, he drove me over every morning to Corbury Flats, and on my return in the afternoon met me again and carried me back through the icy night to Starkfield. The distance each way was barely three miles, but the old bay's pace was slow, and even with firm snow under the runners we were nearly an hour on the way. Ethan Frome drove in silence, the reins loosely held in his left hand, his brown seamed profile, under the helmet-like peak of the cap, relieved against the banks of snow like the bronze image of a hero. He never turned his face to mine, or answered, except in monosyllables, the questions I put, or such slight pleasantries as I ventured. He seemed a part of the mute melancholy landscape, an incarnation of its frozen woe, with all that was warm and sentient in him fast bound below the surface; but there was nothing unfriendly in his silence. I simply felt that he lived in a depth of moral isolation too remote for casual access, and I had the sense that his loneliness was not merely the result of his personal plight, tragic as I guessed that to be, but had in it, as Harmon Gow had hinted, the profound accumulated cold of many Starkfield winters.

Only once or twice was the distance between us bridged for a moment; and the glimpses thus gained confirmed my desire to know more. Once I happened to speak of an engineering job I had been on the previous year in Florida, and of the contrast between the winter landscape about us and that in which I had found myself the year before; and to my surprise Frome said suddenly: "Yes: I was down there once, and for a good while afterward I could call up the sight of it in winter. But now it's all snowed under."

He said no more, and I had to guess the rest from the inflection of his voice and his sharp relapse into silence.

Another day, on getting into my train at the Flats, I missed a volume of popular science—I think it was on some recent discoveries in bio-chemistry—which I had carried with me to read on the way. I thought no more about it till I got into the sleigh again that evening, and saw the book in Frome's hand.

"I found it after you were gone," he said.

I put the volume into my pocket and we dropped back into our usual silence; but as we began to crawl up the long hill from Corbury Flats to the Starkfield ridge I became aware in the dusk that he had turned his face to mine.

"There are things in that book that I didn't know the first word about," he said.

I wondered less at his words than at the queer note of resentment in his voice. He was evidently surprised and slightly aggrieved at his own ignorance.

"Does that sort of thing interest you?" I asked.

"It used to."

"There are one or two rather new things in the book: there have been some big strides lately in that particular line of research." I waited a moment for an answer that did not come; then I said: "If you'd like to look the book through I'd be glad to leave it with you."

He hesitated, and I had the impression that he felt himself about to yield to a stealing tide of inertia; then, "Thank you—I'll take it," he answered shortly.

I hoped that this incident might set up some more direct communication between us. Frome was so simple and straightforward that I was sure his curiosity about the book was based on a genuine interest in its subject. Such tastes and acquirements in a man of his condition made the contrast more poignant between his outer situation and his inner needs, and I hoped that the chance of giving expression to the latter might at least unseal his lips. But something in his past history, or in his present way of living, had apparently driven him too deeply into himself for any casual impulse to draw him back to his kind. At our next meeting he made no allusion to the book, and our intercourse seemed fated to remain as negative and one-sided as if there had been no break in his reserve.

Frome had been driving me over to the Flats for about a week when one morning I looked out of my window into a thick snow-fall. The height of the white waves massed against the garden-fence and along the wall of the church showed that the storm must have been going on all night, and that the drifts were likely to be heavy in the open. I thought it probable that my train would be delayed; but I had to be at the power-house for an hour or two that afternoon, and I decided, if Frome turned up, to push through to the Flats and wait there till my train came in. I don't know why I put it in the conditional, however, for I never doubted that Frome would appear. He was not the kind of man to be turned from his business by any commotion of the elements; and at the appointed hour his sleigh glided up through the snow like a stage-apparition behind thickening veils of gauze.

I was getting to know him too well to express either wonder or gratitude at his keeping his appointment; but I exclaimed in surprise as I saw him turn his horse in a direction opposite to that of the Corbury road.

"The railroad's blocked by a freight-train that got stuck in a drift below the Flats," he explained, as we jogged off into the stinging whiteness.

"But look here—where are you taking me, then?"

"Straight to the Junction, by the shortest way," he answered, pointing up School House Hill with his whip.

"To the Junction—in this storm? Why, it's a good ten miles!"

"The bay'll do it if you give him time. You said you had some business there this afternoon. I'll see you get there."

He said it so quietly that I could only answer: "You're doing me the biggest kind of a favour."

"That's all right," he rejoined.

Abreast of the schoolhouse the road forked, and we dipped down a lane to the left, between hemlock boughs bent inward to their trunks by the weight of the snow. I had often walked that way on Sundays, and knew that the solitary roof showing through bare branches near the bottom of the hill was that of Frome's saw-mill. It looked exanimate enough, with its idle wheel looming above the black stream dashed with yellow-white spume, and its cluster of sheds sagging under their white load. Frome did not even turn his head as we drove by, and still in silence we began to mount the next slope. About a mile farther, on a road I had never travelled, we came to an orchard of starved apple-trees writhing over a hillside among outcroppings of slate that nuzzled up through the snow like animals pushing out their noses to breathe. Beyond the orchard lay a field or two, their boundaries lost under drifts; and above the fields, huddled against the white immensities of land and sky, one of those lonely New England farm-houses that make the landscape lonelier.

"That's my place," said Frome, with a sideway jerk of his lame elbow; and in the distress and oppression of the scene I did not know what to answer. The snow had ceased, and a flash of watery sunlight exposed the house on the slope above us in all its plaintive ugliness. The black wraith of a deciduous creeper flapped from the porch, and the thin wooden walls, under their worn coat of paint, seemed to shiver in the wind that had risen with the ceasing of the snow.

"The house was bigger in my father's time: I had to take down the 'L,' a while back," Frome continued, checking with a twitch of the left rein the bay's evident intention of turning in through the broken-down gate.

I saw then that the unusually forlorn and stunted look of the house was partly due to the loss of what is known in New England as the "L": that long deep-roofed adjunct usually built at right angles to the main house, and connecting it, by way of storerooms and tool-house, with the wood-shed and cowbarn. Whether because of its symbolic sense, the image it presents of a life linked with the soil, and enclosing in itself the chief sources of warmth and nourishment, or whether merely because of the consolatory thought that it enables the dwellers in that harsh climate to get to their morning's work without facing the weather, it is certain that the "L" rather than the house itself seems to be the centre, the actual hearth-stone of the New England farm. Perhaps this connection of ideas, which had often occurred to me in my rambles about Starkfield, caused me to hear a wistful note in Frome's words, and to see in the diminished dwelling the image of his own shrunken body.

"We're kinder side-tracked here now," he added, "but there was considerable passing before the railroad was carried through to the Flats." He roused the lagging bay with another twitch; then, as if the mere sight of the house had let me too deeply into his confidence for any farther pretence of reserve, he went on slowly: "I've always set down the worst of mother's trouble to that. When she got the rheumatism so bad she couldn't move around she used to sit up there and watch the road by the hour; and one year, when they was six months mending the Bettsbridge pike after the floods, and Harmon Gow had to bring his stage round this way, she picked up so that she used to get down to the gate most days to see him. But after the trains begun running nobody ever come by here to speak of, and mother never could get it through her head what had happened, and it preyed on her right along till she died."

As we turned into the Corbury road the snow began to fall again, cutting off our last glimpse of the house; and Frome's silence fell with it, letting down between us the old veil of reticence. This time the wind did not cease with the return of the snow. Instead, it sprang up to a gale which now and then, from a tattered sky, flung pale sweeps of sunlight over a landscape chaotically tossed. But the bay was as good as Frome's word, and we pushed on to the Junction through the wild white scene.

In the afternoon the storm held off, and the clearness in the west seemed to my inexperienced eye the pledge of a fair evening. I finished my business as quickly as possible, and we set out for Starkfield with a good chance of getting there for supper. But at sunset the clouds gathered again, bringing an earlier night, and the snow began to fall straight and steadily from a sky without wind, in a soft universal diffusion more confusing than the gusts and eddies of the morning. It seemed to be a part of the thickening darkness, to be the winter night itself descending on us layer by layer.

The small ray of Frome's lantern was soon lost in this smothering medium, in which even his sense of direction, and the bay's homing instinct, finally ceased to serve us. Two or three times some ghostly landmark sprang up to warn us that we were astray, and then was sucked back into the mist; and when we finally regained our road the old horse began to show signs of exhaustion. I felt myself to blame for having accepted Frome's offer, and after a short discussion I persuaded him to let me get out of the sleigh and walk along through the snow at the bay's side. In this way we struggled on for another mile or two, and at last reached a point where Frome, peering into what seemed to me formless night, said: "That's my gate down yonder."

The last stretch had been the hardest part of the way. The bitter cold and the heavy going had nearly knocked the wind out of me, and I could feel the horse's side ticking like a clock under my hand.

"Look here, Frome," I began, "there's no earthly use in your going any farther—" but he interrupted me: "Nor you neither. There's been about enough of this for anybody."

I understood that he was offering me a night's shelter at the farm, and without answering I turned into the gate at his side, and followed him to the barn, where I helped him to unharness and bed down the tired horse. When this was done he unhooked the lantern from the sleigh, stepped out again into the night, and called to me over his shoulder: "This way."

Far off above us a square of light trembled through the screen of snow. Staggering along in Frome's wake I floundered toward it, and in the darkness almost fell into one of the deep drifts against the front of the house. Frome scrambled up the slippery steps of the porch, digging a way through the snow with his heavily booted foot. Then he lifted his lantern, found the latch, and led the way into the house. I went after him into a low unlit passage, at the back of which a ladder-like staircase rose into obscurity. On our right a line of light marked the door of the room which had sent its ray across the night; and behind the door I heard a woman's voice droning querulously.

Frome stamped on the worn oil-cloth to shake the snow from his boots, and set down his lantern on a kitchen chair which was the only piece of furniture in the hall. Then he opened the door.

"Come in," he said; and as he spoke the droning voice grew still . . .

It was that night that I found the clue to Ethan Frome, and began to put together this vision of his story.

CHAPTER I

The village lay under two feet of snow, with drifts at the windy corners. In a sky of iron the points of the Dipper hung like icicles and Orion flashed his cold fires. The moon had set, but the night was so transparent that the white house-fronts between the elms looked grey against the snow, clumps of bushes made black stains on it, and the basement windows of the church sent shafts of yellow light far across the endless undulations.

Young Ethan Frome walked at a quick pace along the deserted street, past the bank and Michael Eady's new brick store and Lawyer Varnum's house with the two black Norway spruces at the gate. Opposite the Varnum gate, where the road fell away toward the Corbury valley, the church reared its slim white steeple and narrow peristyle. As the young man walked toward it the upper windows drew a black arcade along the side wall of the building, but from the lower openings, on the side where the ground sloped steeply down to the Corbury road, the light shot its long bars, illuminating many fresh furrows in the track leading to the basement door, and showing, under an adjoining shed, a line of sleighs with heavily blanketed horses.

The night was perfectly still, and the air so dry and pure that it gave little sensation of cold. The effect produced on Frome was rather of a complete absence of atmosphere, as though nothing less tenuous than ether intervened between the white earth under his feet and the metallic dome overhead. "It's like being in an exhausted receiver," he thought. Four or five years earlier he had taken a year's course at a technological college at Worcester, and dabbled in the laboratory with a friendly professor of physics; and the images supplied by that experience still cropped up, at unexpected moments, through the totally different associations of thought in which he had since been living. His father's death, and the misfortunes following it, had put a premature end to Ethan's studies; but though they had not gone far enough to be of much practical use they had fed his fancy and made him aware of huge cloudy meanings behind the daily face of things.

As he strode along through the snow the sense of such meanings glowed in his brain and mingled with the bodily flush produced by his sharp tramp. At the end of the village he paused before the darkened front of the church. He stood there a moment, breathing quickly, and looking up and down the street, in which not another figure moved. The pitch of the Corbury road, below lawyer Varnum's spruces, was the favourite coasting-ground of Starksfield, and on clear evenings the church corner rang till late with the shouts of the coasters; but to-night not a sled darkened the whiteness of the long declivity. The hush of midnight lay on the village, and all its waking life was gathered behind the church windows, from which strains of dance-music flowed with the broad bands of yellow light.

The young man, skirting the side of the building, went down the slope toward the basement door. To keep out of range of the revealing rays from within he made a circuit through the untrodden snow and gradually approached the farther angle of the basement wall. Thence, still hugging the shadow, he edged his way cautiously forward to the nearest window, holding back his straight spare body and craning his neck till he got a glimpse of the room.

Seen thus, from the pure and frosty darkness in which he stood, it seemed to be seething in a mist of heat. The metal reflectors of the gas-jets sent crude waves of light against the whitewashed walls, and the iron flanks of the stove at the end of the hall looked as though they were heaving with volcanic fires. The floor was thronged with girls and young men. Down the side wall facing the window stood a row of kitchen chairs from which the older women had just risen. By this time the music had stopped, and the musicians—a fiddler, and the young lady who played the harmonium on Sundays—were hastily refreshing themselves at one corner of the supper-table which aligned its devastated pie-dishes and ice-cream saucers on the platform at the end of the hall. The guests were preparing to leave, and the tide had already set toward the passage where coats and wraps were hung, when a young man with a sprightly foot and a shock of black hair shot into the middle of the floor and clapped his hands. The signal took instant effect. The musicians hurried to their instruments, the dancers—some already half-muffled for departure—fell into line down each side of the room, the older spectators slipped back to their chairs, and the lively young man, after diving about here and there in the throng, drew forth a girl who had already wound a cherry-coloured "fascinator" about her head, and, leading her up to the end of the floor, whirled her down its length to the bounding tune of a Virginia reel.

Frome's heart was beating fast. He had been straining for a glimpse of the dark head under the cherry-coloured scarf and it vexed him that another eye should have been quicker than his. The leader of the reel, who looked as if he had Irish blood in his veins, danced well, and his partner caught his fire. As she passed down the line, her light figure swinging from hand to hand in circles of increasing swiftness, the scarf flew off her head and stood out behind her shoulders, and Frome, at each turn, caught sight of her laughing panting lips, the cloud of dark hair about her forehead, and the dark eyes which seemed the only fixed points in a maze of flying lines.

The dancers were going faster and faster, and the musicians, to keep up with them, belaboured their instruments like jockeys lashing their mounts on the home-stretch; yet it seemed to the young man at the window that the reel would never end. Now and then he turned his eyes from the girl's face to that of her partner, which, in the exhilaration of the dance, had taken on a look of almost impudent ownership. Denis Eady was the son of Michael Eady, the ambitious Irish grocer, whose suppleness and effrontery had given Starkfield its first notion of "smart" business methods, and whose new brick store testified to the success of the attempt. His son seemed likely to follow in his steps, and was meanwhile applying the same arts to the conquest of the Starkfield maidenhood. Hitherto Ethan Frome had been content to think him a mean fellow; but now he positively invited a horse-whipping. It was strange that the girl did not seem aware of it: that she could lift her rapt face to her dancer's, and drop her hands into his, without appearing to feel the offence of his look and touch.

Frome was in the habit of walking into Starkfield to fetch home his wife's cousin, Mattie Silver, on the rare evenings when some chance of amusement drew her to the village. It was his wife who had suggested, when the girl came to live with them, that such opportunities should be put in her way. Mattie Silver came from Stamford, and when she entered the Fromes' household to act as her cousin Zeena's aid it was thought best, as she came without pay, not to let her feel too sharp a contrast between the life she had left and the isolation of a Starkfield farm. But for this—as Frome sardonically reflected—it would hardly have occurred to Zeena to take any thought for the girl's amusement.

When his wife first proposed that they should give Mattie an occasional evening out he had inwardly demurred at having to do the extra two miles to the village and back after his hard day on the farm; but not long afterward he had reached the point of wishing that Starkfield might give all its nights to revelry.

Mattie Silver had lived under his roof for a year, and from early morning till they met at supper he had frequent chances of seeing her; but no moments in her company were comparable to those when, her arm in his, and her light step flying to keep time with his long stride, they walked back through the night to the farm. He had taken to the girl from the first day, when he had driven over to the Flats to meet her, and she had smiled and waved to him from the train, crying out, "You must be Ethan!" as she jumped down with her bundles, while he reflected, looking over her slight person: "She don't look much on housework, but she ain't a fretter, anyhow." But it was not only that the coming to his house of a bit of hopeful young life was like the lighting of a fire on a cold hearth. The girl was more than the bright serviceable creature he had thought her. She had an eye to see and an ear to hear: he could show her things and tell her things, and taste the bliss of feeling that all he imparted left long reverberations and echoes he could wake at will.

It was during their night walks back to the farm that he felt most intensely the sweetness of this communion. He had always been more sensitive than the people about him to the appeal of natural beauty. His unfinished studies had given form to this sensibility and even in his unhappiest moments field and sky spoke to him with a deep and powerful persuasion. But hitherto the emotion had remained in him as a silent ache, veiling with sadness the beauty that evoked it. He did not even know whether any one else in the world felt as he did, or whether he was the sole victim of this mournful privilege. Then he learned that one other spirit had trembled with the same touch of wonder: that at his side, living under his roof and eating his bread, was a creature to whom he could say: "That's Orion down yonder; the big fellow to the right is Aldebaran, and the bunch of little ones—like bees swarming—they're the Pleiades . . ." or whom he could hold entranced before a ledge of granite thrusting up through the fern while he unrolled the huge panorama of the ice age, and the long dim stretches of succeeding time. The fact that admiration for his learning mingled with Mattie's wonder at what he taught was not the least part of his pleasure. And there were other sensations, less definable but more exquisite, which drew them together with a shock of silent joy: the cold red of sunset behind winter hills, the flight of cloud-flocks over slopes of golden stubble, or the intensely blue shadows of hemlocks on sunlit snow. When she said to him once: "It looks just as if it was painted!" it seemed to Ethan that the art of definition could go no farther, and that words had at last been found to utter his secret soul. . . .

As he stood in the darkness outside the church these memories came back with the poignancy of vanished things. Watching Mattie whirl down the floor from hand to hand he wondered how he could ever have thought that his dull talk interested her. To him, who was never gay but in her presence, her gaiety seemed plain proof of indifference. The face she lifted to her dancers was the same which, when she saw him, always looked like a window that has caught the sunset. He even noticed two or three gestures which, in his fatuity, he had thought she kept for him: a way of throwing her head back when she was amused, as if to taste her laugh before she let it out, and a trick of sinking her lids slowly when anything charmed or moved her.

The sight made him unhappy, and his unhappiness roused his latent fears. His wife had never shown any jealousy of Mattie, but of late she had grumbled increasingly over the house-work and found oblique ways of attracting attention to the girl's inefficiency. Zeena had always been what Starkfield called "sickly," and Frome had to admit that, if she were as ailing as she believed, she needed the help of a stronger arm than the one which lay so lightly in his during the night walks to the farm. Mattie had no natural turn for housekeeping, and her training had done nothing to remedy the defect. She was quick to learn, but forgetful and dreamy, and not disposed to take the matter seriously. Ethan had an idea that if she were to marry a man she was fond of the dormant instinct would wake, and her pies and biscuits become the pride of the county; but domesticity in the abstract did not interest her. At first she was so awkward that he could not help laughing at her; but she laughed with him and that made them better friends. He did his best to supplement her unskilled efforts, getting up earlier than usual to light the kitchen fire, carrying in the wood overnight, and neglecting the mill for the farm that he might help her about the house during the day.

He even crept down on Saturday nights to scrub the kitchen floor after the women had gone to bed; and Zeena, one day, had surprised him at the churn and had turned away silently, with one of her queer looks.

Of late there had been other signs of her disfavour, as intangible but more disquieting. One cold winter morning, as he dressed in the dark, his candle flickering in the draught of the ill-fitting window, he had heard her speak from the bed behind him.

"The doctor don't want I should be left without anybody to do for me," she said in her flat whine.

He had supposed her to be asleep, and the sound of her voice had startled him, though she was given to abrupt explosions of speech after long intervals of secretive silence.

He turned and looked at her where she lay indistinctly outlined under the dark calico quilt, her high-boned face taking a greyish tinge from the whiteness of the pillow.

"Nobody to do for you?" he repeated.

"If you say you can't afford a hired girl when Mattie goes."

Frome turned away again, and taking up his razor stooped to catch the reflection of his stretched cheek in the blotched looking-glass above the wash-stand.

"Why on earth should Mattie go?"

"Well, when she gets married, I mean," his wife's drawl came from behind him.

"Oh, she'd never leave us as long as you needed her," he returned, scraping hard at his chin.

"I wouldn't ever have it said that I stood in the way of a poor girl like Mattie marrying a smart fellow like Denis Eady," Zeena answered in a tone of plaintive self-effacement.

Ethan, glaring at his face in the glass, threw his head back to draw the razor from ear to chin. His hand was steady, but the attitude was an excuse for not making an immediate reply.

"And the doctor don't want I should be left without anybody," Zeena continued. "He wanted I should speak to you about a girl he's heard about, that might come——"

Ethan laid down the razor and straightened himself with a laugh.

"Denis Eady! If that's all, I guess there's no such hurry to look round for a girl."

"Well, I'd like to talk to you about it," said Zeena obstinately.

He was getting into his clothes in fumbling haste. "All right. But I haven't got the time now; I'm late as it is," he returned, holding his old silver turnip-watch to the candle.

Zeena, apparently accepting this as final, lay watching him in silence while he pulled his suspenders over his shoulders and jerked his arms into his coat; but as he went toward the door she said, suddenly and incisively: "I guess you're always late, now you shave every morning."

That thrust had frightened him more than any vague insinuations about Denis Eady. It was a fact that since Mattie Silver's coming he had taken to shaving every day; but his wife always seemed to be asleep when he left her side in the winter darkness, and he had stupidly assumed that she would not notice any change in his appearance. Once or twice in the past he had been faintly disquieted by Zenobia's way of letting things happen without seeming to remark them, and then, weeks afterward, in a casual phrase, revealing that she had all along taken her notes and drawn her inferences. Of late, however, there had been no room in his thoughts for such vague apprehensions. Zeena herself, from an oppressive reality, had faded into an insubstantial shade. All his life was lived in the sight and sound of Mattie Silver, and he could no longer conceive of its being otherwise. But now, as he stood outside the church, and saw Mattie spinning down the floor with Denis Eady, a throng of disregarded hints and menaces wove their cloud about his brain. . . .

CHAPTER II

As the dancers poured out of the hall Frome, drawing back behind the projecting storm-door, watched the segregation of the grotesquely muffled groups, in which a moving lantern ray now and then lit up a face flushed with food and dancing. The villagers, being afoot, were the first to climb the slope to the main street, while the country neighbours packed themselves more slowly into the sleighs under the shed.

"Ain't you riding, Mattie?" a woman's voice called back from the throng about the shed, and Ethan's heart gave a jump. From where he stood he could not see the persons coming out of the hall till they had advanced a few steps beyond the wooden sides of the storm-door; but through its cracks he heard a clear voice answer: "Mercy no! Not on such a night."

She was there, then, close to him, only a thin board between. In another moment she would step forth into the night, and his eyes, accustomed to the obscurity, would discern her as clearly as though she stood in daylight. A wave of shyness pulled him back into the dark angle of the wall, and he stood there in silence instead of making his presence known to her. It had been one of the wonders of their intercourse that from the first, she, the quicker, finer, more expressive, instead of crushing him by the contrast, had given him something of her own ease and freedom; but now he felt as heavy and loutish as in his student days, when he had tried to "jolly" the Worcester girls at a picnic.

He hung back, and she came out alone and paused within a few yards of him. She was almost the last to leave the hall, and she stood looking uncertainly about her as if wondering why he did not show himself. Then a man's figure approached, coming so close to her that under their formless wrappings they seemed merged in one dim outline.

"Gentleman friend gone back on you? Say, Matt, that's tough! No, I wouldn't be mean enough to tell the other girls. I ain't as low-down as that." (How Frome hated his cheap banter!) "But look a here, ain't it lucky I got the old man's cutter down there waiting for us?"

Frome heard the girl's voice, gaily incredulous: "What on earth's your father's cutter doin' down there?"

"Why, waiting for me to take a ride. I got the roan colt too. I kinder knew I'd want to take a ride to-night," Eady, in his triumph, tried to put a sentimental note into his bragging voice.

The girl seemed to waver, and Frome saw her twirl the end of her scarf irresolutely about her fingers. Not for the world would he have made a sign to her, though it seemed to him that his life hung on her next gesture.

"Hold on a minute while I unhitch the colt," Denis called to her, springing toward the shed.

She stood perfectly still, looking after him, in an attitude of tranquil expectancy torturing to the hidden watcher. Frome noticed that she no longer turned her head from side to side, as though peering through the night for another figure. She let Denis Eady lead out the horse, climb into the cutter and fling back the bearskin to make room for her at his side; then, with a swift motion of flight, she turned about and darted up the slope toward the front of the church.

"Good-bye! Hope you'll have a lovely ride!" she called back to him over her shoulder.

Denis laughed, and gave the horse a cut that brought him quickly abreast of her retreating figure.

"Come along! Get in quick! It's as slippery as thunder on this turn," he cried, leaning over to reach out a hand to her.

She laughed back at him: "Good-night! I'm not getting in."

By this time they had passed beyond Frome's earshot and he could only follow the shadowy pantomime of their silhouettes as they continued to move along the crest of the slope above him. He saw Eady, after a moment, jump from the cutter and go toward the girl with the reins over one arm. The other he tried to slip through hers; but she eluded him nimbly, and Frome's heart, which had swung out over a black void, trembled back to safety. A moment later he heard the jingle of departing sleigh bells and discerned a figure advancing along toward the empty expanse of snow before the church.

In the black shade of the Varnum spruces he caught up with her and she turned with a quick "Oh!"

"Think I'd forgotten you, Matt?" he asked with sheepish glee.

She answered seriously: "I thought maybe you couldn't come back for me."

"Couldn't? What on earth could stop me?"

"I knew Zeena wasn't feeling any too good to-day."

"Oh, she's in bed long ago." He paused, a question struggling in him. "Then you meant to walk home all alone?"

"Oh, I ain't afraid!" she laughed.

They stood together in the gloom of the spruces, an empty world glimmering about them wide and grey under the stars. He brought his question out.

"If you thought I hadn't come, why didn't you ride back with Denis Eady?"

"Why, where *were* you? How did you know? I never saw you!"

Her wonder and his laughter ran together like spring rills in a thaw. Ethan had the sense of having done something arch and ingenious. To prolong the effect he groped for a dazzling phrase, and brought out, in a growl of rapture: "Come along."

He slipped an arm through hers, as Eady had done, and fancied it was faintly pressed against her side; but neither of them moved. It was so dark under the spruces that he could barely see the shape of her head beside his shoulder. He longed to stoop his cheek and rub it against her scarf. He would have liked to stand there with her all night in the blackness. She moved forward a step or two and then paused again above the dip of the Corbury road. Its icy slope, scored by innumerable runners, looked like a mirror scratched by travellers at an inn.

"There was a whole lot of them coasting before the moon set," she said.

"Would you like to come in and coast with them some night?" he asked.

"Oh, *would* you, Ethan? It would be lovely!"

"We'll come to-morrow if there's a moon."

She lingered, pressing closer to his side. "Ned Hale and Ruth Varnum came just as *near* running into the big elm at the bottom. We were all sure they were killed." Her shiver ran down his arm. "Wouldn't it have been too awful? They're so happy!"

''Oh, Ned ain't much at steering. I guess I can take you down all right!'' he said disdainfully.

He was aware that he was ''talking big,'' like Denis Eady; but his reaction of joy had unsteadied him, and the inflection with which she had said of the engaged couple ''They're so happy!'' made the words sound as if she had been thinking of herself and him.

''The elm *is* dangerous, though. It ought to be cut down,'' she insisted.

''Would you be afraid of it, with me?''

''I told you I ain't the kind to be afraid,'' she tossed back almost indifferently; and suddenly she began to walk on with a rapid step.

These alterations of mood were the despair and joy of Ethan Frome. The motions of her mind were as incalculable as the fli of a bird in the branches. The fact that he had no right to show his feelings, and thus provoke the expression of hers, made him attach a fantastic importance to every change in her look and tone. Now he thought she understood him, and feared; now he was sure she did not, and despaired. To-night the pressure of accumulated misgivings sent the scale drooping toward despair and her indifference was the more chilling after the flush of joy into which she had plunged him by dismissing Denis Eady. He mounted School House Hill at her side and walked on in silence till they reached the lane leading to the saw-mill; then the need of some definite assurance grew too strong for him.

''You'd have found me right off if you hadn't gone back to have that last reel with Denis,'' he brought out awkwardly. He could not pronounce the name without a stiffening of the muscles of his throat.

''Why, Ethan, how could I tell you were there?''

''I suppose what folks say is true,'' he jerked out at her instead of answering.

She stopped short, and he felt, in the darkness, that her face was lifted quickly to his. ''Why, what do folks say?''

''It's natural enough you should be leaving us,'' he floundered on, following his thought.

''Is that what they say?'' she mocked back at him; then, with a sudden drop of her sweet treble: ''You mean that Zeena—ain't suited with me any more?'' she faltered.

Their arms had slipped apart and they stood motionless, each seeking to distinguish the other's face.

''I know I ain't anything like as smart as I ought to be,'' she went on, while he vainly struggled for expression. "There's lots of things a hired girl could do that come awkward to me still—and I haven't got much strength in my arms. But if she'd only tell me I'd try. You know she hardly ever says anything, and sometimes I can see she ain't suited, and yet I don't know why." She turned on him with a sudden flash of indignation. "You'd ought to tell me, Ethan Frome—you'd ought to! Unless *you* want me to go too——"

Unless he wanted her to go too! The cry was balm to his raw wound. The iron heavens seemed to melt and rain down sweetness. Again he struggled for the all-expressive word, and again, his arm in hers, found only a deep "Come along."

They walked on in silence through the blackness of the hemlock-shaded lane, where Ethan's saw-mill gloomed through the night, and out again into the comparative clearness of the fields. On the farther side of the hemlock belt the open country rolled away before them grey and lonely under the stars. Sometimes their way led them under the shade of an overhanging bank or through the thin obscurity of a clump of leafless trees. Here and there a farmhouse stood far back among the fields, mute and cold as a grave-stone. The night was so still that they heard the frozen snow crackle under their feet. The crash of a loaded branch falling far off in the woods reverberated like a musket-shot, and once a fox barked, and Mattie shrank closer to Ethan, and quickened her steps.

At length they sighted the group of larches at Ethan's gate, and as they drew near it the sense that the walk was over brought back his words.

"Then you don't want to leave us, Matt?"

He had to stoop his head to catch her stifled whisper: "Where'd I go, if I did?"

The answer sent a pang through him but the tone suffused him with joy. He forgot what else he had meant to say and pressed her against him so closely that he seemed to feel her warmth in his veins.

"You ain't crying are you, Matt?"

"No, of course I'm not," she quavered.

They turned in at the gate and passed under the shaded knoll where, enclosed in a low fence, the Frome grave-stones slanted at crazy angles through the snow. Ethan looked at them curiously. For years that quiet company had mocked his restlessness, his desire for change and freedom. "We never got away—how should you?" seemed to be written on every headstone; and whenever he went in or out of his gate he thought with a shiver "I shall just go on living here till I join them." But now all desire for change had vanished, and the sight of the little enclosure gave him a warm sense of continuance and stability.

"I guess we'll never let you go, Matt," he whispered, as though even the dead, lovers once, must conspire with him to keep her; and brushing by the graves, he thought: "We'll always go on living here together, and some day she'll lie there beside me."

He let the vision possess him as they climbed the hill to the house. He was never so happy with her as when he abandoned himself to these dreams. Half-way up the slope Mattie stumbled against some unseen obstruction and clutched his sleeve to steady herself. The wave of warmth that went through him was like the prolongation of his vision. For the first time he stole his arm about her, and she did not resist. They walked on as if they were floating on a summer stream.

Zeena always went to bed as soon as she had had her supper, and the shutterless windows of the house were dark. A dead cucumber-vine dangled from the porch like the crape streamer tied to the door for a death, and the thought flashed through Ethan's brain: "If it was there for Zeena—" Then he had a distinct sight of his wife lying in their bedroom asleep, her mouth slightly open, her false teeth in a tumbler by the bed . . .

They walked around to the back of the house, between the rigid gooseberry bushes. It was Zeena's habit, when they came back late from the village, to leave the key of the kitchen door under the mat. Ethan stood before the door, his head heavy with dreams, his arm still about Mattie. "Matt—" he began, not knowing what he meant to say.

She slipped out of his hold without speaking, and he stooped down and felt for the key.

"It's not there!" he said, straightening himself with a start.

They strained their eyes at each other through the icy darkness. Such a thing had never happened before.

"Maybe she's forgotten it," Mattie said in a tremulous whisper; but both of them knew that it was not like Zeena to forget.

"It might have fallen off into the snow," Mattie continued, after a pause during which they had stood intently listening.

"It must have been pushed off, then," he rejoined in the same tone. Another wild thought tore through him. What if tramps had been there—what if . . .

Again he listened, fancying he heard a distant sound in the

house; then he felt in his pocket for a match, and kneeling down, passed its light slowly over the rough edges of snow about the doorstep.

He was still kneeling when his eyes, on a level with the lower panel of the door, caught a faint ray beneath it. Who could be stirring in that silent house? He heard a step on the stairs, and again for an instant the thought of tramps tore through him. Then the door opened and he saw his wife.

Against the dark background of the kitchen she stood up tall and angular, one hand drawing a quilted counterpane to her flat breast, while the other held a lamp. The light, on a level with her chin, drew out of the darkness her puckered throat and the projecting wrist of the hand that clutched the quilt, and deepened fantastically the hollows and prominences of her high-boned face under its ring of crimping-pins. To Ethan, still in the rosy haze of his hour with Mattie, the sight came with the intense precision of the last dream before waking. He felt as if he had never before known what his wife looked like.

She drew aside without speaking, and Mattie and Ethan passed into the kitchen, which had the deadly chill of a vault after the dry cold of the night.

''Guess you forgot about us, Zeena,'' Ethan joked, stamping the snow from his boots.

''No. I just felt so mean I couldn't sleep.''

Mattie came forward, unwinding her wraps, the colour of the cherry scarf in her fresh lips and cheeks. ''I'm so sorry, Zeena! Isn't there anything I can do?''

''No; there's nothing.'' Zeena turned away from her. ''You might 'a' shook off that snow outside,'' she said to her husband.

She walked out of the kitchen ahead of them and pausing in the hall raised the lamp at arm's-length, as if to light them up the stairs.

Ethan paused also, affecting to fumble for the peg on which he hung his coat and cap. The doors of the two bedrooms faced each other across the narrow upper landing, and to-night it was peculiarly repugnant to him that Mattie should see him follow Zeena.

''I guess I won't come up yet awhile,'' he said, turning as if to go back to the kitchen.

Zeena stopped short and looked at him. ''For the land's sake—what you going to do down here?''

''I've got the mill accounts to go over.''

She continued to stare at him, the flame of the unshaded lamp bringing out with microscopic cruelty the fretful lines of her face.

"At this time o' night? You'll ketch your death. The fire's out long ago."

Without answering he moved away toward the kitchen. As he did so his glance crossed Mattie's and he fancied that a fugitive warning gleamed through her lashes. The next moment they sank to her flushed cheeks and she began to mount the stairs ahead of Zeena.

"That's so. It *is* powerful cold down here," Ethan assented; and with lowered head he went up in his wife's wake, and followed her across the threshold of their room.

CHAPTER III

There was some hauling to be done at the lower end of the wood-lot, and Ethan was out early the next day.

The winter morning was as clear as crystal. The sunrise burned red in a pure sky, the shadows on the rim of the wood-lot were darkly blue, and beyond the white and scintillating fields patches of far-off forest hung like smoke.

It was in the early morning stillness, when his muscles were swinging to their familiar task and his lungs expanding with long draughts of mountain air, that Ethan did his clearest thinking. He and Zeena had not exchanged a word after the door of their room had closed on them. She had measured out some drops from a medicine-bottle on a chair by the bed and, after swallowing them, and wrapping her head in a piece of yellow flannel, had lain down with her face turned away. Ethan undressed hurriedly and blew out the light so that he should not see her when he took his place at her side. As he lay there he could hear Mattie moving about in her room, and her candle, sending its small ray across the landing, drew a scarcely perceptible line of light under his door. He kept his eyes fixed on the light till it vanished. Then the room grew perfectly black, and not a sound was audible but Zeena's asthmatic breathing. Ethan felt confusedly that there were many things he ought to think about, but through his tingling veins and tired brain only one sensation throbbed: the warmth of Mattie's shoulder against his. Why had he not kissed her when he held her there? A few hours earlier he would not have asked himself the question. Even a few minutes earlier, when they had stood alone outside the house, he would not have dared to think of kissing her. But since he had seen her lips in the lamplight he felt that they were his.

Now, in the bright morning air, her face was still before him. It was part of the sun's red and of the pure glitter on the snow. How the girl had changed since she had come to Starkfield! He remembered what a colourless slip of a thing she had looked the day he had met her at the station. And all the first winter, how she had shivered with cold when the northerly gales shook the thin clapboards and the snow beat like hail against the loose-hung windows!

He had been afraid that she would hate the hard life, the cold and loneliness; but not a sign of discontent escaped her. Zeena took the view that Mattie was bound to make the best of Starkfield since she hadn't any other place to go to; but this did not strike Ethan as conclusive. Zeena, at any rate, did not apply the principle in her own case.

He felt all the more sorry for the girl because misfortune had, in a sense, indentured her to them. Mattie Silver was the daughter of a cousin of Zenobia Frome's, who had inflamed his clan with mingled sentiments of envy and admiration by descending from the hills to Connecticut, where he had married a Stamford girl and succeeded to her father's thriving "drug" business. Unhappily Orin Silver, a man of far-reaching aims, had died too soon to prove that the end justifies the means. His accounts revealed merely what the means had been; and these were such that it was fortunate for his wife and daughter that his books were examined only after his impressive funeral. His wife died of the disclosure, and Mattie, at twenty, was left alone to make her way on the fifty dollars obtained from the sale of her piano. For this purpose her equipment, though varied, was inadequate. She could trim a hat, make molasses candy, recite "Curfew shall not ring to-night," and play "The Lost Chord" and a pot-pourri from "Carmen." When she tried to extend the field of her activities in the direction of stenography and book-keeping her health broke down, and six months on her feet behind the counter of a department store did not tend to restore it. Her nearest relations had been induced to place their savings in her father's hands, and though, after his death, they ungrudgingly acquitted themselves of the Christian duty of returning good for evil by giving his daughter all the advice at their disposal, they could hardly be expected to supplement it by material aid. But when Zenobia's doctor recommended her looking about for some one to help her with the house-work the clan instantly saw the chance of exacting a compensation from Mattie. Zenobia, though doubtful of the girl's efficiency, was tempted by the freedom to find fault without much risk of losing her; and so Mattie came to Starkfield.

Zenobia's fault-finding was of the silent kind, but not the less penetrating for that. During the first months Ethan alternately burned with the desire to see Mattie defy her and trembled with fear of the result. Then the situation grew less strained. The pure air, and the long summer hours in the open, gave back life and elasticity to Mattie, and Zeena, with more leisure to devote to her complex ailments, grew less watchful of the girl's omissions; so that Ethan, struggling on under the burden of his barren farm and failing saw-mill, could at least imagine that peace reigned in his house.

There was really, even now, no tangible evidence to the contrary; but since the previous night a vague dread had hung on his sky-line. It was formed of Zeena's obstinate silence, of Mattie's sudden look of warning, of the memory of just such fleeting imperceptible signs as those which told him, on certain stainless mornings, that before night there would be rain.

His dread was so strong that, man-like, he sought to postpone certainty. The hauling was not over till mid-day, and as the lumber was to be delivered to Andrew Hale, the Starkfield builder, it was really easier for Ethan to send Jotham Powell, the hired man, back to the farm on foot, and drive the load down to the village himself. He had scrambled up on the logs, and was sitting astride of them, close over his shaggy greys, when, coming between him and their streaming necks, he had a vision of the warning look that Mattie had given him the night before.

"If there's going to be any trouble I want to be there," was his vague reflection, as he threw to Jotham the unexpected order to unhitch the team and lead them back to the barn.

It was a slow trudge home through the heavy fields, and when the two men entered the kitchen Mattie was lifting the coffee from the stove and Zeena was already at the table. Her husband stopped short at sight of her. Instead of her usual calico wrapper and knitted shawl she wore her best dress of brown merino, and above her thin strands of hair, which still preserved the tight undulations of the crimping-pins, rose a hard perpendicular bonnet, as to which Ethan's clearest notion was that he had to pay five dollars for it at the Bettsbridge Emporium. On the floor beside her stood his old valise and a bandbox wrapped in newspapers.

"Why, where are you going, Zeena?" he exclaimed.

"I've got my shooting pains so bad that I'm going over to

Bettsbridge to spend the night with Aunt Martha Pierce and see that new doctor,'' she answered in a matter-of-fact tone, as if she had said she was going into the store-room to take a look at the preserves, or up to the attic to go over the blankets.

In spite of her sedentary habits such abrupt decisions were not without precedent in Zeena's history. Twice or thrice before she had suddenly packed Ethan's valise and started off to Bettsbridge, or even Springfield, to seek the advice of some new doctor, and her husband had grown to dread these expeditions because of their cost. Zeena always came back laden with expensive remedies, and her last visit to Springfield had been commemorated by her paying twenty dollars for an electric battery of which she had never been able to learn the use. But for the moment his sense of relief was so great as to preclude all other feelings. He had now no doubt that Zeena had spoken the truth in saying, the night before, that she had sat up because she felt ''too mean'' to sleep: her abrupt resolve to seek medical advice showed that, as usual, she was wholly absorbed in her health.

As if expecting a protest, she continued plaintively; ''If you're too busy with the hauling I presume you can let Jotham Powell drive me over with the sorrel in time to ketch the train at the Flats.''

Her husband hardly heard what she was saying. During the winter months there was no stage between Starkfield and Bettsbridge, and the trains which stopped at Corbury Flats were slow and infrequent. A rapid calculation showed Ethan that Zeena could not be back at the farm before the following evening. . . .

''If I'd supposed you'd 'a' made any objection to Jotham Powell's driving me over—'' she began again, as though his silence had implied refusal. On the brink of departure she was always seized with a flux of words. ''All I know is,'' she continued, ''I can't go on the way I am much longer. The pains are clear away down to my ankles now, or I'd 'a' walked in to Starkfield on my own feet, sooner'n put you out, and asked Michael Eady to let me ride over on his wagon to the Flats, when he sends to meet the train that brings his groceries. I'd 'a' had two hours to wait in the station, but I'd sooner 'a' done it, even with this cold, than to have you say——''

''Of course Jotham'll drive you over,'' Ethan roused himself to answer. He became suddenly conscious that he was looking at Mattie while Zeena talked to him, and with an effort he turned his eyes to his wife. She sat opposite the window, and the pale light reflected from the banks of snow made her face look more than usually drawn and bloodless, sharpened the three parallel creases between ear and cheek, and drew querulous lines from her thin nose to the corners of her mouth. Though she was but seven years her husband's senior, and he was only twenty-eight, she was already an old woman.

Ethan tried to say something befitting the occasion, but there was only one thought in his mind: the fact that, for the first time since Mattie had come to live with them, Zeena was to be away for a night. He wondered if the girl were thinking of it too. . . .

He knew that Zeena must be wondering why he did not offer to drive her to the Flats and let Jotham Powell take the lumber to Starkfield, and at first he could not think of a pretext for not doing so; then he said: "I'd take you over myself, only I've got to collect the cash for the lumber."

As soon as the words were spoken he regretted them, not only because they were untrue—there being no prospect of his receiving cash payment from Hale—but also because he knew from experience the imprudence of letting Zeena think he was in funds on the eve of one of her therapeutic excursions. At the moment, however, his one desire was to avoid the long drive with her behind the ancient sorrel who never went out of a walk.

Zeena made no reply: she did not seem to hear what he had said. She had already pushed her plate aside, and was measuring out a draught from a large bottle at her elbow.

"It ain't done me a speck of good, but I guess I might as well use it up," she remarked; adding, as she pushed the empty bottle toward Mattie: "If you can get the taste out it'll do for pickles."

CHAPTER IV

As soon as his wife had driven off Ethan took his coat and cap from the peg. Mattie was washing up the dishes, humming one of the dance tunes of the night before. He said "So long, Matt," and she answered gaily "So long, Ethan"; and that was all.

It was warm and bright in the kitchen. The sun slanted through the south window on the girl's moving figure, on the cat dozing in a chair, and on the geraniums brought in from the door-way, where Ethan had planted them in the summer to "make a garden" for Mattie. He would have liked to linger on, watching her tidy up and then settle down to her sewing; but he wanted still more to get the hauling done and be back at the farm before night.

All the way down to the village he continued to think of his return to Mattie. The kitchen was a poor place, not "spruce" and shining as his mother had kept it in his boyhood; but it was surprising what a homelike look the mere fact of Zeena's absence gave it. And he pictured what it would be like that evening, when he and Mattie were there after supper. For the first time they would be alone together indoors, and they would sit there, one on each side of the stove, like a married couple, he in his stocking feet and smoking his pipe, she laughing and talking in that funny way she had, which was always as new to him as if he had never heard her before.

The sweetness of the picture, and the relief of knowing that his fears of "trouble" with Zeena were unfounded, sent up his spirits with a rush, and he, who was usually so silent, whistled and sang aloud as he drove through the snowy fields. There was in him a slumbering spark of sociability which the long Starkfield winters had not yet extinguished. By nature grave and inarticulate, he admired recklessness and gaiety in others and was warmed to the marrow by friendly human intercourse. At Worcester, though he had the name of keeping to himself and not being much of a hand at a good time, he had secretly gloried in being clapped on the back and hailed as "Old Ethe" or "Old Stiff"; and the cessation of such familiarities had increased the chill of his return to Starkfield.

There the silence had deepened about him year by year. Left alone, after his father's accident, to carry the burden of farm and mill, he had had no time for convivial loiterings in the village; and when his mother fell ill the loneliness of the house grew more oppressive than that of the fields. His mother had been a talker in her day, but after her "trouble" the sound of her voice was seldom heard, though she had not lost the power of speech. Sometimes, in the long winter evenings, when in desperation her son asked her why she didn't "say something," she would lift a finger and answer: "Because I'm listening"; and on stormy nights, when the loud wind was about the house, she would complain, if he spoke to her: "They're talking so out there that I can't hear you."

It was only when she drew toward her last illness, and his cousin Zenobia Pierce came over from the next valley to help him nurse her, that human speech was heard again in the house. After the mortal silence of his long imprisonment Zeena's volubility was music in his ears. He felt that he might have "gone like his mother" if the sound of a new voice had not come to steady him. Zeena seemed to understand his case at a glance. She laughed at him for not knowing the simplest sick-bed duties and told him to "go right along out" and leave her to see to things. The mere fact of obeying her orders, of feeling free to go about his business again and talk with other men, restored his shaken balance and magnified his sense of what he owed her. Her efficiency shamed and dazzled him. She seemed to possess by instinct all the household wisdom that his long apprenticeship had not instilled in him. When the end came it was she who had to tell him to hitch up and go for the undertaker, and she thought it "funny" that he had not settled beforehand who was to have his mother's clothes and the sewing-machine. After the funeral, when he saw her preparing to go away, he was seized with an unreasoning dread of being left alone on the farm; and before he knew what he was doing he had asked her to stay there with him. He had often thought since that it would not have happened if his mother had died in spring instead of winter . . .

When they married it was agreed that, as soon as he could straighten out the difficulties resulting from Mrs. Frome's long illness, they would sell the farm and saw-mill and try their luck in a large town. Ethan's love of nature did not take the form of a taste for agriculture. He had always wanted to be an engineer, and to live in towns, where there were lectures and big libraries and "fellows doing things." A slight engineering job in Florida, put in his way during his period of study at Worcester, increased his faith in his ability as well as his eagerness to see the world; and he felt sure that, with a "smart" wife like Zeena, it would not be long before he had made himself a place in it.

Zeena's native village was slightly larger and nearer to the railway than Starkfield, and she had let her husband see from the first that life on an isolated farm was not what she had expected when she married. But purchasers were slow in coming, and while he waited for them Ethan learned the impossibility of transplanting her. She chose to look down on Starkfield, but she could not have lived in a place which looked down on her. Even Bettsbridge or Shadd's Falls would not have been sufficiently aware of her, and in the greater cities which attracted Ethan she would have suffered a complete loss of identity. And within a year of their marriage she developed the "sickliness" which had since made her notable even in a community rich in pathological instances. When she came to take care of his mother she had seemed to Ethan like the very genius of health, but he soon saw that her skill as a nurse had been acquired by the absorbed observation of her own symptoms.

Then she too fell silent. Perhaps it was the inevitable effect of life on the farm, or perhaps, as she sometimes said, it was because Ethan "never listened." The charge was not wholly unfounded. When she spoke it was only to complain, and to complain of things not in his power to remedy; and to check a tendency to impatient retort he had first formed the habit of not answering her, and finally of thinking of other things while she talked. Of late, however, since he had had reasons for observing her more closely, her silence had begun to trouble him. He recalled his mother's growing taciturnity, and wondered if Zeena were also turning "queer." Women did, he knew. Zeena, who had at her fingers' ends the pathological chart of the whole region, had cited many cases of the kind while she was nursing his mother; and he himself knew of certain lonely farm-houses in the neighbourhood where stricken creatures pined, and of others where sudden tragedy had come of their presence. At times, looking at Zeena's shut face, he felt the chill of such forebodings. At other times her silence seemed deliberately assumed to conceal far-reaching intentions, mysterious conclusions drawn from suspicions and resentments impossible to guess. That supposition was even more disturbing than the other; and it was the one which had come to him the night before, when he had seen her standing in the kitchen door.

Now her departure for Bettsbridge had once more eased his mind, and all his thoughts were on the prospect of his evening with Mattie. Only one thing weighed on him, and that was his having told Zeena that he was to receive cash for the lumber. He foresaw so clearly the consequences of this imprudence that with considerable reluctance he decided to ask Andrew Hale for a small advance on his load.

When Ethan drove into Hale's yard the builder was just getting out of his sleigh.

"Hello, Ethe!" he said. "This comes handy."

Andrew Hale was a ruddy man with a big grey moustache and a stubbly double-chin unconstrained by a collar; but his scrupulously clean shirt was always fastened by a small diamond stud. This display of opulence was misleading, for though he did a fairly good business it was known that his easygoing habits and the demands of his large family frequently kept him what Starkfield called "behind." He was an old friend of Ethan's family, and his house one of the few to which Zeena occasionally went, drawn there by the fact that Mrs. Hale, in her youth, had done more "doctoring" than any other woman in Starkfield, and was still a recognised authority on symptoms and treatment.

Hale went up to the greys and patted their sweating flanks.

"Well, sir," he said, "you keep them two as if they was pets."

Ethan set about unloading the logs and when he had finished his job he pushed open the glazed door of the shed which the builder used as his office. Hale sat with his feet up on the stove, his back propped against a battered desk strewn with papers: the place, like the man, was warm, genial and untidy.

"Sit right down and thaw out," he greeted Ethan.

The latter did not know how to begin, but at length he managed to bring out his request for an advance of fifty dollars. The blood rushed to his thin skin under the sting of Hale's astonishment. It was the builder's custom to pay at the end of three months, and there was no precedent between the two men for a cash settlement.

Ethan felt that if he had pleaded an urgent need Hale might have made shift to pay him; but pride, and an instinctive prudence, kept him from resorting to this argument. After his father's death it had taken time to get his head above water, and he did not want Andrew Hale, or any one else in Starkfield, to think he was going under again. Besides, he hated lying; if he wanted the money he wanted it, and it was nobody's business to ask why. He therefore made his demand with the awkwardness of a proud man who will not admit to himself that he is stooping; and he was not much surprised at Hale's refusal.

The builder refused genially, as he did everything else: he treated the matter as something in the nature of a practical joke, and wanted to know if Ethan meditated buying a grand piano or adding a "cupolo" to his house; offering, in the latter case, to give his services free of cost.

Ethan's arts were soon exhausted, and after an embarrassed pause he wished Hale good day and opened the door of the office. As he passed out the builder suddenly called after him: "See here—you ain't in a tight place, are you?"

"Not a bit," Ethan's pride retorted before his reason had time to intervene.

"Well, that's good! Because I *am,* a shade. Fact is, I was going to ask you to give me a little extra time on that payment. Business is pretty slack, to begin with, and then I'm fixing up a little house for Ned and Ruth when they're married. I'm glad to do it for 'em, but it costs." His look appealed to Ethan for sympathy. "The young people like things nice. You know how it is yourself: it's not so long ago since you fixed up your own place for Zeena."

Ethan left the greys in Hale's stable and went about some other business in the village. As he walked away the builder's last phrase lingered in his ears, and he reflected grimly that his seven years with Zeena seemed to Starkfield "not so long."

The afternoon was drawing to an end, and here and there a lighted pane spangled the cold grey dusk and made the snow look whiter. The bitter weather had driven every one indoors and Ethan had the long rural street to himself. Suddenly he heard the brisk play of sleigh-bells and a cutter passed him, drawn by a free-going horse. Ethan recognised Michael Eady's roan colt, and young Denis Eady, in a handsome new fur cap, leaned forward and waved a greeting. "Hello, Ethe!" he shouted and spun on.

The cutter was going in the direction of the Frome farm, and Ethan's heart contracted as he listened to the dwindling bells. What more likely than that Denis Eady had heard of Zeena's departure for Bettsbridge, and was profiting by the opportunity to spend an hour with Mattie? Ethan was ashamed of the storm of jealousy in his breast. It seemed unworthy of the girl that his thoughts of her should be so violent.

He walked on to the church corner and entered the shade of the Varnum spruces, where he had stood with her the night before. As he passed into their gloom he saw an indistinct outline just ahead of him. At his approach it melted for an instant into two separate shapes and then conjoined again, and he heard a kiss, and a half-laughing "Oh!" provoked by the discovery of his presence. Again the outline hastily disunited and the Varnum gate slammed on one half while the other hurried on ahead of him. Ethan smiled at the discomfiture he had caused. What did it matter to Ned Hale and Ruth Varnum if they were caught kissing each other? Everybody in Starkfield knew they were engaged. It pleased Ethan to have surprised a pair of lovers on the spot where he and Mattie had stood with such a thirst for each other in their hearts; but he felt a pang at the thought that these two need not hide their happiness.

He fetched the greys from Hale's stable and started on his long climb back to the farm. The cold was less sharp than earlier in the day and a thick fleecy sky threatened snow for the morrow. Here and there a star pricked through, showing behind it a deep well of blue. In an hour or two the moon would push over the ridge behind the farm, burn a gold-edged rent in the clouds, and then be swallowed by them. A mournful peace hung on the fields, as though they felt the relaxing grasp of the cold and stretched themselves in their long winter sleep.

Ethan's ears were alert for the jingle of sleighbells, but not a sound broke the silence of the lonely road. As he drew near the farm he saw, through the thin screen of larches at the gate, a light twinkling in the house above him. "She's up in her room," he said to himself, "fixing herself up for supper"; and he remembered Zeena's sarcastic stare when Mattie, on the evening of her arrival, had come down to supper with smoothed hair and a ribbon at her neck.

He passed by the graves on the knoll and turned his head to glance at one of the older headstones, which had interested him deeply as a boy because it bore his name.

SACRED TO THE MEMORY OF
ETHAN FROME AND ENDURANCE HIS WIFE,
WHO DWELLED TOGETHER IN PEACE
FOR FIFTY YEARS.

He used to think that fifty years sounded like a long time t live together, but now it seemed to him that they might pass in flash. Then, with a sudden dart of irony, he wondered if, whe their turn came, the same epitaph would be written over him an Zeena.

He opened the barn-door and craned his head into the obscu rity, half-fearing to discover Denis Eady's roan colt in the stal beside the sorrel. But the old horse was there alone, mumblin his crib with toothless jaws, and Ethan whistled cheerfully whil he bedded down the greys and shook an extra measure of oat into their mangers. His was not a tuneful throat, but harsl melodies burst from it as he locked the barn and sprang up th hill to the house. He reached the kitchen-porch and turned th door-handle; but the door did not yield to his touch.

Startled at finding it locked he rattled the handle violently then he reflected that Mattie was alone and that it was natural sh should barricade herself at nightfall. He stood in the darknes expecting to hear her step. It did not come, and after vainl straining his ears he called out in a voice that shook with joy "Hello, Matt!"

Silence answered; but in a minute or two he caught a sound o the stairs and saw a line of light about the door-frame, as he ha seen it the night before. So strange was the precision with whic the incidents of the previous evening were repeating themselve that he half expected, when he heard the key turn, to see his wif before him on the threshold; but the door opened, and Matti faced him.

She stood just as Zeena had stood, a lifted lamp in her hand against the black background of the kitchen. She held the light a the same level, and it drew out with the same distinctness he slim young throat and the brown wrist no bigger than a child's Then, striking upward, it threw a lustrous fleck on her lips edged her eyes with velvet shade, and laid a milky whitenes above the black curve of her brows.

She wore her usual dress of darkish stuff, and there was n bow at her neck; but through her hair she had run a streak o crimson ribbon. This tribute to the unusual transformed an glorified her. She seemed to Ethan taller, fuller, more womanl in shape and motion. She stood aside, smiling silently, while he entered, and then moved away from him with something soft and flowing in her gait. She set the lamp on the table, and he saw that it was carefully laid for supper, with fresh doughnuts, stewed blueberries and his favourite pickles in a dish of gay red glass. A bright fire glowed in the stove and the cat lay stretched before it, watching the table with a drowsy eye.

Ethan was suffocated with the sense of well-being. He went out into the passage to hang up his coat and pull off his wet boots. When he came back Mattie had set the teapot on the table and the cat was rubbing itself persuasively against her ankles.

"Why, Puss! I nearly tripped over you," she cried, the laughter sparkling through her lashes.

Again Ethan felt a sudden twinge of jealousy. Could it be his coming that gave her such a kindled face?

"Well, Matt, any visitors?" he threw off, stooping down carelessly to examine the fastening of the stove.

She nodded and laughed "Yes, one," and he felt a blackness settling on his brows.

"Who was that?" he questioned, raising himself up to slant a glance at her beneath his scowl.

Her eyes danced with malice. "Why, Jotham Powell. He came in after he got back, and asked for a drop of coffee before he went down home."

The blackness lifted and light flooded Ethan's brain. "That all? Well, I hope you made out to let him have it." And after a pause he felt it right to add: "I suppose he got Zeena over to the Flats all right?"

"Oh, yes; in plenty of time."

The name threw a chill between them, and they stood a moment looking sideways at each other before Mattie said with a shy laugh. "I guess it's about time for supper."

They drew their seats up to the table, and the cat, unbidden, jumped between them into Zeena's empty chair. "Oh, Puss!" said Mattie, and they laughed again.

Ethan, a moment earlier, had felt himself on the brink of eloquence; but the mention of Zeena had paralysed him. Mattie seemed to feel the contagion of his embarrassment, and sat with downcast lids, sipping her tea, while he feigned an insatiable appetite for doughnuts and sweet pickles. At last, after casting about for an effective opening, he took a long gulp of tea, cleared his throat, and said: "Looks as if there'd be more snow."

She feigned great interest. "Is that so? Do you suppose it'l interfere with Zeena's getting back?" She flushed red as the question escaped her, and hastily set down the cup she wa lifting.

Ethan reached over for another helping of pickles. "You neve can tell, this time of year, it drifts so bad on the Flats." The name had benumbed him again, and once more he felt as i Zeena were in the room between them.

"Oh, Puss, you're too greedy!" Mattie cried.

The cat, unnoticed, had crept up on muffled paws from Zeena' seat to the table, and was stealthily elongating its body in the direction of the milk-jug, which stood between Ethan and Mattie The two leaned forward at the same moment and their hands me on the handle of the jug. Mattie's hand was underneath, and Ethan kept his clasped on it a moment longer than was neces sary. The cat, profiting by this unusual demonstration, tried to effect an unnoticed retreat, and in doing so backed into the pickle-dish, which fell to the floor with a crash.

Mattie, in an instant, had sprung from her chair and was down on her knees by the fragments.

"Oh, Ethan, Ethan—it's all to pieces! What will Zeena say?"

But this time his courage was up. "Well, she'll have to say i to the cat, any way!" he rejoined with a laugh, kneeling down a Mattie's side to scrape up the swimming pickles.

She lifted stricken eyes to him. "Yes, but, you see, she neve meant it should be used, not even when there was company; and I had to get up on the step-ladder to reach it down from the top shelf of the china-closet, where she keeps it with all her bes things, and of course she'll want to know why I did it——"

The case was so serious that it called forth all of Ethan's laten resolution.

"She needn't know anything about it if you keep quiet. I'll ge another just like it to-morrow. Where did it come from? I'll go to Shadd's Falls for it if I have to!"

"Oh, you'll never get another even there! It was a wedding present—don't you remember? It came all the way from Phila delphia, from Zeena's aunt that married the minister. That's why she wouldn't ever use it. Oh, Ethan, Ethan, what in the world shall I do?"

She began to cry, and he felt as if every one of her tears were pouring over him like burning lead. "Don't, Matt, don't—oh *don't*!" he implored her.

She struggled to her feet, and he rose and followed her

helplessly while she spread out the pieces of glass on the kitchen dresser. It seemed to him as if the shattered fragments of their evening lay there.

"Here, give them to me," he said in a voice of sudden authority.

She drew aside, instinctively obeying his tone. "Oh, Ethan, what are you going to do?"

Without replying he gathered the pieces of glass into his broad palm and walked out of the kitchen to the passage. There he lit a candle-end, opened the china-closet, and, reaching his long arm up to the highest shelf, laid the pieces together with such accuracy of touch that a close inspection convinced him of the impossibility of detecting from below that the dish was broken. If he glued it together the next morning months might elapse before his wife noticed what had happened, and meanwhile he might after all be able to match the dish at Shadd's Falls or Bettsbridge. Having satisfied himself that there was no risk of immediate discovery he went back to the kitchen with a lighter step, and found Mattie disconsolately removing the last scraps of pickle from the floor.

"It's all right, Matt. Come back and finish supper," he commanded her.

Completely reassured, she shone on him through tear-hung lashes, and his soul swelled with pride as he saw how his tone subdued her. She did not even ask what he had done. Except when he was steering a big log down the mountain to his mill he had never known such a thrilling sense of mastery.

CHAPTER V

They finished supper, and while Mattie cleared the table Ethan went to look at the cows and then took a last turn about the house. The earth lay dark under a muffled sky and the air was so still that now and then he heard a lump of snow come thumping down from a tree far off on the edge of the wood-lot.

When he returned to the kitchen Mattie had pushed up his chair to the stove and seated herself near the lamp with a bit of sewing. The scene was just as he had dreamed of it that morning. He sat down, drew his pipe from his pocket and stretched his feet to the glow. His hard day's work in the keen air made him feel at once lazy and light of mood, and he had a confused sense of being in another world, where all was warmth and harmony and time could bring no change. The only drawback to his complete well-being was the fact that he could not see Mattie from where he sat; but he was too indolent to move and after a moment he said: "Come over here and sit by the stove."

Zeena's empty rocking-chair stood facing him. Mattie rose obediently, and seated herself in it. As her young brown head detached itself against the patch-work cushion that habitually framed his wife's gaunt countenance, Ethan had a momentary shock. It was almost as if the other face, the face of the superseded woman, had obliterated that of the intruder. After a moment Mattie seemed to be affected by the same sense of constraint. She changed her position, leaning forward to bend her head above her work, so that he saw only the foreshortened tip of her nose and the streak of red in her hair; then she slipped to her feet, saying "I can't see to sew," and went back to her chair by the lamp.

Ethan made a pretext of getting up to replenish the stove, and when he returned to his seat he pushed it sideways that he might get a view of her profile and of the lamplight falling on her hands. The cat, who had been a puzzled observer of these unusual movements, jumped up into Zeena's chair, rolled itself into a ball, and lay watching them with narrowed eyes.

Deep quiet sank on the room. The clock ticked above the dresser, a piece of charred wood fell now and then in the stove, and the faint sharp scent of the geraniums mingled with the odour of Ethan's smoke, which began to throw a blue haze about the lamp and to hang its greyish cobwebs in the shadowy corners of the room.

All constraint had vanished between the two, and they began to talk easily and simply. They spoke of every-day things, of the prospect of snow, of the next church sociable, of the loves and quarrels of Starkfield. The commonplace nature of what they said produced in Ethan an illusion of long-established intimacy which no outburst of emotion could have given, and he set his imagination adrift on the fiction that they had always spent their evenings thus and would always go on doing so . . .

"This is the night we were to have gone coasting, Matt," he said at length, with the rich sense, as he spoke, that they could go on any other night they chose, since they had all time before them.

She smiled back at him. "I guess you forgot!"

"No, I didn't forget; but it's as dark as Egypt outdoors. We might go to-morrow if there's a moon."

She laughed with pleasure, her head tilted back, the lamplight sparkling on her lips and teeth. "That would be lovely, Ethan!"

He kept his eyes fixed on her, marvelling at the way her face changed with each turn of their talk, like a wheat-field under a summer breeze. It was intoxicating to find such magic in his clumsy words, and he longed to try new ways of using it.

"Would you be scared to go down the Corbury road with me on a night like this?" he asked.

Her cheeks burned redder. "I ain't any more scared than you are!"

"Well, *I'd* be scared, then; I wouldn't do it. That's an ugly corner down by the big elm. If a fellow didn't keep his eyes open he'd go plumb into it." He luxuriated in the sense of protection and authority which his words conveyed. To prolong and intensify the feeling he added: "I guess we're well enough here."

She let her lids sink slowly, in the way he loved. "Yes, we're well enough here," she sighed.

Her tone was so sweet that he took the pipe from his mouth and drew his chair up to the table. Leaning forward, he touched the farther end of the strip of brown stuff that she was hemming. "Say, Matt," he began with a smile, "what do you think I saw under the Varnum spruces, coming along home just now? I saw a friend of yours getting kissed."

The words had been on his tongue all the evening, but now that he had spoken them they struck him as inexpressibly vulgar and out of place.

Mattie blushed to the roots of her hair and pulled her needle rapidly twice or thrice through her work, insensibly drawing the end of it away from him. "I suppose it was Ruth and Ned," she said in a low voice, as though he had suddenly touched on something grave.

Ethan had imagined that his allusion might open the way to the accepted pleasantries, and these perhaps in turn to a harmless caress, if only a mere touch on her hand. But now he felt as if her blush had set a flaming guard about her. He supposed it was his natural awkwardness that made him feel so. He knew that most young men made nothing at all of giving a pretty girl a kiss, and he remembered that the night before, when he had put his arm about Mattie, she had not resisted. But that had been out-of-doors, under the open irresponsible night. Now, in the warm lamplit room, with all its ancient implications of conformity and order, she seemed infinitely farther away from him and more unapproachable.

To ease his constraint he said: "I suppose they'll be setting a date before long."

"Yes. I shouldn't wonder if they got married some time along in the summer." She pronounced the word *married* as if her voice caressed it. It seemed a rustling covert leading to enchanted glades. A pang shot through Ethan, and he said, twisting away from her in his chair: "It'll be your turn next, I wouldn't wonder."

She laughed a little uncertainly. "Why do you keep on saying that?"

He echoed her laugh. "I guess I do it to get used to the idea."

He drew up to the table again and she sewed on in silence, with dropped lashes, while he sat in fascinated contemplation of the way in which her hands went up and down above the strip of stuff, just as he had seen a pair of birds make short perpendicular flights over a nest they were building. At length, without turning her head or lifting her lids, she said in a low tone: "It's not because you think Zeena's got anything against me, is it?"

His former dread started up full-armed at the suggestion. "Why, what do you mean?" he stammered.

She raised distressed eyes to his, her work dropping on the table between them. "I don't know. I thought last night she seemed to have."

"I'd like to know what," he growled.

"Nobody can tell with Zeena." It was the first time they had ever spoken so openly of her attitude toward Mattie, and the repetition of the name seemed to carry it to the farther corners of the room and send it back to them in long repercussions of sound. Mattie waited, as if to give the echo time to drop, and then went on: "She hasn't said anything to *you*?"

He shook his head. "No, not a word."

She tossed the hair back from her forehead with a laugh. "I guess I'm just nervous, then. I'm not going to think about it any more."

"Oh, no—don't let's think about it, Matt!"

The sudden heat of his tone made her colour mount again, not with a rush, but gradually, delicately, like the reflection of a thought stealing slowly across her heart. She sat silent, her hands clasped on her work, and it seemed to him that a warm current flowed toward him along the strip of stuff that still lay unrolled between them. Cautiously he slid his hand palm-downward along the table till his finger-tips touched the end of the stuff. A faint vibration of her lashes seemed to show that she was aware of his gesture, and that it had sent a counter-current back to her; and she let her hands lie motionless on the other end of the strip.

As they sat thus he heard a sound behind him and turned his head. The cat had jumped from Zeena's chair to dart at a mouse in the wainscot, and as a result of the sudden movement the empty chair had set up a spectral rocking.

"She'll be rocking in it herself this time to-morrow," Ethan thought. "I've been in a dream, and this is the only evening we'll ever have together." The return to reality was as painful as the return to consciousness after taking an anæsthetic. His body and brain ached with indescribable weariness, and he could think of nothing to say or to do that should arrest the mad flight of the moments.

His alteration of mood seemed to have communicated itself to Mattie. She looked up at him languidly, as though her lids were weighted with sleep and it cost her an effort to raise them. Her glance fell on his hand, which now completely covered the end of her work and grasped it as if it were a part of herself. He saw a scarcely perceptible tremor cross her face, and without knowing what he did he stooped his head and kissed the bit of stuff in his hold. As his lips rested on it he felt it glide slowly from beneath them, and saw that Mattie had risen and was silently rolling up her work. She fastened it with a pin, and then, finding her thimble and scissors, put them with the roll of stuff into the box covered with fancy paper which he had once brought to her from Bettsbridge.

He stood up also, looking vaguely about the room. The clock above the dresser struck eleven.

"Is the fire all right?" she asked in a low voice.

He opened the door of the stove and poked aimlessly at the embers. When he raised himself again he saw that she was dragging toward the stove the old soap-box lined with carpet in which the cat made its bed. Then she recrossed the floor and lifted two of the geranium pots in her arms, moving them away from the cold window. He followed her and brought the other geraniums, the hyacinth bulbs in a cracked custard bowl and the German ivy trained over an old croquet hoop.

When these nightly duties were performed there was nothing left to do but to bring in the tin candlestick from the passage, light the candle and blow out the lamp. Ethan put the candlestick in Mattie's hand and she went out of the kitchen ahead of him, the light that she carried before her making her dark hair look like a drift of mist on the moon.

"Good night, Matt," he said as she put her foot on the first step of the stairs.

She turned and looked at him a moment. "Good night, Ethan," she answered, and went up.

When the door of her room had closed on her he remembered that he had not even touched her hand.

CHAPTER VI

The next morning at breakfast Jotham Powell was between them, and Ethan tried to hide his joy under an air of exaggerated indifference, lounging back in his chair to throw scraps to the cat, growling at the weather, and not so much as offering to help Mattie when she rose to clear away the dishes.

He did not know why he was so irrationally happy, for nothing was changed in his life or hers. He had not even touched the tip of her fingers or looked her full in the eyes. But their evening together had given him a vision of what life at her side might be, and he was glad now that he had done nothing to trouble the sweetness of the picture. He had a fancy that she knew what had restrained him . . .

There was a last load of lumber to be hauled to the village, and Jotham Powell—who did not work regularly for Ethan in winter—had "come round" to help with the job. But a wet snow, melting to sleet, had fallen in the night and turned the roads to glass. There was more wet in the air and it seemed likely to both men that the weather would "milden" toward afternoon and make the going safer. Ethan therefore proposed to his assistant that they should load the sledge at the wood-lot, as they had done on the previous morning, and put off the "teaming" to Starkfield till later in the day. This plan had the advantage of enabling him to send Jotham to the Flats after dinner to meet Zenobia, while he himself took the lumber down to the village.

He told Jotham to go out and harness up the greys, and for a moment he and Mattie had the kitchen to themselves. She had plunged the breakfast dishes into a tin dish-pan and was bending above it with her slim arms bared to the elbow, the steam from the hot water beading her forehead and tightening her rough hair into little brown rings like the tendrils on the traveller's joy.

Ethan stood looking at her, his heart in his throat. He wanted to say: "We shall never be alone again like this." Instead, he reached down his tobacco-pouch from a shelf of the dresser, put it into his pocket and said: "I guess I can make out to be home for dinner."

She answered "All right, Ethan," and he heard her singing over the dishes as he went.

As soon as the sledge was loaded he meant to send Jotham back to the farm and hurry on foot into the village to buy the glue for the pickle-dish. With ordinary luck he should have had time to carry out this plan; but everything went wrong from the start. On the way over to the wood-lot one of the greys slipped on a glare of ice and cut his knee; and when they got him up again Jotham had to go back to the barn for a strip of rag to bind the cut. Then, when the loading finally began, a sleety rain was coming down once more, and the tree trunks were so slippery that it took twice as long as usual to lift them and get them in place on the sledge. It was what Jotham called a sour morning for work, and the horses, shivering and stamping under their wet blankets, seemed to like it as little as the men. It was long past the dinner-hour when the job was done, and Ethan had to give up going to the village because he wanted to lead the injured horse home and wash the cut himself.

He thought that by starting out again with the lumber as soon as he had finished his dinner he might get back to the farm with the glue before Jotham and the old sorrel had had time to fetch Zenobia from the Flats; but he knew the chance was a slight one. It turned on the state of the roads and on the possible lateness of the Bettsbridge train. He remembered afterward, with a grim flash of self-derision, what importance he had attached to the weighing of these probabilities . . .

As soon as dinner was over he set out again for the wood-lot, not daring to linger till Jotham Powell left. The hired man was still drying his wet feet at the stove, and Ethan could only give Mattie a quick look as he said beneath his breath: "I'll be back early."

He fancied that she nodded her comprehension; and with that scant solace he had to trudge off through the rain.

He had driven his load half-way to the village when Jotham Powell overtook him, urging the reluctant sorrel toward the Flats. "I'll have to hurry up to do it," Ethan mused, as the sleigh dropped down ahead of him over the dip of the schoolhouse hill. He worked like ten at the unloading, and when it was over hastened on to Michael Eady's for the glue. Eady and his assistant were both "down street," and young Denis, who seldom deigned to take their place, was lounging by the stove with a knot of the golden youth of Starkfield. They hailed Ethan with ironic compliment and offers of conviviality; but no one knew where to find the glue. Ethan, consumed with the longing for a last moment alone with Mattie, hung about impatiently while Denis made an ineffectual search in the obscurer corners of the store.

"Looks as if we were all sold out. But if you'll wait around till the old man comes along maybe he can put his hand on it."

"I'm obliged to you, but I'll try if I can get it down at Mrs. Homan's," Ethan answered, burning to be gone.

Denis's commercial instinct compelled him to aver on oath that what Eady's store could not produce would never be found at the widow Homan's; but Ethan, heedless of this boast, had already climbed to the sledge and was driving on to the rival establishment. Here, after considerable search, and sympathetic questions as to what he wanted it for, and whether ordinary flour paste wouldn't do as well if she couldn't find it, the widow Homan finally hunted down her solitary bottle of glue to its hiding-place in a medley of cough-lozenges and corset-laces.

"I hope Zeena ain't broken anything she sets store by," she called after him as he turned the greys toward home.

The fitful bursts of sleet had changed into a steady rain and the horses had heavy work even without a load behind them. Once or twice, hearing sleigh-bells, Ethan turned his head, fancying that Zeena and Jotham might overtake him; but the old sorrel was not in sight, and he set his face against the rain and urged on his ponderous pair.

The barn was empty when the horses turned into it and, after giving them the most perfunctory ministrations they had ever received from him, he strode up to the house and pushed open the kitchen door.

Mattie was there alone, as he had pictured her. She was bending over a pan on the stove; but at the sound of his step she turned with a start and sprang to him.

"See, here, Matt, I've got some stuff to mend the dish with! Let me get at it quick," he cried, waving the bottle in one hand while he put her lightly aside; but she did not seem to hear him.

"Oh, Ethan—Zeena's come," she said in a whisper, clutching his sleeve.

They stood and stared at each other, pale as culprits.

"But the sorrel's not in the barn!" Ethan stammered.

"Jotham Powell brought some goods over from the Flats for his wife, and he drove right on home with them," she explained.

He gazed blankly about the kitchen, which looked cold and squalid in the rainy winter twilight.

"How is she?" he asked, dropping his voice to Mattie's whisper.

She looked away from him uncertainly. "I don't know. She went right up to her room."

"She didn't say anything?"

"No."

Ethan let out his doubts in a low whistle and thrust the bottle back into his pocket. "Don't fret; I'll come down and mend it in the night," he said. He pulled on his wet coat again and went back to the barn to feed the greys.

While he was there Jotham Powell drove up with the sleigh, and when the horses had been attended to Ethan said to him: "You might as well come back up for a bite." He was not sorry to assure himself of Jotham's neutralising presence at the supper table, for Zeena was always "nervous" after a journey. But the hired man, though seldom loth to accept a meal not included in his wages, opened his stiff jaws to answer slowly: "I'm obliged to you, but I guess I'll go along back."

Ethan looked at him in surprise. "Better come up and dry off. Looks as if there'd be something hot for supper."

Jotham's facial muscles were unmoved by this appeal and, his vocabulary being limited, he merely repeated: "I guess I'll go along back."

To Ethan there was something vaguely ominous in this stolid rejection of free food and warmth, and he wondered what had happened on the drive to nerve Jotham to such stoicism. Perhaps Zeena had failed to see the new doctor or had not liked his counsels: Ethan knew that in such cases the first person she met was likely to be held responsible for her grievance.

When he re-entered the kitchen the lamp lit up the same scene of shining comfort as on the previous evening. The table had been as carefully laid, a clear fire glowed in the stove, the cat dozed in its warmth, and Mattie came forward carrying a plate of doughnuts.

She and Ethan looked at each other in silence; then she said, as she had said the night before: "I guess it's about time for supper."

CHAPTER VII

Ethan went out into the passage to hang up his wet garments. He listened for Zeena's step and, not hearing it, called her name up the stairs. She did not answer, and after a moment's hesitation he went up and opened her door. The room was almost dark, but in the obscurity he saw her sitting by the window, bolt upright, and knew by the rigidity of the outline projected against the pane that she had not taken off her travelling dress.

"Well, Zeena," he ventured from the threshold.

She did not move, and he continued: "Supper's about ready. Ain't you coming?"

She replied: "I don't feel as if I could touch a morsel."

It was the consecrated formula, and he expected it to be followed, as usual, by her rising and going down to supper. But she remained seated, and he could think of nothing more felicitous than: "I presume you're tired after the long ride."

Turning her head at this, she answered solemnly: "I'm a great deal sicker than you think."

Her words fell on his ear with a strange shock of wonder. He had often heard her pronounce them before—what if at last they were true?

He advanced a step or two into the dim room. "I hope that's not so, Zeena," he said.

She continued to gaze at him through the twilight with a mien of wan authority, as of one consciously singled out for a great fate. "I've got complications," she said.

Ethan knew the word for one of exceptional import. Almost everybody in the neighbourhood had "troubles," frankly localized and specified; but only the chosen had "complications." To have them was in itself a distinction, though it was also, in most cases, a death-warrant. People struggled on for years with "troubles," but they almost always succumbed to "complications."

Ethan's heart was jerking to and fro between two extremities of feeling, but for the moment compassion prevailed. His wife looked so hard and lonely, sitting there in the darkness with such thoughts.

"Is that what the new doctor told you?" he asked, instinctively lowering his voice.

"Yes. He says any regular doctor would want me to have an operation."

Ethan was aware that, in regard to the important question of surgical intervention, the female opinion of the neighbourhood was divided, some glorying in the prestige conferred by operations while others shunned them as indelicate. Ethan, from motives of economy, had always been glad that Zeena was of the latter faction.

In the agitation caused by the gravity of her announcement he sought a consolatory short cut. "What do you know about this doctor anyway? Nobody ever told you that before."

He saw his blunder before she could take it up: she wanted sympathy, not consolation.

"I didn't need to have anybody tell me I was losing ground every day. Everybody but you could see it. And everybody in Bettsbridge knows about Dr. Buck. He has his office in Worcester, and comes over once a fortnight to Shadd's Falls and Bettsbridge for consultations. Eliza Spears was wasting away with kidney trouble before she went to him, and now she's up and around, and singing in the choir."

"Well, I'm glad of that. You must do just what he tells you," Ethan answered sympathetically.

She was still looking at him. "I mean to," she said. He was struck by a new note in her voice. It was neither whining nor reproachful, but drily resolute.

"What does he want you should do?" he asked, with a mounting vision of fresh expenses.

"He wants I should have a hired girl. He says I oughtn't to have to do a single thing around the house."

"A hired girl?" Ethan stood transfixed.

"Yes. And Aunt Martha found me one right off. Everybody said I was lucky to get a girl to come away out here, and I agreed to give her a dollar extry to make sure. She'll be over to-morrow afternoon."

Wrath and dismay contended in Ethan. He had foreseen an

immediate demand for money, but not a permanent drain on hi scant resources. He no longer believed what Zeena had told hir of the supposed seriousness of her state: he saw in her expeditio to Bettsbridge only a plot hatched between herself and her Pierc relations to foist on him the cost of a servant; and for th moment wrath predominated.

"If you meant to engage a girl you ought to have told m before you started," he said.

"How could I tell you before I started? How did I know wha Dr. Buck would say?"

"Oh, Dr. Buck—" Ethan's incredulity escaped in a short laugh "Did Dr. Buck tell you how I was to pay her wages?"

Her voice rose furiously with his. "No, he didn't. For I'd 'a been ashamed to tell *him* that you grudged me the money to ge back my health, when I lost it nursing your own mother!"

"*You* lost your health nursing mother?"

"Yes; and my folks all told me at the time you couldn't do n less than marry me after——"

"Zeena!"

Through the obscurity which hid their faces their thought seemed to dart at each other like serpents shooting venom. Etha was seized with horror of the scene and shame at his own shar in it. It was as senseless and savage as a physical fight betwee two enemies in the darkness.

He turned to the shelf above the chimney, groped for matche and lit the one candle in the room. At first its weak flame mad no impression on the shadows; then Zeena's face stood griml out against the uncurtained pane, which had turned from grey t black.

It was the first scene of open anger between the couple in the sad seven years together, and Ethan felt as if he had lost a irretrievable advantage in descending to the level of recrimina tion. But the practical problem was there and had to be dea with.

"You know I haven't got the money to pay for a girl, Zeena You'll have to send her back: I can't do it."

"The doctor says it'll be my death if I go on slaving the wa I've had to. He doesn't understand how I've stood it as long as have."

"Slaving!—" He checked himself again, "You sha'n't lift hand, if he says so. I'll do everything round the house myself——

She broke in: "You're neglecting the farm enough already, and this being true, he found no answer, and left her time to ad ironically: "Better send me over to the almshouse and done with it . . . I guess there's been Fromes there afore now."

The taunt burned into him, but he let it pass. "I haven't got the money. That settles it."

There was a moment's pause in the struggle, as though the combatants were testing their weapons. Then Zeena said in a level voice: "I thought you were to get fifty dollars from Andrew Hale for that lumber."

"Andrew Hale never pays under three months." He had hardly spoken when he remembered the excuse he had made for not accompanying his wife to the station the day before; and the blood rose to his frowning brows.

"Why, you told me yesterday you'd fixed it up with him to pay cash down. You said that was why you couldn't drive me over to the Flats."

Ethan had no suppleness in deceiving. He had never before been convicted of a lie, and all the resources of evasion failed him. "I guess that was a misunderstanding," he stammered.

"You ain't got the money?"

"No."

"And you ain't going to get it?"

"No."

"Well, I couldn't know that when I engaged the girl, could I?"

"No." He paused to control his voice. "But you know it now. I'm sorry, but it can't be helped. You're a poor man's wife, Zeena; but I'll do the best I can for you."

For a while she sat motionless, as if reflecting, her arms stretched along the arms of her chair, her eyes fixed on vacancy. "Oh, I guess we'll make out," she said mildly.

The change in her tone reassured him. "Of course we will! There's a whole lot more I can do for you, and Mattie——"

Zeena, while he spoke, seemed to be following out some elaborate mental calculation. She emerged from it to say: "There'll be Mattie's board less, anyhow——"

Ethan, supposing the discussion to be over, had turned to go down to supper. He stopped short, not grasping what he heard. "Mattie's board less—?" he began.

Zeena laughed. It was an odd unfamiliar sound—he did not remember ever having heard her laugh before. "You didn't suppose I was going to keep two girls, did you? No wonder you were scared at the expense!"

He still had but a confused sense of what she was saying.

From the beginning of the discussion he had instinctively avoided the mention of Mattie's name, fearing he hardly knew what criticism, complaints, or vague allusions to the imminent probability of her marrying. But the thought of a definite rupture had never come to him, and even now could not lodge itself in hi mind.

"I don't know what you mean," he said. "Mattie Silver's no a hired girl. She's your relation."

"She's a pauper that's hung onto us all after her father'd done his best to ruin us. I've kep' her here a whole year: it's somebody else's turn now."

As the shrill words shot out Ethan heard a tap on the door which he had drawn shut when he turned back from the threshold

"Ethan—Zeena!" Mattie's voice sounded gaily from the landing, "do you know what time it is? Supper's been ready half an hour."

Inside the room there was a moment's silence; then Zeen called out from her seat: "I'm not coming down to supper."

"Oh, I'm sorry! Aren't you well? Sha'n't I bring you up a bit of something?"

Ethan roused himself with an effort and opened the door. "Go along down, Matt. Zeena's just a little tired. I'm coming."

He heard her "All right!" and her quick step on the stairs then he shut the door and turned back into the room. His wife' attitude was unchanged, her face inexorable, and he was seized with the despairing sense of his helplessness.

"You ain't going to do it, Zeena?"

"Do what?" she emitted between flattened lips.

"Send Mattie away—like this?"

"I never bargained to take her for life!"

He continued with rising vehemence: "You can't put her ou of the house like a thief—a poor girl without friends or money She's done her best for you and she's got no place to go to. Yo may forget she's your kin but everybody else'll remember it. I you do a thing like that what do you suppose folks'll say o you?"

Zeena waited a moment, as if giving him time to feel the full force of the contrast between his own excitement and her composure. Then she replied in the same smooth voice: "I know wel enough what they say of my having kep' her here as long as have."

Ethan's hand dropped from the door-knob, which he had held clenched since he had drawn the door shut on Mattie. His wife' retort was like a knife-cut across the sinews and he felt suddenly weak and powerless. He had meant to humble himself, to argue that Mattie's keep didn't cost much, after all, that he could make out to buy a stove and fix up a place in the attic for the hired girl—but Zeena's words revealed the peril of such pleadings.

"You mean to tell her she's got to go—at once?" he faltered out, in terror of letting his wife complete her sentence.

As if trying to make him see reason she replied impartially: "The girl will be over from Bettsbridge to-morrow, and I presume she's got to have somewheres to sleep."

Ethan looked at her with loathing. She was no longer the listless creature who had lived at his side in a state of sullen self-absorption, but a mysterious alien presence, an evil energy secreted from the long years of silent brooding. It was the sense of his helplessness that sharpened his antipathy. There had never been anything in her that one could appeal to; but as long as he could ignore and command he had remained indifferent. Now she had mastered him and he abhorred her. Mattie was her relation, not his: there were no means by which he could compel her to keep the girl under her roof. All the long misery of his baffled past, of his youth of failure, hardship and vain effort, rose up in his soul in bitterness and seemed to take shape before him in the woman who at every turn had barred his way. She had taken everything else from him; and now she meant to take the one thing that made up for all the others. For a moment such a flame of hate rose in him that it ran down his arm and clenched his fist against her. He took a wild step forward and then stopped.

"You're—you're not coming down?" he said in a bewildered voice.

"No. I guess I'll lay down on the bed a little while," she answered mildly; and he turned and walked out of the room.

In the kitchen Mattie was sitting by the stove, the cat curled up on her knees. She sprang to her feet as Ethan entered and carried the covered dish of meat-pie to the table.

"I hope Zeena isn't sick?" she asked.

"No."

She shone at him across the table. "Well, sit right down then. You must be starving." She uncovered the pie and pushed it over to him. So they were to have one more evening together, her happy eyes seemed to say!

He helped himself mechanically and began to eat; then disgust took him by the throat and he laid down his fork.

Mattie's tender gaze was on him and she marked the gesture.

"Why, Ethan, what's the matter? Don't it taste right?"

"Yes—it's first-rate. Only I—" He pushed his plate away, rose from his chair, and walked around the table to her side. She started up with frightened eyes.

"Ethan, there's something wrong! I *knew* there was!"

She seemed to melt against him in her terror, and he caught her in his arms, held her fast there, felt her lashes beat his cheek like netted butterflies.

"What is it—what is it?" she stammered; but he had found her lips at last and was drinking unconscious of everything but the joy they gave him.

She lingered a moment, caught in the same strong current; then she slipped from him and drew back a step or two, pale and troubled. Her look smote him with compunction, and he cried out, as if he saw her drowning in a dream: "You can't go, Matt! I'll never let you!"

"Go—go?" she stammered. "Must I go?"

The words went on sounding between them as though a torch of warning flew from hand to hand through a black landscape.

Ethan was overcome with shame at his lack of self-control in flinging the news at her so brutally. His head reeled and he had to support himself against the table. All the while he felt as if he were still kissing her, and yet dying of thirst for her lips.

"Ethan, what has happened? Is Zeena mad with me?"

Her cry steadied him, though it deepened his wrath and pity. "No, no," he assured her, "it's not that. But this new doctor has scared her about herself. You know she believes all they say the first time she sees them. And this one's told her she won't get well unless she lays up and don't do a thing about the house—not for months——"

He paused, his eyes wandering from her miserably. She stood silent a moment, drooping before him like a broken branch. She was so small and weak-looking that it wrung his heart; but suddenly she lifted her head and looked straight at him. "And she wants somebody handier in my place? Is that it?"

"That's what she says to-night."

"If she says it to-night she'll say it to-morrow."

Both bowed to the inexorable truth: they knew that Zeena never changed her mind, and that in her case a resolve once taken was equivalent to an act performed.

There was a long silence between them; then Mattie said in a low voice: "Don't be too sorry, Ethan."

"Oh, God—oh, God," he groaned. The glow of passion he had felt for her had melted to an aching tenderness. He saw her quick lids beating back the tears, and longed to take her in his arms and soothe her.

"You're letting your supper get cold," she admonished him with a pale gleam of gaiety.

"Oh, Matt—Matt—where'll you go to?"

Her lids sank and a tremor crossed her face. He saw that for the first time the thought of the future came to her distinctly. "I might get something to do over at Stamford," she faltered, as if knowing that he knew she had no hope.

He dropped back into his seat and hid his face in his hands. Despair seized him at the thought of her setting out alone to renew the weary quest for work. In the only place where she was known she was surrounded by indifference or animosity; and what chance had she, inexperienced and untrained, among the million bread-seekers of the cities? There came back to him miserable tales he had heard at Worcester, and the faces of girls whose lives had begun as hopefully as Mattie's. . . . It was not possible to think of such things without a revolt of his whole being. He sprang up suddenly.

"You can't go, Matt! I won't let you! She's always had her way, but I mean to have mine now——"

Mattie lifted her hand with a quick gesture, and he heard his wife's step behind him.

Zeena came into the room with her dragging down-at-the-heel step, and quietly took her accustomed seat between them.

"I felt a little mite better, and Dr. Buck says I ought to eat all I can to keep my strength up, even if I ain't got any appetite," she said in her flat whine, reaching across Mattie for the teapot. Her "good" dress had been replaced by the black calico and brown knitted shawl which formed her daily wear, and with them she had put on her usual face and manner. She poured out her tea, added a great deal of milk to it, helped herself largely to pie and pickles, and made the familiar gesture of adjusting her false teeth before she began to eat. The cat rubbed itself ingratiatingly against her, and she said "Good Pussy," stooped to stroke it and gave it a scrap of meat from her plate.

Ethan sat speechless, not pretending to eat, but Mattie nibbled valiantly at her food and asked Zeena one or two questions about her visit to Bettsbridge. Zeena answered in her every-day tone and, warming to the theme, regaled them with several vivid descriptions of intestinal disturbances among her friends and relatives. She looked straight at Mattie as she spoke, a faint smile deepening the vertical lines between her nose and chin.

When supper was over she rose from her seat and pressed her hand to the flat surface over the region of her heart. "That pie of yours always sets a mite heavy, Matt," she said, not ill-naturedly. She seldom abbreviated the girl's name, and when she did so it was always a sign of affability.

"I've a good mind to go and hunt up those stomach powders I got last year over in Springfield," she continued. "I ain't tried them for quite a while, and maybe they'll help the heartburn."

Mattie lifted her eyes. "Can't I get them for you, Zeena?" she ventured.

"No. They're in a place you don't know about," Zeena answered darkly, with one of her secret looks.

She went out of the kitchen and Mattie, rising, began to clear the dishes from the table. As she passed Ethan's chair their eyes met and clung together desolately. The warm still kitchen looked as peaceful as the night before. The cat had sprung to Zeena's rocking-chair, and the heat of the fire was beginning to draw out the faint sharp scent of the geraniums. Ethan dragged himself wearily to his feet.

"I'll go out and take a look around," he said, going toward the passage to get his lantern.

As he reached the door he met Zeena coming back into the room, her lips twitching with anger, a flush of excitement on her sallow face. The shawl had slipped from her shoulders and was dragging at her down-trodden heels, and in her hands she carried the fragments of the red glass pickle-dish.

"I'd like to know who done this," she said, looking sternly from Ethan to Mattie.

There was no answer, and she continued in a trembling voice: "I went to get those powders I'd put away in father's old spectacle-case, top of the china-closet, where I keep the things I set store by, so's folks sha'n't meddle with them—" Her voice broke, and two small tears hung on her lashless lids and ran slowly down her cheeks. "It takes the step-ladder to get at the top shelf, and I put Aunt Philura Maple's pickle-dish up there o' purpose when we was married, and it's never been down since, 'cept for the spring cleaning, and then I always lifted it with my own hands, so's 't shouldn't get broke." She laid the fragments reverently on the table. "I want to know who done this," she quavered.

At the challenge Ethan turned back into the room and faced her. "I can tell you, then. The cat done it."

"The *cat*?"

"That's what I said."

She looked at him hard, and then turned her eyes to Mattie, who was carrying the dish-pan to the table.

"I'd like to know how the cat got into my china-closet," she said.

"Chasin' mice, I guess," Ethan rejoiced. "There was a mouse round the kitchen all last evening."

Zeena continued to look from one to the other; then she emitted her small strange laugh. "I knew the cat was a smart cat," she said in a high voice, "but I didn't know he was smart enough to pick up the pieces of my pickle-dish and lay 'em edge to edge on the very shelf he knocked 'em off of."

Mattie suddenly drew her arms out of the steaming water. "It wasn't Ethan's fault, Zeena! The cat *did* break the dish; but I got it down from the china-closet, and I'm the one to blame for its getting broken."

Zeena stood beside the ruin of her treasure, stiffening into a stony image of resentment. "*You* got down my pickle-dish—what for?"

A bright flush flew to Mattie's cheeks. "I wanted to make the supper-table pretty," she said.

"You wanted to make the supper-table pretty; and you waited till my back was turned, and took the thing I set most store by of everything I've got, and wouldn't never use it, not even when the minister come to dinner, or Aunt Martha Pierce come over from Bettsbridge—" Zeena paused with a gasp, as if terrified by her own evocation of the sacrilege. "You're a bad girl, Mattie Silver, and I always known it. It's the way your father begun, and I was warned of it when I took you, and I tried to keep my things where you couldn't get at 'em—and now you've took from me the one I cared for most of all—" She broke off in a short spasm of sobs that passed and left her more than ever like a shape of stone.

"If I'd 'a' listened to folks, you'd 'a' gone before now, and this wouldn't 'a' happened," she said; and gathering up the bits of broken glass she went out of the room as if she carried a dead body . . .

CHAPTER VIII

When Ethan was called back to the farm by his father's illness his mother gave him, for his own use, a small room behind the untenanted "best parlour." Here he had nailed up shelves for his books, built himself a box-sofa out of boards and a mattress, laid out his papers on a kitchen-table, hung on the rough plaster wall an engraving of Abraham Lincoln and a calendar with "Thoughts from the Poets," and tried, with these meagre properties, to produce some likeness to the study of a "minister" who had been kind to him and lent him books when he was at Worcester. He still took refuge there in summer, but when Mattie came to live at the farm he had had to give her his stove, and consequently the room was uninhabitable for several months of the year.

To this retreat he descended as soon as the house was quiet, and Zeena's steady breathing from the bed had assured him that there was to be no sequel to the scene in the kitchen. After Zeena's departure he and Mattie had stood speechless, neither seeking to approach the other. Then the girl had returned to her task of clearing up the kitchen for the night and he had taken his lantern and gone on his usual round outside the house. The kitchen was empty when he came back to it; but his tobacco-pouch and pipe had been laid on the table, and under them was a scrap of paper torn from the back of a seedsman's catalogue, on which three words were written: "Don't trouble, Ethan."

Going into his cold dark "study" he placed the lantern on the table and, stooping to its light, read the message again and again. It was the first time that Mattie had ever written to him, and the possession of the paper gave him a strange new sense of her nearness; yet it deepened his anguish by reminding him that henceforth they would have no other way of communicating with each other. For the life of her smile, the warmth of her voice, only cold paper and dead words!

Confused motions of rebellion stormed in him. He was too young, too strong, too full of the sap of living, to submit so easily to the destruction of his hopes. Must he wear out all his years at the side of a bitter querulous woman? Other possibilities had been in him, possibilities sacrificed, one by one, to Zeena's narrow-mindedness and ignorance. And what good had come of it? She was a hundred times bitterer and more discontented than when he had married her: the one pleasure left her was to inflict pain on him. All the healthy instincts of self-defence rose up in him against such waste . . .

He bundled himself into his old coon-skin coat and lay down on the box-sofa to think. Under his cheek he felt a hard object with strange protuberances. It was a cushion which Zeena had made for him when they were engaged—the only piece of needlework he had ever seen her do. He flung it across the floor and propped his head against the wall . . .

He knew a case of a man over the mountain—a young fellow of about his own age—who had escaped from just such a life of misery by going West with the girl he cared for. His wife had divorced him, and he had married the girl and prospered. Ethan had seen the couple the summer before at Shadd's Falls, where they had come to visit relatives. They had a little girl with fair curls, who wore a gold locket and was dressed like a princess. The deserted wife had not done badly either. Her husband had given her the farm and she had managed to sell it, and with that and the alimony she had started a lunch-room at Bettsbridge and bloomed into activity and importance. Ethan was fired by the thought. Why should he not leave with Mattie the next day, instead of letting her go alone? He would hide his valise under the seat of the sleigh, and Zeena would suspect nothing till she went upstairs for her afternoon nap and found a letter on the bed . . .

His impulses were still near the surface, and he sprang up, re-lit the lantern, and sat down at the table. He rummaged in the drawer for a sheet of paper, found one, and began to write.

"Zeena, I've done all I could for you, and I don't see as it's been any use. I don't blame you, nor I don't blame myself. Maybe both of us will do better separate. I'm going to try my luck West, and you can sell the farm and mill, and keep the money——"

His pen paused on the word, which brought home to him the

relentless conditions of his lot. If he gave the farm and mill to Zeena what would be left him to start his own life with? Once in the West he was sure of picking up work—he would not have feared to try his chance alone. But with Mattie depending on him the case was different. And what of Zeena's fate? Farm and mill were mortgaged to the limit of their value, and even if she found a purchaser—in itself an unlikely chance—it was doubtful if she could clear a thousand dollars on the sale. Meanwhile, how could she keep the farm going? It was only by incessant labour and personal supervision that Ethan drew a meagre living from his land, and his wife, even if she were in better health than she imagined, could never carry such a burden alone.

Well, she could go back to her people, then, and see what they would do for her. It was the fate she was forcing on Mattie—why not let her try it herself? By the time she had discovered his whereabouts, and brought suit for divorce, he would probably—wherever he was—be earning enough to pay her a sufficient alimony. And the alternative was to let Mattie go forth alone, with far less hope of ultimate provision . . .

He had scattered the contents of the table-drawer in his search for a sheet of paper, and as he took up his pen his eye fell on an old copy of the *Bettsbridge Eagle*. The advertising sheet was folded uppermost, and he read the seductive words: "Trips to the West: Reduced Rates."

He drew the lantern nearer and eagerly scanned the fares; then the paper fell from his hand and he pushed aside his unfinished letter. A moment ago he had wondered what he and Mattie were to live on when they reached the West; now he saw that he had not even the money to take her there. Borrowing was out of the question: six months before he had given his only security to raise funds for necessary repairs to the mill, and he knew that without security no one at Starkfield would lend him ten dollars. The inexorable facts closed in on him like prison-warders handcuffing a convict. There was no way out—none. He was a prisoner for life, and now his one ray of light was to be extinguished.

He crept back heavily to the sofa, stretching himself out with limbs so leaden that he felt as if they would never move again. Tears rose in his throat and slowly burned their way to his lids.

As he lay there, the window-pane that faced him, growing gradually lighter, inlaid upon the darkness a square of moon-suffused sky. A crooked tree-branch crossed it, a branch of the apple-tree under which, on summer evenings, he had sometimes found Mattie sitting when he came up from the mill. Slowly the rim of the rainy vapours caught fire and burnt away, and a pure moon swung into the blue. Ethan, rising on his elbow, watched the landscape whiten and shape itself under the sculpture of the moon. This was the night on which he was to have taken Mattie coasting, and there hung the lamp to light them! He looked out at the slopes bathed in lustre, the silver-edged darkness of the woods, the spectral purple of the hills against the sky, and it seemed as though all the beauty of the night had been poured out to mock his wretchedness . . .

He fell asleep, and when he woke the chill of the winter dawn was in the room. He felt cold and stiff and hungry, and ashamed of being hungry. He rubbed his eyes and went to the window. A red sun stood over the grey rim of the fields, behind trees that looked black and brittle. He said to himself: "This is Matt's last day," and tried to think what the place would be without her.

As he stood there he heard a step behind him and she entered.

"Oh, Ethan—were you here all night?"

She looked so small and pinched, in her poor dress, with the red scarf wound about her, and the cold light turning her paleness sallow, that Ethan stood before her without speaking.

"You must be frozen," she went on, fixing lustreless eyes on him.

He drew a step nearer. "How did you know I was here?"

"Because I heard you go down stairs again after I went to bed, and I listened all night, and you didn't come up."

All his tenderness rushed to his lips. He looked at her and said: "I'll come right along and make up the kitchen fire."

They went back to the kitchen, and he fetched the coal and kindlings and cleared out the stove for her, while she brought in the milk and the cold remains of the meat-pie. When warmth began to radiate from the stove, and the first ray of sunlight lay on the kitchen floor, Ethan's dark thoughts melted in the mellower air. The sight of Mattie going about her work as he had seen her on so many mornings made it seem impossible that she should ever cease to be a part of the scene. He said to himself that he had doubtless exaggerated the significance of Zeena's threats, and that she too, with the return of daylight, would come to a saner mood.

He went up to Mattie as she bent above the stove, and laid his hand on her arm. "I don't want you should trouble either," he said, looking down into her eyes with a smile.

She flushed up warmly and whispered back: "No, Ethan, I ain't going to trouble."

"I guess things'll straighten out," he added.

There was no answer but a quick throb of her lids, and he went on: "She ain't said anything this morning?"

"No. I haven't seen her yet."

"Don't you take any notice when you do."

With this injunction he left her and went out to the cow-barn. He saw Jotham Powell walking up the hill through the morning mist, and the familiar sight added to his growing conviction of security.

As the two men were clearing out the stalls Jotham rested on his pitch-fork to say: "Dan'l Byrne's goin' over to the Flats to-day noon, an' he c'd take Mattie's trunk along, and make it easier ridin' when I take her over in the sleigh."

Ethan looked at him blankly, and he continued: "Mis' Frome said the new girl'd be at the Flats at five, and I was to take Mattie then, so's 't she could ketch the six o'clock train for Stamford."

Ethan felt the blood drumming in his temples. He had to wait a moment before he could find voice to say: "Oh, it ain't so sure about Mattie's going——"

"That so?" said Jotham indifferently; and they went on with their work.

When they returned to the kitchen the two women were already at breakfast. Zeena had an air of unusual alertness and activity. She drank two cups of coffee and fed the cat with the scraps left in the pie-dish; then she rose from her seat and, walking over to the window, snipped two or three yellow leaves from the geraniums. "Aunt Martha's ain't got a faded leaf on 'em; but they pine away when they ain't cared for," she said reflectively. Then she turned to Jotham and asked: "What time'd you say Dan'l Byrne'd be along?"

The hired man threw a hesitating glance at Ethan. "Round about noon," he said.

Zeena turned to Mattie. "That trunk of yours is too heavy for the sleigh, and Dan'l Byrne'll be round to take it over to the Flats," she said.

"I'm much obliged to you, Zeena," said Mattie.

"I'd like to go over things with you first," Zeena continued in an unperturbed voice. "I know there's a huckabuck towel missing; and I can't take out what you done with that match-safe 't used to stand behind the stuffed owl in the parlour."

She went out, followed by Mattie, and when the men were alone Jotham said to his employer: "I guess I better let Dan'l come round, then."

Ethan finished his usual morning tasks about the house and barn; then he said to Jotham: "I'm going down to Starkfield. Tell them not to wait dinner."

The passion of rebellion had broken out in him again. That which had seemed incredible in the sober light of day had really come to pass, and he was to assist as a helpless spectator at Mattie's banishment. His manhood was humbled by the part he was compelled to play and by the thought of what Mattie must think of him. Confused impulses struggled in him as he strode along to the village. He had made up his mind to do something, but he did not know what it would be.

The early mist had vanished and the fields lay like a silver shield under the sun. It was one of the days when the glitter of winter shines through a pale haze of spring. Every yard of the road was alive with Mattie's presence, and there was hardly a branch against the sky or a tangle of brambles on the bank in which some bright shred of memory was not caught. Once, in the stillness, the call of a bird in a mountain ash was so like her laughter that his heart tightened and then grew large; and all these things made him see that something must be done at once.

Suddenly it occurred to him that Andrew Hale, who was a kind-hearted man, might be induced to reconsider his refusal and advance a small sum on the lumber if he were told that Zeena's ill-health made it necessary to hire a servant. Hale, after all, knew enough of Ethan's situation to make it possible for the latter to renew his appeal without too much loss of pride; and, moreover, how much did pride count in the ebullition of passions in his breast?

The more he considered his plan the more hopeful it seemed. If he could get Mrs. Hale's ear he felt certain of success, and with fifty dollars in his pocket nothing could keep him from Mattie . . .

His first object was to reach Starkfield before Hale had started for his work; he knew the carpenter had a job down the Corbury road and was likely to leave his house early. Ethan's long strides grew more rapid with the accelerated beat of his thoughts, and as he reached the foot of School House Hill he caught sight of Hale's sleigh in the distance. He hurried forward to meet it, but as it drew nearer he saw that it was driven by the carpenter's youngest boy and that the figure at his side, looking like a large upright cocoon in spectacles, was that of Mrs. Hale. Ethan signed to them to stop, and Mrs. Hale leaned forward, her pink wrinkles twinkling with benevolence.

"Mr. Hale? Why, yes, you'll find him down home now. He ain't going to his work this forenoon. He woke up with a touch o' lumbago, and I just made him put on one of old Dr. Kidder's plasters and set right up into the fire."

Beaming maternally on Ethan, she bent over to add: "I on'y just heard from Mr. Hale 'bout Zeena's going over to Bettsbridge to see that new doctor. I'm real sorry she's feeling so bad again! I hope he thinks he can do something for her. I don't know anybody round here's had more sickness than Zeena. I always tell Mr. Hale I don't know what she'd 'a' done if she hadn't 'a' had you to look after her; and I used to say the same thing 'bout your mother. You've had an awful mean time, Ethan Frome."

She gave him a last nod of sympathy while her son chirped to the horse; and Ethan, as she drove off, stood in the middle of the road and stared after the retreating sleigh.

It was a long time since any one had spoken to him as kindly as Mrs. Hale. Most people were either indifferent to his troubles, or disposed to think it natural that a young fellow of his age should have carried without repining the burden of three crippled lives. But Mrs. Hale had said, "You've had an awful mean time, Ethan Frome," and he felt less alone with his misery. If the Hales were sorry for him they would surely respond to his appeal . . .

He started down the road toward their house, but at the end of a few yards he pulled up sharply, the blood in his face. For the first time, in the light of the words he had just heard, he saw what he was about to do. He was planning to take advantage of the Hales' sympathy to obtain money from them on false pretences. That was a plain statement of the cloudy purpose which had driven him in headlong to Starkfield.

With the sudden perception of the point to which his madness had carried him, the madness fell and he saw his life before him as it was. He was a poor man, the husband of a sickly woman, whom his desertion would leave alone and destitute; and even if he had had the heart to desert her he could have done so only by deceiving two kindly people who had pitied him.

He turned and walked slowly back to the farm.

CHAPTER IX

At the kitchen door Daniel Byrne sat in his sleigh behind a big-boned grey who pawed the snow and swung his long head restlessly from side to side.

Ethan went into the kitchen and found his wife by the stove. Her head was wrapped in her shawl, and she was reading a book called "Kidney Troubles and Their Cure" on which he had had to pay extra postage only a few days before.

Zeena did not move or look up when he entered, and after a moment he asked: "Where's Mattie?"

Without lifting her eyes from the page she replied: "I presume she's getting down her trunk."

The blood rushed to his face. "Getting down her trunk—alone?"

"Jotham Powell's down in the wood-lot, and Dan'l Byrne says he darsn't leave that horse," she returned.

Her husband, without stopping to hear the end of the phrase, had left the kitchen and sprung up the stairs. The door of Mattie's room was shut, and he wavered a moment on the landing. "Matt," he said in a low voice; but there was no answer, and he put his hand on the door-knob.

He had never been in her room except once, in the early summer, when he had gone there to plaster up a leak in the eaves, but he remembered exactly how everything had looked: the red-and-white quilt on her narrow bed, the pretty pin-cushion on the chest of drawers, and over it the enlarged photograph of her mother, in an oxydized frame, with a bunch of dyed grasses at the back. Now these and all other tokens of her presence had vanished and the room looked as bare and comfortless as when Zeena had shown her into it on the day of her arrival. In the middle of the floor stood her trunk, and on the trunk she sat in her Sunday dress, her back turned to the door and her face in her hands. She had not heard Ethan's call because she was sobbing and she did not hear his step till he stood close behind her and laid his hands on her shoulders.

"Matt—oh, don't—oh, *Matt*!"

She started up, lifting her wet face to his. "Ethan—I thought I wasn't ever going to see you again!"

He took her in his arms, pressing her close, and with a trembling hand smoothed away the hair from her forehead.

"Not see me again? What do you mean?"

She sobbed out: "Jotham said you told him we wasn't to wait dinner for you, and I thought——"

"You thought I meant to cut it?" he finished for her grimly.

She clung to him without answering, and he laid his lips on her hair, which was soft yet springy, like certain mosses on warm slopes, and had the faint woody fragrance of fresh sawdust in the sun.

Through the door they heard Zeena's voice calling out from below: "Dan'l Byrne says you better hurry up if you want him to take that trunk."

They drew apart with stricken faces. Words of resistance rushed to Ethan's lips and died there. Mattie found her handkerchief and dried her eyes; then, bending down, she took hold of a handle of the trunk.

Ethan put her aside. "You let go, Matt," he ordered her.

She answered: "It takes two to coax it round the corner"; and submitting to this argument he grasped the other handle, and together they manœuvred the heavy trunk out to the landing.

"Now let go," he repeated; then he shouldered the trunk and carried it down the stairs and across the passage to the kitchen. Zeena, who had gone back to her seat by the stove, did not lift her head from her book as he passed. Mattie followed him out of the door and helped him to lift the trunk into the back of the sleigh. When it was in place they stood side by side on the door-step, watching Daniel Byrne plunge off behind his fidgety horse.

It seemed to Ethan that his heart was bound with cords which an unseen hand was tightening with every tick of the clock. Twice he opened his lips to speak to Mattie and found no breath. At length, as she turned to re-enter the house, he laid a detaining hand on her.

"I'm going to drive you over, Matt," he whispered.

She murmured back: "I think Zeena wants I should go with Jotham."

"I'm going to drive you over," he repeated; and she went into the kitchen without answering.

At dinner Ethan could not eat. If he lifted his eyes they rested on Zeena's pinched face, and the corners of her straight lips seemed to quiver away into a smile. She ate well, declaring that the mild weather made her feel better, and pressed a second helping of beans on Jotham Powell, whose wants she generally ignored.

Mattie, when the meal was over, went about her usual task of clearing the table and washing up the dishes. Zeena, after feeding the cat, had returned to her rocking-chair by the stove, and Jotham Powell, who always lingered last, reluctantly pushed back his chair and moved toward the door.

On the threshold he turned back to say to Ethan: "What time'll I come round for Mattie?"

Ethan was standing near the window, mechanically filling his pipe while he watched Mattie move to and fro. He answered: "You needn't come round; I'm going to drive her over myself."

He saw the rise of the colour in Mattie's averted cheek, and the quick lifting of Zeena's head.

"I want you should stay here this afternoon, Ethan," his wife said. "Jotham can drive Mattie over."

Mattie flung an imploring glance at him, but he repeated curtly: "I'm going to drive her over myself."

Zeena continued in the same even tone: "I wanted you should stay and fix up that stove in Mattie's room afore the girl gets here. It ain't been drawing right for nigh on a month now."

Ethan's voice rose indignantly. "If it was good enough for Mattie I guess it's good enough for a hired girl."

"That girl that's coming told me she was used to a house where they had a furnace," Zeena persisted with the same monotonous mildness.

"She'd better ha' stayed there then," he flung back at her; and turning to Mattie he added in a hard voice: "You be ready by three, Matt; I've got business at Corbury."

Jotham Powell had started for the barn, and Ethan strode down after him aflame with anger. The pulses in his temples throbbed and a fog was in his eyes. He went about his task without knowing what force directed him, or whose hands and feet were fulfilling its orders. It was not till he led out the sorrel and backed him between the shafts of the sleigh that he once more became conscious of what he was doing. As he passed the bridle over the horse's head, and wound the traces around the shafts, he remembered the day when he had made the same preparations in order to drive over and meet his wife's cousin at the Flats. It was little more than a year ago, on just such a soft afternoon, with a "feel" of spring in the air. The sorrel, turning the same big ringed eye on him, nuzzled the palm of his hand in the same way; and one by one all the days between rose up and stood before him . . .

He flung the bearskin into the sleigh, climbed to the seat, and drove up to the house. When he entered the kitchen it was empty, but Mattie's bag and shawl lay ready by the door. He went to the foot of the stairs and listened. No sound reached him from above, but presently he thought he heard some one moving about in his deserted study, and pushing open the door he saw Mattie, in her hat and jacket, standing with her back to him near the table.

She started at his approach and turning quickly, said: "Is it time?"

"What are you doing here, Matt?" he asked her.

She looked at him timidly. "I was just taking a look round—that's all," she answered, with a wavering smile.

They went back into the kitchen without speaking, and Ethan picked up her bag and shawl.

"Where's Zeena?" he asked.

"She went upstairs right after dinner. She said she had those shooting pains again, and didn't want to be disturbed."

"Didn't she say good-bye to you?"

"No. That was all she said."

Ethan, looking slowly about the kitchen, said to himself with a shudder that in a few hours he would be returning to it alone. Then the sense of unreality overcame him once more, and he could not bring himself to believe that Mattie stood there for the last time before him.

"Come on," he said almost gaily, opening the door and putting her bag into the sleigh. He sprang to his seat and bent over to tuck the rug about her as she slipped into the place at his side. "Now then, go 'long," he said, with a shake of the reins that sent the sorrel placidly jogging down the hill.

"We got lots of time for a good ride, Matt!" he cried, seeking her hand beneath the fur and pressing it in his. His face tingled and he felt dizzy, as if he had stopped in at the Starkfield saloon on a zero day for a drink.

At the gate, instead of making for Starkfield, he turned the sorrel to the right, up the Bettsbridge road. Mattie sat silent, giving no sign of surprise; but after a moment she said: "Are you going round by Shadow Pond?"

He laughed and answered: "I knew you'd know!"

She drew closer under the bearskin, so that, looking sideways around his coat-sleeve, he could just catch the tip of her nose and a blown brown wave of hair. They drove slowly up the road between fields glistening under the pale sun, and then bent to the right down a lane edged with spruce and larch. Ahead of them, a long way off, a range of hills stained by mottlings of black forest flowed away in round white curves against the sky. The lane passed into a pine-wood with boles reddening in the afternoon sun and delicate blue shadows on the snow. As they entered it the breeze fell and a warm stillness seemed to drop from the branches with the dropping needles. Here the snow was so pure that the tiny tracks of wood-animals had left on it intricate lace-like patterns, and the bluish cones caught in its surface stood out like ornaments of bronze.

Ethan drove on in silence till they reached a part of the wood where the pines were more widely spaced, then he drew up and helped Mattie to get out of the sleigh. They passed between the aromatic trunks, the snow breaking crisply under their feet, till they came to a small sheet of water with steep wooded sides. Across its frozen surface, from the farther bank, a single hill rising against the western sun threw the long conical shadow which gave the lake its name. It was a shy secret spot, full of the same dumb melancholy that Ethan felt in his heart.

He looked up and down the little pebbly beach till his eye lit on a fallen tree-trunk half submerged in snow.

"There's where we sat at the picnic," he reminded her.

The entertainment of which he spoke was one of the few that they had taken part in together: a "church picnic" which, on a long afternoon of the preceding summer, had filled the retired place with merry-making. Mattie had begged him to go with her but he had refused. Then, toward sunset, coming down from the mountain where he had been felling timber, he had been caught by some strayed revellers and drawn into the group by the lake, where Mattie, encircled by facetious youths, and bright as a blackberry under her spreading hat, was brewing coffee over a gipsy fire. He remembered the shyness he had felt at approaching her in his uncouth clothes, and then the lighting up of her face, and the way she had broken through the group to come to him with a cup in her hand. They had sat for a few minutes on the fallen log by the pond, and she had missed her gold locket, and set the young men searching for it; and it was Ethan who had spied it in the moss. . . . That was all; but all their intercourse had been made up of just such inarticulate flashes, when they seemed to come suddenly upon happiness as if they had surprised a butterfly in the winter woods . . .

"It was right there I found your locket," he said, pushing his foot into a dense tuft of blueberry bushes.

"I never saw anybody with such sharp eyes!" she answered.

She sat down on the tree-trunk in the sun and he sat down beside her.

"You were as pretty as a picture in that pink hat," he said.

She laughed with pleasure. "Oh, I guess it was the hat!" she rejoined

They had never before avowed their inclination so openly, and Ethan, for a moment, had the illusion that he was a free man, wooing the girl he meant to marry. He looked at her hair and longed to touch it again, and to tell her that it smelt of the woods; but he had never learned to say such things.

Suddenly she rose to her feet and said: "We mustn't stay here any longer."

He continued to gaze at her vaguely, only half-roused from his dream. "There's plenty of time," he answered.

They stood looking at each other as if the eyes of each were straining to absorb and hold fast the other's image. There were things he had to say to her before they parted, but he could not say them in that place of summer memories, and he turned and followed her in silence to the sleigh. As they drove away the sun sank behind the hill and the pine-boles turned from red to grey.

By a devious track between the fields they wound back to the Starkfield road. Under the open sky the light was still clear, with a reflection of cold red on the eastern hills. The clumps of trees in the snow seemed to draw together in ruffled lumps, like birds with their heads under their wings; and the sky, as it paled, rose higher, leaving the earth more alone.

As they turned into the Starkfield road Ethan said: "Matt, what do you mean to do?"

She did not answer at once, but at length she said: "I'll try to get a place in a store."

"You know you can't do it. The bad air and the standing all day nearly killed you before."

"I'm a lot stronger than I was before I came to Starkfield."

"And now you're going to throw away all the good it's done you!"

There seemed to be no answer to this, and again they drove on for a while without speaking. With every yard of the way some spot where they had stood, and laughed together or been silent, clutched at Ethan and dragged him back.

"Isn't there any of your father's folks could help you?"

"There isn't any of 'em I'd ask."

He lowered his voice to say: "You know there's nothing I wouldn't do for you if I could."

"I know there isn't."

"But I can't——"

She was silent, but he felt a slight tremor in the shoulder against his.

"Oh, Matt," he broke out, "if I could ha' gone with you now I'd ha' done it——"

She turned to him, pulling a scrap of paper from her breast. "Ethan—I found this," she stammered. Even in the failing light he saw it was the letter to his wife that he had begun the night before and forgotten to destroy. Through his astonishment there ran a fierce thrill of joy. "Matt—" he cried; "if I could ha' done it, would you?"

"Oh, Ethan, Ethan—what's the use?" With a sudden movement she tore the letter in shreds and sent them fluttering off into the snow.

"Tell me, Matt! Tell me!" he adjured her.

She was silent for a moment; then she said, in such a low tone that he had to stoop his head to hear her: "I used to think of it sometimes, summer nights, when the moon was so bright I couldn't sleep."

His heart reeled with the sweetness of it. "As long ago as that?"

She answered, as if the date had long been fixed for her: "The first time was at Shadow Pond."

"Was that why you gave me my coffee before the others?"

"I don't know. Did I? I was dreadfully put out when you wouldn't go to the picnic with me; and then, when I saw you coming down the road, I thought maybe you'd gone home that way o' purpose; and that made me glad."

They were silent again. They had reached the point where the road dipped to the hollow by Ethan's mill and as they descended the darkness descended with them, dropping down like a black veil from the heavy hemlock boughs.

"I'm tied hand and foot, Matt. There isn't a thing I can do," he began again.

"You must write to me sometimes, Ethan."

"Oh, what good'll writing do? I want to put my hand out and touch you. I want to do for you and care for you. I want to be there when you're sick and when you're lonesome."

"You mustn't think but what I'll do all right."

"You won't need me, you mean? I suppose you'll marry!"

"Oh, Ethan!" she cried.

"I don't know how it is you make me feel, Matt. I'd a'most rather have you dead than that!"

"Oh, I wish I was, I wish I was!" she sobbed.

The sound of her weeping shook him out of his dark anger, and he felt ashamed.

"Don't let's talk that way," he whispered.

"Why shouldn't we, when it's true? I've been wishing it every minute of the day."

"Matt! You be quiet! Don't you say it."

"There's never anybody been good to me but you."

"Don't say that either, when I can't lift a hand for you!"

"Yes; but it's true just the same."

They had reached the top of School House Hill and Starkfield lay below them in the twilight. A cutter, mounting the road from the village, passed them by in a joyous flutter of bells, and they straightened themselves and looked ahead with rigid faces. Along the main street lights had begun to shine from the house-fronts and stray figures were turning in here and there at the gates. Ethan, with a touch of his whip, roused the sorrel to a languid trot.

As they drew near the end of the village the cries of children reached them, and they saw a knot of boys, with sleds behind them, scattering across the open space before the church.

"I guess this'll be their last coast for a day or two," Ethan said, looking up at the mild sky.

Mattie was silent, and he added: "We were to have gone down last night."

Still she did not speak and, prompted by an obscure desire to help himself and her through their miserable last hour, he went on discursively: "Ain't it funny we haven't been down together but just that once last winter?"

She answered: "It wasn't often I got down to the village."

"That's so," he said.

They had reached the crest of the Corbury road, and between

the indistinct white glimmer of the church and the black curtain of the Varnum spruces the slope stretched away below them without a sled on its length. Some erratic impulse prompted Ethan to say: "How'd you like me to take you down now?"

She forced a laugh. "Why, there isn't time!"

"There's all the time we want. Come along!" His one desire now was to postpone the moment of turning the sorrel toward the Flats.

"But the girl," she faltered. "The girl'll be waiting at the station."

"Well, let her wait. You'd have to if she didn't. Come!"

The note of authority in his voice seemed to subdue her, and when he had jumped from the sleigh she let him help her out, saying only, with a vague feint of reluctance: "But there isn't a sled round anywheres."

"Yes, there is! Right over there under the spruces."

He threw the bearskin over the sorrel, who stood passively by the roadside, hanging a meditative head. Then he caught Mattie's hand and drew her after him toward the sled.

She seated herself obediently and he took his place behind her, so close that her hair brushed his face. "All right, Matt?" he called out, as if the width of the road had been between them.

She turned her head to say: "It's dreadfully dark. Are you sure you can see?"

He laughed contemptuously: "I could go down this coast with my eyes tied!" and she laughed with him, as if she liked his audacity. Nevertheless he sat still a moment, straining his eyes down the long hill, for it was the most confusing hour of the evening, the hour when the last clearness from the upper sky is merged with the rising night in a blur that disguises landmarks and falsifies distances.

"Now!" he cried.

The sled started with a bound, and they flew on through the dusk, gathering smoothness and speed as they went, with the hollow night opening out below them and the air singing by like an organ. Mattie sat perfectly still, but as they reached the bend at the foot of the hill, where the big elm thrust out a deadly elbow, he fancied that she shrank a little closer.

"Don't be scared, Matt!" he cried exultantly, as they spun safely past it and flew down the second slope; and when they reached the level ground beyond, and the speed of the sled began to slacken, he heard her give a little laugh of glee.

They sprang off and started to walk back up the hill. Ethan

dragged the sled with one hand and passed the other through Mattie's arm.

"Were you scared I'd run you into the elm?" he asked with a boyish laugh.

"I told you I was never scared with you," she answered.

The strange exaltation of his mood had brought on one of his rare fits of boastfulness. "It *is* a tricky place, though. The least swerve, and we'd never ha' come up again. But I can measure distances to a hair's-breadth—always could."

She murmured: "I always say you've got the surest eye . . ."

Deep silence had fallen with the starless dusk, and they leaned on each other without speaking; but at every step of their climb Ethan said to himself: "It's the last time we'll ever walk together."

They mounted slowly to the top of the hill. When they were abreast of the church he stooped his head to her to ask: "Are you tired?" and she answered, breathing quickly: "It was splendid!"

With a pressure of his arm he guided her toward the Norway spruces. "I guess this sled must be Ned Hale's. Anyhow I'll leave it where I found it." He drew the sled up to the Varnum gate and rested it against the fence. As he raised himself he suddenly felt Mattie close to him among the shadows.

"Is this where Ned and Ruth kissed each other?" she whispered breathlessly, and flung her arms about him. Her lips, groping for his, swept over his face, and he held her fast in a rapture of surprise.

"Good-bye—good-bye," she stammered, and kissed him again.

"Oh, Matt, I can't let you go!" broke from him in the same old cry.

She freed herself from his hold and he heard her sobbing. "Oh, I can't go either!" she wailed.

"Matt! What'll we do? What'll we do?"

They clung to each other's hands like children, and her body shook with desperate sobs.

Through the stillness they heard the church clock striking five.

"Oh, Ethan, it's time!" she cried.

He drew her back to him. "Time for what? You don't suppose I'm going to leave you now?"

"If I missed my train where'd I go?"

"Where are you going if you catch it?"

She stood silent, her hands lying cold and relaxed in his.

"What's the good of either of us going anywheres without the other one now?" he said.

She remained motionless, as if she had not heard him. Then

she snatched her hands from his, threw her arms about his neck, and pressed a sudden drenched cheek against his face. "Ethan! Ethan! I want you to take me down again!"

"Down where?"

"The coast. Right off," she panted. "So 't we'll never come up any more."

"Matt! What on earth do you mean?"

She put her lips close against his ear to say: "Right into the big elm. You said you could. So 't we'd never have to leave each other any more."

"Why, what are you talking of? You're crazy!"

"I'm not crazy; but I will be if I leave you."

"Oh, Matt, Matt—" he groaned.

She tightened her fierce hold about his neck. Her face lay close to his face.

"Ethan, where'll I go if I leave you? I don't know how to get along alone. You said so yourself just now. Nobody but you was ever good to me. And there'll be that strange girl in the house . . . and she'll sleep in my bed, where I used to lay nights and listen to hear you come up the stairs . . ."

The words were like fragments torn from his heart. With them came the hated vision of the house he was going back to—of the stairs he would have to go up every night, of the woman who would wait for him there. And the sweetness of Mattie's avowal, the wild wonder of knowing at last that all that had happened to him had happened to her too, made the other vision more abhorrent, the other life more intolerable to return to . . .

Her pleadings still came to him between short sobs, but he no longer heard what she was saying. Her hat had slipped back and he was stroking her hair. He wanted to get the feeling of it into his hand, so that it would sleep there like a seed in winter. Once he found her mouth again, and they seemed to be by the pond together in the burning August sun. But his cheek touched hers, and it was cold and full of weeping, and he saw the road to the Flats under the night and heard the whistle of the train up the line.

The spruces swathed them in blackness and silence. They might have been in their coffins underground. He said to himself: "Perhaps it'll feel like this . . ." and then again: "After this I sha'n't feel anything . . ."

Suddenly he heard the old sorrel whinny across the road, and thought: "He's wondering why he doesn't get his supper . . ."

"Come," Mattie whispered, tugging at his hand.

Her sombre violence constrained him: she seemed the embodied instrument of fate. He pulled the sled out, blinking like a night-bird as he passed from the shade of the spruces into the transparent dusk of the open. The slope below them was deserted. All Starkfield was at supper, and not a figure crossed the open space before the church. The sky, swollen with the clouds that announce a thaw, hung as low as before a summer storm. He strained his eyes through the dimness, and they seemed less keen, less capable than usual.

He took his seat on the sled and Mattie instantly placed herself in front of him. Her hat had fallen into the snow and his lips were in her hair. He stretched out his legs, drove his heels into the road to keep the sled from slipping forward, and bent her head back between his hands. Then suddenly he sprang up again.

"Get up," he ordered her.

It was the tone she always heeded, but she cowered down in her seat, repeating vehemently: "No, no, no!"

"Get up!"

"Why?"

"I want to sit in front."

"No, no! How can you steer in front?"

"I don't have to. We'll follow the track."

They spoke in smothered whispers, as though the night were listening.

"Get up! Get up!" he urged her; but she kept on repeating: "Why do you want to sit in front?"

"Because I—because I want to feel you holding me," he stammered, and dragged her to her feet.

The answer seemed to satisfy her, or else she yielded to the power of his voice. He bent down, feeling in the obscurity for the glassy slide worn by preceding coasters, and placed the runners carefully between its edges. She waited while he seated himself with crossed legs in the front of the sled; then she crouched quickly down at his back and clasped her arms about him. Her breath in his neck set him shuddering again, and he almost sprang from his seat. But in a flash he remembered the alternative. She was right: this was better than parting. He leaned back and drew her mouth to his . . .

Just as they started he heard the sorrel's whinny again, and the familiar wistful call, and all the confused images it brought with it, went with him down the first reach of the road. Half-way down there was a sudden drop, then a rise, and after that another long delirious descent. As they took wing for this it seemed to him that they were flying indeed, flying far up into the cloudy night, with Starkfield immeasurably below them, falling away like a speck in space . . . Then the big elm shot up ahead, lying in wait for them at the bend of the road, and he said between his teeth: "We can fetch it; I know we can fetch it——"

As they flew toward the tree Mattie pressed her arms tighter, and her blood seemed to be in his veins. Once or twice the sled swerved a little under them. He slanted his body to keep it headed for the elm, repeating to himself again and again: "I know we can fetch it"; and little phrases she had spoken ran through his head and danced before him on the air. The big tree loomed bigger and closer, and as they bore down on it he thought: "It's waiting for us: it seems to know." But suddenly his wife's face, with twisted monstrous lineaments, thrust itself between him and his goal, and he made an instinctive movement to brush it aside. The sled swerved in response, but he righted it again, kept it straight, and drove down on the black projecting mass. There was a last instant when the air shot past him like millions of fiery wires; and then the elm . . .

The sky was still thick, but looking straight up he saw a single star, and tried vaguely to reckon whether it were Sirius, or—or— The effort tired him too much, and he closed his heavy lids and thought that he would sleep . . . The stillness was so profound that he heard a little animal twittering somewhere near by under the snow. It made a small frightened *cheep* like a field mouse, and he wondered languidly if it were hurt. Then he understood that it must be in pain: pain so excruciating that he seemed, mysteriously, to feel it shooting through his own body. He tried in vain to roll over in the direction of the sound, and stretched his left arm out across the snow. And now it was as though he felt rather than heard the twittering; it seemed to be under his palm, which rested on something soft and springy. The thought of the animal's suffering was intolerable to him and he struggled to raise himself, and could not because a rock, or some huge mass, seemed to be lying on him. But he continued to finger about cautiously with his left hand, thinking he might get hold of the little creature and help it; and all at once he knew that the soft thing he had touched was Mattie's hair and that his hand was on her face.

He dragged himself to his knees, the monstrous load on him moving with him as he moved, and his hand went over and over her face, and he felt that the twittering came from her lips . . .

He got his face down close to hers, with his ear to her mouth, and in the darkness he saw her eyes open and heard her say his name.

"Oh, Matt, I thought we'd fetched it," he moaned; and far off, up the hill, he heard the sorrel whinny, and thought: "I ought to be getting him his feed . . ."

The querulous drone ceased as I entered Frome's kitchen, and of the two women sitting there I could not tell which had been the speaker.

One of them, on my appearing, raised her tall bony figure from her seat, not as if to welcome me—for she threw me no more than a brief glance of surprise—but simply to set about preparing the meal which Frome's absence had delayed. A slatternly calico wrapper hung from her shoulders and the wisps of her thin grey hair were drawn away from a high forehead and fastened at the back by a broken comb. She had pale opaque eyes which revealed nothing and reflected nothing, and her narrow lips were of the same sallow colour as her face.

The other woman was much smaller and slighter. She sat huddled in an arm-chair near the stove, and when I came in she turned her head quickly toward me, without the least corresponding movement of her body. Her hair was as grey as her companion's, her face as bloodless and shrivelled, but amber-tinted, with swarthy shadows sharpening the nose and hollowing the temples. Under her shapeless dress her body kept its limp immobility, and her dark eyes had the bright witch-like stare that disease of the spine sometimes gives.

Even for that part of the country the kitchen was a poor-looking place. With the exception of the dark-eyed woman's chair, which looked like a soiled relic of luxury bought at a country auction, the furniture was of the roughest kind. Three coarse china plates and a broken-nosed milk-jug had been set on a greasy table scored with knife-cuts, and a couple of straw-bottomed chairs and a kitchen dresser of unpainted pine stood meagrely against the plaster walls.

"My, it's cold here! The fire must be 'most out," Frome said, glancing about him apologetically as he followed me in.

The tall woman, who had moved away from us toward the dresser, took no notice; but the other, from her cushioned niche, answered complainingly, in a high thin voice. "It's on'y just been made up this very minute. Zeena fell asleep and slep' ever so long, and I thought I'd be frozen stiff before I could wake her up and get her to 'tend to it."

I knew then that it was she who had been speaking when we entered.

Her companion, who was just coming back to the table with the remains of a cold mince-pie in a battered pie-dish, set down her unappetising burden without appearing to hear the accusation brought against her.

Frome stood hesitatingly before her as she advanced; then he looked at me and said: "This is my wife, Mis' Frome." After another interval he added, turning toward the figure in the arm-chair: "And this is Miss Mattie Silver . . ."

Mrs. Hale, tender soul, had pictured me as lost in the Flats and buried under a snow-drift; and so lively was her satisfaction on seeing me safely restored to her the next morning that I felt my peril had caused me to advance several degrees in her favour.

Great was her amazement, and that of old Mrs. Varnum, on learning that Ethan Frome's old horse had carried me to and from Corbury Junction through the worst blizzard of the winter; greater still their surprise when they heard that his master had taken me in for the night.

Beneath their wondering exclamations I felt a secret curiosity to know what impressions I had received from my night in the Frome household, and divined that the best way of breaking down their reserve was to let them try to penetrate mine. I therefore confined myself to saying, in a matter-of-fact tone, that I had been received with great kindness, and that Frome had made a bed for me in a room on the ground-floor which seemed in happier days to have been fitted up as a kind of writing-room or study.

"Well," Mrs. Hale mused, "in such a storm I suppose he felt he couldn't do less than take you in—but I guess it went hard with Ethan. I don't believe but what you're the only stranger has set foot in that house for over twenty years. He's that proud he don't even like his oldest friends to go there; and I don't know as any do, any more, except myself and the doctor . . ."

"You still go there, Mrs. Hale?" I ventured.

"I used to go a good deal after the accident, when I was first married; but after awhile I got to think it made 'em feel worse to see us. And then one thing and another came, and my own troubles . . . But I generally make out to drive over there round about New Year's, and once in the summer. Only I always try to pick a day when Ethan's off somewheres. It's bad enough to see the two women sitting there—but *his* face, when he looks round that bare place, just kills me . . . You see, I can look back and call it up in his mother's day, before their troubles."

Old Mrs. Varnum, by this time, had gone up to bed, and her daughter and I were sitting alone, after supper, in the austere seclusion of the horse-hair parlour. Mrs. Hale glanced at me tentatively, as though trying to see how much footing my conjectures gave her; and I guessed that if she had kept silence till now it was because she had been waiting, through all the years, for some one who should see what she alone had seen.

I waited to let her trust in me gather strength before I said: "Yes, it's pretty bad, seeing all three of them there together."

She drew her mild brows into a frown of pain. "It was just awful from the beginning. I was here in the house when they were carried up—they laid Mattie Silver in the room you're in. She and I were great friends, and she was to have been my bridesmaid in the spring . . . When she came to I went up to her and stayed all night. They gave her things to quiet her, and she didn't know much till to'rd morning, and then all of a sudden she woke up just like herself, and looked straight at me out of her big eyes, and said . . . Oh, I don't know why I'm telling you all this," Mrs. Hale broke off, crying.

She took off her spectacles, wiped the moisture from them, and put them on again with an unsteady hand. "It got about the next day," she went on, "that Zeena Frome had sent Mattie off in a hurry because she had a hired girl coming, and the folks here could never rightly tell what she and Ethan were doing that night coasting, when they'd ought to have been on their way to the Flats to ketch the train . . . I never knew myself what Zeena thought—I don't to this day. Nobody knows Zeena's thoughts. Anyhow, when she heard o' the accident she came right in and stayed with Ethan over to the minister's, where they'd carried him. And as soon as the doctors said that Mattie could be moved, Zeena sent for her and took her back to the farm."

"And there she's been ever since?"

Mrs. Hale answered simply: "There was nowhere else for her to go;" and my heart tightened at the thought of the hard compulsions of the poor.

"Yes, there she's been," Mrs. Hale continued, "and Zeena's done for her, and done for Ethan, as good as she could. It was a miracle, considering how sick she was—but she seemed to be raised right up just when the call came to her. Not as she's ever given up doctoring, and she's had sick spells right along; but she's had the strength given her to care for those two for over twenty years, and before the accident came she thought she couldn't even care for herself."

Mrs. Hale paused a moment, and I remained silent, plunged in the vision of what her words evoked. "It's horrible for them all," I murmured.

"Yes: it's pretty bad. And they ain't any of 'em easy people either. Mattie *was,* before the accident; I never knew a sweeter nature. But she's suffered too much—that's what I always say when folks tell me how she's soured. And Zeena, she was always cranky. Not but what she bears with Mattie wonderful—I've seen that myself. But sometimes the two of them get going at each other, and then Ethan's face'd break your heart . . . When I see that, I think it's *him* that suffers most . . . anyhow it ain't Zeena, because she ain't got the time . . . It's a pity, though," Mrs. Hale ended, sighing, "that they're all shut up there'n that one kitchen. In the summertime, on pleasant days, they move Mattie into the parlour, or out in the door-yard, and that makes it easier . . . but winters there's the fires to be thought of; and there ain't a dime to spare up at the Fromes'."

Mrs. Hale drew a deep breath, as though her memory were eased of its long burden, and she had no more to say; but suddenly an impulse of complete avowal seized her.

She took off her spectacles again, leaned toward me across the bead-work table-cover, and went on with lowered voice: "There was one day, about a week after the accident, when they all thought Mattie couldn't live. Well, I say it's a pity she *did.* I said it right out to our minister once, and he was shocked at me. Only he wasn't with me that morning when she first came to . . . And I say, if she'd ha' died, Ethan might ha' lived; and the way they are now, I don't see's there's much difference between the Fromes up at the farm and the Fromes down in the graveyard; 'cept that down there they're all quiet, and the women have got to hold their tongues."

THE TOUCHSTONE

I

Professor Joslin, who, as our readers are doubtless aware, is engaged in writing the life of Mrs. Aubyn, asks us to state that he will be greatly indebted to any of the famous novelist's friends who will furnish him with information concerning the period previous to her coming to England. Mrs. Aubyn had so few intimate friends, and consequently so few regular correspondents, that letters will be of special value. Professor Joslin's address is 10 Augusta Gardens, Kensington, and he begs us to say that he will promptly return any documents entrusted to him.

Glennard dropped the *Spectator* and sat looking into the fire. The club was filling up, but he still had to himself the small inner room with its darkening outlook down the rain-streaked prospect of Fifth Avenue. It was all dull and dismal enough, yet a moment earlier his boredom had been perversely tinged by a sense of resentment at the thought that, as things were going, he might in time have to surrender even the despised privilege of boring himself within those particular four walls. It was not that he cared much for the club, but that the remote contingency of having to give it up stood to him, just then, perhaps by very reason of its insignificance and remoteness, for the symbol of his increasing abnegations; of that perpetual paring-off that was gradually reducing existence to the naked business of keeping himself alive. It was the futility of his multiplied shifts and privations that made them seem unworthy of a high attitude—the sense that, however rapidly he eliminated the superfluous, his cleared horizon was likely to offer no nearer view of the one prospect toward which he strained. To give up things in order to marry the woman one loves is easier than to give them up without being brought appreciably nearer to such a conclusion.

Through the open door he saw young Hollingsworth rise with a yawn from the ineffectual solace of a brandy-and-soda and transport his purposeless person to the window. Glennard measured his course with a contemptuous eye. It was so like Hollingsworth to get up and look out of the window just as it was growing too dark to see anything! There was a man rich enough to do what he pleased—had he been capable of being pleased—yet barred from all conceivable achievement by his own impervious dulness; while, a few feet off, Glennard, who wanted only enough to keep a decent coat on his back and a roof over the head of the woman he loved—Glennard, who had sweated, toiled, denied himself for the scant measure of opportunity that his zeal would have converted into a kingdom—sat wretchedly calculating that, even when he had resigned from the club, and knocked off his cigars, and given up his Sundays out of town, he would still be no nearer to attainment.

The *Spectator* had slipped to his feet, and as he picked it up his eye fell again on the paragraph addressed to the friends of Mrs. Aubyn. He had read it for the first time with a scarcely perceptible quickening of attention: her name had so long been public property that his eye passed it unseeingly, as the crowd in the street hurries without a glance by some familiar monument.

"Information concerning the period previous to her coming to England. . . ." The words were an evocation. He saw her again as she had looked at their first meeting, the poor woman of genius with her long pale face and short-sighted eyes, softened a little by the grace of youth and inexperience, but so incapable even then of any hold upon the pulses. When she spoke, indeed, she was wonderful, more wonderful, perhaps, than when later, to Glennard's fancy at least, the consciousness of memorable things uttered seemed to take from even her most intimate speech the perfect bloom of privacy. It was in those earliest days, if ever, that he had come near loving her; though even then his sentiment had lived only in the intervals of its expression. Later, when to be loved by her had been a state to touch any man's imagination, the physical reluctance had, inexplicably, so overborne the intellectual attraction, that the last years had been, to both of them, an agony of conflicting impulses. Even now, if, in turning over old papers his hand lit on her letters, the touch filled him with inarticulate misery.

"She had so few intimate friends . . . that letters will be of special value.'' So few intimate friends! For years she had had but one; one who in the last years had requited her wonderful pages, her tragic outpourings of love, humility and pardon, with the scant phrases by which a man evades the vulgarest of sentimental importunities. He had been a brute in spite of himself, and sometimes, now that the remembrance of her face had faded, and only her voice and words remained with him, he chafed at his own inadequacy, his stupid inability to rise to the height of her passion. His egoism was not of a kind to mirror its complacency in the adventure. To have been loved by the most brilliant woman of her day, and to have been incapable of loving her, seemed to him, in looking back, derisive evidence of his limitations; and his remorseful tenderness for her memory was complicated with a sense of irritation against her for having given him once for all the measure of his emotional capacity. It was not often, however, that he thus probed the past. The public, in taking possession of Mrs. Aubyn, had eased his shoulders of their burden. There was something fatuous in an attitude of sentimental apology toward a memory already classic: to reproach one's self for not having loved Margaret Aubyn was a good deal like being disturbed by an inability to admire the Venus of Milo. From her cold niche of fame she looked down ironically enough on his self-flagellations. . . . It was only when he came on something that belonged to her that he felt a sudden renewal of the old feeling, the strange dual impulse that drew him to her voice but drove him from her hand, so that even now, at sight of anything she had touched, his heart contracted painfully. It happened seldom nowadays. Her little presents, one by one, had disappeared from his room, and her letters, kept from some unacknowledged puerile vanity in the possession of such treasures, seldom came beneath his hand.

''Her letters will be of special value—'' Her letters! Why, he must have hundreds of them—enough to fill a volume. Sometimes it used to seem to him that they came with every post—he used to avoid looking in his letter-box when he came home to his rooms—but her writing seemed to spring out at him as he put his key in the door.

He stood up and strolled into the other room. Hollingsworth, lounging away from the window, had joined himself to a languidly convivial group of men, to whom, in phrases as halting as though they struggled to define an ultimate idea, he was expounding the cursed nuisance of living in a hole with such a damned climate that one had to get out of it by February, with the contingent difficulty of there being no place to take one's yacht to in winter but that other played-out hole, the Riviera. From the outskirts of this group Glennard wandered to another, where a voice as different as possible from Hollingsworth's colorless organ dominated another circle of languid listeners.

"Come and hear Dinslow talk about his patent: admission free," one of the men sang out in a tone of mock resignation.

Dinslow turned to Glennard the confident pugnacity of his smile. "Give it another six months and it'll be talking about itself," he declared. "It's pretty nearly articulate now."

"Can it say papa?" someone else inquired.

Dinslow's smile broadened. "You'll be deuced glad to say papa to *it* a year from now," he retorted. "It'll be able to support even you in affluence. Look here, now, just let me explain to you—"

Glennard moved away impatiently. The men at the club—all but those who were "in it"—were proverbially "tired" of Dinslow's patent, and none more so than Glennard, whose knowledge of its merits made it loom large in the depressing catalogue of lost opportunities. The relations between the two men had always been friendly, and Dinslow's urgent offers to "take him in on the ground floor" had of late intensified Glennard's sense of his own inability to meet good luck half-way. Some of the men who had paused to listen were already in evening clothes, others on their way home to dress; and Glennard, with an accustomed twinge of humiliation, said to himself that if he lingered among them it was in the miserable hope that one of the number might ask him to dine. Miss Trent had told him that she was to go to the opera that evening with her rich aunt; and if he should have the luck to pick up a dinner invitation he might join her there without extra outlay.

He moved about the room, lingering here and there in a tentative affectation of interest; but though the men greeted him pleasantly, no one asked him to dine. Doubtless they were all engaged, these men who could afford to pay for their dinners, who did not have to hunt for invitations as a beggar rummages for a crust in an ash-barrel! But no—as Hollingsworth left the lessening circle about the table, an admiring youth called out, "Holly, stop and dine!"

Hollingsworth turned on him the crude countenance that looked like the wrong side of a more finished face. "Sorry I can't. I'm in for a beastly banquet."

Glennard threw himself into an armchair. Why go home in the

rain to dress? It was folly to take a cab to the opera, it was worse folly to go there at all. His perpetual meetings with Alexa Trent were as unfair to the girl as they were unnerving to himself. Since he couldn't marry her, it was time to stand aside and give a better man the chance—and his thought admitted the ironical implication that in the terms of expediency the phrase might stand for Hollingsworth.

II

He dined alone and walked home to his rooms in the rain. As he turned into Fifth Avenue he caught the wet gleam of carriages on their way to the opera, and he took the first side street, in a moment of irritation against the petty restrictions that thwarted every impulse. It was ridiculous to give up the opera, not because one might possibly be bored there, but because one must pay for the experiment.

In his sitting-room, the tacit connivance of the inanimate had centred the lamplight on a photograph of Alexa Trent, placed, in the obligatory silver frame, just where, as memory officiously reminded him, Margaret Aubyn's picture had long throned in its stead. Miss Trent's features cruelly justified the usurpation. She had the kind of beauty that comes of a happy accord of face and spirit. It is not given to many to have the lips and eyes of their rarest mood, and some women go through life behind a mask expressing only their anxiety about the butcher's bill or their inability to see a joke. With Miss Trent, face and mind had the same high serious contour. She looked like a throned Justice by some grave Florentine painter; and it seemed to Glennard that her most salient attribute, or that at least to which her conduct gave most consistent expression, was a kind of passionate justness—the intuitive feminine justness that is so much rarer than a reasoned impartiality. Circumstances had tragically combined to develop this instinct into a conscious habit. She had seen more than most girls of the shabby side of life, of the perpetual tendency of want to cramp the noblest attitude. Poverty and misfortune had overhung her childhood, and she had none of the pretty delusions about life that are supposed to be the crowning grace of girlhood. This very competence, which gave her a touching reasonableness, made Glennard's situation more difficult than if he had aspired to a princess. Between them they asked so little—they knew so well how to make that little do; but they understood also, and she especially did not for a moment let him forget, that without that little the future they dreamed of was impossible.

The sight of her photograph quickened Glennard's exasperation. He was sick and ashamed of the part he was playing. He had loved her now for two years, with the tranquil tenderness that gathers depth and volume as it nears fulfilment; he knew that she would wait for him—but the certitude was an added pang. There are times when the constancy of the woman one cannot marry is almost as trying as that of the woman one does not want to.

Glennard turned up his reading-lamp and stirred the fire. He had a long evening before him, and he wanted to crowd out thought with action. He had brought some papers from his office and he spread them out on his table and squared himself to the task.

It must have been an hour later that he found himself automatically fitting a key into a locked drawer. He had no more notion than a somnambulist of the mental process that had led up to this action. He was just dimly aware of having pushed aside the papers and the heavy calf volumes that a moment before had bounded his horizon, and of laying in their place, without a trace of conscious volition, the parcel he had taken from the drawer.

The letters were tied in packets of thirty or forty. There were a great many packets. On some of the envelopes the ink was fading; on others, which bore the English postmark, it was still fresh. She had been dead hardly three years, and she had written, at lengthening intervals, to the last.

He undid one of the early packets—little notes written during their first acquaintance at Hillbridge. Glennard, on leaving college, had begun life in his uncle's law office in the old university town. It was there that, at the house of her father, Professor Forth, he had first met the young lady then chiefly distinguished for having, after two years of a conspicuously unhappy marriage, returned to the protection of the paternal roof.

Mrs. Aubyn was at that time an eager and somewhat tragic young woman, of complex mind and undeveloped manners, whom her crude experience of matrimony had fitted out with a stock of generalizations that exploded like bombs in the academic air of Hillbridge. In her choice of a husband she had been fortunate enough, if the paradox be permitted, to light on one so signally gifted with the faculty of putting himself in the wrong that her leaving him had the dignity of a manifesto—made her, as it were, the spokeswoman of outraged wifehood. In this light she was cherished by that dominant portion of Hillbridge society which was least indulgent to conjugal differences, and which found a proportionate pleasure in being for once able to feast openly on a dish liberally seasoned with the outrageous. So much did this endear Mrs. Aubyn to the university ladies, that they were disposed from the first to allow her more latitude of speech and action than the ill-used wife was generally accorded in Hillbridge, where misfortune was still regarded as a visitation designed to put people in their proper place and make them feel the superiority of their neighbors. The young woman so privileged combined with a kind of personal shyness an intellectual audacity that was like a deflected impulse of coquetry: one felt that if she had been prettier she would have had emotions instead of ideas. She was in fact even then what she had always remained: a genius capable of the acutest generalizations, but curiously undiscerning where her personal susceptibilities were concerned. Her psychology failed her just where it serves most women, and one felt that her brains would never be a guide to her heart. Of all this, however, Glennard thought little in the first year of their acquaintance. He was at an age when all the gifts and graces are but so much undiscriminated food to the ravening egoism of youth In seeking Mrs. Aubyn's company he was prompted by an intuitive taste for the best as a pledge of his own superiority. The sympathy of the cleverest woman in Hillbridge was balm to his craving for distinction; it was public confirmation of his secret sense that he was cut out for a bigger place. It must not be understood that Glennard was vain. Vanity contents itself with the coarsest diet; there is no palate so fastidious as that of self-distrust. To a youth of Glennard's aspirations the encouragement of a clever woman stood for the symbol of all success. Later, when he had begun to feel his way, to gain a foothold, he would not need such support; but it served to carry him lightly and easily over what is often a period of insecurity and discouragement.

It would be unjust, however, to represent his interest in Mrs. Aubyn as a matter of calculation. It was as instinctive as love, and it missed being love by just such a hair-breadth deflection from the line of beauty as had determined the curve of Mrs. Aubyn's lips. When they met she had just published her first novel, and Glennard, who afterward had an ambitious man's impatience of distinguished women, was young enough to be dazzled by the semi-publicity it gave her. It was the kind of book that makes elderly ladies lower their voices and call each other "my dear" when they furtively discuss it; and Glennard exulted in the superior knowledge of the world that enabled him to take as a matter of course sentiments over which the university shook its head. Still more delightful was it to hear Mrs. Aubyn waken the echoes of academic drawing-rooms with audacities surpassing those of her printed page. Her intellectual independence gave a touch of comradeship to their intimacy, prolonging the illusion of college friendships based on a joyous interchange of heresies. Mrs. Aubyn and Glennard represented to each other the augur's wink behind the Hillbridge idol: they walked together in that light of young omniscience from which fate so curiously excludes one's elders.

Husbands, who are notoriously inopportune, may even die inopportunely, and this was the revenge that Mr. Aubyn, some two years after her return to Hillbridge, took upon his injured wife. He died precisely at the moment when Glennard was beginning to criticise her. It was not that she bored him; she did what was infinitely worse—she made him feel his inferiority. The sense of mental equality had been gratifying to his raw ambition; but as his self-knowledge defined itself, his understanding of her also increased; and if man is at times indirectly flattered by the moral superiority of woman, her mental ascendency is extenuated by no such oblique tribute to his powers. The attitude of looking up is a strain on the muscles; and it was becoming more and more Glennard's opinion that brains, in a woman, should be merely the obverse of beauty. To beauty Mrs. Aubyn could lay no claim; and while she had enough prettiness to exasperate him by her incapacity to make use of it, she seemed invincibly ignorant of any of the little artifices whereby women contrive to hide their defects and even to turn them into graces. Her dress never seemed a part of her; all her clothes had an impersonal air, as though they had belonged to someone else and been borrowed in an emergency that had somehow become chronic. She was conscious enough of her deficiencies to try to amend them by rash imitations of the most approved models; but no woman who does not dress well intuitively will ever do so by the light of reason, and Mrs. Aubyn's plagiarisms, to borrow a metaphor of her trade, somehow never seemed to be incorporated with the text.

Genius is of small use to a woman who does not know how to

do her hair. The fame that came to Mrs. Aubyn with her second book left Glennard's imagination untouched, or had at most the negative effect of removing her still farther from the circle of his contracting sympathies. We are all the sport of time; and fate had so perversely ordered the chronology of Margaret Aubyn's romance that when her husband died Glennard felt as though he had lost a friend.

It was not in his nature to be needlessly unkind; and though he was in the impregnable position of the man who has given a woman no more definable claim on him than that of letting her fancy that he loves her, he would not for the world have accentuated his advantage by any betrayal of indifference. During the first year of her widowhood their friendship dragged on with halting renewals of sentiment, becoming more and more a banquet of empty dishes from which the covers were never removed; then Glennard went to New York to live and exchanged the faded pleasures of intercourse for the comparative novelty of correspondence. Her letters, oddly enough, seemed at first to bring her nearer than her presence. She had adopted, and she successfully maintained, a note as affectionately impersonal as his own; she wrote ardently of her work, she questioned him about his, she even bantered him on the inevitable pretty girl who was certain before long to divert the current of his confidences. To Glennard, who was almost a stranger in New York, the sight of Mrs. Aubyn's writing was like a voice of reassurance in surroundings as yet insufficiently aware of him. His vanity found a retrospective enjoyment in the sentiment his heart had rejected, and this factitious emotion drove him once or twice to Hillbridge, whence, after scenes of evasive tenderness, he returned dissatisfied with himself and her. As he made room for himself in New York and peopled the space he had cleared with the sympathies at the disposal of agreeable and self-confident young men, it seemed to him natural to infer that Mrs. Aubyn had refurnished in the same manner the void he was not unwilling his departure should have left. But in the dissolution of sentimental partnerships it is seldom that both associates are able to withdraw their funds at the same time; and Glennard gradually learned that he stood for the venture on which Mrs. Aubyn had irretrievably staked her all. It was not the kind of figure he cared to cut. He had no fancy for leaving havoc in his wake and would have preferred to sow a quick growth of oblivion in the spaces wasted by his unconsidered inroads; but if he supplied the seed, it was clearly Mrs. Aubyn's business to see to the raising of the crop. Her attitude seemed indeed to throw his own reasonableness into distincter relief; so that they might have stood for thrift and improvidence in an allegory of the affections.

It was not that Mrs. Aubyn permitted herself to be a pensioner on his bounty. He knew she had no wish to keep herself alive on the small change of sentiment; she simply fed on her own funded passion, and the luxuries it allowed her made him, even then, dimly aware that she had the secret of an inexhaustible alchemy.

Their relations remained thus negatively tender till she suddenly wrote him of her decision to go abroad to live. Her father had died, she had no near ties in Hillbridge, and London offered more scope than New York to her expanding personality. She was already famous, and her laurels were yet unharvested.

For a moment the news roused Glennard to a jealous sense of lost opportunities. He wanted, at any rate, to reassert his power before she made the final effort of escape. They had not met for over a year, but of course he could not let her sail without seeing her. She came to New York the day before her departure, and they spent its last hours together. Glennard had planned no course of action—he simply meant to let himself drift. They both drifted, for a long time, down the languid current of reminiscence; she seemed to sit passive, letting him push his way back through the overgrown channels of the past. At length she reminded him that they must bring their explorations to an end. He rose to leave, and stood looking at her with the same uncertainty in his heart. He was tired of her already—he was always tired of her—yet he was not sure that he wanted her to go.

"I may never see you again," he said, as though confidently appealing to her compassion.

Her look enveloped him. "And I shall see you always—always!"

"Why go then—?" escaped him.

"To be nearer you," she answered; and the words dismissed him like a closing door.

The door was never to reopen; but through its narrow crack Glennard, as the years went on, became more and more conscious of an inextinguishable light directing its small ray toward the past which consumed so little of his own commemorative oil. The reproach was taken from this thought by Mrs. Aubyn's gradual translation into terms of universality. In becoming a personage she so naturally ceased to be a person that Glennard could almost look back to his explorations of her spirit as on a visit to some famous shrine, immortalized, but in a sense desecrated, by popular veneration.

Her letters from London continued to come with the same tender punctuality; but the altered conditions of her life, the vistas of new relationships disclosed by every phrase, made her communications as impersonal as a piece of journalism. It was as though the state, the world, indeed, had taken her off his hands, assuming the maintenance of a temperament that had long exhausted his slender store of reciprocity.

In the retrospective light shed by the letters he was blinded to their specific meaning. He was not a man who concerned himself with literature, and they had been to him, at first, simply the extension of her brilliant talk, later the dreaded vehicle of a tragic importunity. He knew, of course, that they were wonderful; that, unlike the authors who give their essence to the public and keep only a dry rind for their friends, Mrs. Aubyn had stored of her rarest vintage for this hidden sacrament of tenderness. Sometimes, indeed, he had been oppressed, humiliated almost, by the multiplicity of her allusions, the wide scope of her interests, her persistence in forcing her superabundance of thought and emotion into the shallow receptacle of his sympathy; but he had never thought of the letters objectively, as the production of a distinguished woman; had never measured the literary significance of her oppressive prodigality. He was almost frightened now at the wealth in his hands; the obligation of her love had never weighed on him like this gift of her imagination; it was as though he had accepted from her something to which even a reciprocal tenderness could not have justified his claim.

He sat a long time staring at the scattered pages on his desk; and in the sudden realization of what they meant he could almost fancy some alchemistic process changing them to gold as he stared.

He had the sense of not being alone in the room, of the presence of another self observing from without the stirring of subconscious impulses that sent flushes of humiliation to his forehead. At length he stood up, and with the gesture of a man who wishes to give outward expression to his purpose—to establish, as it were, a moral alibi—swept the letters into a heap and carried them toward the grate. But it would have taken too long to burn all the packets. He turned back to the table and one by one fitted the pages into their envelopes; then he tied up the letters and put them back into the locked drawer.

III

It was one of the laws of Glennard's intercourse with Miss Trent that he always went to see her the day after he had resolved to give her up. There was a special charm about the moments thus snatched from the jaws of renunciation; and his sense of their significance was on this occasion so keen that he hardly noticed the added gravity of her welcome.

His feeling for her had become so vital a part of him that her nearness had the quality of imperceptibly readjusting his point of view, of making the jumbled phenomena of experience fall at once into a rational perspective. In this redistribution of values the sombre retrospect of the previous evening shrank to a mere cloud on the edge of consciousness. Perhaps the only service an unloved woman can render the man she loves is to enhance and prolong his illusions about her rival. It was the fate of Margaret Aubyn's memory to serve as a foil to Miss Trent's presence, and never had the poor lady thrown her successor into more vivid relief.

Miss Trent had the charm of still waters that are felt to be renewed by rapid currents. Her attention spread a tranquil surface to the demonstrations of others, and it was only in days of storm that one felt the pressure of the tides. This inscrutable composure was perhaps her chief grace in Glennard's eyes. Reserve, in some natures, implies merely the locking of empty rooms or the dissimulation of awkward encumbrances; but Miss Trent's reticence was to Glennard like the closed door to the sanctuary, and his certainty of divining the hidden treasure made him content to remain outside in the happy expectancy of the neophyte.

"You didn't come to the opera last night," she began, in the tone that seemed always rather to record a fact than to offer a reflection on it.

He answered with a discouraged gesture. "What was the use? We couldn't have talked."

"Not as well as here," she assented; adding, after a meditative pause, "As you didn't come I talked to Aunt Virginia instead."

"Ah!" he returned, the fact being hardly striking enough to detach him from the contemplation of her hands, which had fallen, as was their wont, into an attitude full of plastic possibilities. One felt them to be hands that, moving only to some purpose, were capable of intervals of serene inaction.

"We had a long talk," Miss Trent went on; and she waited again before adding, with the increased absence of stress that marked her graver communications, "Aunt Virginia wants me to go abroad with her."

Glennard looked up with a start. "Abroad? When?"

"Now—next month. To be gone two years."

He permitted himself a movement of tender derision. "Does she really? Well, I want you to go abroad with *me*—for any number of years. Which offer do you accept?"

"Only one of them seems to require immediate consideration," she returned with a smile.

Glennard looked at her again. "You're not thinking of it?"

Her gaze dropped and she unclasped her hands. Her movements were so rare that they might have been said to italicize her words. "Aunt Virginia talked to me very seriously. It will be a great relief to mother and the others to have me provided for in that way for two years. I must think of that, you know." She glanced down at her gown, which, under a renovated surface, dated back to the first days of Glennard's wooing. "I try not to cost much—but I do."

"Good Lord!" Glennard groaned.

They sat silent till at length she gently took up the argument. "As the eldest, you know, I'm bound to consider these things. Women are such a burden. Jim does what he can for mother, but with his own children to provide for it isn't very much. You see we're all poor together."

"Your aunt isn't. She might help your mother."

"She does—in her own way."

"Exactly—that's the rich relation all over! You may be miserable in any way you like, but if you're to be happy, you must be so in her way—and in her old gowns."

"I could be very happy in Aunt Virginia's old gowns," Miss Trent interposed.

"Abroad, you mean?"

"I mean wherever I felt that I was helping. And my going abroad will help."

"Of course—I see that. And I see your considerateness in putting its advantages negatively."

"Negatively?"

"In dwelling simply on what the going will take you from, not on what it will bring you to. It means a lot to a woman, of course, to get away from a life like this.'' He summed up in a disparaging glance the background of indigent furniture. ''The question is how you'll like coming back to it.''

She seemed to accept the full consequences of his thought. ''I only know I don't like leaving it.''

He flung back sombrely, ''You don't even put it conditionally then?''

Her gaze deepened. ''On what?''

He stood up and walked across the room. Then he came back and paused before her. ''On the alternative of marrying me.''

The slow color—even her blushes seemed deliberate—rose to her lower lids; her lips stirred, but the words resolved themselves into a smile and she waited.

He took another turn, with the thwarted step of the man whose nervous exasperation escapes through his muscles.

''And to think that in fifteen years I shall have a big practice!''

Her eyes triumphed for him. ''In less!''

''The cursed irony of it! What do I care for the man I shall be then? It's slaving one's life away for a stranger!'' He took her hands abruptly. ''You'll go to Cannes, I suppose, or Monte Carlo? I heard Hollingsworth say today that he meant to take his yacht over to the Mediterranean—''

She released herself. ''If you think that—''

''I don't. I almost wish I did. It would be easier, I mean.'' He broke off incoherently. ''I believe your Aunt Virginia does, though. She somehow connotes Hollingsworth and the Mediterranean.'' He caught her hands again. ''Alexa—if we could manage a little hole somewhere out of town?''

''Could we?'' she sighed, half yielding.

''In one of those places where they make jokes about the mosquitoes,'' he pressed her. ''Could you get on with one servant?''

''Could you get on without varnished boots?''

''Promise me you won't go, then!''

''What are you thinking of, Stephen?''

''I don't know,'' he stammered, the question giving unexpected form to his intention. ''It's all in the air yet, of course; but I picked up a tip the other day—''

''You're not speculating?'' she cried, with a kind of superstitious terror.

''Lord, no. This is a sure thing—I almost wish it wasn't: I mean if I can work it—'' He had a sudden vision of the comprehensiveness of the temptation. If only he had been less sure of

Dinslow! His assurance gave the situation the base element of safety.

"I don't understand you," she faltered.

"Trust me, instead!" he adjured her with sudden energy; and turning on her abruptly, "If you go, you know, you go free," he concluded.

She drew back, paling a little. "Why do you make it harder for me?"

"To make it easier for myself," he retorted.

IV

The next afternoon Glennard, leaving his office earlier than usual, turned, on his way home, into one of the public libraries.

He had the place to himself at that closing hour, and the librarian was able to give an undivided attention to his tentative request for letters—collections of letters. The librarian suggested Walpole.

"I meant women—women's letters."

The librarian proffered Hannah More and Miss Martineau.

Glennard cursed his own inarticulateness. "I mean letters to—to some one person—a man: their husband—or—"

"Ah," said the inspired librarian. "Eloise and Abelard."

"Well—something a little nearer, perhaps," said Glennard, with lightness. "Didn't Mérimée—"

"The lady's letters, in that case, were not published."

"Of course not," said Glennard, vexed at his blunder.

"There are George Sand's letters to Flaubert."

"Ah!" Glennard hesitated. "Was she—were they—?" He chafed at his own ignorance of the sentimental by-paths of literature.

"If you want love-letters, perhaps some of the French eighteenth-century correspondences might suit you better—Mlle. Aïssé or Madame de Sabran—"

But Glennard insisted. "I want something modern—English or American. I want to look something up," he lamely concluded.

The librarian could only suggest George Eliot.

"Well, give me some of the French things, then—and I'll

have Mérimée's letters. It was the woman who published them, wasn't it?''

He caught up his armful, transferring it, on the doorstep, to a cab which carried him to his rooms. He dined alone, hurriedly, at a small restaurant nearby, and returned at once to his books.

Late that night, as he undressed, he wondered what contemptible impulse had forced from him his last words to Alexa Trent. It was bad enough to interfere with the girl's chances by hanging about her to the obvious exclusion of other men, but it was worse to seem to justify his weakness by dressing up the future in delusive ambiguities. He saw himself sinking from depth to depth of sentimental cowardice in his reluctance to renounce his hold on her; and it filled him with self-disgust to think that the highest feeling of which he supposed himself capable was blent with such base elements.

His awakening was hardly cheered by the sight of her writing. He tore her note open and took in the few lines—she seldom exceeded the first page—with the lucidity of apprehension that is the forerunner of evil.

''My aunt sails on Saturday and I must give her my answer the day after tomorrow. Please don't come till then—I want to think the question over by myself. I know I ought to go. Won't you help me to be reasonable?''

It was settled, then. Well, he would help her to be reasonable; he wouldn't stand in her way; he would let her go. For two years he had been living some other, luckier man's life; the time had come when he must drop back into his own. He no longer tried to look ahead, to grope his way through the endless labyrinth of his material difficulties; a sense of dull resignation closed in on him like a fog.

''Hullo, Glennard!'' a voice said, as an electric car, late that afternoon, dropped him at an uptown corner.

He looked up and met the interrogative smile of Barton Flamel, who stood on the curbstone watching the retreating car with the eye of a man philosophic enough to remember that it will be followed by another.

Glennard felt his usual impulse of pleasure at meeting Flamel; but it was not in this case curtailed by the reaction of contempt that habitually succeeded it. Probably even the few men who had known Flamel since his youth could have given no good reason for the vague mistrust that he inspired. Some people are judged by their actions, others by their ideas; and perhaps the shortest way of defining Flamel is to say that his well-known leniency of view was vaguely divined to include himself. Simple minds may have resented the discovery that his opinions were based on his perceptions; but there was certainly no more definite charge against him than that implied in the doubt as to how he would behave in an emergency, and his company was looked upon as one of those mildly unwholesome dissipations to which the prudent may occasionally yield. It now offered itself to Glennard as an easy escape from the obsession of moral problems, which somehow could no more be worn in Flamel's presence than a surplice in the street.

"Where are you going? To the club?" Flamel asked, adding, as the younger man assented, "Why not come to my studio instead? You'll see one bore instead of twenty."

The apartment which Flamel described as his studio showed, as its one claim to the designation, a perennially empty easel, the rest of its space being filled with the evidences of a comprehensive dilettantism. Against this background, which seemed the visible expression of its owner's intellectual tolerance, rows of fine books detached themselves with a prominence showing them to be Flamel's chief care.

Glennard glanced with the eye of untrained curiosity at the lines of warm-toned morocco, while his host busied himself with the uncorking of Apollinaris.

"You've got a splendid lot of books," he said.

"They're fairly decent," the other assented, in the curt tone of the collector who will not talk of his passion for fear of talking of nothing else; then, as Glennard, his hands in his pockets, began to stroll perfunctorily down the long line of bookcases—"Some men," Flamel irresistibly added, "think of books merely as tools, others as tooling. I'm between the two; there are days when I use them as scenery, other days when I want them as society; so that, as you see, my library represents a makeshift compromise between looks and brains, and the collectors look down on me almost as much as the students."

Glennard, without answering, was mechanically taking one book after another from the shelves. His hands slipped curiously over the smooth covers and the noiseless subsidence of opening pages. Suddenly he came on a thin volume of faded manuscript.

"What's this?" he asked with a listless sense of wonder.

"Ah, you're at my manuscript shelf. I've been going in for that sort of thing lately." Flamel came up and looked over his shoulders. "That's a bit of Stendhal—one of the Italian stories—and here are some letters of Balzac to Madame Surville."

Glennard took the book with sudden eagerness. "Who was Madame Surville?"

"His sister." He was conscious that Flamel was looking at him with the smile that was like an interrogation point. "I didn't know you cared for this kind of thing."

"I don't—at least I've never had the chance. Have you many collections of letters?"

"Lord, no—very few. I'm just beginning, and most of the interesting ones are out of my reach. Here's a queer little collection, though—the rarest thing I've got—half a dozen of Shelley's letters to Harriet Westbrook. I had a devil of a time getting them—a lot of collectors were after them."

Glennard, taking the volume from his hand, glanced with a kind of repugnance at the interleaving of yellow crisscrossed sheets. "She was the one who drowned herself, wasn't she?"

Flamel nodded. "I suppose that little episode adds about fifty per cent to their value," he said meditatively.

Glennard laid the book down. He wondered why he had joined Flamel. He was in no humor to be amused by the older man's talk, and a recrudescence of personal misery rose about him like an icy tide.

"I believe I must take myself off," he said. "I'd forgotten an engagement."

He turned to go; but almost at the same moment he was conscious of a duality of intention wherein his apparent wish to leave revealed itself as a last effort of the will against the overmastering desire to stay and unbosom himself to Flamel.

The older man, as though divining the conflict, laid a detaining pressure on his arm.

"Won't the engagement keep? Sit down and try one of these cigars. I don't often have the luck of seeing you here."

"I'm rather driven just now," said Glennard vaguely. He found himself seated again, and Flamel had pushed to his side a low stand holding a bottle of Apollinaris and a decanter of cognac.

Flamel, thrown back in his capacious armchair, surveyed him through a cloud of smoke with the comfortable tolerance of the man to whom no inconsistencies need be explained. Connivance was implicit in the air. It was the kind of atmosphere in which the outrageous loses its edge. Glennard felt a gradual relaxing of his nerves.

"I suppose one has to pay a lot for letters like that?" he heard himself asking, with a glance in the direction of the volume he had laid aside.

"Oh, so-so—depends on circumstances." Flamel viewed him thoughtfully. "Are you thinking of collecting?"

Glennard laughed. "Lord, no. The other way round."

"Selling?"

"Oh, I hardly know. I was thinking of a poor chap—"

Flamel filled the pause with a nod of interest.

"A poor chap I used to know—who died—he died last year—and who left me a lot of letters, letters he thought a great deal of—he was fond of me and left 'em to me outright with the idea, I suppose, that they might benefit me somehow—I don't know—I'm not much up on such things—" He reached his hand to the tall glass his host had filled.

"A collection of autograph letters, eh? Any big names?"

"Oh, only one name. They're all letters written to him—by one person, you understand; a woman, in fact—"

"Oh, a woman," said Flamel negligently.

Glennard was nettled by his obvious loss of interest. "I rather think they'd attract a good deal of notice if they were published."

Flamel still looked uninterested. "Love-letters, I suppose?"

"Oh, just—the letters a woman would write to a man she knew well. They were tremendous friends, he and she."

"And she wrote a clever letter?"

"Clever? It was Margaret Aubyn."

A great silence filled the room. It seemed to Glennard that the words had burst from him as blood gushes from a wound.

"Great Scott!" said Flamel sitting up. "A collection of Margaret Aubyn's letters? Did you say *you* had them?"

"They were left me—by my friend."

"I see. Was he—well, no matter. You're to be congratulated, at any rate. What are you going to do with them?"

Glennard stood up with a sense of weariness in all his bones. "Oh, I don't know. I haven't thought much about it. I just happened to see that some fellow was writing her life—"

"Joslin; yes. You didn't think of giving them to him?"

Glennard lounged across the room and stood staring up at a bronze Bacchus who drooped his garlanded head above the pediment of an Italian cabinet. "What ought I to do? You're just the fellow to advise me." He felt the blood in his cheek as he spoke.

Flamel sat with meditative eye. "What do you *want* to do with them?" he asked.

"I want to publish them," said Glennard, swinging round with sudden energy—"If I can—"

"If you can? They're yours, you say?"

"They're mine fast enough. There's no one to prevent—I mean there are no restrictions—" he was arrested by the sense that these accumulated proofs of impunity might precisely stand as the strongest check on his action.

"And Mrs. Aubyn had no family, I believe?"

"No."

"Then I don't see who's to interfere," said Flamel, studying his cigar-tip.

Glennard had turned his unseeing stare on an ecstatic Saint Catherine framed in tarnished gilding.

"It's just this way," he began again, with an effort. "When letters are as personal as—as these of my friend's. . . . Well, I don't mind telling you that the cash would make a heap of difference to me; such a lot that it rather obscures my judgment—the fact is, if I could lay my hand on a few thousands now I could get into a big thing, and without appreciable risk; and I'd like to know whether you think I'd be justified—under the circumstances. . . ." He paused with a dry throat. It seemed to him at the moment that it would be impossible for him ever to sink lower in his own estimation. He was in truth less ashamed of weighing the temptation than of submitting his scruples to a man like Flamel, and affecting to appeal to sentiments of delicacy on the absence of which he had consciously reckoned. But he had reached a point where each word seemed to compel another, as each wave in a stream is forced forward by the pressure behind it; and before Flamel could speak he had faltered out—"You don't think people could say . . . could criticise the man. . . ."

"But the man's dead, isn't he?"

"He's dead—yes; but can I assume the responsibility without—"

Flamel hesitated; and almost immediately Glennard's scruples gave way to irritation. If at this hour Flamel were to affect an inopportune reluctance—!

The older man's answer reassured him. "Why need you assume any responsibility? Your name won't appear, of course; and as to your friend's, I don't see why his should either. He wasn't a celebrity himself, I suppose?"

"No, no."

"Then the letters can be addressed to Mr. Blank. Doesn't that make it all right?"

Glennard's hesitation revived. "For the public, yes. But I don't see that it alters the case for me. The question is, ought I to publish them at all?"

"Of course you ought to." Flamel spoke with invigorating emphasis. "I doubt if you'd be justified in keeping them back. Anything of Margaret Aubyn's is more or less public property by this time. She's too great for any one of us. I was only wondering how you could use them to the best advantage—to yourself, I mean. How many are there?"

"Oh, a lot; perhaps a hundred—I haven't counted. There may be more. . . ."

"Gad! What a haul! When were they written?"

"I don't know—that is—they corresponded for years. What's the odds?" He moved toward his hat with a vague impulse of flight.

"It all counts," said Flamel imperturbably. "A long correspondence—one, I mean, that covers a great deal of time—is obviously worth more than if the same number of letters had been written within a year. At any rate, you won't give them to Joslin? They'd fill a book, wouldn't they?"

"I suppose so. I don't know how much it takes to fill a book."

"Not love-letters, you say?"

"Why?" flashed from Glennard.

"Oh, nothing—only the big public is sentimental, and if they *were*—why, you could get any money for Margaret Aubyn's love-letters."

Glennard was silent.

"Are the letters interesting in themselves? I mean apart from the association with her name?"

"I'm no judge." Glennard took up his hat and thrust himself into his overcoat. "I dare say I shan't do anything about it. And, Flamel—you won't mention this to any one?"

"Lord, no. Well, I congratulate you. You've got a big thing." Flamel was smiling at him from the hearth.

Glennard, on the threshold, forced a response to the smile, while he questioned with loitering indifference—"Financially, eh?"

"Rather; I should say so."

Glennard's hand lingered on the knob. "How much—should you say? You know about such things."

"Oh, I should have to see the letters; but I should say—well, if you've got enough to fill a book and they're fairly readable, and the book is brought out at the right time—say ten thousand down from the publisher, and possibly one or two more in royalties. If you got the publishers bidding against each other you might do even better; but of course I'm talking in the dark."

"Of course," said Glennard, with sudden dizziness. His hand had slipped from the knob and he stood staring down at the exotic spirals of the Persian rug beneath his feet.

"I'd have to see the letters," Flamel repeated.

"Of course—you'd have to see them. . . ." Glennard stammered; and, without turning, he flung over his shoulder an inarticulate "Good-bye. . . ."

V

The little house, as Glennard strolled up to it between the trees, seemed no more than a gay tent pitched against the sunshine. It had the crispness of a freshly starched summer gown, and the geraniums on the veranda bloomed as simultaneously as the flowers in a bonnet. The garden was prospering absurdly. Seed they had sown at random—amid laughing countercharges of incompetence—had shot up in fragrant defiance of their blunders. He smiled to see the clematis unfolding its punctual wings about the porch. The tiny lawn was smooth as a shaven cheek, and a crimson rambler mounted to the nursery window of a baby who never cried. A breeze shook the awning above the tea-table, and his wife, as he drew near, could be seen bending above a kettle that was just about to boil. So vividly did the whole scene suggest the painted bliss of a stage setting, that it would have been hardly surprising to see her step forward among the flowers and trill out her virtuous happiness from the veranda rail.

The stale heat of the long day in town, the dusty promiscuity of the suburban train, were now but the requisite foil to an evening of scented breezes and tranquil talk. They had been married more than a year, and each homecoming still reflected the freshness of their first day together. If, indeed, their happiness had a flaw, it was in resembling too closely the bright impermanence of their surroundings. Their love as yet was but the gay tent of holiday-makers.

His wife looked up with a smile. The country life suited her, and her beauty had gained depth from a stillness in which certain faces might have grown opaque.

"Are you very tired?" she asked, pouring his tea.

"Just enough to enjoy this." He rose from the chair in which he had thrown himself and bent over the tray for his cream. "You've had a visitor?" he commented, noticing a half-empty cup beside her own.

"Only Mr. Flamel," she said indifferently.

"Flamel? Again?"

She answered without show of surprise. "He left just now. His yacht is down at Laurel Bay and he borrowed a trap of the Dreshams to drive over here."

Glennard made no comment, and she went on, leaning her head back against the cushions of her bamboo seat, "He wants us to go for a sail with him next Sunday."

Glennard meditatively stirred his tea. He was trying to think of the most natural and unartificial thing to say, and his voice seemed to come from the outside, as though he were speaking behind a marionette. "Do you want to?"

"Just as you please," she said compliantly. No affectation of indifference could have been as baffling as her compliance. Glennard, of late, was beginning to feel that the surface which, a year ago, he had taken for a sheet of clear glass, might, after all, be a mirror reflecting merely his own conception of what lay behind it.

"Do you like Flamel?" he suddenly asked; to which, still engaged with her tea, she returned the feminine answer—"I thought you did."

"I do, of course," he agreed, vexed at his own incorrigible tendency to magnify Flamel's importance by hovering about the topic. "A sail would be rather jolly; let's go."

She made no reply and he drew forth the rolled-up evening papers which he had thrust into his pocket on leaving the train. As he smoothed them out his own countenance seemed to undergo the same process. He ran his eye down the list of stocks, and Flamel's importunate personality receded behind the rows of figures pushing forward into notice like so many bearers of good news. Glennard's investments were flowering like his garden: the dryest shares blossomed into dividends and a golden harvest awaited his sickle.

He glanced at his wife with the tranquil air of a man who digests good luck as naturally as the dry ground absorbs a shower. "Things are looking uncommonly well. I believe we shall be able to go to town for two or three months next winter if we can find something cheap."

She smiled luxuriously: it was pleasant to be able to say, with an air of balancing relative advantages, "Really, on the baby's account I shall be almost sorry; but if we do go, there's Kate Erskine's house . . . she'll let us have it for almost nothing. . . ."

"Well, write her about it," he recommended, his eye travelling on in search of the weather report. He had turned to the wrong page; and suddenly a line of black characters leapt out at him as from an ambush.

MARGARET AUBYN'S LETTERS

Two volumes. Out Today. First Edition of five thousand sold out before leaving the press. Second Edition ready next week. The Book of the Year. . . .

He looked up stupidly. His wife still sat with her head thrown back, her pure profile detached against the cushions. She was smiling a little over the prospect his last words had opened. Behind her head shivers of sun and shade ran across the striped awning. A row of maples and a privet hedge hid their neighbor's gables, giving them undivided possession of their leafy half-acre; and life, a moment before, had been like their plot of ground, shut off, hedged in from importunities, impenetrably his and hers. Now it seemed to him that every maple-leaf, every privet-bud, was a relentless human gaze, pressing close upon their privacy. It was as though they sat in a brightly lit room, uncurtained from a darkness full of hostile watchers. . . . His wife still smiled; and her unconsciousness of danger seemed in some horrible way to put her beyond the reach of rescue.

He had not known that it would be like this. After the first odious weeks, spent in preparing the letters for publication, in submitting them to Flamel, and in negotiating with the publishers, the transaction had dropped out of his consciousness into that unvisited limbo to which we relegate the deeds we would rather not have done but have no notion of undoing. From the moment he had obtained Miss Trent's promise not to sail with her aunt he had tried to imagine himself irrevocably committed. After that, he argued, his first duty was to her—she had become his conscience. The sum obtained from the publishers by Flamel's manipulations, and opportunely transferred to Dinslow's successful venture, already yielded a return which, combined with Glennard's professional earnings, took the edge of compulsion from their way of living, making it appear the expression of a graceful preference for simplicity. It was the mitigated poverty which can subscribe to a review or two and have a few flowers on the dinner-table. And already in a small way Glennard was beginning to feel the magnetic quality of prosperity. Clients who had passed his door in the hungry days sought it out now that it bore the name of a successful man. It was understood that a small inheritance, cleverly invested, was the source of his fortune; and there was a feeling that a man who could do so well for himself was likely to know how to turn over other people's money.

But it was in the more intimate reward of his wife's happiness that Glennard tasted the full flavor of success. Coming out of conditions so narrow that those he offered her seemed spacious, she fitted into her new life without any of those manifest efforts at adjustment that are as sore to a husband's pride as the critical rearrangement of the bridal furniture. She had given him, instead, the delicate pleasure of watching her expand like a sea-creature restored to its element, stretching out the atrophied tentacles of girlish vanity and enjoyment to the rising tide of opportunity. And somehow—in the windowless inner cell of his consciousness where self-criticism cowered—Glennard's course seemed justified by its merely material success. How could such a crop of innocent blessedness have sprung from tainted soil?

Now he had the injured sense of a man entrapped into a disadvantagous bargain. He had not known it would be like this; and a dull anger gathered at his heart. Anger against whom? Against his wife, for not knowing what he suffered? Against Flamel, for being the unconscious instrument of his wrongdoing? Or against that mute memory to which his own act had suddenly given a voice of accusation? Yes, that was it; and his punishment henceforth would be the presence, the unescapable presence, of the woman he had so persistently evaded. She would always be there now. It was as though he had married her instead of the other. It was what she had always wanted—to be with him—and she had gained her point at last.

He sprang up, as though in an impulse of flight. The sudden movement lifted his wife's lids, and she asked, in the incurious voice of the woman whose life is enclosed in a magic circle of prosperity—"Any news?"

"No—none—" he said, roused to a sense of immediate peril. The papers lay scattered at his feet—what if she were to see them? He stretched his arm to gather them up, but his next thought showed him the futility of such concealment. The same advertisement would appear every day, for weeks to come, in every newspaper; how could he prevent her seeing it? He could not always be hiding the papers from her. . . . Well, and what if she did see it? It would signify nothing to her; the chances were that she would never even read the book. . . . As she ceased to be an element of fear in his calculations the distance between them seemed to lessen and he took her again, as it were, into the circle of his conjugal protection. . . . Yet a moment before he had almost hated her! . . . He laughed aloud at his senseless terrors. . . . He was off his balance, decidedly.

"What are you laughing at?" she asked.

He explained, elaborately, that he was laughing at the recollection of an old woman in the train, an old woman with a lot of bundles, who couldn't find her ticket. . . . But somehow, in the telling, the humor of the story seemed to evaporate, and he felt the conventionality of her smile. He glanced at his watch. "Isn't it time to dress?"

She rose with serene reluctance. "It's a pity to go in. The garden looks so lovely."

They lingered side by side, surveying their domain. There was not space in it, at this hour, for the shadow of the elm tree in the angle of the hedge: it crossed the lawn, cut the flower-border in two, and ran up the side of the house to the nursery window. She bent to flick a caterpillar from the honeysuckle; then, as they turned indoors, "If we mean to go on the yacht next Sunday," she suggested, "oughtn't you to let Mr. Flamel know?"

Glennard's exasperation deflected suddenly. "Of course I shall let him know. You always seem to imply that I'm going to do something rude to Flamel."

The words reverberated through her silence; she had a way of thus leaving one space in which to contemplate one's folly at arm's length. Glennard turned on his heel and went upstairs. As he dropped into a chair before his dressing-table, he said to himself that in the last hour he had sounded the depths of his humiliation, and that the lowest dregs of it, the very bottom-slime, was the hateful necessity of having always, as long as the two men lived, to be civil to Barton Flamel.

VI

The week in town had been sultry, and the men, in the Sunday emancipation of white flannel and duck, filled the deck chairs of the yacht with their outstretched apathy, following, through a mist of cigarette smoke, the flitting inconsequences of the women. The party was a small one—Flamel had few intimate friends—but composed of more heterogeneous atoms than the little pools into which society usually runs. The reaction from the chief episode of his earlier life had bred in Glennard an uneasy distaste for any kind of personal saliency. Cleverness was useful in business; but in society it seemed to him as futile as the sham cascades formed by a stream that might have been used to drive a mill. He liked the collective point of view that goes with the civilized uniformity of dress clothes, and his wife's attitude implied the same preference; yet they found themselves slipping more and more into Flamel's intimacy. Alexa had once or twice said that she enjoyed meeting clever people; but her enjoyment took the negative form of a smiling receptivity; and Glennard felt a growing preference for the kind of people who have their thinking done for them by the community.

Still, the deck of the yacht was a pleasant refuge from the heat on shore, and his wife's profile, serenely projected against the changing blue, lay on his retina like a cool hand on the nerves. He had never been more impressed by the kind of absoluteness that lifted her beauty above the transient effects of other women, making the most harmonious face seem an accidental collocation of features.

The ladies who directly suggested this comparison were of a kind accustomed to take similar risks with more gratifying results. Mrs. Armiger had in fact long been the triumphant alternative of those who couldn't "see" Alexa Glennard's looks; and Mrs. Touchett's claims to consideration were founded on that distribution of effects which is the wonder of those who admire a highly cultivated country. The third lady of the trio which Glennard's fancy had put to such unflattering uses was bound by circumstances to support the claims of the other two. This was Mrs. Dresham, the wife of the editor of the *Radiator*. Mrs. Dresham was a lady who had rescued herself from social obscurity by assuming the role of her husband's exponent and interpreter; and Dresham's leisure being devoted to the cultivation of remarkable women, his wife's attitude committed her to the public celebration of their remarkableness. For the conceivable tedium of this duty, Mrs. Dresham was repaid by the fact that there were people who took *her* for a remarkable woman; and who in turn probably purchased similar distinction with the small change of her reflected importance. As to the other ladies of the party, they were simply the wives of some of the men—the kind of women who expect to be talked to collectively and to have their questions left unanswered.

Mrs. Armiger, the latest embodiment of Dresham's instinct for the remarkable, was an innocent beauty who for years had distilled dulness among a set of people now self-condemned by their inability to appreciate her. Under Dresham's tutelage she had developed into a "thoughtful woman," who read his leaders in the *Radiator* and bought the works he recommended. When a new book appeared, people wanted to know what Mrs. Armiger thought of it; and a young gentleman who had made a trip in Touraine had recently inscribed to her the wide-margined result of his explorations.

Glennard, leaning back with his head against the rail and a slit of fugitive blue between his half-closed lids, vaguely wished she wouldn't spoil the afternoon by making people talk; though he reduced his annoyance to the minimum by not listening to what was said, there remained a latent irritation against the general futility of words.

His wife's gift of silence seemed to him the most vivid commentary on the clumsiness of speech as a means of intercourse, and his eyes had turned to her in renewed appreciation of this finer faculty when Mrs. Armiger's voice abruptly brought home to him the underrated potentialities of language.

"You've read them, of course, Mrs. Glennard?" he heard her ask: and, in reply to Alexa's vague interrogation—"Why, the *Aubyn Letters*—it's the only book people are talking of this week."

Mrs. Dresham immediately saw her advantage. "You *haven't* read them? How very extraordinary! As Mrs. Armiger says, the book's in the air: one breathes it in like the influenza."

Glennard sat motionless, watching his wife.

"Perhaps it hasn't reached the suburbs yet," she said with her unruffled smile.

"Oh, *do* let me come to you, then!" Mrs. Touchett cried; "anything for a change of air! I'm positively sick of the book and I can't put it down. Can't you sail us beyond its reach, Mr. Flamel?"

Flamel shook his head. "Not even with this breeze. Literature travels faster than steam nowadays. And the worst of it is that we can't any of us give up reading; it's as insidious as a vice and as tiresome as a virtue."

"I believe it *is* a vice, almost, to read such a book as the *Letters,*" said Mrs. Touchett. "It's the woman's soul, absolutely torn up by the roots—her whole self laid bare; and to a man who evidently didn't care; who couldn't have cared. I don't mean to read another line: it's too much like listening at a keyhole."

"But if she wanted it published?"

"Wanted it? How do we know she did?"

"Why, I heard she'd left the letters to the man—whoever he is—with directions that they should be published after his death—"

"I don't believe it," Mrs. Touchett declared.

"He's dead then, is he?" one of the men asked.

"Why, you don't suppose if he were alive he could ever hold up his head again, with these letters being read by everybody?" Mrs. Touchett protested. "It must have been horrible enough to know they'd been written to him; but to publish them! No man could have done it and no woman could have told him to—"

"Oh, come, come," Dresham judicially interposed; "after all, they're not love-letters."

"No—that's the worst of it; they're unloved letters," Mrs. Touchett retorted.

"Then, obviously, she needn't have written them; whereas the man, poor devil, could hardly help receiving them."

"Perhaps he counted on the public to save him the trouble of reading them," said young Hartly, who was in the cynical stage.

Mrs. Armiger turned her reproachful loveliness to Dresham. "From the way you defend him I believe you know who he is."

Everyone looked at Dresham, and his wife smiled with the superior air of the woman who is in her husband's professional secrets. Dresham shrugged his shoulders.

"What have I said to defend him?"

"You called him a poor devil—you pitied him."

"A man who could let Margaret Aubyn write to him in that way? Of course I pity him."

"Then you *must* know who he is," cried Mrs. Armiger with a triumphant air of penetration.

Hartly and Flamel laughed and Dresham shook his head. "No one knows; not even the publishers; so they tell me at least."

"So they tell you to tell us," Hartly astutely amended; and Mrs. Armiger added, with the appearance of carrying the argument a point farther, "But even if *he's* dead and *she's* dead, somebody must have given the letters to the publishers."

"A little bird, probably," said Dresham, smiling indulgently on her deduction.

"A little bird of prey then—a vulture, I should say—" another man interpolated.

"Oh, I'm not with you there," said Dresham easily. "Those letters belonged to the public."

"How can any letters belong to the public that weren't written to the public?" Mrs. Touchett interposed.

"Well, these were, in a sense. A personality as big as Margaret Aubyn's belongs to the world. Such a mind is part of the general fund of thought. It's the penalty of greatness—one becomes a *monument historique*. Posterity pays the cost of keeping one up, but on condition that one is always open to the public."

"I don't see that that exonerates the man who gives up the keys of the sanctuary, as it were."

"Who *was* he?" another voice inquired.

"Who was he? Oh, nobody, I fancy—the letter-box, the slit in the wall through which the letters passed to posterity. . . ."

"But she never meant them for posterity!"

"A woman shouldn't write such letters if she doesn't mean them to be published. . . ."

"She shouldn't write them to such a man!" Mrs. Touchett scornfully corrected.

"I never keep letters," said Mrs. Armiger, under the obvious impression that she was contributing a valuable point to the discussion.

There was a general laugh, and Flamel, who had not spoken, said lazily, "You women are too incurably subjective. I venture to say that most men would see in those letters merely their immense literary value, their significance as documents. The personal side doesn't count where there's so much else."

"Oh, we all know you haven't any principles," Mrs. Armiger declared; and Alexa Glennard, lifting an indolent smile, said: "I shall never write you a love-letter, Mr. Flamel."

Glennard moved away impatiently. Such talk was as tedious as the buzzing of gnats. He wondered why his wife had wanted to drag him on such a senseless expedition. . . . He hated Flamel's crowd—and what business had Flamel himself to interfere in that way, standing up for the publication of the letters as though Glennard needed his defence?

Glennard turned his head and saw that Flamel had drawn a seat to Alexa's elbow and was speaking to her in a low tone. The other groups had scattered, straying in twos along the deck. It came over Glennard that he should never again be able to see Flamel speaking to his wife without the sense of sick mistrust that now loosened his joints.

Alexa, the next morning, over their early breakfast, surprised her husband by an unexpected request.

"Will you bring me those letters from town?" she asked.

"What letters?" he said, putting down his cup. He felt himself as vulnerable as a man who is lunged at in the dark.

"Mrs. Aubyn's. The book they were all talking about yesterday."

Glennard, carefully measuring his second cup of tea, said with deliberation, "I didn't know you cared about that sort of thing."

She was, in fact, not a great reader, and a new book seldom reached her till it was, so to speak, on the home stretch; but she replied with a gentle tenacity, "I think it would interest me because I read her life last year."

"Her life? Where did you get that?"

"Someone lent it to me when it came out—Mr. Flamel, I think."

His first impulse was to exclaim, "Why the devil do you borrow books of Flamel? I can buy you all you want—" but he felt himself irresistibly forced into an attitude of smiling compliance. "Flamel always has the newest books going, hasn't he? You must be careful, by the way, about returning what he lends you. He's rather crotchety about his library."

"Oh, I'm always very careful," she said, with a touch of competence that struck him; and she added, as he caught up his hat: "Don't forget the letters."

Why had she asked for the book? Was her sudden wish to see it the result of some hint of Flamel's? The thought turned Glennard sick, but he preserved sufficient lucidity to tell himself, a moment later, that his last hope of self-control would be lost if he yielded to the temptation of seeing a hidden purpose in everything she said and did. How much Flamel guessed, he had no means of divining; nor could he predicate, from what he knew of the man, to what use his inferences might be put. The very qualities that had made Flamel a useful adviser made him the most dangerous of accomplices. Glennard felt himself agrope among alien forces that his own act had set in motion.

Alexa was a woman of few requirements; but her wishes, even in trifles, had a definiteness that distinguished them from the fluid impulses of her kind. He knew that, having once asked for the book, she would not forget it; and he put aside, as an ineffectual expedient, his momentary idea of applying for it at the circulating library and telling her that all the copies were out. If the book was to be bought, it had better be bought at once. He left his office earlier than usual and turned in at the first bookshop on his way to the train. The show-window was stacked with conspicuously lettered volumes. *Margaret Aubyn* flashed back at him in endless iteration. He plunged into the shop and came on a counter where the name repeated itself on row after row of bindings. It seemed to have driven the rest of literature to the back shelves. He caught up a copy, tossing the money to an astonished clerk, who pursued him to the door with the unheeded offer to wrap up the volumes.

In the street he was seized with a sudden apprehension. What if he were to meet Flamel? The thought was intolerable. He called a cab and drove straight to the station, where, amid the palm-leaf fans of a perspiring crowd, he waited a long half-hour for his train to start.

He had thrust a volume in either pocket, and in the train he dared not draw them out; but the detested words leaped at him from the folds of the evening paper. The air seemed full of Margaret Aubyn's name; the motion of the train set it dancing up and down on the page of a magazine that a man in front of him was reading.

At the door he was told that Mrs. Glennard was still out, and he went upstairs to his room and dragged the books from his pocket. They lay on the table before him like live things that he feared to touch. . . . At length he opened the first volume. A familiar letter sprang out at him, each word quickened by its glaring garb of type. The little broken phrases fled across the page like wounded animals in the open. . . . It was a horrible sight . . . a *battue* of helpless things driven savagely out of shelter. He had not known it would be like this.

He understood now that, at the moment of selling the letters, he had viewed the transaction solely as it affected himself: as an unfortunate blemish on an otherwise presentable record. He had scarcely considered the act in relation to Margaret Aubyn; for death, if it hallows, also makes innocuous. Glennard's God was a god of the living, of the immediate, the actual, the tangible; all his days he had lived in the presence of that god, heedless of the divinities who, below the surface of our deeds and passions, silently forge the fatal weapons of the dead.

VII

A knock roused him, and looking up he saw his wife. He met her glance in silence, and she faltered out, "Are you ill?"

The words restored his self-possession. "Ill? Of course not. They told me you were out and I came upstairs."

The books lay between them on the table; he wondered when she would see them. She lingered tentatively on the threshold, with the air of leaving his explanation on his hands. She was not the kind of woman who could be counted on to fortify an excuse by appearing to dispute it.

"Where have you been?" Glennard asked, moving forward so that he obstructed her vision of the books.

"I walked over to the Dreshams' for tea."

"I can't think what you see in those people," he said with a shrug; adding, uncontrollably—"I suppose Flamel was there?"

"No; he left on the yacht this morning."

An answer so obstructing to the natural escape of his irritation left Glennard with no momentary resource but that of strolling impatiently to the window. As her eyes followed him they lit on the books.

"Ah, you've brought them! I'm so glad," she said.

He answered over his shoulder, "For a woman who never reads you make the most astounding exceptions!"

Her smile was an exasperating concession to the probability that it had been hot in town or that something had bothered him.

"Do you mean it's not nice to want to read the book?" she asked. "It was not nice to publish it, certainly; but after all, I'm not responsible for that, am I?" She paused, and, as he made no answer, went on, still smiling, "I do read sometimes, you know; and I'm very fond of Margaret Aubyn's books. I was reading *Pomegranate Seed* when we first met. Don't you remember? It was then you told me all about her."

Glennard had turned back into the room and stood staring at his wife. "All about her?" he repeated, and with the words remembrance came to him. He had found Miss Trent one afternoon with the novel in her hand, and moved by the lover's fatuous impulse to associate himself in some way with whatever fills the mind of the beloved, had broken through his habitual silence about the past. Rewarded by the consciousness of figuring impressively in Miss Trent's imagination, he had gone on from one anecdote to another, reviving dormant details of his old Hillbridge life, and pasturing his vanity on the eagerness with which she listened to his reminiscences of a being already clothed in the impersonality of greatness.

The incident had left no trace in his mind; but it sprang up now like an old enemy, the more dangerous for having been forgotten. The instinct of self-preservation—sometimes the most perilous that man can exercise—made him awkwardly declare: "Oh, I used to see her at people's houses, that was all," and her silence as usual leaving room for a multiplicatiion of blunders, he added, with increased indifference, "I simply can't see what you can find to interest you in such a book."

She seemed to consider this intently. "You've read it, then?"

"I glanced at it—I never read such things."

"Is it true that she didn't wish the letters to be published?"

Glennard felt the sudden dizziness of the mountaineer on a narrow ledge, and with it the sense that he was lost if he looked more than a step ahead.

"I'm sure I don't know," he said; then, summoning a smile, he passed his hand through her arm. "*I* didn't have tea at the Dreshams', you know; won't you give me some now?" he suggested.

That evening Glennard, under pretext of work to be done, shut himself into the small study opening off the drawing-room. As he gathered up his papers he said to his wife: "You're not going to sit indoors on such a night as this? I'll join you presently outside."

But she had drawn her armchair to the lamp. "I want to look at my book," she said, taking up the first volume of the *Letters*.

Glennard, with a shrug, withdrew into the study. "I'm going to shut the door; I want to be quiet," he explained from the threshold; and she nodded without lifting her eyes from the book.

He sank into a chair, staring aimlessly at the outspread papers. How was he to work, while on the other side of the door she sat with that volume in her hand? The door did not shut her out—he saw her distinctly, felt her close to him in a contact as painful as the pressure on a bruise.

The sensation was part of the general strangeness that made him feel like a man waking from a long sleep to find himself in an unknown country among people of alien tongue. We live in our own souls as in an unmapped region, a few acres of which we have cleared for our habitation; while of the nature of those nearest us we know but the boundaries that march with ours. Of the points in his wife's character not in direct contact with his own, Glennard now discerned his ignorance; and the baffling sense of her remoteness was intensified by the discovery that, in one way, she was closer to him than ever before. As one may live for years in happy unconsciousness of the possession of a sensitive nerve, he had lived beside his wife unaware that her individuality had become a part of the texture of his life, ineradicable as some growth on a vital organ; and he now felt himself at once incapable of forecasting her judgment and powerless to evade its effects.

To escape, the next morning, the confidences of the breakfast-table, he went to town earlier than usual. His wife, who read slowly, was given to talking over what she read, and at present his first object in life was to postpone the inevitable discussion of the letters. This instinct of protection, in the afternoon, on his way up town, guided him to the club in search of a man who might be persuaded to come out to the country to dine. The only man in the club was Flamel.

Glennard, as he heard himself almost involuntarily pressing Flamel to come and dine, felt the full irony of the situation. To use Flamel as a shield against his wife's scrutiny was only a shade less humiliating than to reckon on his wife as a defence against Flamel.

He felt a contradictory movement of annoyance at the latter's ready acceptance, and the two men drove in silence to the station. As they passed the bookstall in the waiting-room Flamel lingered a moment, and the eyes of both fell on Margaret Aubyn's name, conspicuously displayed above a counter stacked with the familiar volumes.

"We shall be late, you know," Glennard remonstrated, pulling out his watch.

"Go ahead," said Flamel imperturbably. "I want to get something—"

Glennard turned on his heel and walked down the platform. Flamel rejoined him with an innocent-looking magazine in his hand; but Glennard dared not even glance at the cover, lest it should show the syllables he feared.

The train was full of people they knew, and they were kept apart till it dropped them at the little suburban station. As they strolled up the shaded hill, Glennard talked volubly, pointing out the improvements in the neighborhood, deploring the threatened approach of an electric railway, and screening himself by a series of reflex adjustments from the risk of any allusion to the *Letters*. Flamel suffered his discourse with the bland inattention that we accord to the affairs of someone else's suburb, and they reached the shelter of Alexa's tea-table without a perceptible turn toward the dreaded topic.

The dinner passed off safely. Flamel, always at his best in Alexa's presence, gave her the kind of attention which is like a becoming light thrown on the speaker's words: his answers seemed to bring out a latent significance in her phrases, as the sculptor draws his statue from the block. Glennard, under his wife's composure, detected a sensibility to this manœuvre, and the discovery was like the lightning-flash across a nocturnal landscape. Thus far these momentary illuminations had served only to reveal the strangeness of the intervening country: each fresh observation seemed to increase the sum-total of his ignorance. Her simplicity of outline was more puzzling than a complex surface. One may conceivably work one's way through a labyrinth; but Alexa's candor was like a snow-covered plain where, the road once lost, there are no landmarks to travel by.

Dinner over, they returned to the veranda, where a moon, rising behind the old elm, was combining with that complaisant tree a romantic enlargement of their borders. Glennard had forgotten the cigars. He went to his study to fetch them, and in passing through the drawing-room he saw the second volume of the *Letters* lying open on his wife's table. He picked up the book and looked at the date of the letter she had been reading. It was one of the last . . . he knew the few lines by heart. He dropped the book and leaned against the wall. Why had he included that one among the others? Or was it possible that now they would all seem like that?

Alexa's voice came suddenly out of the dusk. "May Touchett was right—it *is* like listening at a keyhole. I wish I hadn't read it!"

Flamel returned, in the leisurely tone of the man whose phrases are punctuated by a cigarette, "It seems so to us, perhaps; but to another generation the book will be a classic."

"Then it ought not to have been published till it had time to become a classic. It's horrible, it's degrading almost, to read the secrets of a woman one might have known." She added, in a lower tone, "Stephen *did* know her—"

"Did he?" came from Flamel.

"He knew her very well, at Hillbridge, years ago. The book has made him feel dreadfully . . . he wouldn't read it . . . he didn't want me to read it. I didn't understand at first, but now I can see how horribly disloyal it must seem to him. It's so much worse to surprise a friend's secrets than a stranger's."

"Oh, Glennard's such a sensitive chap," Flamel said easily; and Alexa almost rebukingly rejoined, "If you'd known her I'm sure you'd feel as he does. . . ."

Glennard stood motionless, overcome by the singular infelicity with which he had contrived to put Flamel in possession of the two points most damaging to his case: the fact that he had been a friend of Margaret Aubyn's and that he had concealed from Alexa his share in the publication of the letters. To a man of less than Flamel's astuteness it must now be clear to whom the letters were addressed; and the possibility once suggested, nothing could be easier than to confirm it by discreet research. An impulse of self-accusal drove Glennard to the window. Why not anticipate betrayal by telling his wife the truth in Flamel's presence? If the man had a drop of decent feeling in him, such a course would be the surest means of securing his silence; and above all, it would rid Glennard of the necessity of defending himself against the perpetual criticism of his wife's belief in him.

The impulse was strong enough to carry him to the window; but there a reaction of defiance set in. What had he done, after all, to need defence and explanation? Both Dresham and Flamel had, in his hearing, declared the publication of the letters to be not only justifiable but obligatory; and if the disinterestedness of Flamel's verdict might be questioned, Dresham's at least represented the impartial view of the man of letters. As to Alexa's words, they were simply the conventional utterance of the "nice" woman on a question already decided for her by other "nice" women. She had said the proper thing as mechanically as she would have put on the appropriate gown or written the correct form of dinner invitation. Glennard had small faith in the abstract judgments of the other sex: he knew that half the women who were horrified by the publication of Mrs. Aubyn's letters would have betrayed her secrets without a scruple.

The sudden lowering of his emotional pitch brought a proportionate relief. He told himself that now the worst was over an things would fall into perspective again. His wife and Flamel ha turned to other topics, and coming out on the veranda, he hande the cigars to Flamel, saying cheerfully—and yet he could hav sworn they were the last words he meant to utter!—"Look here old man, before you go down to Newport you must come ou and spend a few days with us—mustn't he, Alexa?"

VIII

Glennard, perhaps unconsciously, had counted on the continu ance of this easier mood. He had always taken pride in a certai robustness of fibre that enabled him to harden himself against th inevitable, to convert his failures into the building materials o success. Though it did not even now occur to him that what h called the inevitable had hitherto been the alternative he hap pened to prefer, he was yet obscurely aware that his presen difficulty was one not to be conjured by any affectation o indifference. Some griefs build the soul a spacious house, but i this misery of Glennard's he could not stand upright. It presse against him at every turn. He told himself that this was becaus there was no escape from the visible evidences of his act. Th *Letters* confronted him everywhere. People who had never opene a book discussed them with critical reservations; to have rea them had become a social obligation in circles to which literatur never penetrates except in a personal guise.

Glennard did himself injustice. It was from the unexpecte discovery of his own pettiness that he chiefly suffered. Ou self-esteem is apt to be based on the hypothetical great act w have never had occasion to perform; and even the most self scrutinizing modesty credits itself negatively with a high stan dard of conduct. Glennard had never thought himself a hero; bu he had been certain that he was incapable of baseness. We al like our wrong-doings to have a becoming cut, to be made t order, as it were; and Glennard found himself suddenly thrus into a garb of dishonor surely meant for a meaner figure.

The immediate result of his first weeks of wretchedness wa the resolve to go to town for the winter. He knew that such course was just beyond the limit of prudence; but it was easy t allay the fears of Alexa, who, scrupulously vigilant in the management of the household, preserved the American wife's usual aloofness from her husband's business cares. Glennard felt that he could not trust himself to a winter's solitude with her. He had an unspeakable dread of her learning the truth about the letters, yet could not be sure of steeling himself against the suicidal impulse of avowal. His very soul was parched for sympathy; he thirsted for a voice of pity and comprehension. But would his wife pity? Would she understand? Again he found himself brought up abruptly against his incredible ignorance of her nature. The fact that he knew well enough how she would behave in the ordinary emergencies of life, that he could count, in such contingencies, on the kind of high courage and directness he had always divined in her, made him the more hopeless of her entering into the tortuous psychology of an act that he himself could no longer explain or understand. It would have been easier had she been more complex, more feminine—if he could have counted on her imaginative sympathy or her moral obtuseness—but he was sure of neither. He was sure of nothing but that, for a time, he must avoid her. Glennard could not rid himself of the delusion that by and by his action would cease to make its consequences felt. He would not have cared to own to himself that he counted on the dulling of his sensibilities: he preferred to indulge the vague hypothesis that extraneous circumstances would somehow efface the blot upon his conscience. In his worst moments of self-abasement he tried to find solace in the thought that Flamel had sanctioned his course. Flamel, at the outset, must have guessed to whom the letters were addressed; yet neither then nor afterward had he hesitated to advise their publication. This thought drew Glennard to him in fitful impulses of friendliness, from each of which there was a sharper reaction of distrust and aversion. When Flamel was not at the house, he missed the support of his tacit connivance; when he was there, his presence seemed the assertion of an intolerable claim.

Early in the winter the Glennards took possession of the little house that was to cost them almost nothing. The change brought Glennard the relief of seeing less of his wife, and of being protected, in her presence, by the multiplied preoccupations of town life. Alexa, who could never appear hurried, showed the smiling abstraction of a pretty woman to whom the social side of married life has not lost its novelty. Glennard, with the recklessness of a man fresh from his first financial imprudence, encouraged her in such little extravagances as her good sense at first resisted. Since they had come to town, he argued, they might as well enjoy themselves. He took a sympathetic view of the necessity of new gowns, he gave her a set of furs at Christmas, and before the New Year they had agreed on the necessity of adding a parlormaid to their small establishment.

Providence the very next day hastened to justify this measure by placing on Glennard's breakfast-plate an envelope bearing the name of the publishers to whom he had sold Mrs. Aubyn's letters. It happened to be the only letter the early post had brought, and he glanced across the table at his wife, who had come down before him and had probably laid the envelope on his plate. She was not the woman to ask awkward questions, but he felt the conjecture of her glance, and he was debating whether to affect surprise at the receipt of the letter, or to pass it off as a business communication that had strayed to his house, when a check fell from the envelope. It was the royalty on the first edition of the letters. His first feeling was one of simple satisfaction. The money had come with such infernal opportuneness that he could not help welcoming it. Before long, too, there would be more; he knew the book was still selling far beyond the publishers' previsions. He put the check in his pocket and left the room without looking at his wife.

On the way to his office the habitual reaction set in. The money he had received was the first tangible reminder that he was living on the sale of his self-esteem. The thought of material benefit had been overshadowed by his sense of the intrinsic baseness of making the letters known: now he saw what an element of sordidness it added to the situation and how the fact that he needed the money, and must use it, pledged him more irrevocably than ever to the consequences of his act. It seemed to him, in that first hour of misery, that he had betrayed his friend anew.

When, that afternoon, he reached home earlier than usual, Alexa's drawing-room was full of a gayety that overflowed to the stairs. Flamel, for a wonder, was not there; but Dresham and young Hartly, grouped about the tea-table, were receiving with resonant mirth a narrative delivered in the fluttered staccato that made Mrs. Armiger's conversation like the ejaculations of a startled aviary.

She paused as Glennard entered, and he had time to notice that his wife, who was busied about the tea-tray, had not joined in the laughter of the men.

"Oh, go on, go on," young Hartly rapturously groaned; and

Irs. Armiger met Glennard's inquiry with the deprecating cry that eally she didn't see what there was to laugh at. "I'm sure I feel nore like crying. I don't know what I should have done if Alexa adn't been at home to give me a cup of tea. My nerves are in hreds—yes, another, dear, please—" and as Glennard looked is perplexity, she went on, after pondering on the selection of a econd lump of sugar, "Why, I've just come from the reading, ou know—the reading at the Waldorf."

"I haven't been in town long enough to know anything," said Glennard, taking the cup his wife handed him. "Who has been eading what?"

"That lovely girl from the South—Georgie—Georgie What's-er-name—Mrs. Dresham's protégée—unless she's *yours,* Mr. Dresham! Why, the big ballroom was *packed,* and all the women vere crying like idiots—it was the most harrowing thing I ever eard—"

"What *did* you hear?" Glennard asked; and his wife interposed: "Won't you have another bit of cake, Julia? Or, Stephen, ing for some hot toast, please." Her tone betrayed a polite veariness of the topic under discussion. Glennard turned to the ell, but Mrs. Armiger pursued him with her lovely amazement.

"Why, the *Aubyn Letters*—didn't you know about it? She ead them so beautifully that it was quite horrible—I should have ainted if there'd been a man near enough to carry me out."

Hartly's glee redoubled, and Dresham said jovially, "How ike you women to raise a shriek over the book and then do all ou can to encourage the blatant publicity of the readings!"

Mrs. Armiger met him more than half-way on a torrent of elf-accusal. "It *was* horrid; it was disgraceful. I told your wife ve ought all to be ashamed of ourselves for going, and I think Alexa was quite right to refuse to take any tickets—even if it was or a charity."

"Oh," her hostess murmured indifferently, "with me charity egins at home. I can't afford emotional luxuries."

"A charity? A charity?" Hartly exulted. "I hadn't seized the ull beauty of it. Reading poor Margaret Aubyn's love-letters at he Waldorf before five hundred people for a charity! *What* harity, dear Mrs. Armiger?"

"Why, the Home for Friendless Women——"

"It was well chosen," Dresham commented; and Hartly bur-ed his mirth in the sofa cushions.

* * *

When they were alone Glennard, still holding his untouched cup of tea, turned to his wife, who sat silently behind the kettle. "Who asked you to take a ticket for that reading?"

"I don't know, really—Kate Dresham, I fancy. It was she who got it up."

"It's just the sort of damnable vulgarity she's capable of! It's loathsome—it's monstrous—"

His wife, without looking up, answered gravely, "I thought so too. It was for that reason I didn't go. But you must remember that very few people feel about Mrs. Aubyn as you do—"

Glennard managed to set down his cup with a steady hand, but the room swung round with him and he dropped into the nearest chair. "As I do?" he repeated.

"I mean that very few people knew her when she lived in New York. To most of the women who went to the reading she was a mere name, too remote to have any personality. With me, of course, it was different—"

Glennard gave her a startled look. "Different? Why different?"

"Since you were her friend—"

"Her friend!" He stood up. "You speak as if she had had only one—the most famous woman of her day!" He moved vaguely about the room, bending down to look at some books on the table. "I hope," he added, "you didn't give that as a reason?"

"A reason?"

"For not going. A woman who gives reasons for getting out of social obligations is sure to make herself unpopular or ridiculous."

The words were uncalculated; but in an instant he saw that they had strangely bridged the distance between his wife and himself. He felt her close on him, like a panting foe, and her answer was a flash that showed the hand on the trigger.

"I seem," she said from the threshold, "to have done both in giving my reason to you."

The fact that they were dining out that evening made it easy for him to avoid Alexa till she came downstairs in her opera-cloak. Mrs. Touchett, who was going to the same dinner, had offered to call for her, and Glennard, refusing a precarious seat between the ladies' draperies, followed on foot. The evening was interminable. The reading at the Waldorf, at which all the women had been present, had revived the discussion of the *Aubyn Letters*, and Glennard, hearing his wife questioned as to her absence, felt himself miserably wishing that she had gone, rather than that her staying away should have been remarked. He was rapidly losing all sense of proportion where the *Letters* were concerned. He could no longer hear them mentioned without suspecting a purpose in the allusion; he even yielded himself for a moment to the extravagance of imagining that Mrs. Dresham, whom he disliked, had organized the reading in the hope of making him betray himself—for he was already sure that Dresham had divined his share in the transaction.

The attempt to keep a smooth surface on this inner tumult was as endless and unavailing as efforts made in a nightmare. He lost all sense of what he was saying to his neighbors; and once when he looked up his wife's glance struck him cold.

She sat nearly opposite him, at Flamel's side, and it appeared to Glennard that they had built about themselves one of those airy barriers of talk behind which two people can say what they please. While the reading was discussed they were silent. Their silence seemed to Glennard almost cynical—it stripped the last disguise from their complicity. A throb of anger rose in him, but suddenly it fell, and he felt, with a curious sense of relief, that at bottom he no longer cared whether Flamel had told his wife or not. The assumption that Flamel knew about the letters had become a fact to Glennard; and it now seemed to him better that Alexa should know too.

He was frightened at first by the discovery of his own indifference. The last barriers of his will seemed to be breaking down before a flood of moral lassitude. How could he continue to play his part, how keep his front to the enemy, with this poison of indifference stealing through his veins? He tried to brace himself with the remembrance of his wife's scorn. He had not forgotten the note on which their conversation had closed. If he had ever wondered how she would receive the truth he wondered no longer—she would despise him. But this lent a new insidiousness to his temptation, since her contempt would be a refuge from his own. He said to himself that, since he no longer cared for the consequences, he could at least acquit himself of speaking in self-defence. What he wanted now was not immunity but castigation: his wife's indignation might still reconcile him to himself. Therein lay his one hope of regeneration; her scorn was the moral antiseptic that he needed, her comprehension the one balm that could heal him.

When they left the dinner he was so afraid of speaking that he let her drive home alone, and went to the club with Flamel.

IX

He rose next morning with the resolve to know what Alexa thought of him. It was not anchoring in a haven but lying to in a storm—he felt the need of a temporary lull in the turmoil of his sensations.

He came home late, for they were dining alone and he knew that they would have the evening together. When he followed her to the drawing-room after dinner he thought himself on the point of speaking; but as she handed him his coffee he said involuntarily: "I shall have to carry this off to the study; I've got a lot of work tonight."

Alone in the study he cursed his cowardice. What was it that had withheld him? A certain bright unapproachableness seemed to keep him at arm's length. She was not the kind of woman whose compassion could be circumvented; there was no chance of slipping past the outposts—he would never take her by surprise. Well—why not face her, then? What he shrank from could be no worse than what he was enduring. He had pushed back his chair and turned to go upstairs when a new expedient presented itself. What if, instead of telling her, he were to let her find out for herself and watch the effect of the discovery before speaking? In this way he made over to chance the burden of the revelation.

The idea had been suggested by the sight of the formula enclosing the publisher's check. He had deposited the money, but the notice accompanying it dropped from his note-case as he cleared his table for work. It was the formula usual in such cases, and revealed clearly enough that he was the recipient of a royalty on Margaret Aubyn's letters. It would be impossible for Alexa to read it without understanding at once that the letters had been written to him and that he had sold them.

He sat downstairs till he heard her ring for the parlormaid to put out the lights; then he went up to the drawing-room with a bundle of papers in his hand. Alexa was just rising from her seat, and the lamplight fell on the deep roll of hair that overhung her brow like the eaves of a temple. Her face had often the high secluded look of a shrine; and it was this touch of awe in her beauty that now made him feel himself on the brink of sacrilege.

Lest the feeling should control him, he spoke at once. "I've brought you a piece of work—a lot of old bills and things that I want you to sort for me. Some are not worth keeping—but you'll be able to judge of that. There may be a letter or two among them—nothing of much account; but I don't like to throw away the whole lot without having them looked over, and I haven't time to do it myself."

He held out the papers, and she took them with a smile that seemed to recognize in the service he asked the tacit intention of making amends for the incident of the previous day.

"Are you sure I shall know which to keep?"

"Oh, quite sure," he answered easily; "and besides, none are of much importance."

The next morning he invented an excuse for leaving the house without seeing her, and when he returned, just before dinner, he found a visitor's hat and stick in the hall. The visitor was Flamel, who was just taking leave.

He had risen, but Alexa remained seated; and their attitude gave the impression of a colloquy that had prolonged itself beyond the limits of speech. Both turned a surprised eye on Glennard, and he had the sense of walking into a room grown suddenly empty, as though their thoughts were conspirators dispersed by his approach. He felt the clutch of his old fear. What if his wife had already sorted the papers and had told Flamel of her discovery? Well, it was no news to Flamel that Glennard was in receipt of a royalty on the *Aubyn Letters*.

A sudden resolve to know the worst made him lift his eyes to his wife as the door closed on Flamel. But Alexa had risen also, and bending over her writing-table, with her back to Glennard, was beginning to speak precipitately.

"I'm dining out tonight—you don't mind my deserting you? Julia Armiger sent me word just now that she had an extra ticket for the last Ambrose concert. She told me to say how sorry she was that she hadn't two, but I knew *you* wouldn't be sorry!" She ended with a laugh that had the effect of being a strayed echo of Mrs. Armiger's; and before Glennard could speak she had added, with her hand on the door, "Mr. Flamel stayed so late that I've hardly time to dress. The concert begins ridiculously early, and Julia dines at half-past seven."

Glennard stood alone in the empty room that seemed somehow full of an ironical consciousness of what was happening. "She hates me," he murmured. "She hates me . . ."

The next day was Sunday, and Glennard purposely lingered late in his room. When he came downstairs his wife was already seated at the breakfast-table. She lifted her usual smile to his entrance and they took shelter in the nearest topic, like wayfarers overtaken by a storm. While he listened to her account of the concert he began to think that, after all, she had not yet sorted the papers, and that her agitation of the previous day must be ascribed to another cause, in which perhaps he had but an indirect concern. He wondered it had never before occurred to him that Flamel was the kind of man who might very well please a woman at his own expense, without need of fortuitous assistance. If this possibility cleared the outlook it did not brighten it. Glennard merely felt himself left alone with his baseness.

Alexa left the breakfast-table before him, and when he went up to the drawing-room he found her dressed to go out.

"Aren't you a little early for church?" he asked.

She replied that, on the way there, she meant to stop a moment at her mother's; and while she drew on her gloves he fumbled among the knickknacks on the mantelpiece for a match to light his cigarette.

"Well, goodbye," she said, turning to go; and from the threshold she added: "By the way, I've sorted the papers you gave me. Those that I thought you would like to keep are on your study table." She went downstairs and he heard the door close behind her.

She had sorted the papers—she knew, then—she *must* know—and she had made no sign!

Glennard, he hardly knew how, found himself once more in the study. On the table lay the packet he had given her. It was much smaller—she had evidently gone over the papers with care, destroying the greater number. He loosened the elastic band and spread the remaining envelopes on his desk. The publisher's notice was among them.

X

His wife knew and she made no sign. Glennard found himself in the case of the seafarer who, closing his eyes at nightfall on a scene he thinks to put leagues behind him before day, wakes to a porthole framing the same patch of shore. From the kind of exaltation to which his resolve had lifted him he dropped to an unreasoning apathy. His impulse of confession had acted as a drug to self-reproach. He had tried to shift a portion of his burden to his wife's shoulders; and now that she had tacitly refused to carry it, he felt the load too heavy to be taken up.

A fortunate interval of hard work brought respite from this phase of sterile misery. He went West to argue an important case, won it, and came back to fresh preoccupations. His own affairs were thriving enough to engross him in the pauses of his professional work, and for over two months he had little time to look himself in the face. Not unnaturally—for he was as yet unskilled in the subtleties of introspection—he mistook his temporary insensibility for a gradual revival of moral health.

He told himself that he was recovering his sense of proportion, getting to see things in their true light; and if he now thought of his rash appeal to his wife's sympathy it was as an act of folly from the consequences of which he had been saved by the providence that watches over madmen. He had little leisure to observe Alexa; but he concluded that the common sense momentarily denied him had counselled her silent acceptance of the inevitable. If such a quality was a poor substitute for the passionate justness that had once seemed to distinguish her, he accepted the alternative as a part of that general lowering of the key that seems needful to the maintenance of the matrimonial duet. What woman ever retained her abstract sense of justice where another woman was concerned? Possibly the thought that he had profited by Mrs. Aubyn's tenderness was not wholly disagreeable to his wife.

When the pressure of work began to lessen, and he found himself, in the lengthening afternoons, able to reach home somewhat earlier, he noticed that the little drawing-room was always full and that he and his wife seldom had an evening alone together. When he was tired, as often happened, she went out alone; the idea of giving up an engagement to remain with him seemed not to occur to her. She had shown, as a girl, little fondness for society, nor had she seemed to regret it during the year they had spent in the country. He reflected, however, that he was sharing the common lot of husbands, who proverbially mistake the early ardors of housekeeping for a sign of settled domesticity. Alexa, at any rate, was refuting his theory as inconsiderately as a seedling defeats the gardener's expectations. An undefinable change had come over her. In one sense it was a happy one, since she had grown, if not handsomer, at least more vivid and expressive; her beauty had become more communicable: it was as though she had learned the conscious exercise of intuitive attributes and now used her effects with the discrimination of an artist skilled in values. To a dispassionate critic (as Glennard now rated himself) the art may at times have been a little too obvious. Her attempts at lightness lacked spontaneity, and she sometimes rasped him by laughing like Julia Armiger; but he had enough imagination to perceive that, in respect of his wife's social arts, a husband necessarily sees the wrong side of the tapestry.

In this ironical estimate of their relation Glennard found himself strangely relieved of all concern as to his wife's feelings for Flamel. From an Olympian pinnacle of indifference he calmly surveyed their inoffensive antics. It was surprising how his cheapening of his wife put him at ease with himself. Far as he and she were from each other they had yet had, in a sense, the tacit nearness of complicity. Yes, they were accomplices; he could no more be jealous of her than she could despise him. The jealousy that would once have seemed a blur on her whiteness now appeared like a tribute to ideals in which he no longer believed.

Glennard was little given to exploring the outskirts of literature. He always skipped the "literary notices" in the papers, and he had small leisure for the intermittent pleasures of the periodical. He had therefore no notion of the prolonged reverberations which the *Aubyn Letters* had awakened. When the book ceased to be talked about he supposed it had ceased to be read; and this apparent subsidence of the agitation about it brought the reassuring sense that he had exaggerated its vitality. The conviction, if it did not ease his conscience, at least offered him the relative relief of obscurity; he felt like an offender taken down from the pillory and thrust into the soothing darkness of a cell.

But one evening, when Alexa had left him to go to a dance, he chanced to turn over the magazines on her table, and the copy of the *Horoscope* to which he settled down with his cigar confronted him, on its first page, with a portrait of Margaret Aubyn. It was a reproduction of the photograph that had stood so long on his desk. The desiccating air of memory had turned her into the mere abstraction of a woman, and this unexpected evocation seemed to bring her nearer than she had ever been in life. Was it because he understood her better? He looked long into her eyes; little personal traits reached out to him like caresses—the tired droop of her lids, her quick way of leaning forward as she spoke, the movements of her long expressive hands. All that was feminine in her, the quality he had always missed, stole toward him from her unreproachful gaze; and now that it was too late, life had developed in him the subtler perceptions which could detect it in even this poor semblance of herself. For a moment he found consolation in the thought that, at any cost, they had thus been brought together; then a sense of shame rushed over him. Face to face with her, he felt himself laid bare to the inmost fold of consciousness. The shame was deep, but it was a renovating anguish: he was like a man whom intolerable pain has roused from the creeping lethargy of death.

He rose next morning to as fresh a sense of life as though his hour of communion with Margaret Aubyn had been a more exquisite renewal of their earlier meetings. His waking thought was that he must see her again; and as consciousness affirmed itself he felt an intense fear of losing the sense of her nearness. But she was still close to him: her presence remained the one reality in a world of shadows. All through his working hours he was re-living with incredible minuteness every incident of their obliterated past: as a man who has mastered the spirit of a foreign tongue turns with renewed wonder to the pages his youth has plodded over. In this lucidity of retrospection the most trivial detail had its meaning, and the joy of recovery was embittered to Glennard by the perception of all that he had missed. He had been pitiably, grotesquely stupid; and there was irony in the thought that, but for the crisis through which he was passing, he might have lived on in complacent ignorance of his loss. It was as though she had bought him with her blood.

That evening he and Alexa dined alone. After dinner he followed her to the drawing-room. He no longer felt the need of avoiding her; he was hardly conscious of her presence. After a few words they lapsed into silence, and he sat smoking with his eyes on the fire. It was not that he was unwilling to talk to her; he felt a curious desire to be as kind as possible; but he was always forgetting that she was there. Her full bright presence, through which the currents of life flowed so warmly, had grown as tenuous as a shadow, and he saw so far beyond her.

Presently she rose and began to move about the room. She seemed to be looking for something, and he roused himself to ask what she wanted.

"Only the last number of the *Horoscope*. I thought I'd left it on this table." He said nothing, and she went on: "You haven't seen it?"

"No," he returned coldly. The magazine was locked in his desk.

His wife had moved to the mantelpiece. She stood facing him, and as he looked up he met her tentative gaze. "I was reading an article in it—a review of Mrs. Aubyn's *Letters,*" she added slowly, with her deep deliberate blush.

Glennard stooped to toss his cigar into the fire. He felt a savage wish that she would not speak the other woman's name; nothing else seemed to matter.

"You seem to do a lot of reading," he said.

She still confronted him. "I was keeping this for you—I thought it might interest you," she said with an air of gentle insistence.

He stood up and turned away. He was sure she knew that he had taken the review, and he felt that he was beginning to hate her again.

"I haven't time for such things," he said indifferently. As he moved to the door he heard her take a hurried step forward; then she paused, and sank without speaking into the chair from which he had risen.

XI

As Glennard, in the raw February sunlight, mounted the road to the cemetery, he felt the beatitude that comes with an abrupt cessation of physical pain. He had reached the point where self-analysis ceases; the impulse that moved him was purely intuitive. He did not even seek a reason for it, beyond the obvious one that his desire to stand by Margaret Aubyn's grave was prompted by no attempt at a sentimental reparation, but rather by the need to affirm in some way the reality of the tie between them.

The ironical promiscuity of death had brought Mrs. Aubyn back to share the hospitality of her husband's last lodging; but though Glennard knew she had been buried near New York he had never visited her grave. He was oppressed, as he now threaded the long avenues, by a chilling vision of her return. There was no family to follow her hearse; she had died alone, as she had lived; and the "distinguished mourners" who had formed the escort of the famous writer knew nothing of the woman they were committing to the grave. Glennard could not even remember at what season she had been buried; but his mood indulged the fancy that it must have been on some such day of harsh sunlight, the incisive February brightness that gives perspicuity without warmth. The white avenues stretched before him interminably, lined with stereotyped emblems of affliction, as though all the platitudes ever uttered had been turned to marble and set up over the unresisting dead. Here and there, no doubt, a frigid urn or an insipid angel imprisoned some fine-fibred grief, as the most hackneyed words may become the vehicle of rare meanings; but for the most part the endless alignment of monuments seemed to embody those easy generalizations about death that do not disturb the repose of the living. Glennard's eye, as he followed the way pointed out to him, had instinctively sought some low mound with a quiet headstone. He had forgotten that the dead seldom plan their own houses, and with a pang he discovered the name he sought on the cyclopean base of a shaft rearing its aggressive height at the angle of two avenues.

"How she would have hated it!" he murmured.

A bench stood near and he seated himself. The monument rose before him like some pretentious uninhabited dwelling: he could not believe that Margaret Aubyn lay there. It was a Sunday morning, and black figures moved among the paths, placing flowers on the frost-bound hillocks. Glennard noticed that the neighboring graves had been thus newly dressed, and he fancied a blind stir of expectancy through the sod, as though the bare mounds spread a parched surface to that commemorative rain. He rose presently and walked back to the entrance of the cemetery. Several greenhouses stood near the gates, and turning in at the first he asked for some flowers.

"Anything in the emblematic line?" asked the anæmic man behind the dripping counter.

Glennard shook his head.

"Just cut flowers? This way then." The florist unlocked a glass door and led him down a moist green aisle. The hot air was choked with the scent of white azaleas, white lilies, white lilacs; all the flowers were white: they were like a prolongation, a mystic efflorescence, of the long rows of marble tombstones, and their perfume seemed to cover an odor of decay. The rich atmosphere made Glennard dizzy. As he leaned in the doorway, waiting for the flowers, he had a penetrating sense of Margaret Aubyn's nearness—not the imponderable presence of his inner vision, but a life that beat warm in his arms.

The sharp air caught him as he stepped out into it again. He walked back and scattered the flowers over the grave. The edges of the white petals shrivelled like burnt paper in the cold; and as he watched them the illusion of her nearness faded, shrank back frozen.

XII

The motive of his visit to the cemetery remained undefined save as a final effort of escape from his wife's inexpressive acceptance of his shame. It seemed to him that as long as he could keep himself alive to that shame he would not wholly have succumbed to its consequences. His chief fear was that he should become the creature of his act. His wife's indifference degraded him: it seemed to put him on a level with his dishonor. Margaret Aubyn would have abhorred the deed in proportion to her pity for the man. The sense of her potential pity drew him back to her. The one woman knew but did not understand; the other, it sometimes seemed, understood without knowing.

In its last disguise of retrospective remorse, his self-pity affected a desire for solitude and meditation. He lost himself in morbid musings, in futile visions of what life with Margaret Aubyn might have been. There were moments when, in the strange dislocation of his view, the wrong he had done her seemed a tie between them.

To indulge these emotions he fell into the habit, on Sunday afternoons, of solitary walks prolonged till after dusk. The days were lengthening, there was a touch of spring in the air, and his wanderings now usually led him to the Park and its outlying regions.

One Sunday, tired of aimless locomotion, he took a cab at the Park gates and let it carry him out to the Riverside Drive. It was a gray afternoon streaked with east wind. Glennard's cab advanced slowly, and as he leaned back, gazing with absent intentness at the deserted paths that wound under bare boughs between grass banks of premature vividness, his attention was arrested by two figures walking ahead of him. This couple, who had the path to themselves, moved at an uneven pace, as though adapting their gait to a conversation marked by meditative intervals. Now and then they paused, and in one of these pauses the lady, turning toward her companion, showed Glennard the outline of his wife's profile. The man was Flamel.

The blood rushed to Glennard's forehead. He sat up with a jerk and pushed back the lid in the roof of the hansom; but when the cabman bent down he dropped into his seat without speaking. Then, becoming conscious of the prolonged interrogation of the lifted lid, he called out—"Turn—drive back—anywhere—I'm in a hurry—"

As the cab swung round he caught a last glimpse of the two figures. They had not moved; Alexa, with bent head, stood listening.

"My God, my God—" he groaned.

It was hideous—it was abominable—he could not understand it. The woman was nothing to him—less than nothing—yet the blood hummed in his ears and hung a cloud before him. He knew it was only the stirring of the primal instinct, that it had no more to do with his reasoning self than any reflex impulse of the body; but that merely lowered anguish to disgust. Yes, it was disgust he felt—almost a physical nausea. The poisonous fumes of life were in his lungs. He was sick, unutterably sick.

He drove home and went to his room. They were giving a little dinner that night, and when he came down the guests were arriving. He looked at his wife: her beauty was extraordinary, but it seemed to him the beauty of a smooth sea along an unlit coast. She frightened him.

He sat late in his study. He heard the parlormaid lock the front door; then his wife went upstairs and the lights were put out. His brain was like some great empty hall with an echo in it: one thought reverberated endlessly. . . . At length he drew his chair to the table and began to write. He addressed an envelope and then slowly re-read what he had written.

My dear Flamel

Many apologies for not sending you sooner the enclosed check, which represents the customary percentage on the sale of the "Letters."

Trusting you will excuse the oversight.

Yours truly

Stephen Glennard.

He let himself out of the darkened house and dropped the letter in the post-box at the corner.

* * *

The next afternoon he was detained late at his office, and as he was preparing to leave he heard someone asking for him in the outer room. He seated himself again and Flamel was shown in.

The two men, as Glennard pushed aside an obstructive chair, had a moment to measure each other; then Flamel advanced, and drawing out his note-case, laid a slip of paper on the desk.

"My dear fellow, what on earth does this mean?"

Glennard recognized his check.

"That I was remiss, simply. It ought to have gone to you before."

Flamel's tone had been that of unaffected surprise, but at this his accent changed and he asked quickly: "On what ground?"

Glennard had moved away from the desk and stood leaning against the calf-backed volumes of the bookcase. "On the ground that you sold Mrs. Aubyn's letters for me, and that I find the intermediary in such cases is entitled to a percentage on the sale."

Flamel paused before answering. "You find, you say. It's a recent discovery?"

"Obviously, from my not sending the check sooner. You see I'm new to the business."

"And since when have you discovered that there was any question of business, as far as I was concerned?"

Glennard flushed and his voice rose slightly. "Are you reproaching me for not having remembered it sooner?"

Flamel, who had spoken in the rapid repressed tone of a man on the verge of anger, stared a moment at this and then, in his natural voice, rejoined good-humoredly, "Upon my soul, I don't understand you!"

The change of key seemed to disconcert Glennard. "It's simple enough," he muttered.

"Simple enough—your offering me money in return for a friendly service? I don't know what your other friends expect!"

"Some of my friends wouldn't have undertaken the job. Those who would have done so would probably have expected to be paid."

He lifted his eyes to Flamel and the two men looked at each other. Flamel had turned white and his lips stirred, but he held his temperate note. "If you mean to imply that the job was not a nice one you lay yourself open to the retort that you proposed it.

But for my part I've never seen, I never shall see, any reason for not publishing the letters."

"That's just it!"

"What—?"

"The certainty of your not seeing was what made me go to you. When a man's got stolen goods to pawn he doesn't take them to the police-station."

"Stolen?" Flamel echoed. "The letters were stolen?"

Glennard burst into a laugh. "How much longer do you expect me to keep up that pretence about the letters? You know well enough they were written to me."

Flamel looked at him in silence. "Were they?" he said at length. "I didn't know it."

"And didn't suspect it, I suppose," Glennard sneered.

The other was again silent; then he said, "I may remind you that, supposing I had felt any curiosity about the matter, I had no way of finding out that the letters were written to you. You never showed me the originals."

"What does that prove? There were fifty ways of finding out. It's the kind of thing one can easily do."

Flamel glanced at him with contempt. "Our ideas probably differ as to what a man can easily do. It would not have been easy for me."

Glennard's anger vented itself in the words uppermost in his thought. "It may, then, interest you to hear that my wife *does* know about the letters—has known for some months. . . ."

"Ah," said the other, slowly.

Glennard saw that, in his blind clutch at a weapon, he had seized the one most apt to wound. Flamel's muscles were under control, but his face showed the undefinable change produced by the slow infiltration of poison. Every implication that the words contained had reached its mark; but Glennard felt that their obvious intent was lost in the anguish of what they suggested. He was sure now that Flamel would never have betrayed him, but the inference only made a wider outlet for his anger. He paused breathlessly for Flamel to speak.

"If she knows it's not through me." It was what Glennard had waited for.

"Through you, by God? Who said it was through you? Do you suppose I leave it to you, or to anybody else, for that matter, to keep my wife informed of my actions? I didn't suppose even such egregious conceit as yours could delude a man to that degree!" Struggling for a foothold in the landslide of his dignity, he added in a steadier tone, "My wife learned the facts from me."

Flamel received this in silence. The other's outbreak seemed to have restored his self-control, and when he spoke it was with a deliberation implying that his course was chosen. "In that case I understand still less—"

"Still less—?"

"The meaning of this." He pointed to the check. "When you began to speak I supposed you had meant it as a bribe; now I can only infer it was intended as a random insult. In either case, here's my answer."

He tore the slip of paper in two and tossed the fragments across the desk to Glennard. Then he turned and walked out of the office.

Glennard dropped his head on his hands. If he had hoped to restore his self-respect by the simple expedient of assailing Flamel's, the result had not justified his expectation. The blow he had struck had blunted the edge of his anger, and the unforeseen extent of the hurt inflicted did not alter the fact that his weapon had broken in his hands. He now saw that his rage against Flamel was only the last projection of a passionate self-disgust. This consciousness did not dull his dislike of the man; it simply made reprisals ineffectual. Flamel's unwillingness to quarrel with him was the last stage of his abasement.

In the light of this final humiliation his assumption of his wife's indifference struck him as hardly so fatuous as the sentimental resuscitation of his past. He had been living in a factitious world wherein his emotions were the sycophants of his vanity, and it was with instinctive relief that he felt its ruins crash about his head.

It was nearly dark when he left his office, and he walked slowly homeward in the complete mental abeyance that follows on such a crisis. He was not aware that he was thinking of his wife; yet when he reached his own door he found that, in the involuntary readjustment of his vision, she had once more become the central point of consciousness.

XIII

It had never before occurred to him that she might, after all, have missed the purport of the document he had put in her way. What if, in her hurried inspection of the papers, she had passed it over as related to the private business of some client? What, for instance, was to prevent her concluding that Glennard was the counsel of the unknown person who had sold the *Aubyn Letters*? The subject was one not likely to fix her attention—she was not a curious woman.

Glennard at this point laid down his fork and glanced at her between the candle-shades. The alternative explanation of her indifference was not slow in presenting itself. Her head had the same listening droop as when he had caught sight of her the day before in Flamel's company; the attitude revived the vividness of his impression. It was simple enough, after all. She had ceased to care for him because she cared for someone else.

As he followed her upstairs he felt a sudden stirring of his dormant anger. His sentiments had lost their artificial complexity. He had already acquitted her of any connivance in his baseness, and he felt only that he loved her and that she had escaped him. This was now, strangely enough, his dominant thought: the sense that he and she had passed through the fusion of love and had emerged from it as incommunicably apart as though the transmutation had never taken place. Every other passion, he mused, left some mark upon the nature, but love passed like the flight of a ship across the waters.

She dropped into her usual seat near the lamp, and he leaned against the chimney, moving about with an inattentive hand the knickknacks on the mantel.

Suddenly he caught sight of her reflection in the mirror. She was looking at him. He turned and their eyes met.

He moved across the room.

"There's something that I want to say to you," he began.

She held his gaze, but her color deepened. He noticed again, with a jealous pang, how her beauty had gained in warmth and meaning. It was as though a transparent cup had been filled with wine. He looked at her ironically.

"I've never prevented your seeing your friends here," he broke out. "Why do you meet Flamel in out-of-the-way places? Nothing makes a woman so cheap—"

She rose abruptly and they faced each other a few feet apart.

"What do you mean?" she asked.

"I saw you with him last Sunday on the Riverside Drive," he went on, the utterance of the charge reviving his anger.

"Ah," she murmured. She sank into her chair again and began to play with a paper-knife that lay on the table at her elbow.

Her silence exasperated him.

"Well?" he burst out. "Is that all you have to say?"

"Do you wish me to explain?" she asked proudly.

"Do you imply I haven't the right to?"

"I imply nothing. I will tell you whatever you wish to know. I went for a walk with Mr. Flamel because he asked me to."

"I didn't suppose you went uninvited. But there are certain things a sensible woman doesn't do. She doesn't slink about in out-of-the-way streets with men. Why couldn't you have seen him here?"

She hesitated. "Because he wanted to see me alone."

"Did he indeed? And may I ask if you gratify all his wishes with equal alacrity?"

"I don't know that he has any others where I am concerned." She paused again and then continued, in a voice that somehow had an under-note of warning, "He wished to bid me good-bye. He's going away."

Glennard turned on her a startled glance. "Going away?"

"He's going to Europe tomorrow. He goes for a long time. I supposed you knew."

The last phrase revived his irritation. "You forget that I depend on you for my information about Flamel. He's your friend and not mine. In fact, I've sometimes wondered at your going out of your way to be so civil to him when you must see plainly enough that I don't like him."

Her answer to this was not immediate. She seemed to be choosing her words with care, not so much for her own sake as for his, and his exasperation was increased by the suspicion that she was trying to spare him.

"He was your friend before he was mine. I never knew him till I was married. It was you who brought him to the house and who seemed to wish me to like him."

Glennard gave a short laugh. The defense was feebler than he had expected: she was certainly not a clever woman.

"Your deference to my wishes is really beautiful; but it's not the first time in history that a man had made a mistake in introducing his friends to his wife. You must, at any rate, have seen since then that my enthusiasm had cooled; but so, perhaps, has your eagerness to oblige me.''

She met this with a silence that seemed to rob the taunt of half its efficacy.

''Is that what you imply?'' he pressed her.

''No,'' she answered with sudden directness. ''I noticed some time ago that you seemed to dislike him, but since then—''

''Well—since then?''

''I've imagined that you had reasons for still wishing me to be civil to him, as you call it.''

''Ah,'' said Glennard with an effort at lightness; but his irony dropped, for something in her voice made him feel that he and she stood at last in that naked desert of apprehension where meaning skulks vainly behind speech.

''And why did you imagine this?'' The blood mounted to his forehead. ''Because he told you that I was under obligations to him?''

She turned pale. ''Under obligations?''

''Oh, don't let's beat about the bush. Didn't he tell you it was I who published Mrs. Aubyn's letters? Answer me that.''

''No,'' she said; and after a moment which seemed given to the weighing of alternatives, she added: ''No one told me.''

''You didn't know, then?''

She seemed to speak with an effort. ''Not until—not until—''

''Till I gave you those papers to sort?''

Her head sank.

''You understood then?''

''Yes.''

He looked at her immovable face. ''Had you suspected—before?'' was slowly wrung from him.

''At times—yes—.'' Her voice dropped to a whisper.

''Why? From anything that was said—?''

There was a shade of pity in her glance. ''No one said anything—no one told me anything.'' She looked away from him. ''It was your manner—''

''My manner?''

''Whenever the book was mentioned. Things you said—once or twice—your irritation—I can't explain.''

Glennard, unconsciously, had moved nearer. He breathed like a man who has been running. ''You knew, then, you knew—'' he stammered. The avowal of her love for Flamel would have hurt him less, would have rendered her less remote. ''You knew—you knew—'' he repeated, and suddenly his anguish gathered voice. ''My God!'' he cried, ''you suspected it first, you say—and then you knew it—this damnable, this accursed thing; you knew it months ago—it's months since I put that paper in your way—and yet you've done nothing, you've said nothing, you've made no sign, you've lived alongside of me as if it had made no difference—no difference in either of our lives. What are you made of, I wonder? Don't you see the hideous ignominy of it? Don't you see how you've shared in my disgrace? Or haven't you any sense of shame?''

He preserved sufficient lucidity, as the words poured from him, to see how fatally they invited her derision; but something told him they had both passed beyond the phase of obvious retaliations, and that if any chord in her responded it would not be that of scorn.

He was right. She rose slowly and moved toward him.

''Haven't you had enough—without that?'' she said in a strange voice of pity.

He stared at her. ''Enough—?''

''Of misery . . . .''

An iron band seemed loosened from his temples. ''You saw then . . ?'' he whispered.

''Oh, God—oh, God—'' she sobbed. She dropped beside him and hid her anguish against his knees. They clung thus in silence a long time, driven together down the same fierce blast of shame.

When at length she lifted her face he averted his. Her scorn would have hurt him less than the tears on his hands.

She spoke languidly, like a child emerging from a passion of weeping. ''It was for the money—?''

His lips shaped an assent.

''That was the inheritance—that we married on?''

''Yes.''

She drew back and rose to her feet. He sat watching her as she wandered away from him.

''You hate me,'' broke from him.

She made no answer.

''Say you hate me!'' he persisted.

''That would have been so simple,'' she answered with a strange smile. She dropped into a chair near the writing-table and rested a bowed forehead on her hand.

''Was it much?'' she began at length.

''Much—?'' he returned vaguely.

"The money."

"The money?" That part of it seemed to count so little that for a moment he did not follow her thought.

"It must be paid back," she insisted. "Can you do it?"

"Oh, yes," he returned listlessly. "I can do it."

"I would make any sacrifice for that!" she urged.

He nodded. "Of course." He sat staring at her in dry-eyed self-contempt. "Do you count on its making much difference?"

"Much difference?"

"In the way I feel—or you feel about me?"

She shook her head.

"It's the least part of it," he groaned.

"It's the only part we can repair."

"Good heavens! If there were any reparation—" He rose quickly and crossed the space that divided them. "Why did you never speak?"

"Haven't you answered that yourself?"

"Answered it?"

"Just now—when you told me you did it for me."

She paused a moment and then went on with a deepening note—"I would have spoken if I could have helped you."

"But you must have despised me."

"I've told you that would have been simpler."

"But how could you go on like this—hating the money?"

"I knew you'd speak in time. I wanted you, first, to hate it as I did."

He gazed at her with a kind of awe. "You're wonderful," he murmured. "But you don't yet know the depths I've reached."

She raised an entreating hand. "I don't want to!"

"You're afraid, then, that you'll hate me?"

"No—but that you'll hate *me*. Let me understand without your telling me."

"You can't. It's too base. I thought you didn't care because you loved Flamel."

She blushed deeply. "Don't—don't—" she warned him.

"I haven't the right to, you mean?"

"I mean that you'll be sorry."

He stood imploringly before her. "I want to say something worse—something more outrageous. If you don't understand *this* you'll be perfectly justified in ordering me out of the house."

She answered him with a glance of divination. "I shall understand—but you'll be sorry."

"I must take my chance of that." He moved away and tossed

the books about the table. Then he swung round and faced her. "Does Flamel care for you?" he asked.

Her flush deepened, but she still looked at him without anger. "What would be the use?" she said with a note of sadness.

"Ah, I didn't ask *that,*" he penitently murmured.

"Well, then—"

To this adjuration he made no response beyond that of gazing at her with an eye which seemed now to view her as a mere factor in an immense redistribution of meanings.

"I insulted Flamel today. I let him see that I suspected him of having told you. I hated him because he knew about the letters."

He caught the spreading horror of her eyes, and for an instant he had to grapple with the new temptation they lit up. Then he said with an effort—"Don't blame him—he's impeccable. He helped me to get them published; but I lied to him too; I pretended they were written to another man . . . a man who was dead . . ."

She raised her arms in a gesture that seemed to ward off his blows.

"You *do* despise me!" he insisted.

"Ah, that poor woman—that poor woman—" he heard her murmur.

"I spare no one, you see!" he triumphed over her. She kept her face hidden.

"You do hate me, you do despise me!" he strangely exulted.

"Be silent!" she commanded him; but he seemed no longer conscious of any check on his gathering purpose.

"He cared for you—he cared for you," he repeated, "and he never told you of the letters—"

She sprang to her feet. "How can you?" she flamed. "How dare you? *That—!*"

Glennard was ashy pale. "It's a weapon . . . like another . . ."

"A scoundrel's!"

He smiled wretchedly. "I should have used it in his place."

"Stephen! Stephen!" she cried, as though to drown the blasphemy on his lips. She swept to him with a rescuing gesture. "Don't say such things. I forbid you! It degrades us both."

He put her back with trembling hands. "Nothing that I say of myself can degrade you. We're on different levels."

"I'm on yours, wherever it is!"

He lifted his head and their gaze flowed together.

XIV

The great renewals take effect as imperceptibly as the first workings of spring. Glennard, though he felt himself brought nearer to his wife, was still, as it were, hardly within speaking distance. He was but laboriously acquiring the rudiments of a new language, and he had to grope for her through the dense fog of his humiliation, the distorting vapor against which her personality loomed grotesque and mean.

Only the fact that we are unaware how well our nearest know us enables us to live with them. Love is the most impregnable refuge of self-esteem, and we hate the eye that reaches to our nakedness. If Glennard did not hate his wife it was slowly, sufferingly, that there was born in him that profounder passion which made his earlier feeling seem a mere commotion of the blood. He was like a child coming back to the sense of an enveloping presence: her nearness was a breast on which he leaned.

They did not, at first, talk much together, and each beat a devious track about the outskirts of the subject that lay between them like a haunted wood. But every word, every action, seemed to glance at it, to draw toward it, as though a fount of healing sprang in its poisoned shade. If only they might cut a way through the thicket to that restoring spring!

Glennard, watching his wife with the intentness of a wanderer to whom no natural sign is negligible, saw that she had taken temporary refuge in the purpose of renouncing the money. If both, theoretically, owned the inefficacy of such amends, the woman's instinctive subjectiveness made her find relief in this crude form of penance. Glennard saw that she meant to live as frugally as possible till what she deemed their debt was discharged, and he prayed she might not discover how far-reaching, in its merely material sense, was the obligation she thus hoped to acquit. Her mind was fixed on the sum originally paid for the letters, and this he knew he could lay aside in a year or two. He was touched, meanwhile, by the spirit that made her discard the petty luxuries which she regarded as the sign of their bondage. Their shared renunciations drew her nearer to him, helped, in their evidence of her helplessness, to restore the full protecting stature of his love. And still they did not speak.

* * *

It was several weeks later that, one afternoon by the drawing-room fire, she handed him a letter that she had been reading when he entered.

"I've heard from Mr. Flamel," she said.

It was as though a latent presence had become visible to both. Glennard took the letter mechanically.

"It's from Smyrna," she said. "Won't you read it?"

He handed it back. "You can tell me about it—his hand's so illegible." He wandered to the other end of the room and then turned and stood before her. "I've been thinking of writing to Flamel," he said.

She looked up.

"There's one point," he continued slowly, "that I ought to clear up. I told him you'd known about the letters all along; for a long time, at least; and I saw how it hurt him. It was just what I meant to do, of course; but I can't leave him to that false impression; I must write him."

She received this without outward movement, but he saw that the depths were stirred. At length she returned in a hesitating tone, "Why do you call it a false impression? I did know."

"Yes, but I implied you didn't care."

"Ah!"

He still stood looking down on her. "Don't you want me to set that right?" he pursued.

She lifted her head and fixed him bravely. "It isn't necessary," she said.

Glennard flushed with the shock of the retort, then, with a gesture of comprehension, "No," he said, "with you it couldn't be; but I might still set myself right."

She looked at him gently. "Don't I," she murmured, "do that?"

"In being yourself merely? Alas, the rehabilitation's too complete! You make me seem—to myself even—what I'm not; what I can never be. I can't, at times, defend myself from the delusion; but I can at least enlighten others."

The flood was loosened, and kneeling by her he caught her hands. "Don't you see that it's become an obsession with me? That if I could strip myself down to the last lie—only there'd always be another one left under it!—and do penance naked in the market-place, I should at least have the relief of easing one anguish by another? Don't you see that the worst of my torture is the impossibility of such amends?"

Her hands lay in his without returning pressure. ''Ah, poor woman, poor woman,'' he heard her sigh.

''Don't pity her, pity me! What have I done to her or to you, after all? You're both inaccessible! It was myself I sold.''

He took an abrupt turn away from her; then halted before her again. ''How much longer,'' he burst out, ''do you suppose you can stand it? You've been magnificent, you've been inspired, but what's the use? You can't wipe out the ignominy of it. It's miserable for you and it does *her* no good!''

She lifted a vivid face. ''That's the thought I can't bear!'' she cried.

''What thought?''

''That it does her no good—all you're feeling, all you're suffering. Can it be that it makes no difference?''

He avoided her challenging glance. ''What's done is done,'' he muttered.

''Is it ever, quite, I wonder?'' she mused. He made no answer and they lapsed into one of the pauses that are a subterranean channel of communication.

It was she who, after a while, began to speak, with a new suffusing diffidence that made him turn a roused eye on her.

''Don't they say,'' she asked, feeling her way as in a kind of tender apprehensiveness, ''that the early Christians, instead of pulling down the heathen temples—the temples of the unclean gods—purified them by turning them to their own uses? I've always thought one might do that with one's actions—the actions one loathes but can't undo. One can make, I mean, a wrong the door to other wrongs or an impassable wall against them . . .'' Her voice wavered on the word. ''We can't always tear down the temples we've built to the unclean gods, but we can put good spirits in the house of evil—the spirits of mercy and shame and understanding, that might never have come to us if we hadn't been in such great need . . .''

She moved over to him and laid a hand on his. His head was bent and he did not change his attitude. She sat down beside him without speaking; but their silences were now fertile as rainclouds—they quickened the seeds of understanding.

At length he looked up. ''I don't know,'' he said, ''what spirits have come to live in the house of evil that I built—but you're there and that's enough. It's strange,'' he went on after another pause, ''she wished the best for me so often, and now, at last, it's through her that it's come to me. But for her I shouldn't have known you—it's through her that I've found you. Sometimes—

do you know?—that makes it hardest—makes me most intolerable to myself. Can't you see that it's the worst thing I've got to face? I sometimes think I could have borne it better if you hadn't understood! I took everything from her—everything—even to the poor shelter of loyalty she's trusted in—the only thing I *could* have left her!—I took everything from her, I deceived her, I despoiled her, I destroyed her—and she's given me *you* in return!''

His wife's cry caught him up. ''It isn't that she's given *me* to you—it is that she's given you to yourself.'' She leaned to him as though swept forward on a wave of pity. ''Don't you see,'' she went on, as his eyes hung on her, ''that that's the gift you can't escape from, the debt you're pledged to acquit? Don't you see that you've never before been what she thought you, and that now, so wonderfully, she's made you into the man she loved? *That's* worth suffering for, worth dying for, to a woman—that's the gift she would have wished to give!''

''Ah,'' he cried, ''but woe to him by whom it cometh. What did I ever give her?''

''The happiness of giving,'' she said.

THE LAST ASSET

I

"The devil!" Paul Garnett exclaimed as he re-read his note; and the dry old gentleman who was at the moment his only neighbour in the modest restaurant they both frequented, remarked with a smile: "You don't seem particularly disturbed at meeting him."

Garnett returned the smile. "I don't know why I apostrophised him, for he's not in the least present—except inasmuch as he may prove to be at the bottom of anything unexpected."

The old gentleman who, like Garnett, was an American, and spoke in the thin rarefied voice which seems best fitted to emit sententious truths, twisted his lean neck round to cackle out: "Ah, it's generally a woman who's at the bottom of the unexpected. Not," he added, leaning forward with deliberation to select a tooth-pick, "that that precludes the devil's being there too."

Garnett uttered the requisite laugh, and his neighbour, pushing back his plate, called out with a perfectly unbending American intonation: "Gassong! L'addition, silver play."

His repast, as usual, had been a simple one, and he left only thirty centimes in the plate on which his account was presented; but the waiter, to whom he was evidently a familiar presence, received the tribute with Latin amenity, and hovered helpfully about the table while the old gentleman cut and lighted his cigar.

"Yes," the latter proceeded, revolving the cigar meditatively between his thin lips, "they're generally both in the same hole, like the owl and the prairie-dog in the natural history books of my youth. I believe it was all a mistake about the owl and the prairie-dog, but it isn't about the unexpected. The fact is, the unexpected *is* the devil—the sooner you find that out, the happier you'll be." He leaned back, tilting his bald head against the blotched mirror behind him, and rambling on with gentle garrulity while Garnett attacked his omelet.

"Get your life down to routine—eliminate surprises. Arrange things so that, when you get up in the morning, you'll know exactly what's going to happen to you during the day—and the next day and the next. I don't say it's funny—it ain't. But it's better than being hit on the head by a brickbat. That's why I always take my meals at this restaurant. I know just how much onion they put in things—if I went to the next place I shouldn't. And I always take the same streets to come here—I've been doing it for ten years now. I know at which crossing to look out—I know what I'm going to see in the shop-windows. It saves a lot of wear and tear to know what's coming. For a good many years I never *did* know, from one minute to another, and now I like to think that everything's cut-and-dried, and nothing unexpected can jump out at me like a tramp from a ditch."

He paused calmly to knock the ashes from his cigar and Garnett said with a smile: "Doesn't such a plan of life cut off nearly all the possibilities?"

The old gentleman made a contemptuous motion. "Possibilities of what? Of being multifariously miserable? There are lots of ways of being miserable, but there's only one way of being comfortable, and that is to stop running round after happiness. If you make up your mind not to be happy there's no reason why you shouldn't have a fairly good time."

"That was Schopenhauer's idea, I believe," the young man said, pouring his wine with the smile of youthful incredulity.

"I guess he hadn't the monopoly," responded his friend. "Lots of people have found out the secret—the trouble is that so few live up to it."

He rose from his seat, pushing the table forward, and standing passive while the waiter advanced with his shabby overcoat and umbrella. Then he nodded to Garnett, lifted his hat to the broad-bosomed lady behind the desk, and passed out into the street.

Garnett looked after him with a musing smile. The two had exchanged views on life for two years without so much as knowing each other's names. Garnett was a newspaper correspondent whose work kept him mainly in London, but on his periodic visits to Paris he lodged in a dingy hotel of the Latin quarter, the chief merit of which was its nearness to the cheap and excellent restaurant where the two Americans had made acquaintance. But Garnett's assiduity in frequenting the place arose, in the end, less from the excellence of the food than from the enjoyment of his old friend's conversation. Amid the flashy sophistications of the Parisian life to which Garnett's trade introduced him, the American sage's conversation had the crisp and homely flavour of a native dish—one of the domestic compounds for which the exiled palate is supposed to yearn. It was a mark of the old man's impersonality that, in spite of the interest he inspired, Garnett had never got beyond idly wondering who he might be, where he lived, and what his occupations were. He was presumably a bachelor—a man of family ties, however relaxed, though he might have been as often absent from home would not have been as regularly present in the same place—and there was about him a boundless desultoriness which renewed Garnett's conviction that there is no one on earth as idle as an American who is not busy. From certain allusions it was plain that he had lived many years in Paris, yet he had not taken the trouble to adapt his tongue to the local inflections, but spoke French with the accent of one who has formed his notion of the language from a phrase-book.

The city itself seemed to have made as little impression on him as its speech. He appeared to have no artistic or intellectual curiosities, to remain untouched by the complex appeal of Paris, while preserving, perhaps the more strikingly from his very detachment, that odd American astuteness which seems the fruit of innocence rather than of experience. His nationality revealed itself again in a mild interest in the political problems of his adopted country, though they appeared to preoccupy him only as illustrating the boundless perversity of mankind. The exhibition of human folly never ceased to divert him, and though his examples of it seemed mainly drawn from the columns of one exiguous daily paper, he found there matter for endless variations on his favourite theme. If this monotony of topic did not weary the younger man, it was because he fancied he could detect under it the tragic note of the fixed idea—of some great moral upheaval which had flung his friend stripped and starving on the desert island of the little restaurant where they met. He hardly knew wherein he read this revelation—whether in the shabbiness of the sage's dress, the impersonal courtesy of his manner, or the shade of apprehension which lurked, indescribably, in his guileless yet suspicious eye. There were moments when Garnett could only define him by saying that he looked like a man who had seen a ghost.

II

An apparition almost as startling had come to Garnett himself in the shape of the mauve note handed to him by his *concierge* as he was leaving the hotel for luncheon.

Not that, on the face of it, a missive announcing Mrs. Sam Newell's arrival at Ritz's, and her need of his presence there that day at five, carried any mark of the portentous. It was not her being at Ritz's that surprised him. The fact that she was chronically hard up, and had once or twice lately been so harshly confronted with the consequences as to accept—indeed solicit—a loan of five pounds from him: this circumstance, as Garnett knew, would never be allowed to affect the general tenor of her existence. If one came to Paris, where could one go but to Ritz's? Did he see her in some grubby hole across the river? Or in a family *pension* near the Place de l'Etoile? There was no affectation in her tendency to gravitate toward what was costliest and most conspicuous. In doing so she obeyed one of the profoundest instincts of her nature, and it was another instinct which taught her to gratify the first at any cost, even to that of dipping into the pocket of an impecunious journalist. It was a part of her strength—and of her charm, too—that she did such things naturally, openly, without any of the grimaces of dissimulation or compunction.

Her recourse to Garnett had of course marked a specially low ebb in her fortunes. Save in moments of exceptional dearth she had richer sources of supply; and he was nearly sure that by running over the "society column" of the Paris *Herald* he should find an explanation, not perhaps of her presence at Ritz's, but of her means of subsistence there. What perplexed him was not the financial but the social aspect of the case. When Mrs. Newell had left London in July she had told him that, between Cowes and Scotland, she and Hermy were provided for till the middle of October: after that, as she put it, they would have to look about. Why, then, when she had in her hand the opportunity of living for three months at the expense of the British aristocracy, did she rush off to Paris at heaven knew whose expense in the beginning of September? She was not a woman to act incoherently; if she made mistakes they were not of that kind. Garnett felt sure she would never willingly relax her hold on her distinguished friends—was it possible that it was they who had somewhat violently let go of her?

As Garnett reviewed the situation he began to see that this possibility had for some time been latent in it. He had felt that something might happen at any moment—and was not this the something he had obscurely foreseen? Mrs. Newell really moved too fast: her position was as perilous as that of an invading army without a base of supplies. She used up everything too quickly—friends, credit, influence, forbearance. It was so easy for her to acquire all these—what a pity she had never learned to keep them! He himself, for instance—the most insignificant of her acquisitions—was beginning to feel like a squeezed sponge at the mere thought of her; and it was this sense of exhaustion, of the inability to provide more, either materially or morally, which had provoked his exclamation on opening her note. From the first days of their acquaintance her prodigality had amazed him, but he had believed it to be surpassed by the infinity of her resources. If she exhausted old supplies she always had new ones to replace them. When one set of people began to find her impossible, another was always beginning to find her indispensable. Yes—but there were limits—there were only so many sets of people, at least in her classification, and when she came to an end of them, what then? Was this flight to Paris a sign that she had come to an end—was she going to try Paris because London had failed her? The time of year precluded such a conjecture. Mrs. Newell's Paris was non-existent in September. The town was a desert of gaping trippers—he could as soon think of her seeking social restoration at Margate.

For a moment it occurred to him that she might have come over to renew her wardrobe; but he knew her dates too well to dwell long on this. It was in April and December that she visited the dressmakers: before December, he had heard her explain, one got nothing but "the American fashions." Mrs. Newell's scorn of all things American was somewhat illogically coupled with the determination to use her own Americanism to the utmost as a means of social advance. She had found out long ago that, on certain lines, it paid in London to be American, and she had manufactured for herself a personality independent of geographical or social demarcations, and presenting that remarkable blend of plantation dialect, Bowery slang and hyperbolic statement, which expresses the British idea of an unadulterated Americanism. Mrs. Newell, for all her talents, was not by nature either humourous or hyperbolic, and there were times when it would doubtless have been a relief to her to be as stolid as some of the persons whose dulness it was her fate to enliven. It was perhaps the need of relaxing which had drawn her into her odd intimacy with Garnett, with whom she did not have to be either scrupulously English or artificially American, since the impression she made on him was of no more consequence than that which she produced on her footman. Garnett was aware that he owed his success to his insignificance, but the fact affected him only as adding one more element to his knowledge of Mrs. Newell's character. He was as ready to sacrifice his personal vanity in such a cause as he had been, at the outset of their acquaintance, to sacrifice his professional pride to the opportunity of knowing her.

When he had accepted the position of "London correspondent" (with an occasional side-glance at Paris) to the New York *Searchlight,* he had not understood that his work was to include the obligation of "interviewing"; indeed, had the possibility presented itself in advance, he would have met it by packing his valise and returning to the drudgery of his assistant-editorship in New York. But when, after three months in Europe, he received a letter from his chief, suggesting that he should enliven the Sunday *Searchlight* by a series of "Talks with Smart Americans in London" (beginning say, with Mrs. Sam Newell), the change of focus already enabled him to view the proposal without passion. For his life on the edge of the great world-caldron of art, politics and pleasure—of that high-spiced brew which is nowhere else so subtly and variously compounded—had bred in him an eagerness to taste of the heady mixture. He knew he should never have the full spoon at his lips, but he recalled the peasant-girl in one of Browning's plays, who boasts of having eaten polenta cut with a knife which has carved an ortolan. Might not Mrs. Newell, who had so successfully cut a way into the dense and succulent mass of English society, serve as the knife to season his polenta?

He had expected, as the result of the interview, to which she promptly, almost eagerly, agreed, no more than the glimpse of brightly lit vistas which a waiting messenger may catch through open doors; but instead he had found himself drawn at once into the inner sanctuary, not of London society, but of Mrs. Newell's relation to it. She had been candidly charmed by the idea of the interview: it struck him that she was conscious of the need of being freshened up. Her appearance was brilliantly fresh, with the inveterate freshness of the toilet-table; her paint was as impenetrable as armour. But her personality was a little tarnished: she was in want of social renovation. She had been doing and saying the same things for too long a time. London, Cowes, Homburg, Scotland, Monte Carlo—that had been the round since Hermy was a baby. Hermy was her daughter, Miss Hermione Newell, who was called in presently to be shown off to the interviewer and add a paragraph to the celebration of her mother's charms.

Miss Newell's appearance was so full of an unassisted freshness that for a moment Garnett made the mistake of fancying that she could fill a paragraph of her own. But he soon found that her vague personality was merely tributary to her parent's; that her youth and grace were, in some mysterious way, her mother's rather than her own. She smiled obediently on Garnett, but could contribute little beyond her smile, and the general sweetness of her presence, to the picture of Mrs. Newell's existence that it was the young man's business to draw. And presently he found that she had left the room without his noticing it.

He learned in time that this unnoticeableness was the most conspicuous thing about her. Burning at best with a mild light, she became invisible in the glare of her mother's personality. It was in fact only as a product of her environment that poor Hermione struck the imagination. With the smartest woman in London as her guide and example she had never developed a taste for dress, and with opportunities for enlightenment from which Garnett's fancy recoiled she remained simple, unsuspicious and tender, with an inclination to good works and afternoon church, a taste for the society of dull girls, and a clinging fidelity to old governesses and retired nurse-maids. Mrs. Newell, whose boast it was that she looked facts in the face, frankly owned that she had not been able to make anything of Hermione. "If she has a rôle I haven't discovered it," she confessed to Garnett. "I've tried everything, but she doesn't fit in anywhere."

Mrs. Newell spoke as if her daughter were a piece of furniture acquired without due reflection, and for which no suitable place could be found. She got, of course, what she could out of Hermione, who wrote her notes, ran her errands, saw tiresome people for her, and occupied an intermediate office between that of lady's maid and secretary; but such small returns on her investment were not what Mrs. Newell had counted on. What was the use of producing and educating a handsome daughter if she did not, in some more positive way, contribute to her parent's advancement?

III

"It's about Hermy," Mrs. Newell said, rising from the heap of embroidered cushions which formed the background of her afternoon repose.

Her sitting-room at Ritz's was full of warmth and fragrance. Long-stemmed roses filled the vases on the chimney-piece, in which a fire sparkled with that effect of luxury which fires produce when the weather is not cold enough to justify them. On the writing-table, among notes and cards, and signed photographs of celebrities, Mrs. Newell's gold inkstand, her jewelled penholder, her heavily monogrammed despatch-box, gave back from their expensive surfaces the glint of the flame, which sought out and magnified the orient of the pearls among the lady's laces and found a mirror in the pinky polish of her fingertips. It was just such a scene as a little September fire, lit for show and not for warmth, would delight to dwell on and pick out in all its opulent details; and even Garnett, inured to Mrs. Newell's capacity for extracting manna from the desert, reflected that she must have found new fields to glean.

"It's about Hermy," she repeated, making room for him at her side. "I had to see you at once. We came over yesterday from London."

Garnett, seating himself, continued his leisurely survey of the room. In the blaze of Mrs. Newell's refulgence Hermione, as usual, faded out of sight, and he hardly noticed her mother's allusion.

"I've never seen you more resplendent," he remarked.

She received the tribute with complacency. "The rooms are not bad, are they? We came over with the Woolsey Hubbards (you've heard of them, of course?—they're from Detroit), and really they do things very decently. Their motor met us at Boulogne, and the courier always wires ahead to have the rooms filled with flowers. This *salon* is really a part of their suite. I simply couldn't have afforded it myself."

She delivered these facts in a high decisive voice, which had a note like the clink of her many bracelets and the rattle of her ringed hands against the enamelled cigarette-case that she held out to Garnett after helping herself from its contents.

"You are always meeting such charming people," said the

young man with mild irony; and, reverting to her first remark, he bethought himself to add: "I hope Miss Hermione is not ill?"

"Ill? She was never ill in her life," exclaimed Mrs. Newell, as though her daughter had been accused of an indelicacy.

"It was only that you said you had come over on her account."

"So I have. Hermione is to be married."

Mrs. Newell brought out the words impressively, drawing back to observe their effect on her visitor. It was such that he received them with a long silent stare, which finally passed into a cry of wonder. "Married? For heaven's sake, to whom?"

Mrs. Newell continued to regard him with a smile so serene and victorious that he saw she took his somewhat unseemly astonishment as a merited tribute to her genius. Presently she extended a glittering hand and took a sheet of note-paper from the blotter.

"You can have that put in to-morrow's *Herald,*" she said.

Garnett, receiving the paper, read in Hermione's own finished hand: "A marriage has been arranged, and will shortly take place, between the Comte Louis du Trayas, son of the Marquis du Trayas de la Baume, and Miss Hermione Newell, daughter of Samuel C. Newell Esqre., of Elmira, N. Y. Comte Louis du Trayas belongs to one of the oldest and most distinguished families in France, and is equally well connected in England, being the nephew of Lord Saint Priscoe and a cousin of the Countess of Morningfield, whom he frequently visits at Adham and Portlow."

The perusal of this document filled Garnett with such deepening wonder that he could not, for the moment, even do justice to the strangeness of its being written out for publication in the bride's own hand. Hermione a bride! Hermione a future countess! Hermione on the brink of a marriage which would give her not only a great "situation" in the Parisian world but a footing in some of the best houses in England! Regardless of its unflattering implications, Garnett prolonged his stare of amazement till Mrs. Newell somewhat sharply exclaimed—"Well, didn't I always tell you she'd marry a Frenchman?"

Garnett, in spite of himself, smiled at this revised version of his hostess's frequent assertion that Hermione was too goody-goody to take in England, but that with her little dowdy air she might very well "go off" in the Faubourg if only a *dot* could be raked up—and the recollection flashed a new light on the versatility of Mrs. Newell's genius.

"But how did you do it—?" was on the tip of his tongue; and

he had barely time to give the query the more conventional turn of: "How did it happen?"

"Oh, we were up at Glaish with the Edmund Fitzarthurs. Lady Edmund is a sort of cousin of the Morningfields', who have a shooting-lodge near Glaish—a place called Portlow—and young Trayas was there with them. Lady Edmund, who is a dear, drove Hermy over to Portlow, and the thing was done in no time. He simply fell over head and ears in love with her. You know Hermy is really very handsome in her peculiar way. I don't think you've ever appreciated her," Mrs. Newell summed up with a note of reproach.

"I've appreciated her, I assure you; but one somehow didn't think of her marrying—so soon."

"Soon? She's three and twenty; but you've no imagination," said Mrs. Newell; and Garnett inwardly admitted that he had not enough to soar to the heights of her invention. For the marriage, of course, was her invention, a superlative stroke of business in which he was sure the principal parties had all been passive agents, in which every one, from the bankrupt and disreputable Fitzarthurs to the rich and immaculate Morningfields, had by some mysterious sleight of hand been made to fit into Mrs. Newell's designs. But it was not enough for Garnett to marvel at her work—he wanted to understand it, to take it apart, to find out how the trick had been done. It was true that Mrs. Newell had always said Hermy might go off in the Faubourg if she had a *dot*—but even Mrs. Newell's juggling could hardly conjure up a *dot;* such feats as she was able to perform in this line were usually made to serve her own urgent necessities. And besides, who was likely to take sufficient interest in Hermione to supply her with the means of marrying a French nobleman? The flowers ordered in advance by the Woolsey Hubbards' courier made Garnett wonder if that accomplished functionary had also wired over to have Miss Newell's settlements drawn up. But of all the comments hovering on his lips the only one he could decently formulate was the remark that he supposed Mrs. Newell and her daughter had come over to see the young man's family and make the final arrangements.

"Oh, they're made—everything's settled," said Mrs. Newell, looking him squarely in the eye. "You're wondering, of course, about the *dot*—Frenchmen never go off their heads to the extent of forgetting *that;* or at least their parents don't allow them to."

Garnett murmured a vague assent, and she went on without the least appearance of resenting his curiosity: "It all came about so fortunately. Only fancy, just the week they met I got a little legacy from an aunt in Elmira—a good soul I hadn't seen or heard of for years. I suppose I ought to have put on mourning for her, by the way, but it would have eaten up a good bit of the legacy, and I really needed it all for poor Hermy. Oh, it's not a fortune, you understand—but the young man is madly in love, and has always had his own way, so after a lot of correspondence it's been arranged. They saw Hermy this morning, and they're enchanted."

"And the marriage takes place very soon?"

"Yes, in a few weeks, here. His mother is an invalid and couldn't have gone to England. Besides, the French don't travel. And as Hermy has become a Catholic—"

"Already?"

Mrs. Newell stared. "It doesn't take long. And it suits Hermy exactly—she can go to church so much oftener. So I thought," Mrs. Newell concluded with dignity, "that a wedding at Saint Philippe du Roule would be the most suitable thing at this season."

"Dear me," said Garnett, "I am left breathless—I can't catch up with you. I suppose even the day is fixed, though Miss Hermione doesn't mention it," and he indicated the official announcement in his hand.

Mrs. Newell laughed. "Hermy had to write that herself, poor dear, because my scrawl's too hideous—but I dictated it. No, the day's not fixed—that's why I sent for you." There was a splendid directness about Mrs. Newell. It would never have occurred to her to pretend to Garnett that she had summoned him for the pleasure of his company.

"You've sent for me—to fix the day?" he enquired humourously.

"To remove the last obstacle to its being fixed."

"I? What kind of an obstacle could I have the least effect on?"

Mrs. Newell met his banter with a look which quelled it. "I want you to find her father."

"Her father? Miss Hermione's—?"

"My husband, of course. I suppose you know he's living."

Garnett blushed at his own clumsiness. "I—yes—that is, I really knew nothing—" he stammered, feeling that each word added to it. If Hermione was unnoticeable, Mr. Newell had always been invisible. The young man had never so much as given him a thought, and it was awkward to come on him so suddenly at a turn of the talk.

"Well, he is—living here in Paris," said Mrs. Newell, with a note of asperity which seemed to imply that her friend might have taken the trouble to post himself on this point.

"In Paris? But in that case isn't it quite simple—?"

"To find him? I dare say it won't be difficult, though he's rather mysterious. But the point is that I can't go to him—and that if I write to him he won't answer."

"Ah," said Garnett thoughtfully.

"And so you've got to find him for me, and tell him."

"Tell him what?"

"That he must come to the wedding—that we must show ourselves together at church and afterward in the sacristy."

She delivered the behest in her sharp imperative key, the tone of the born commander. But for once Garnett ventured to question her orders.

"And supposing he won't come?"

"He must if he cares for his daughter's happiness. She can't be married without him."

"Can't be married?"

"The French are like that—especially the old families. I was given to understand at once that my husband must appear—if only to establish the fact that we're not divorced."

"Ah—you're *not*, then?" escaped from Garnett.

"Mercy no! Divorce is stupid. They don't like it in Europe. And in this case it would have been the end of Hermy's marriage. They wouldn't think of letting their son marry the child of divorced parents."

"How fortunate, then—"

"Yes; but I always think of such things beforehand. And of course I've told them that my husband will be present."

"You think he will consent?"

"No; not at first; but you must make him. You must tell him how sweet Hermione is—and you must see Louis, and be able to describe their happiness. You must dine here to-night—he's coming. We're all dining with the Hubbards, and they expect you. They've given Hermy some very good diamonds—though I should have preferred a cheque, as she'll be horribly poor. But I think Kate Hubbard means to do something about the trousseau—Hermy is at Paquin's with her now. You've no idea how delightful all our friends have been.—Ah, here is one of them now," she broke off smiling, as the door opened to admit, without preliminary announcement, a gentleman so glossy and ancient, with such a fixed unnatural freshness of smile and eye, that he gave Garnett the effect of having been embalmed and then enamelled. It needed not the exotic-looking ribbon in the visitor's buttonhole, nor Mrs. Newell's introduction of him as her friend Baron Schenkelderff, to assure Garnett of his connection with a race as ancient as his appearance.

Baron Schenkelderff greeted his hostess with paternal playfulness, and the young man with an ease which might have been acquired on the Stock Exchange and in the dressing-rooms of "leading ladies." He spoke a faultless colourless English, from which one felt he might pass with equal mastery to half a dozen other languages. He inquired patronisingly for the excellent Hubbards, asked his hostess if she did not mean to give him a drop of tea and a cigarette, remarked that he need not ask if Hermione was still closeted with the dress-maker, and, on the waiter's coming in answer to his ring, ordered the tea himself, and added a request for *fine champagne*. It was not the first time that Garnett had seen such minor liberties taken in Mrs. Newell's drawing-room, but they had hitherto been taken by persons who had at least the superiority of knowing what they were permitting themselves, whereas the young man felt almost sure that Baron Schenkelderff's manner was the most distinguished he could achieve; and this deepened the disgust with which, as the minutes passed, he yielded to the conviction that the Baron was Mrs. Newell's aunt.

IV

Garnett had always foreseen that Mrs. Newell might some day ask him to do something he should greatly dislike. He had never gone so far as to conjecture what it might be, but had simply felt that if he allowed his acquaintance with her to pass from spectatorship to participation he must be prepared to find himself, at any moment, in a queer situation.

The moment had come; and he was relieved to find that he could meet it by refusing her request. He had not always been sure that she would leave him this alternative. She had a way of involving people in her complications without their being aware of it; and Garnett had pictured himself in holes so tight that there might not be room for a wriggle. Happily in this case he could still move freely. Nothing compelled him to act as an intermediary between Mrs. Newell and her husband, and it was preposterous to suppose that, even in a life of such perpetual upheaval as hers, there were no roots which struck deeper than her casual intimacy with himself. She had simply laid hands on him because he happened to be within reach, and he would put himself out of reach by leaving for London on the morrow.

Having thus inwardly asserted his independence, he felt free to let his fancy dwell on the strangeness of the situation. He had always supposed that Mrs. Newell, in her flight through life, must have thrown a good many victims to the wolves, and had assumed that Mr. Newell had been among the number. That he had been dropped overboard at an early stage in the lady's career seemed probable from the fact that neither his wife nor his daughter ever mentioned him. Mrs. Newell was incapable of reticence, and if her husband had still been an active element in her life he would certainly have figured in her conversation. Garnett, if he thought of the matter at all, had concluded that divorce must long since have eliminated Mr. Newell; but he now saw how he had underrated his friend's faculty for using up the waste material of life. She had always struck him as the most extravagant of women, yet it turned out that by a miracle of thrift she had for years kept a superfluous husband on the chance that he might some day be useful. The day had come, and Mr. Newell was to be called from his obscurity. Garnett wondered what had become of him in the interval, and in what shape he would respond to the evocation. The fact that his wife feared he might not respond to it at all seemed to show that his exile was voluntary, or had at least come to appear preferable to other alternatives; but if that were the case it was curious he should not have taken legal means to free himself. He could hardly have had his wife's motives for wishing to maintain the vague tie between them; but conjecture lost itself in trying to picture what his point of view was likely to be, and Garnett, on his way to the Hubbards' dinner that evening, could not help regretting that circumstances denied him the opportunity of meeting so enigmatic a person. The young man's knowledge of Mrs. Newell's methods made him feel that her husband might be an interesting study. This, however, did not affect his resolve to keep clear of the business. He entered the Hubbards' dining-room with the firm intention of refusing to execute Mrs. Newell's commission, and if he changed his mind in the course of the evening it was not owing to that lady's persuasions.

Garnett's curiosity as to the Hubbards' share in Hermione's marriage was appeased before he had been five minutes at their table.

Mrs. Woolsey Hubbard was an expansive blonde, whose ample but disciplined outline seemed the result of a well-matched struggle between her cook and her corset-maker. She talked a great deal of what was appropriate in dress and conduct, and seemed to regard Mrs. Newell as a final arbiter on both points. To do or to wear anything inappropriate would have been extremely mortifying to Mrs. Hubbard, and she was evidently resolved, at the price of eternal vigilance, to prove her familiarity with what she frequently referred to as "the right thing." Mr. Hubbard appeared to have no such preoccupations. Garnett, if called on to describe him, would have done so by saying that he was the American who always pays. The young man, in the course of his foreign wanderings, had come across many fellow-citizens of Mr. Hubbard's type in the most diverse company and surroundings; and wherever they were to be found, they always had their hands in their pockets. Mr. Hubbard's standard of gentility was the extent of a man's capacity to "foot the bill"; and as no one but an occasional compatriot cared to dispute the privilege with him he seldom had reason to doubt his social superiority.

Garnett, nevertheless, did not believe that this lavish pair were, as Mrs. Newell would have phrased it, "putting up" Hermione's *dot*. They would go very far in diamonds but they would hang back from securities. Their readiness to pay was indefinably mingled with a dread of being expected to, and their prodigalities would take flight at the first hint of coercion. Mrs. Newell, who had had a good deal of experience in managing this type of millionaire, could be trusted not to arouse their susceptibilities, and Garnett was therefore certain that the chimerical legacy had been extracted from other pockets. There were none in view but those of Baron Schenkelderff, who, seated at Mrs. Hubbard's right, with a new order in his buttonhole, and a fresh glaze upon his features, enchanted that lady by his careless references to crowned heads and his condescending approval of the champagne. Garnett was more than ever certain that it was the Baron who was paying; and it was this conviction which made him suddenly resolve that, at any cost, Hermione's marriage must take place. He had felt no special interest in the marriage except as one more proof of Mrs. Newell's extraordinary capacity; but now it appealed to him from the girl's own stand-point. For he saw, with a touch of compunction, that in the mephitic air of her surroundings a love-story of miraculous freshness had flowered. He had only to intercept the glances which the young couple exchanged to find himself transported to the candid region of romance. It was evident that Hermione adored and was adored; that the lovers believed in each other and in every one about them, and that even the legacy of the defunct aunt had not been too great a strain on their faith in human nature.

His first glance at the Comte Louis du Trayas showed Garnett that, by some marvel of fitness, Hermione had happened on a kindred nature. If the young man's long mild features and short-sighted glance revealed no special force of character, they showed a benevolence and simplicity as incorruptible as her own, and declared that their possessor, whatever his failings, would never imperil the illusions she had so wondrously preserved. The fact that the girl took her good fortune naturally, and did not regard herself as suddenly snatched from the jaws of death, added poignancy to the situation; for if she missed this way of escape, and was thrown back on her former life, the day of discovery could not be long deferred. It made Garnett shiver to think of her growing old between her mother and Schenkelderff, or such successors of the Baron's as might probably attend on Mrs. Newell's waning fortunes; for it was clear to him that the Baron marked the first stage in his friend's decline. When Garnett took leave that evening he had promised Mrs. Newell that he would try to find her husband.

V

If Mr. Newell read in the papers the announcement of his daughter's marriage it did not cause him to lift the veil of seclusion in which his wife represented him as shrouded.

A round of the American banks in Paris failed to give Garnett his address, and it was only in chance talk with one of the young secretaries of the Embassy that he was put on Mr. Newell's track. The secretary's father, it appeared, had known the Newells some twenty years earlier. He had had business relations with Mr. Newell, who was then a man of property, with factories or something of the kind, the narrator thought, somewhere in

Western New York. There had been at this period, for Mrs. Newell, a phase of large hospitality and showy carriages in Washington and at Narragansett. Then her husband had had reverses, had lost heavily in Wall Street, and had finally drifted abroad and disappeared from sight. The young man did not know at what point in his financial decline Mr. Newell had parted company with his wife and daughter; "though you may bet your hat," he philosophically concluded, "that the old girl hung on as long as there were any pickings." He did not himself know Mr. Newell's address, but opined that it might be extracted from a certain official of the Consulate, if Garnett could give a sufficiently good reason for the request; and here in fact Mrs. Newell's emissary learned that her husband was to be found in an obscure street of the Luxembourg quarter.

In order to be near the scene of action, Garnett went to breakfast at his usual haunt, determined to despatch his business as early in the day as politeness allowed. The head waiter welcomed him to a table near that of the transatlantic sage, who sat in his customary corner, his head tilted back against the blistered mirror at an angle suggesting that in a freer civilisation his feet would have sought the same level. He greeted Garnett affably and the two exchanged their usual generalisations on life till the sage rose to go; whereupon it occurred to Garnett to accompany him. His friend took the offer in good part, merely remarking that he was going to the Luxembourg gardens, where it was his invariable habit, on good days, to feed the sparrows with the remains of his breakfast roll; and Garnett replied that, as it happened, his own business lay in the same direction.

"Perhaps, by the way," he added, "you can tell me how to find the rue Panonceaux, where I must go presently. I thought I knew this quarter fairly well, but I have never heard of it."

His companion came to a halt on the narrow pavement, to the confusion of the dense and desultory traffic which flows through the old streets of the Latin quarter. He fixed his mild eye on Garnett and gave a twist to the cigar which lingered in the corner of his mouth.

"The rue Panonceaux? It *is* an out-of-the-way hole, but I can tell you how to find it," he answered.

He made no motion to do so, however, but continued to bend on the young man the full force of his interrogative gaze; then he added: "Would you mind telling me your object in going there?"

Garnett looked at him with surprise: a question so unblushingly personal was strangely out of keeping with his friend's usual attitude of detachment. Before he could reply, however, the other had continued: ''Do you happen to be in search of Samuel C. Newell?''

''Why, yes, I am,'' said Garnett with a start of conjecture.

His companion uttered a sigh. ''I supposed so,'' he said resignedly; ''and in that case,'' he added, ''we may as well have the matter out in the Luxembourg.''

Garnett had halted before him with deepening astonishment. ''But you don't mean to tell me—?'' he stammered.

The little man made a motion of assent. ''I am Samuel C. Newell,'' he said; ''and if you have no objection, I prefer not to break through my habit of feeding the sparrows. We are five minutes late as it is.''

He quickened his pace without awaiting a reply from Garnett, who walked beside him in unsubdued wonder till they reached the Luxembourg gardens, where Mr. Newell, making for one of the less frequented alleys, seated himself on a bench and drew the fragment of a roll from his pocket. His coming was evidently expected, for a shower of little dusky bodies at once descended on him, and the gravel fluttered with battling beaks and wings as he distributed his dole.

It was not till the ground was white with crumbs, and the first frenzy of his pensioners appeased, that he turned to Garnett and said: ''I presume, sir, that you come from my wife.''

Garnett coloured with embarrassment: the more simply the old man took his mission the more complicated it appeared to himself.

''From your wife—and from Miss Newell,'' he said at length. ''You have perhaps heard that your daughter is to be married.''

''Oh, yes—I read the *Herald* pretty faithfully,'' said Miss Newell's parent, shaking out another handful of crumbs.

Garnett cleared his throat. ''Then you have no doubt thought it natural that, under the circumstances, they should wish to communicate with you.''

The sage continued to fix his attention on the sparrows. ''My wife,'' he remarked, ''might have written to me.''

''Mrs. Newell was afraid she might not hear from you in reply.''

''In reply? Why should she? I suppose she merely wishes to announce the marriage. She knows I have no money left to buy wedding-presents,'' said Mr. Newell astonishingly.

Garnett felt his colour deepen: he had a vague sense of standing as the representative of something guilty and enormous, with which he had rashly identified himself.

"I don't think you understand," he said. "Mrs. Newell and your daughter have asked me to see you because they're anxious that you should consent to appear at the wedding."

Mr. Newell, at this, ceased to give his attention to the birds, and turned a compassionate gaze on Garnett.

"My dear sir—I don't know your name—" he remarked, "would you mind telling me how long you've been acquainted with Mrs. Newell?" And without waiting for an answer he added: "If you wait long enough she will ask you to do some very disagreeable things for her."

This echo of his own thoughts gave Garnett a twinge of discomfort, but he made shift to answer good-humouredly: "If you refer to my present errand, I must tell you that I don't find it disagreeable to do anything which may be of service to Miss Hermione."

Mr. Newell fumbled in his pocket, as though searching unavailingly for another morsel of bread; then he said: "From her point of view I shall not be the most important person at the ceremony."

Garnett smiled. "That is hardly a reason—" he began; but he was checked by the brevity of tone with which his companion replied: "I am not aware that I am called upon to give you my reasons."

"You are certainly not," the young man rejoined, "except in so far as you are willing to consider me as the messenger of your wife and daughter."

"Oh, I accept your credentials," said the other with his dry smile; "what I don't recognise is their right to send a message."

This reduced Garnett to silence, and after a moment's pause Mr. Newell drew his watch from his pocket.

"I am sorry to cut the conversation short, but my days are mapped out with a certain regularity, and this is the hour for my nap." He rose as he spoke and held out his hand with a glint of melancholy humour in his small clear eyes.

"You dismiss me, then? I am to take back a refusal?" the young man exclaimed.

"My dear sir, those ladies have got on very well without me for a number of years: I imagine they can put through this wedding without my help."

"You're mistaken, then; if it were not for that I shouldn't have undertaken this errand."

Mr. Newell paused as he was turning away. "Not for what?" he inquired.

"The fact that, as it happens, the wedding can't be put through without your help."

Mr. Newell's thin lips formed a noiseless whistle. "They've got to have my consent, have they? Well, is he a good young man?"

"The bridegroom?" Garnett echoed in surprise. "I hear the best accounts of him—and Miss Newell is very much in love."

Her parent met this with an odd smile. "Well, then, I give my consent—it's all I've got left to give," he added philosophically.

Garnett hesitated. "But if you consent—if you approve—why do you refuse your daughter's request?"

Mr. Newell looked at him a moment. "Ask Mrs. Newell!" he said. And as Garnett was again silent, he turned away with a slight gesture of leave-taking.

But in an instant the young man was at his side. "I will not ask your reasons, sir," he said, "but I will give you mine for being here. Miss Newell cannot be married unless you are present at the ceremony. The young man's parents know that she has a father living, and they give their consent only on condition that he appears at her marriage. I believe it is customary in old French families—"

"Old French families be damned!" said Mr. Newell. "She had better marry an American." And he made a more decided motion to free himself from Garnett's importunities.

But his resistance only strengthened the young man's. The more unpleasant the latter's task became, the more unwilling he grew to see his efforts end in failure. During the three days which had been consumed in his quest it had become clear to him that the bridegroom's parents, having been surprised to a reluctant consent, were but too ready to withdraw it on the plea of Mr. Newell's nonappearance. Mrs. Newell, on the last edge of tension, had confided to Garnett that the Morningfields were "being nasty"; and he could picture the whole powerful clan, on both sides of the Channel, arrayed in a common resolve to exclude poor Hermione from their ranks. The very inequality of the contest stirred his blood, and made him vow that in this case at least the sins of the parents should not be visited on the children. In his talk with the young secretary he had obtained certain glimpses of Baron Schenkelderff's past that fortified this resolve. The Baron, at one time a familiar figure in a much-observed London set, had been mixed up in an ugly money-lending business ending in suicide, which had excluded him from the society most accessible to his race. His alliance with

Mrs. Newell was doubtless a desperate attempt at rehabilitation, a forlorn hope on both sides, but likely to be an enduring tie because it represented, to both partners, their last chance of escape from social extinction. That Hermione's marriage was a mere stake in their game did not in the least affect Garnett's view of its urgency. If on their part it was a sordid speculation, to her it had the freshness of the first wooing. If it made of her a mere pawn in their hands, it would put her, so Garnett hoped, beyond farther risk of such base uses; and to achieve this had become a necessity to him.

The sense that, if he lost sight of Mr. Newell, the latter might not easily be found again, nerved Garnett to hold his ground in spite of the resistance he encountered; and he tried to put the full force of his plea into the tone with which he cried: "Ah, you don't know your daughter!"

VI

Mrs. Newell, that afternoon, met him on the threshold of her sitting-room with a "Well?" of pent-up anxiety.

In the room itself, Baron Schenkelderff sat with crossed legs and head thrown back, in an attitude which he did not see fit to alter at the young man's approach.

Garnett hesitated; but it was not the summariness of the Baron's greeting which he resented.

"You've found him?" Mrs. Newell exclaimed.

"Yes; but—"

She followed his glance and answered it with a slight shrug. "I can't take you into my room, because there's a dress-maker there, and she won't go because she's waiting to be paid. Schenkelderff," she exclaimed, "you're not wanted; please go and look out of the window."

The Baron rose, and lighting a cigarette, laughingly retired to the embrasure. Mrs. Newell flung herself down and signed to Garnett to take a seat at her side.

"Well—you've found him? You've talked with him?"

"Yes; I've talked with him—for an hour."

She made an impatient movement. "That's too long! Does he refuse?"

"He doesn't consent."

"Then you mean—?"

"He wants time to think it over."

"Time? There *is* no time—did you tell him so?"

"I told him so; but you must remember that he has plenty. He has taken twenty-four hours."

Mrs. Newell groaned. "Oh, that's too much. When he thinks things over he always refuses."

"Well, he would have refused at once if I had not agreed to the delay."

She rose nervously from her seat and pressed her hands to her forehead. "It's too hard, after all I've done! The trousseau is ordered—think how disgraceful! You must have managed him badly; I'll go and see him myself."

The Baron, at this, turned abruptly from his study of the Place Vendôme.

"My dear creature, for heaven's sake don't spoil everything!" he exclaimed.

Mrs. Newell coloured furiously. "What's the meaning of that brilliant speech?"

"I was merely putting myself in the place of a man on whom you have ceased to smile."

He picked up his hat and stick, nodded knowingly to Garnett, and walked toward the door with an air of creaking jauntiness.

But on the threshold Mrs. Newell waylaid him.

"Don't go—I must speak to you," she said, following him into the ante-chamber; and Garnett remembered the dress-maker who was not to be dislodged from her bedroom.

In a moment Mrs. Newell returned, with a small flat packet which she vainly sought to dissemble in an inaccessible pocket.

"He makes everything too odious!" she exclaimed; but whether she referred to her husband or the Baron it was left to Garnett to decide.

She sat silent, nervously twisting her cigarette-case between her fingers, while her visitor rehearsed the details of his conversation with Mr. Newell. He did not indeed tell her the arguments he had used to shake her husband's resolve, since in his eloquent sketch of Hermione's situation there had perforce entered hints unflattering to her mother; but he gave the impression that his hearer had in the end been moved, and for that reason had consented to defer his refusal.

"Ah, it's not that—it's to prolong our misery!" Mrs. Newell

exclaimed; and after a moment she added drearily: "He's been waiting for such an opportunity for years."

It seemed needless for Garnett to protract his visit, and he took leave with the promise to report at once the result of his final talk with Mr. Newell. But as he was passing through the antechamber a side door opened and Hermione stood before him. Her face was flushed and shaken out of its usual repose, and he saw at once that she had been waiting for him.

"Mr. Garnett!" she said in a whisper.

He paused, considering her with surprise: he had never supposed her capable of such emotion as her voice and eyes revealed.

"I want to speak to you; we are quite safe here. Mamma is with the dress-maker," she explained, closing the door behind her, while Garnett laid aside his hat and stick.

"I am at your service," he said.

"You have seen my father? Mamma told me that you were to see him to-day," the girl went on, standing close to him in order that she might not have to raise her voice.

"Yes; I've seen him," Garnett replied with increasing wonder. Hermione had never before mentioned her father to him, and it was by a slight stretch of veracity that he had included her name in her mother's plea to Mr. Newell. He had supposed her to be either unconscious of the transaction, or else too much engrossed in her own happiness to give it a thought; and he had forgiven her the last alternative in consideration of the abnormal character of her filial relations. But he now saw that he must readjust his view of her.

"You went to ask him to come to my wedding; I know about it," Hermione continued. "Of course it's the custom—people will think it odd if he does not come." She paused, and then asked: "Does he consent?"

"No; he has not yet consented."

"Ah, I thought so when I saw Mamma just now!"

"But he hasn't quite refused—he has promised to think it over."

"But he hated it—he hated the idea?"

Garnett hesitated. "It seemed to arouse painful associations."

"Ah, it would—it would!" she exclaimed.

He was astonished at the passion of her accent; astonished still more at the tone with which she went on, laying her hand on his arm: "Mr. Garnett, he must not be asked—he has been asked too often to do things that he hated!"

Garnett looked at the girl with a shock of awe. What abysses of knowledge did her purity hide?

"But, my dear Miss Hermione—" he began.

"I know what you are going to say," she interrupted him. "It is necessary that he should be present at the marriage, or the du Trayas will break it off. They don't want it very much, at any rate," she added with a strange candour, "and they'll not be sorry, perhaps—for of course Louis would have to obey them."

"So I explained to your father," Garnett assured her.

"Yes—yes; I knew you would put it to him. But that makes no difference. He must not be forced to come unwillingly."

"But if he sees the point—after all, no one can force him!"

"No; but if it's painful to him—if it reminds him too much. . . . Oh, Mr. Garnett, I was not a child when he left us. . . . I was old enough to see . . . to see how it must hurt him even now to be reminded. Peace was all he asked for, and I want him to be left in peace!"

Garnett paused in deep embarrassment. "My dear child, there is no need to remind you that your own future—"

She had a gesture that recalled her mother. "My future must take care of itself; he must not be made to see us!" she said imperatively. And as Garnett remained silent she went on: "I have always hoped he didn't hate me, but he would hate me now if he were forced to see me."

"Not if he could see you at this moment!"

She lifted her face with swimming eyes.

"Well, go to him, then; tell him what I've said to you!"

Garnett continued to stand before her, deeply struck. "It might be the best thing," he reflected inwardly; but he did not give utterance to the thought. He merely put out his hand, holding Hermione's in a long pressure.

"I will do whatever you wish," he replied.

"You understand that I'm in earnest?" she urged.

"I'm quite sure of it."

"Then I want you to repeat to him what I've said—I want him to be left undisturbed. I don't want him ever to hear of us again!"

The next day, at the appointed hour, Garnett resorted to the Luxembourg gardens, which Mr. Newell had named as a meeting-place in preference to his own lodgings. It was clear that he did not wish to admit the young man any farther into his privacy than the occasion required, and the extreme shabbiness of his dress hinted that pride might be the cause of his reluctance.

Garnett found him feeding the sparrows, but he desisted at the young man's approach, and said at once: "You won't thank me for bringing you all this distance."

"If that means that you're going to send me away with a refusal, I have come to spare you the necessity," Garnett answered.

Mr. Newell turned on him a glance of undisguised wonder, in which a tinge of disappointment might almost have been detected.

"Ah—they've got no use for me, after all?" he said ironically.

Garnett, in reply, related without comment his conversation with Hermione, and the message with which she had charged him. He remembered her words exactly and repeated them without modification, heedless of what they implied or revealed.

Mr. Newell listened with an immovable face, occasionally casting a crumb to his flock. When Garnett ended he asked: "Does her mother know of this?"

"Assuredly not!" cried Garnett with a movement of disgust.

"You must pardon me; but Mrs. Newell is a very ingenious woman." Mr. Newell shook out his remaining crumbs and turned thoughtfully toward Garnett.

"You believe it's quite clear to Hermione that these people will use my refusal as a pretext for backing out of the marriage?"

"Perfectly clear—she told me so herself."

"Doesn't she consider the young man rather chicken-hearted?"

"No; he has already put up a big fight for her, and you know the French look at these things differently. He's only twenty-three, and his marrying against his parents' approval is in itself an act of heroism."

"Yes; I believe they look at it that way," Mr. Newell assented. He rose and picked up the half-smoked cigar which he had laid on the bench beside him.

"What do they wear at these French weddings, anyhow? A dress-suit, isn't it?" he asked.

The question was such a surprise to Garnett that for the moment he could only stammer out—"You consent then? I may go and tell her?"

"You may tell my girl—yes." He gave a vague laugh and added: "One way or another, my wife always gets what she wants."

VII

Mr. Newell's consent brought with it no accompanying concessions. In the first flush of his success Garnett had pictured himself as bringing together the father and daughter, and hovering in an attitude of benediction over a family group in which Mrs. Newell did not very distinctly figure.

But Mr. Newell's conditions were inflexible. He would "see the thing through" for his daughter's sake; but he stipulated that in the meantime there should be no meetings of further communications of any kind. He agreed to be ready when Garnett called for him, at the appointed hour on the wedding-day; but until then he begged to be left alone. To this decision he adhered immovably, and when Garnett conveyed it to Hermione she accepted it with a deep look of understanding. As for Mrs. Newell she was too much engrossed in the nuptial preparations to give her husband another thought. She had gained her point, she had disarmed her foes, and in the first flush of success she had no time to remember by what means her victory had been won. Even Garnett's services received little recognition, unless he found them sufficiently compensated by the new look in Hermione's eyes.

The principal figures in Mrs. Newell's foreground were the Woolsey Hubbards and Baron Schenkelderff. With these she was in hourly consultation, and Mrs. Hubbard went about aureoled with the importance of her close connection with an "aristocratic marriage," and dazzled by the Baron's familiarity with the intricacies of the Almanach de Gotha. In his society and Mrs. Newell's, Mrs. Hubbard evidently felt that she had penetrated to the sacred precincts where "the right thing" flourished in its native soil. As for Hermione, her look of happiness had returned, but with it an undertint of melancholy, visible perhaps only to Garnett, but to him always hauntingly present. Outwardly she sank back into her passive self, resigned to serve as the brilliant lay-figure on which Mrs. Newell hung the trophies of conquest. Preparations for the wedding were zealously pressed. Mrs. Newell knew the danger of giving people time to think things over, and her fears about her husband being allayed, she began to dread a new attempt at evasion on the part of the bridegroom's family.

"The sooner it's over the sounder I shall sleep!" she declared to Garnett; and all the mitigations of art could not conceal the fact that she was desperately in need of that restorative. There were moments, indeed, when he was sorrier for her than for her husband or her daughter; so black and unfathomable appeared the abyss into which she must slip back if she lost her hold on this last spar of safety.

But she did not lose her hold; his own experience, as well as her husband's declaration, might have told him that she always got what she wanted. How much she had wanted this particular thing was shown by the way in which, on the last day, when all peril was over, she bloomed out in renovated splendour. It gave Garnett a shivering sense of the ugliness of the alternative which had confronted her.

The day came; the showy coupé provided by Mrs. Newell presented itself punctually at Garnett's door, and the young man entered it and drove to the rue Panonceaux. It was a little melancholy back street, with lean old houses sweating rust and damp, and glimpses of pit-like gardens, black and sunless, between walls bristling with iron spikes. On the narrow pavement a blind man pottered along led by a red-eyed poodle: a little farther on a dishevelled woman sat grinding coffee on the threshold of a *buvette*. The bridal carriage stopped before one of the doorways, with a clatter of hoofs and harness which drew the neighbourhood to its windows, and Garnett started to mount the ill-smelling stairs to the fourth floor, on which he learned from the *concierge* that Mr. Newell lodged. But half-way up he met the latter descending, and they turned and went down together.

Hermione's parent wore his usual imperturbable look, and his eye seemed as full as ever of generalisations on human folly; but there was something oddly shrunken and submerged in his appearance, as though he had grown smaller or his clothes larger. And on the last hypothesis Garnett paused—for it became evident to him that Mr. Newell had hired his dress-suit.

Seated at the young man's side on the satin cushions, he remained silent while the carriage rolled smoothly and rapidly through the net-work of streets leading to the Boulevard Saint-Germain; only once he remarked, glancing at the elaborate fittings of the coupé: "Is this Mrs. Newell's carriage?"

"I believe so—yes," Garnett assented, with the guilty sense that in defining that lady's possessions it was impossible not to trespass on those of her friends.

Mr. Newell made no farther comment, but presently requested his companion to rehearse to him once more the exact duties which were to devolve on him during the coming ceremony. Having mastered these he remained silent, fixing a dry speculative eye on the panorama of the brilliant streets, till the carriage drew up at the entrance of Saint Philippe du Roule.

With the same air of composure he followed his guide through the mob of spectators, and up the crimson velvet steps, at the head of which, but for a word from Garnett, a formidable Suisse, glittering with cocked hat and mace, would have checked the advance of the small crumpled figure so oddly out of keeping with the magnificence of the bridal party. The French fashion prescribing that the family *cortège* shall follow the bride to the altar, the vestibule of the church was thronged with the participators in the coming procession; but if Mr. Newell felt any nervousness at his sudden projection into this unfamiliar group, nothing in his look or manner betrayed it. He stood beside Garnett till a white-favoured carriage, dashing up to the church with a superlative glitter of highly groomed horse-flesh and silver-plated harness, deposited the snowy apparition of the bride, supported by her mother; then, as Hermione entered the vestibule, he went forward quietly to meet her.

The girl, wrapped in the haze of her bridal veil, and a little confused, perhaps, by the anticipation of the meeting, paused a moment, as if in doubt, before the small oddly-clad figure which blocked her path—a horrible moment to Garnett, who felt a pang of misery at this satire on the infallibility of the filial instinct. He longed to make some sigh, to break in some way the pause of uncertainty; but before he could move he saw Mrs. Newell give her daughter a sharp push, he saw a blush of compunction flood Hermione's face, and the girl, throwing back her veil, bent her tall head and flung her arms about her father.

Mr. Newell emerged unshaken from the embrace: it seemed to have no effect beyond giving an odder twist to his tie. He stood beside his daughter till the church doors were thrown open; then, at a sign from the verger, he gave her his arm, and the strange couple, with the long train of fashion and finery behind them, started on their march to the altar.

Garnett had already slipped into the church and secured a post of vantage which gave him a side-view over the assemblage. The building was thronged—Mrs. Newell had attained her ambition and given Hermione a smart wedding. Garnett's eye travelled curiously from one group to another—from the numerous representatives of the bridegroom's family, all stamped with the same air of somewhat dowdy distinction, the air of having had their thinking done for them for so long that they could no longer perform the act individually, and the heterogeneous company of Mrs. Newell's friends, who presented, on the opposite side of the nave, every variety of individual conviction in dress and conduct. Of the two groups the latter was decidedly the more interesting to Garnett, who observed that it comprised not only such recent acquisitions as the Woolsey Hubbards and the Baron, but also sundry more important figures which of late had faded to the verge of Mrs. Newell's horizon. Hermione's marriage had drawn them back, had once more made her mother a social entity, had in short already accomplished the object for which it had been planned and executed.

And as he looked about him Garnett saw that all the other actors in the show faded into insignificance beside the dominant figure of Mrs. Newell, became mere marionettes pulled hither and thither by the hidden wires of her intention. One and all they were there to serve her ends and accomplish her purpose: Schenkelderff and the Hubbards to pay for the show, the bride and bridegroom to seal and symbolize her social rehabilitation, Garnett himself as the humble instrument adjusting the different parts of the complicated machinery, and her husband, finally, as the last stake in her game, the last asset on which she could draw to rebuild her fallen fortunes. At the thought Garnett was filled with a deep disgust for what the scene signified, and for his own share in it. He had been her tool and dupe like the others; if he imagined that he was serving Hermione, it was for her mother's ends that he had worked. What right had he to sentimentalise a marriage founded on such base connivances, and how could he have imagined that in so doing he was acting a disinterested part?

While these thoughts were passing through his mind the ceremony had already begun, and the principal personages in the drama were ranged before him in the row of crimson velvet chairs which fills the foreground of a Catholic marriage. Through the glow of lights and the perfumed haze about the altar, Garnett's eyes rested on the central figures of the group, and gradually the others disappeared from his view and his mind. After all, neither Mrs. Newell's schemes nor his own share in them could ever unsanctify Hermione's marriage. It was one more testimony to life's indefatigable renewals, to nature's secret of drawing fragrance from corruption; and as his eyes turned from the girl's illuminated presence to the resigned and stoical figure sunk in the adjoining chair, it occurred to him that he had perhaps worked better than he knew in placing them, if only for a moment, side by side.

XINGU

I

Mrs. Ballinger is one of the ladies who pursue Culture in bands, as though it were dangerous to meet alone. To this end she had founded the Lunch Club, an association composed of herself and several other indomitable huntresses of erudition. The Lunch Club after three or four winters of lunching and debate, had acquired such local distinction that the entertainment of distinguished strangers became one of its accepted functions; in recognition of which it duly extended to the celebrated "Osric Dane," on the day of her arrival in Hillbridge, an invitation to be present at the next meeting.

The club was to meet at Mrs. Ballinger's. The other members, behind her back, were of one voice in deploring her unwillingness to cede her rights in favor of Mrs. Plinth, whose house made a more impressive setting for the entertainment of celebrities; while, as Mrs. Leveret observed, there was always the picture-gallery to fall back on.

Mrs. Plinth made no secret of sharing this view. She had always regarded it as one of her obligations to entertain the Lunch Club's distinguished guests. Mrs. Plinth was almost as proud of her obligations as she was of her picture-gallery; she was in fact fond of implying that the one possession implied the other, and that only a woman of her wealth could afford to live up to a standard as high as that which she had set herself. An all-round sense of duty, roughly adaptable to various ends, was, in her opinion, all that Providence exacted of the more humbly stationed; but the power which had predestined Mrs. Plinth to keep a footman clearly intended her to maintain an equally specialized staff of responsibilities. It was the more to be regretted that Mrs. Ballinger, whose obligations to society were bounded by the narrow scope of two parlour-maids, should have been so tenacious of the right to entertain Osric Dane.

The question of that lady's reception had for a month past profoundly moved the members of the Lunch Club. It was not that they felt themselves unequal to the task, but that their sense of the opportunity plunged them into the agreeable uncertainty of the lady who weighs the alternatives of a well-stocked wardrobe. If such subsidiary members as Mrs. Leveret were fluttered by the thought of exchanging ideas with the author of "The Wings of Death," no forebodings disturbed the conscious adequacy of Mrs. Plinth, Mrs. Ballinger and Miss Van Vluyck. "The Wings of Death" had, in fact, at Miss Van Vluyck's suggestion, been chosen as the subject of discussion at the last club meeting, and each member had thus been enabled to express her own opinion or to appropriate whatever sounded well in the comments of the others.

Mrs. Roby alone had abstained from profiting by the opportunity; but it was now openly recognised that, as a member of the Lunch Club, Mrs. Roby was a failure. "It all comes," as Miss Van Vluyck put it, "of accepting a woman on a man's estimation." Mrs. Roby, returning to Hillbridge from a prolonged sojourn in exotic lands—the other ladies no longer took the trouble to remember where—had been heralded by the distinguished biologist, Professor Foreland, as the most agreeable woman he had ever met; and the members of the Lunch Club, impressed by an encomium that carried the weight of a diploma, and rashly assuming that the Professor's social sympathies would follow the line of his professional bent, had seized the chance of annexing a biological member. Their disillusionment was complete. At Miss Van Vluyck's first off-hand mention of the pterodactyl Mrs. Roby had confusedly murmured: "I know so little about metres—" and after that painful betrayal of incompetence she had prudently withdrawn from further participation in the mental gymnastics of the club.

"I suppose she flattered him," Miss Van Vluyck summed up—"or else it's the way she does her hair."

The dimensions of Miss Van Vluyck's dining-room having restricted the membership of the club to six, the non-conductiveness of one member was a serious obstacle to the exchange of ideas, and some wonder had already been expressed that Mrs. Roby should care to live, as it were, on the intellectual bounty of the others. This feeling was increased by the discovery that she had not yet read "The Wings of Death." She owned to having heard the name of Osric Dane; but that—incredible as it appeared—was the extent of her acquaintance with the celebrated novelist. The ladies could not conceal their surprise; but Mrs. Ballinger, whose pride in the club made her wish to put even Mrs. Roby in the best possible light, gently insinuated that, though she had not had time to acquaint herself with "The Wings of Death," she must at least be familiar with its equally remarkable predecessor, "The Supreme Instant."

Mrs. Roby wrinkled her sunny brows in a conscientious effort of memory, as a result of which she recalled that, oh, yes, she *had* seen the book at her brother's, when she was staying with him in Brazil, and had even carried it off to read one day on a boating party; but they had all got to shying things at each other in the boat, and the book had gone overboard, so she had never had the chance—

The picture evoked by this anecdote did not increase Mrs. Roby's credit with the club, and there was a painful pause, which was broken by Mrs. Plinth's remarking: "I can understand that, with all your other pursuits, you should not find much time for reading; but I should have thought you might at least have *got up* 'The Wings of Death' before Osric Dane's arrival."

Mrs. Roby took this rebuke good-humouredly. She had meant, she owned, to glance through the book; but she had been so absorbed in a novel of Trollope's that—

"No one reads Trollope now," Mrs. Ballinger interrupted.

Mrs. Roby looked pained. "I'm only just beginning," she confessed.

"And does he interest you?" Mrs. Plinth enquired.

"He amuses me."

"Amusement," said Mrs. Plinth, "is hardly what I look for in my choice of books."

"Oh, certainly, 'The Wings of Death' is not amusing," ventured Mrs. Leveret, whose manner of putting forth an opinion was like that of an obliging salesman with a variety of other styles to submit if his first selection does not suit.

"Was it *meant* to be?" enquired Mrs. Plinth, who was fond of asking questions that she permitted no one but herself to answer. "Assuredly not."

"Assuredly not—that is what I was going to say," assented Mrs. Leveret, hastily rolling up her opinion and reaching for another. "It was meant to—to elevate."

Miss Van Vluyck adjusted her spectacles as though they were the black cap of condemnation. "I hardly see," she interposed, "how a book steeped in the bitterest pessimism can be said to elevate, however much it may instruct."

"I meant of course, to instruct," said Mrs. Leveret, flurried by the unexpected distinction between two terms which she had supposed to be synonymous. Mrs. Leveret's enjoyment of the Lunch Club was frequently marred by such surprise; and not knowing her own value to the other ladies as a mirror for their mental complacency she was sometimes troubled by a doubt of her worthiness to join in their debates. It was only the fact of having a dull sister who thought her clever that saved her from a sense of hopeless inferiority.

"Do they get married in the end?" Mrs. Roby interposed.

"They—who?" the Lunch Club collectively exclaimed.

"Why, the girl and man. It's a novel, isn't it? I always think that's the one thing that matters. If they're parted it spoils my dinner."

Mrs. Plinth and Mrs. Ballinger exchanged scandalised glances, and the latter said: "I should hardly advise you to read 'The Wings of Death' in that spirit. For my part, when there are so many books one *has* to read, I wonder how any one can find time for those that are merely amusing."

"The beautiful part of it," Laura Glyde murmured, "is surely just this—that no one can tell *how* 'The Wings of Death' ends. Osric Dane, overcome by the awful significance of her own meaning, has mercifully veiled it—perhaps even from herself—as Apelles, in representing the sacrifice of Iphigenia, veiled the face of Agamemnon."

"What's that? Is it poetry?" whispered Mrs. Leveret to Mrs. Plinth, who, disdaining a definite reply, said coldly: "You should look it up. I always make it a point to look things up." Her tone added—"though I might easily have it done for me by the footman."

"I was about to say," Miss Van Vluyck resumed, "that it must always be a question whether a book *can* instruct unless it elevates."

"Oh—" murmured Mrs. Leveret, now feeling herself hopelessly astray.

"I don't know," said Mrs. Ballinger, scenting in Miss Van Vluyck's tone a tendency to depreciate the coveted distinction of entertaining Osric Dane; "I don't know that such a question can seriously be raised as to a book which has attracted more attention among thoughtful people than any novel since 'Robert Elsmere.' "

"Oh, but don't you see," exclaimed Laura Glyde, "that it's just the dark hopelessness of it all—the wonderful tone-scheme of black on black—that makes it such an artistic achievement? It reminded me when I read it of Prince Rupert's *manière noire* . . . the book is etched, not painted, yet one feels the colour-values so intensely. . . ."

"Who is *he*?" Mrs. Leveret whispered to her neighbour. "Some one she's met abroad?"

"The wonderful part of the book," Mrs. Ballinger conceded, "is that it may be looked at from so many points of view. I hear that as a study of determinism Professor Lupton ranks it with 'The Data of Ethics.' "

"I'm told that Osric Dane spent ten years in preparatory studies before beginning to write it," said Mrs. Plinth. "She looks up everything—verifies everything. It has always been my principle, as you know. Nothing would induce me, now, to put aside a book before I'd finished it, just because I can buy as many more as I want."

"And what do *you* think of 'The Wings of Death'?" Mrs. Roby abruptly asked her.

It was the kind of question that might be termed out of order, and the ladies glanced at each other as though disclaiming any share in such a breach of discipline. They all knew there was nothing Mrs. Plinth so much disliked as being asked her opinion of a book. Books were written to read; if one read them what more could be expected? To be questioned in detail regarding the contents of a volume seemed to her as great an outrage as being searched for smuggled laces at the Custom House. The club had always respected this idiosyncrasy of Mrs. Plinth's. Such opinions as she had were imposing and substantial: her mind, like her house, was furnished with monumental "pieces" that were not meant to be disarranged; and it was one of the unwritten rules of the Lunch Club that, within her own province, each member's habits of thought should be respected. The meeting therefore closed with an increased sense, on the part of the other ladies, of Mrs. Roby's hopeless unfitness to be one of them.

II

Mrs. Leveret, on the eventful day, arrived early at Mrs. Ballinger's, her volume of Appropriate Allusions in her pocket.

It always flustered Mrs. Leveret to be late at the Lunch Club: she liked to collect her thoughts and gather a hint, as the others assembled, of the turn the conversation was likely to take. Today, however, she felt herself completely at a loss; and even the familiar contact of Appropriate Allusions, which stuck into her as she sat down, failed to give her any reassurance. It was an admirable little volume, compiled to meet all the social emergencies; so that, whether on the occasion of Anniversaries, joyful or melancholy (as the classification ran), of Banquets, social or municipal, or of Baptisms, Church of England or sectarian, its student need never be at a loss for a pertinent reference. Mrs. Leveret, though she had for years devoutly conned its pages, valued it, however, rather for its moral support than for its practical services; for though in the privacy of her own room she commanded an army of quotations, these invariably deserted her at the critical moment, and the only phrase she retained—*Canst thou draw out leviathan with a hook?*—was one she had never yet found occasion to apply.

To-day she felt that even the complete mastery of the volume would hardly have insured her self-possession; for she thought it probable that, even if she *did,* in some miraculous way, remember an Allusion, it would be only to find that Osric Dane used a different volume (Mrs. Leveret was convinced that literary people always carried them), and would consequently not recognise her quotations.

Mrs. Leveret's sense of being adrift was intensified by the appearance of Mrs. Ballinger's drawing-room. To a careless eye its aspect was unchanged; but those acquainted with Mrs. Ballinger's way of arranging her books would instantly have detected the marks of recent perturbation. Mrs. Ballinger's province, as a member of the Lunch Club, was the Book of the Day. On that, whatever it was, from a novel to a treatise on experimental psychology, she was confidently, authoritatively "up." What became of last year's books, or last week's even; what she did with the "subjects" she had previously professed with equal authority; no one had ever yet discovered. Her mind was an hotel where facts came and went like transient lodgers, without leaving their address behind, and frequently without paying for their board. It was Mrs. Ballinger's boast that she was "abreast with the Thought of the Day," and her pride that this advanced position should be expressed by the books on her table. These volumes, frequently renewed, and almost always damp from the press, bore names generally unfamiliar to Mrs. Leveret, and giving her, as she furtively scanned them, a disheartened glimpse of new fields of knowledge to be breathlessly traversed in Mrs. Ballinger's wake. But to-day a number of maturer-looking volumes were adroitly mingled with the *primeurs* of the press—Karl Marx jostled Professor Bergson, and the "Confessions of St. Augustine" lay beside the last work on "Mendelism"; so that even to Mrs. Leveret's fluttered perceptions it was clear that Mrs. Ballinger didn't in the least know what Osric Dane was likely to talk about, and had taken measures to be prepared for anything. Mrs. Leveret felt like a passenger on an ocean steamer who is told that there is no immediate danger, but that she had better put on her life-belt.

It was a relief to be roused from these forebodings by Miss Van Vluyck's arrival.

"Well, my dear," the new-comer briskly asked her hostess, "what subjects are we to discuss to-day?"

Mrs. Ballinger was furtively replacing a volume of Wordsworth by a copy of Verlaine. "I hardly know," she said, somewhat nervously. "Perhaps we had better leave that to circumstances."

"Circumstances?" said Miss Van Vluyck drily. "That means, I suppose, that Laura Glyde will take the floor as usual, and we shall be deluged with literature."

Philanthropy and statistics were Miss Van Vluyck's province, and she resented any tendency to divert their guest's attention from these topics.

Mrs. Plinth at this moment appeared.

"Literature?" she protested in a tone of remonstrance. "But this is perfectly unexpected. I understood we were to talk of Osric Dane's novel."

Mrs. Ballinger winced at the discrimination, but let it pass. "We hardly make that our chief subject—at least not *too* intentionally," she suggested. "Of course we can let our talk *drift* in that direction, but we ought to have some other topic as an introduction, and that is what I wanted to consult you about. The fact is, we know so little of Osric Dane's tastes and interests that it is difficult to make any special preparation."

"It may be difficult," said Mrs. Plinth with decision, "but it is necessary. I know what that happy-go-lucky principle leads to. As I told one of my nieces the other day, there are certain emergencies for which a lady should always be prepared. It's in shocking taste to wear colours when one pays a visit of condolence, or a last year's dress when there are reports that one's husband is on the wrong side of the market; and so it is with conversation. All I ask is that I should know beforehand what is to be talked about; then I feel sure of being able to say the proper thing."

"I quite agree with you," Mrs. Ballinger assented: "but—"

And at that instant, heralded by the fluttered parlour-maid, Osric Dane appeared upon the threshold.

Mrs. Leveret told her sister afterward that she had known at a glance what was coming. She saw that Osric Dane was not going to meet them half way. That distinguished personage had indeed entered with an air of compulsion not calculated to promote the easy exercise of hospitality. She looked as though she were about to be photographed for a new edition of her books.

The desire to propitiate a divinity is generally in inverse ratio to its responsiveness, and the sense of discouragement produced by Osric Dane's entrance visibly increased the Lunch Club's eagerness to please her. Any lingering idea that she might consider herself under an obligation to her entertainers was at once dispelled by her manner: as Mrs. Leveret said afterward to her sister, she had a way of looking at you that made you feel as if there was something wrong with your hat. This evidence of greatness produced such an immediate impression on the ladies that a shudder of awe ran through them when Mrs. Roby, as their hostess led the great personage into the dining-room, turned back to whisper to the others: "What a brute she is!"

The hour about the table did not tend to revise this verdict. It was passed by Osric Dane in the silent deglutition of Mrs. Ballinger's menu, and by the members of the club in the emission of tentative platitudes which their guest seemed to swallow as perfunctorily as the successive courses of the luncheon.

Mrs. Ballinger's reluctance to fix a topic had thrown the club into a mental disarray which increased with the return to the drawing-room, where the actual business of discussion was to open. Each lady waited for the other to speak; and there was a general shock of disappointment when their hostess opened the conversation by the painfully commonplace enquiry: "Is this your first visit to Hillbridge?"

Even Mrs. Leveret was conscious that this was a bad beginning; and a vague impulse of deprecation made Miss Glyde interject: "It is a very small place indeed."

Mrs. Plinth bristled. "We have a great many representative people," she said, in the tone of one who speaks for her order.

Osric Dane turned to her. "What do they represent?" she asked.

Mrs. Plinth's constitutional dislike to being questioned was intensified by her sense of unpreparedness; and her reproachful glance passed the question on to Mrs. Ballinger.

"Why," said that lady, glancing in turn at the other members, "as a community I hope it is not too much to say that we stand for culture."

"For art—" Miss Glyde interjected.

"For art and literature," Mrs. Ballinger emended.

"And for sociology, I trust," snapped Miss Van Vluyck.

"We have a standard," said Mrs. Plinth, feeling herself suddenly secure on the vast expanse of a generalisation; and Mrs. Leveret, thinking there must be room for more than one on so broad a statement, took courage to murmur: "Oh, certainly; we have a standard."

"The object of our little club," Mrs. Ballinger continued, "is to concentrate the highest tendencies of Hillbridge—to centralise and focus its intellectual effort."

This was felt to be so happy that the ladies drew an almost audible breath of relief.

"We aspire," the President went on, "to be in touch with whatever is highest in art, literature and ethics."

Osric Dane again turned to her. "What ethics?" she asked.

A tremor of apprehension encircled the room. None of the ladies required any preparation to pronounce on a question of morals; but when they were called ethics it was different. The club, when fresh from the "Encyclopædia Britannica," the "Reader's Handbook" or Smith's "Classical Dictionary," could deal confidently with any subject; but when taken unawares it had been known to define agnosticism as a heresy of the Early Church and Professor Froude as a distinguished histologist; and such minor members as Mrs. Leveret still secretly regarded ethics as something vaguely pagan.

Even to Mrs. Ballinger, Osric Dane's question was unsettling, and there was a general sense of gratitude when Laura Glyde leaned forward to say, with her most sympathetic accent: "You must excuse us, Mrs. Dane, for not being able, just at present, to talk of anything but 'The Wings of Death.' "

"Yes," said Miss Van Vluyck, with a sudden resolve to carry the war into the enemy's camp. "We are so anxious to know the exact purpose you had in mind in writing your wonderful book."

"You will find," Mrs. Plinth interposed, "that we are not superficial readers."

"We are eager to hear from you," Miss Van Vluyck continued, "if the pessimistic tendency of the book is an expression of your own convictions or—"

"Or merely," Miss Glyde thrust in, "a sombre background brushed in to throw your figures into more vivid relief. *Are* you not primarily plastic?"

"*I* have always maintained," Mrs. Ballinger interposed, "that you represent the purely objective method—"

Osric Dane helped herself critically to coffee. "How do you define objective?" she then enquired.

There was a flurried pause before Laura Glyde intensely murmured: "In reading *you* we don't define, we feel."

Osric Dane smiled. "The cerebellum," she remarked, "is not infrequently the seat of the literary emotions." And she took a second lump of sugar.

The sting that this remark was vaguely felt to conceal was almost neutralised by the satisfaction of being addressed in such technical language.

"Ah, the cerebellum," said Miss Van Vluyck complacently. "The club took a course in psychology last winter."

"Which psychology?" asked Osric Dane.

There was an agonising pause, during which each member of the club secretly deplored the distressing inefficiency of the others. Only Mrs. Roby went on placidly sipping her chartreuse. At last Mrs. Ballinger said, with an attempt at a high tone: "Well, really, you know, it was last year that we took psychology, and this winter we have been so absorbed in—"

She broke off, nervously trying to recall some of the club's discussions; but her faculties seemed to be paralysed by the petrifying stare of Osric Dane. What *had* the club been absorbed in? Mrs. Ballinger, with a vague purpose of gaining time, repeated slowly: "We've been so intensely absorbed in— "

Mrs. Roby put down her liqueur glass and drew near the group with a smile.

"In Xingu?" she gently prompted.

A thrill ran through the other members. They exchanged

confused glances, and then, with one accord, turned a gaze of mingled relief and interrogation on their rescuer. The expression of each denoted a different phase of the same emotion. Mrs. Plinth was the first to compose her features to an air of reassurance: after a moment's hasty adjustment her look almost implied that it was she who had given the word to Mrs. Ballinger.

"Xingu, of course!" exclaimed the latter with her accustomed promptness, while Miss Van Vluyck and Laura Glyde seemed to be plumbing the depths of memory, and Mrs. Leveret, feeling apprehensively for Appropriate Allusions, was somehow reassured by the uncomfortable pressure of its bulk against her person.

Osric Dane's change of countenance was no less striking than that of her entertainers. She too put down her coffee-cup, but with a look of distinct annoyance; she too wore, for a brief moment, what Mrs. Roby afterward described as the look of feeling for something in the back of her head; and before she could dissemble these momentary signs of weakness, Mrs. Roby, turning to her with a deferential smile, had said: "And we've been so hoping that to-day you would tell us just what you think of it."

Osric Dane received the homage of the smile as a matter of course; but the accompanying question obviously embarrassed her, and it became clear to her observers that she was not quick at shifting her facial scenery. It was as though her countenance had so long been set in an expression of unchallenged superiority that the muscles had stiffened, and refused to obey her orders.

"Xingu—" she said, as if seeking in her turn to gain time.

Mrs. Roby continued to press her. "Knowing how engrossing the subject is, you will understand how it happens that the club has let everything else go to the wall for the moment. Since we took up Xingu I might almost say—were it not for your books—that nothing else seems to us worth remembering."

Osric Dane's stern features were darkened rather than lit up by an uneasy smile. "I am glad to hear that you make one exception," she gave out between narrowed lips.

"Oh, of course," Mrs. Roby said prettily; "but as you have shown us that—so very naturally!—you don't care to talk of your own things, we really can't let you off from telling us exactly what you think about Xingu; especially," she added, with a still more persuasive smile, "as some people say that one of your last books was saturated with it."

It was an *it,* then—the assurance sped like fire through the parched minds of the other members. In their eagerness to gain the least little clue to Xingu they almost forgot the joy of assisting at the discomfiture of Mrs. Dane.

The latter reddened nervously under her antagonist's challenge. "May I ask," she faltered out, "to which of my books you refer?"

Mrs. Roby did not falter. "That's just what I want you to tell us; because, though I was present, I didn't actually take part."

"Present at what?" Mrs. Dane took her up; and for an instant the trembling members of the Lunch Club thought that the champion Providence had raised up for them had lost a point. But Mrs. Roby explained herself gaily: "At the discussion, of course. And so we're dreadfully anxious to know just how it was that you went into the Xingu."

There was a portentous pause, a silence so big with incalculable dangers that the members with one accord checked the words on their lips, like soldiers dropping their arms to watch a single combat between their leaders. Then Mrs. Dane gave expression to their inmost dread by saying sharply: "Ah—you say *the* Xingu, do you?"

Mrs. Roby smiled undauntedly. "It *is* a shade pedantic, isn't it? Personally, I always drop the article; but I don't know how the other members feel about it."

The other members looked as though they would willingly have dispensed with this appeal to their opinion, and Mrs. Roby, after a bright glance about the group, went on: "They probably think, as I do, that nothing really matters except the thing itself—except Xingu."

No immediate reply seemed to occur to Mrs. Dane, and Mrs. Ballinger gathered courage to say: "Surely every one must feel that about Xingu."

Mrs. Plinth came to her support with a heavy murmur of assent, and Laura Glyde sighed out emotionally: "I have known cases where it has changed a whole life."

"It has done me worlds of good," Mrs. Leveret interjected, seeming to herself to remember that she had either taken it or read it the winter before.

"Of course," Mrs. Roby admitted, "the difficulty is that one must give up so much time to it. It's very long."

"I can't imagine," said Miss Van Vluyck, "grudging the time given to such a subject."

"And deep in places," Mrs. Roby pursued; (so then it was a book!) "And it isn't easy to skip."

"I never skip," said Mrs. Plinth dogmatically.

"Ah, it's dangerous to, in Xingu. Even at the start there are places where one can't. One must just wade through."

"I should hardly call it *wading,*" said Mrs. Ballinger sarcastically.

Mrs. Roby sent her a look of interest. "Ah—you always found it went swimmingly?"

Mrs. Ballinger hesitated. "Of course there are difficult passages," she conceded.

"Yes; some are not at all clear—even," Mrs. Roby added, "if one is familiar with the original."

"As I suppose you are?" Osric Dane interposed, suddenly fixing her with a look of challenge.

Mrs. Roby met it by a deprecating gesture. "Oh, it's really not difficult up to a certain point; though some of the branches are very little known, and it's almost impossible to get at the source."

"Have you ever tried?" Mrs. Plinth enquired, still distrustful of Mrs. Roby's thoroughness.

Mrs. Roby was silent for a moment; then she replied with lowered lids: "No—but a friend of mine did; a very brilliant man; and he told me it was best for women—not to. . . ."

A shudder ran around the room. Mrs. Leveret coughed so that the parlour-maid, who was handing the cigarettes, should not hear; Miss Van Vluyck's face took on a nauseated expression, and Mrs. Plinth looked as if she were passing some one she did not care to bow to. But the most remarkable result of Mrs. Roby's words was the effect they produced on the Lunch Club's distinguished guest. Osric Dane's impassive features suddenly softened to an expression of the warmest human sympathy, and edging her chair toward Mrs. Roby's she asked: "Did he really? And—did you find he was right?"

Mrs. Ballinger, in whom annoyance at Mrs. Roby's unwonted assumption of prominence was beginning to displace gratitude for the aid she had rendered, could not consent to her being allowed, by such dubious means, to monopolise the attention of their guest. If Osric Dane had not enough self-respect to resent Mrs. Roby's flippancy, at least the Lunch Club would do so in the person of its President.

Mrs. Ballinger laid her hand on Mrs. Roby's arm. "We must not forget," she said with a frigid amiability, "that absorbing as Xingu is to *us,* it may be less interesting to—"

"Oh, no, on the contrary, I assure you," Osric Dane intervened.

"—to others," Mrs. Ballinger finished firmly; "and we must

not allow our little meeting to end without persuading Mrs. Dane to say a few words to us on a subject which, to-day, is much more present in all our thoughts. I refer, of course, to 'The Wings of Death.' "

The other members, animated by various degrees of the same sentiment, and encouraged by the humanised mien of their redoubtable guest, repeated after Mrs. Ballinger: "Oh, yes, you really *must* talk to us a little about your book."

Osric Dane's expression became as bored, though not as haughty, as when her work had been previously mentioned. But before she could respond to Mrs. Ballinger's request, Mrs. Roby had risen from her seat, and was pulling down her veil over her frivolous nose.

"I'm so sorry," she said, advancing toward her hostess with outstretched hand, "but before Mrs. Dane begins I think I'd better run away. Unluckily, as you know, I haven't read her books, so I should be at a terrible disadvantage among you all, and besides, I've an engagement to play bridge."

If Mrs. Roby had simply pleaded her ignorance of Osric Dane's works as a reason for withdrawing, the Lunch Club, in view of her recent prowess, might have approved such evidence of discretion; but to couple this excuse with the brazen announcement that she was foregoing the privilege for the purpose of joining a bridge-party was only one more instance of her deplorable lack of discrimination.

The ladies were disposed, however, to feel that her departure—now that she had performed the sole service she was ever likely to render them—would probably make for greater order and dignity in the impending discussion, besides relieving them of the sense of self-distrust which her presence always mysteriously produced. Mrs. Ballinger therefore restricted herself to a formal murmur of regret, and the other members were just grouping themselves comfortably about Osric Dane when the latter, to their dismay, started up from the sofa on which she had been seated.

"Oh wait—do wait, and I'll go with you!" she called out to Mrs. Roby; and, seizing the hands of the disconcerted members, she administered a series of farewell pressures with the mechanical haste of a railway-conductor punching tickets.

"I'm so sorry—I'd quite forgotten—" she flung back at them from the threshold; and as she joined Mrs. Roby, who had turned in surprise at her appeal, the other ladies had the mortification of hearing her say, in a voice which she did not take the pains to lower: "If you'll let me walk a little way with you, I should so like to ask you a few more questions about Xingu . . ."

III

The incident had been so rapid that the door closed on the departing pair before the other members had time to understand what was happening. Then a sense of the indignity put upon them by Osric Dane's unceremonious desertion began to contend with the confused feeling that they had been cheated out of their due without exactly knowing how or why.

There was a silence, during which Mrs. Ballinger, with a perfunctory hand, rearranged the skilfully grouped literature at which her distinguished guest had not so much as glanced; then Miss Van Vluyck tartly pronounced: "Well, I can't say that I consider Osric Dane's departure a great loss."

This confession crystallised the resentment of the other members, and Mrs. Leveret exclaimed: "I do believe she came on purpose to be nasty!"

It was Mrs. Plinth's private opinion that Osric Dane's attitude toward the Lunch Club might have been very different had it welcomed her in the majestic setting of the Plinth drawing-rooms; but not liking to reflect on the inadequacy of Mrs. Ballinger's establishment she sought a roundabout satisfaction in depreciating her lack of foresight.

"I said from the first that we ought to have had a subject ready. It's what always happens when you're unprepared. Now if we'd only got up Xingu—"

The slowness of Mrs. Plinth's mental processes was always allowed for by the club; but this instance of it was too much for Mrs. Ballinger's equanimity.

"Xingu!" she scoffed. "Why, it was the fact of our knowing so much more about it than she did—unprepared though we were—that made Osric Dane so furious. I should have thought that was plain enough to everybody!"

This retort impressed even Mrs. Plinth, and Laura Glyde, moved by an impulse of generosity, said: "Yes, we really ought to be grateful to Mrs. Roby for introducing the topic. It may have made Osric Dane furious, but at least it made her civil."

"I am glad we were able to show her," added Miss Van Vluyck, "that a broad and up-to-date culture is not confined to the great intellectual centres."

This increased the satisfaction of the other members, and they began to forget their wrath against Osric Dane in the pleasure of having contributed to her discomfiture.

Miss Van Vluyck thoughtfully rubbed her spectacles. "What surprised me most," she continued, "was that Fanny Roby should be so up on Xingu."

This remark threw a slight chill on the company, but Mrs. Ballinger said with an air of indulgent irony: "Mrs. Roby always has the knack of making a little go a long way; still, we certainly owe her a debt for happening to remember that she'd heard of Xingu." And this was felt by the other members to be a graceful way of cancelling once for all the club's obligation to Mrs. Roby.

Even Mrs. Leveret took courage to speed a timid shaft of irony. "I fancy Osric Dane hardly expected to take a lesson in Xingu at Hillbridge!"

Mrs. Ballinger smiled. "When she asked me what we represented—do you remember?—I wish I'd simply said we represented Xingu!"

All the ladies laughed appreciatively at this sally, except Mrs. Plinth, who said, after a moment's deliberation: "I'm not sure it would have been wise to do so."

Mrs. Ballinger, who was already beginning to feel as if she had launched at Osric Dane the retort which had just occurred to her, turned ironically on Mrs. Plinth. "May I ask why?" she enquired.

Mrs. Plinth looked grave. "Surely," she said, "I understood from Mrs. Roby herself that the subject was one it was as well not to go into too deeply?"

Miss Van Vluyck rejoined with precision: "I think that applied only to an investigation of the origin of the—of the—"; and suddenly she found that her usually accurate memory had failed her. "It's a part of the subject I never studied myself," she concluded.

"Nor I," said Mrs. Ballinger.

Laura Glyde bent toward them with widened eyes. "And yet it seems—doesn't it?—the part that is fullest of an esoteric fascination?"

"I don't know on what you base that," said Miss Van Vluyck argumentatively.

"Well, didn't you notice how intensely interested Osric Dane became as soon as she heard what the brilliant foreigner—he *was* a foreigner, wasn't he?—had told Mrs. Roby about the origin—the origin of the rite—or whatever you call it?"

Mrs. Plinth looked disapproving, and Mrs. Ballinger visibly wavered. Then she said: "It may not be desirable to touch on the—on that part of the subject in general conversation; but, from the importance it evidently has to a woman of Osric Dane's distinction, I feel as if we ought not to be afraid to discuss it among ourselves—without gloves—though with closed doors, if necessary."

"I'm quite of your opinion," Miss Van Vluyck came briskly to her support; "on condition, that is, that all grossness of language is avoided."

"Oh, I'm sure we shall understand without that," Mrs. Leveret tittered; and Laura Glyde added significantly: "I fancy we can read between the lines," while Mrs. Ballinger rose to assure herself that the doors were really closed.

Mrs. Plinth had not yet given her adhesion. "I hardly see," she began, "what benefit is to be derived from investigating such peculiar customs—"

But Mrs. Ballinger's patience had reached the extreme limit of tension. "This at least," she returned; "that we shall not be placed again in the humiliating position of finding ourselves less up on our own subjects than Fanny Roby!"

Even to Mrs. Plinth this argument was conclusive. She peered furtively about the room and lowered her commanding tones to ask: "Have you got a copy?"

"A—a copy?" stammered Mrs. Ballinger. She was aware that the other members were looking at her expectantly, and that this answer was inadequate, so she supported it by asking another question. "A copy of what?"

Her companions bent their expectant gaze on Mrs. Plinth, who, in turn, appeared less sure of herself than usual. "Why, of—of—the book," she explained.

"What book?" snapped Miss Van Vluyck, almost as sharply as Osric Dane.

Mrs. Ballinger looked at Laura Glyde, whose eyes were interrogatively fixed on Mrs. Leveret. The fact of being deferred to was so new to the latter that it filled her with an insane temerity. "Why, Xingu, of course!" she exclaimed.

A profound silence followed this challenge to the resources of Mrs. Ballinger's library, and the latter, after glancing nervously toward the Books of the Day, returned with dignity: "It's not a thing one cares to leave about."

"I should think *not*!" exclaimed Mrs. Plinth.

"It *is* a book, then?" said Miss Van Vluyck.

This again threw the company into disarray, and Mrs. Ballinger, with an impatient sigh, rejoined: "Why—there *is* a book—naturally. . . ."

"Then why did Miss Glyde call it a religion?"

Laura Glyde started up. "A religion? I never—"

"Yes, you did," Miss Van Vluyck insisted; "you spoke of rites; and Mrs. Plinth said it was a custom."

Miss Glyde was evidently making a desperate effort to recall her statement; but accuracy of detail was not her strongest point. At length she began in a deep murmur: "Surely they used to do something of the kind at the Eleusinian mysteries—"

"Oh—" said Miss Van Vluyck, on the verge of disapproval; and Mrs. Plinth protested: "I understood there was to be no indelicacy!"

Mrs. Ballinger could not control her irritation. "Really, it is too bad that we should not be able to talk the matter over quietly among ourselves. Personally, I think that if one goes into Xingu at all—"

"Oh, so do I!" cried Miss Glyde.

"And I don't see how one can avoid doing so, if one wishes to keep up with the Thought of the Day—"

Mrs. Leveret uttered an exclamation of relief. "There—that's it!" she interposed.

"What's it?" the President took her up.

"Why—it's a—a Thought: I mean a philosophy."

This seemed to bring a certain relief to Mrs. Ballinger and Laura Glyde, but Miss Van Vluyck said: "Excuse me if I tell you that you're all mistaken. Xingu happens to be a language."

"A language!" the Lunch Club cried.

"Certainly. Don't you remember Fanny Roby's saying that there were several branches, and that some were hard to trace? What could that apply to but dialects?"

Mrs. Ballinger could no longer restrain a contemptuous laugh. "Really, if the Lunch Club has reached such a pass that it has to go to Fanny Roby for instruction on a subject like Xingu, it had almost better cease to exist!"

"It's really her fault for not being clearer," Laura Glyde put in.

"Oh, clearness and Fanny Roby!" Mrs. Ballinger shrugged. "I daresay we shall find she was mistaken on almost every point."

"Why not look it up?" said Mrs. Plinth.

As a rule this recurrent suggestion of Mrs. Plinth's was ignored in the heat of discussion, and only resorted to afterward in the privacy of each member's home. But on the present occasion the desire to ascribe their own confusion of thought to the vague and contradictory nature of Mrs. Roby's statements caused the members of the Lunch Club to utter a collective demand for a book of reference.

At this point the production of her treasured volume gave Mrs. Leveret, for a moment, the unusual experience of occupying the centre front; but she was not able to hold it long, for Appropriate Allusions contained no mention of Xingu.

"Oh, that's not the kind of thing we want!" exclaimed Miss Van Vluyck. She cast a disparaging glance over Mrs. Ballinger's assortment of literature, and added impatiently: "Haven't you any useful books?"

"Of course I have," replied Mrs. Ballinger indignantly; "I keep them in my husband's dressingroom."

From this region, after some difficulty and delay, the parlourmaid produced the W-Z volume of an Encyclopædia and, in deference to the fact that the demand for it had come from Miss Van Vluyck, laid the ponderous tome before her.

There was a moment of painful suspense while Miss Van Vluyck rubbed her spectacles, adjusted them, and turned to Z; and a murmur of surprise when she said: "It isn't here."

"I suppose," said Mrs. Plinth, "it's not fit to be put in a book of reference."

"Oh, nonsense!" exclaimed Mrs. Ballinger. "Try X."

Miss Van Vluyck turned back through the volume, peering short-sightedly up and down the pages, till she came to a stop and remained motionless, like a dog on a point.

"Well, have you found it?" Mrs. Ballinger enquired after a considerable delay.

"Yes. I've found it," said Miss Van Vluyck in a queer voice.

Mrs. Plinth hastily interposed: "I beg you won't read it aloud if there's anything offensive."

Miss Van Vluyck, without answering, continued her silent scrutiny.

"Well, what *is* it?" exclaimed Laura Glyde excitedly.

"*Do* tell us!" urged Mrs. Leveret, feeling that she would have something awful to tell her sister.

Miss Van Vluyck pushed the volume aside and turned slowly toward the expectant group.

"It's a river."

"A *river*?"

"Yes: in Brazil. Isn't that where she's been living?"

"Who? Fanny Roby? Oh, but you must be mistaken. You've been reading the wrong thing," Mrs. Ballinger exclaimed, leaning over her to seize the volume.

"It's the only *Xingu* in the Encyclopædia; and she *has* been living in Brazil," Miss Van Vluyck persisted.

"Yes: her brother has a consulship there," Mrs. Leveret interposed.

"But it's too ridiculous! I—we—why we *all* remember studying Xingu last year—or the year before last," Mrs. Ballinger stammered.

"I thought I did when *you* said so," Laura Glyde avowed.

"*I* said so?" cried Mrs. Ballinger.

"Yes. You said it had crowded everything else out of your mind."

"Well *you* said it had changed your whole life!"

"For that matter, Miss Van Vluyck said she had never grudged the time she'd given it."

Mrs. Plinth interposed: "I made it clear that I knew nothing whatever of the original."

Mrs. Ballinger broke off the dispute with a groan. "Oh, what does it all matter if she's been making fools of us? I believe Miss Van Vluyck's right—she was talking of the river all the while!"

"How could she? It's too preposterous," Miss Glyde exclaimed.

"Listen." Miss Van Vluyck had repossessed herself of the Encyclopædia, and restored her spectacles to a nose reddened by excitement. " 'The Xingu, one of the principal rivers of Brazil, rises on the plateau of Mato Grosso, and flows in a northerly direction for a length of no less than one thousand one hundred and eighteen miles, entering the Amazon near the mouth of the latter river. The upper course of the Xingu is auriferous and fed by numerous branches. Its source was first discovered in 1884 by the German explorer von den Steinen, after a difficult and dangerous expedition through a region inhabited by tribes still in the Stone Age of culture.' "

The ladies received this communication in a state of stupefied silence from which Mrs. Leveret was the first to rally. "She certainly *did* speak of its having branches."

The word seemed to snap the last thread of their incredulity. "And of its great length," gasped Mrs. Ballinger.

"She said it was awfully deep, and you couldn't skip—you just had to wade through," Miss Glyde added.

The idea worked its way more slowly through Mrs. Plinth's compact resistances. "How could there be anything improper about a river?" she enquired.

"Improper?"

"Why, what she said about the source—that it was corrupt?"

"Not corrupt, but hard to get at," Laura Glyde corrected. "Some one who'd been there had told her so. I daresay it was the explorer himself—doesn't it say the expedition was dangerous?"

" 'Difficult and dangerous,' " read Miss Van Vluyck.

Mrs. Ballinger pressed her hands to her throbbing temples. "There's nothing she said that wouldn't apply to a river—to this river!" She swung about excitedly to the other members. "Why, do you remember her telling us that she hadn't read 'The Supreme Instant' because she'd taken it on a boating party while she was staying with her brother, and some one had 'shied' it overboard—'shied' of course was her own expression."

The ladies breathlessly signified that the expression had not escaped them.

"Well—and then didn't she tell Osric Dane that one of her books was simply saturated with Xingu? Of course it was, if one of Mrs. Roby's rowdy friends had thrown it into the river!"

This surprising reconstruction of the scene in which they had just participated left the members of the Lunch Club inarticulate. At length, Mrs. Plinth, after visibly labouring with the problem, said in a heavy tone: "Osric Dane was taken in too."

Mrs. Leveret took courage at this. "Perhaps that's what Mrs. Roby did it for. She said Osric Dane was a brute, and she may have wanted to give her a lesson."

Miss Van Vluyck frowned. "It was hardly worth while to do it at our expense."

"At least," said Miss Glyde with a touch of bitterness, "she succeeded in interesting her, which was more than we did."

"What chance had we?" rejoined Mrs. Ballinger. "Mrs. Roby monopolised her from the first. And *that*, I've no doubt, was her purpose—to give Osric Dane a false impression of her own standing in the club. She would hesitate at nothing to attract attention: we all know how she took in poor Professor Foreland."

"She actually makes him give bridge-teas every Thursday," Mrs. Leveret piped up.

Laura Glyde struck her hands together. "Why, this is Thursday, and it's *there* she's gone, of course; and taken Osric with her!"

"And they're shrieking over us at this moment," said Mrs. Ballinger between her teeth.

This possibility seemed too preposterous to be admitted. "She would hardly dare," said Miss Van Vluyck, "confess the imposture to Osric Dane."

"I'm not so sure: I thought I saw her make a sign as she left. If she hadn't made a sign, why should Osric Dane have rushed out after her?"

"Well, you know, we'd all been telling her how wonderful Xingu was, and she said she wanted to find out more about it," Mrs. Leveret said, with a tardy impulse of justice to the absent.

This reminder, far from mitigating the wrath of the other members, gave it a stronger impetus.

"Yes—and that's exactly what they're both laughing over now," said Laura Glyde ironically.

Mrs. Plinth stood up and gathered her expensive furs about her monumental form. "I have no wish to criticise," she said; "but unless the Lunch Club can protect its members against the recurrence of such—such unbecoming scenes, I for one—"

"Oh, so do I!" agreed Miss Glyde, rising also.

Miss Van Vluyck closed the Encyclopædia and proceeded to button herself into her jacket. "My time is really too valuable—" she began.

"I fancy we are all of one mind," said Mrs. Ballinger, looking searchingly at Mrs. Leveret, who looked at the others.

"I always deprecate anything like a scandal—" Mrs. Plinth continued.

"She has been the cause of one to-day!" exclaimed Miss Glyde.

Mrs. Leveret moaned: "I don't see how she *could*!" and Miss Van Vluyck said, picking up her note-book: "Some women stop at nothing."

"—but if," Mrs. Plinth took up her argument impressively, "anything of the kind had happened in *my* house" (it never would have, her tone implied), "I should have felt that I owed it to myself either to ask for Mrs. Roby's resignation—or to offer mine."

"Oh, Mrs. Plinth—" gasped the Lunch Club.

"Fortunately for me," Mrs. Plinth continued with an awful magnanimity, "the matter was taken out of my hands by our President's decision that the right to entertain distinguished guests was a privilege vested in her office; and I think the other members will agree that, as she was alone in this opinion, she ought to be alone in deciding on the best way of effacing its—its really deplorable consequences."

A deep silence followed this outbreak of Mrs. Plinth's long-stored resentment.

"I don't see why *I* should be expected to ask her to resign—" Mrs. Ballinger at length began; but Laura Glyde turned back to remind her: "You know she made you say that you'd got on swimmingly in Xingu."

An ill-timed giggle escaped from Mrs. Leveret, and Mrs. Ballinger energetically continued "—but you needn't think for a moment that I'm afraid to!"

The door of the drawing-room closed on the retreating backs of the Lunch Club, and the President of that distinguished association, seating herself at her writing-table, and pushing away a copy of "The Wings of Death" to make room for her elbow, drew forth a sheet of the club's note-paper, on which she began to write: "My dear Mrs. Roby—"

THE OTHER TWO

I

Waythorn, on the drawing-room hearth, waited for his wife to come down to dinner.

It was their first night under his own roof, and he was surprised at his thrill of boyish agitation. He was not so old, to be sure—his glass gave him little more than the five-and-thirty years to which his wife confessed—but he had fancied himself already in the temperate zone; yet here he was listening for her step with a tender sense of all it symbolised, with some old trail of verse about the garlanded nuptial door-posts floating through his enjoyment of the pleasant room and the good dinner just beyond it.

They had been hastily recalled from their honeymoon by the illness of Lily Haskett, the child of Mrs. Waythorn's first marriage. The little girl, at Waythorn's desire, had been transferred to his house on the day of her mother's wedding, and the doctor, on their arrival, broke the news that she was ill with typhoid, but declared that all the symptoms were favourable. Lily could show twelve years of unblemished health, and the case promised to be a light one. The nurse spoke as reassuringly, and after a moment of alarm Mrs. Waythorn had adjusted herself to the situation. She was very fond of Lily—her affection for the child had perhaps been her decisive charm in Waythorn's eyes—but she had the perfectly balanced nerves which her little girl had inherited, and no woman ever wasted less tissue in unproductive worry. Waythorn was therefore quite prepared to see her come in presently, a little late because of a last look at Lily, but as serene and well-appointed as if her good-night kiss had been laid on the brow of health. Her composure was restful to him; it acted as ballast to his somewhat unstable sensibilities. As he pictured her bending over the child's bed he thought how soothing her presence must be in illness: her very step would prognosticate recovery.

His own life had been a gray one, from temperament rather than circumstance, and he had been drawn to her by the unperturbed gaiety which kept her fresh and elastic at an age when most women's activities are growing either slack or febrile. He knew what was said about her; for, popular as she was, there had always been a faint undercurrent of detraction. When she had appeared in New York, nine or ten years earlier, as the pretty Mrs. Haskett whom Gus Varick had unearthed somewhere—was it in Pittsburgh or Utica?—society, while promptly accepting her, had reserved the right to cast a doubt on its own indiscrimination. Enquiry, however, established her undoubted connection with a socially reigning family, and explained her recent divorce as the natural result of a runaway match at seventeen; and as nothing was known of Mr. Haskett it was easy to believe the worst of him.

Alice Haskett's remarriage with Gus Varick was a passport to the set whose recognition she coveted, and for a few years the Varicks were the most popular couple in town. Unfortunately, the alliance was brief and stormy, and this time the husband had his champions. Still, even Varick's staunchest supporters admitted that he was not meant for matrimony, and Mrs. Varick's grievances were of a nature to bear the inspection of the New York courts. A New York divorce is in itself a diploma of virtue, and in the semi-widowhood of this second separation Mrs. Varick took on an air of sanctity, and was allowed to confide her wrongs to some of the most scrupulous ears in town. But when it was known that she was to marry Waythorn there was a momentary reaction. Her best friends would have preferred to see her remain in the rôle of the injured wife, which was as becoming to her as crape to a rosy complexion. True, a decent time had elapsed, and it was not even suggested that Waythorn had supplanted his predecessor. People shook their heads over him, however, and one grudging friend, to whom he affirmed that he took the step with his eyes open, replied oracularly: "Yes—and with your ears shut."

Waythorn could afford to smile at these innuendoes. In the Wall Street phrase, he had "discounted" them. He knew that society has not yet adapted itself to the consequences of divorce, and that till the adaptation takes place every woman who uses the freedom the law accords her must be her own social justification.

Waythorn had an amused confidence in his wife's ability to justify herself. His expectations were fulfilled, and before the wedding took place Alice Varick's group had rallied openly to her support. She took it all imperturbably: she had a way of surmounting obstacles without seeming to be aware of them, and Waythorn looked back with wonder at the trivialities over which he had worn his nerves thin. He had the sense of having found refuge in a richer, warmer nature than his own, and his satisfaction, at the moment, was humorously summed up in the thought that his wife, when she had done all she could for Lily, would not be ashamed to come down and enjoy a good dinner.

The anticipation of such enjoyment was not, however, the sentiment expressed by Mrs. Waythorn's charming face when she presently joined him. Though she had put on her most engaging tea-gown she had neglected to assume the smile that went with it, and Waythorn thought he had never seen her look so nearly worried.

"What is it?" he asked. "Is anything wrong with Lily?"

"No; I've just been in and she's still sleeping." Mrs. Waythorn hesitated. "But something tiresome has happened."

He had taken her two hands, and now perceived that he was crushing a paper between them.

"This letter?"

"Yes—Mr. Haskett has written—I mean his lawyer has written."

Waythorn felt himself flush uncomfortably. He dropped his wife's hands.

"What about?"

"About seeing Lily. You know the courts—"

"Yes, yes," he interrupted nervously.

Nothing was known about Haskett in New York. He was vaguely supposed to have remained in the outer darkness from which his wife had been rescued, and Waythorn was one of the few who were aware that he had given up his business in Utica and followed her to New York in order to be near his little girl. In the days of his wooing, Waythorn had often met Lily on the doorstep, rosy and smiling, on her way "to see papa."

"I am so sorry," Mrs. Waythorn murmured.

He roused himself. "What does he want?"

"He wants to see her. You know she goes to him once a week."

"Well—he doesn't expect her to go to him now, does he?"

"No—he has heard of her illness; but he expects to come here."

"Here?"

Mrs. Waythorn reddened under his gaze. They looked away from each other.

"I'm afraid he has the right. . . . You'll see. . . ." She made a proffer of the letter.

Waythorn moved away with a gesture of refusal. He stood staring about the softly lighted room, which a moment before had seemed so full of bridal intimacy.

"I'm so sorry," she repeated. "If Lily could have been moved—"

"That's out of the question," he returned impatiently.

"I suppose so."

Her lip was beginning to tremble, and he felt himself a brute.

"He must come, of course," he said. "When is—his day?"

"I'm afraid—to-morrow."

"Very well. Send a note in the morning."

The butler entered to announce dinner.

Waythorn turned to his wife. "Come—you must be tired. It's beastly, but try to forget about it," he said, drawing her hand through his arm.

"You're so good, dear. I'll try," she whispered back.

Her face cleared at once, and as she looked at him across the flowers, between the rosy candle-shades, he saw her lips waver back into a smile.

"How pretty everything is!" she sighed luxuriously.

He turned to the butler. "The champagne at once, please. Mrs. Waythorn is tired."

In a moment or two their eyes met above the sparkling glasses. Her own were quite clear and untroubled: he saw that she had obeyed his injunction and forgotten.

II

Waythorn, the next morning, went down town earlier than usual. Haskett was not likely to come till the afternoon, but the instinct of flight drove him forth. He meant to stay away all day—he had thoughts of dining at his club. As his door closed behind him he reflected that before he opened it again it would have admitted another man who had as much right to enter it as himself, and the thought filled him with a physical repugnance.

He caught the "elevated" at the employees' hour, and found himself crushed between two layers of pendulous humanity. At Eighth Street the man facing him wriggled out, and another took his place. Waythorn glanced up and saw that it was Gus Varick. The men were so close together that it was impossible to ignore the smile of recognition on Varick's handsome overblown face. And after all—why not? They had always been on good terms, and Varick had been divorced before Waythorn's attentions to his wife began. The two exchanged a word on the perennial grievance of the congested trains, and when a seat at their side was miraculously left empty the instinct of self-preservation made Waythorn slip into it after Varick.

The latter drew the stout man's breath of relief. "Lord—I was beginning to feel like a pressed flower." He leaned back, looking unconcernedly at Waythorn. "Sorry to hear that Sellers is knocked out again."

"Sellers?" echoed Waythorn, starting at his partner's name.

Varick looked surprised. "You didn't know he was laid up with the gout?"

"No. I've been away—I only got back last night." Waythorn felt himself reddening in anticipation of the other's smile.

"Ah—yes; to be sure. And Sellers's attack came on two days ago. I'm afraid he's pretty bad. Very awkward for me, as it happens, because he was just putting through a rather important thing for me."

"Ah?" Waythorn wondered vaguely since when Varick had been dealing in "important things." Hitherto he had dabbled only in the shallow pools of speculation, with which Waythorn's office did not usually concern itself.

It occurred to him that Varick might be talking at random, to relieve the strain of their propinquity. That strain was becoming momentarily more apparent to Waythorn, and when, at Cortlandt Street, he caught sight of an acquaintance and had a sudden vision of the picture he and Varick must present to an initiated eye, he jumped up with a muttered excuse.

"I hope you'll find Sellers better," said Varick civilly, and he stammered back: "If I can be of any use to you—" and let the departing crowd sweep him to the platform.

At his office he heard that Sellers was in fact ill with the gout, and would probably not be able to leave the house for some weeks.

"I'm sorry it should have happened so, Mr. Waythorn," the senior clerk said with affable significance. "Mr. Sellers was very much upset at the idea of giving you such a lot of extra work just now."

"Oh, that's no matter," said Waythorn hastily. He secretly welcomed the pressure of additional business, and was glad to think that, when the day's work was over, he would have to call at his partner's on the way home.

He was late for luncheon, and turned in at the nearest restaurant instead of going to his club. The place was full, and the waiter hurried him to the back of the room to capture the only vacant table. In the cloud of cigar-smoke Waythorn did not at once distinguish his neighbours; but presently, looking about him, he saw Varick seated a few feet off. This time, luckily, they were too far apart for conversation, and Varick, who faced another way, had probably not even seen him; but there was an irony in their renewed nearness.

Varick was said to be fond of good living, and as Waythorn sat despatching his hurried luncheon he looked across half enviously at the other's leisurely degustation of his meal. When Waythorn first saw him he had been helping himself with critical deliberation to a bit of Camembert at the ideal point of liquefaction, and now, the cheese removed, he was just pouring his *café double* from its little two-storied earthen pot. He poured slowly, his ruddy profile bent above the task, and one beringed white hand steadying the lid of the coffee-pot; then he stretched his other hand to the decanter of cognac at his elbow, filled a liqueur-glass, took a tentative sip, and poured the brandy into his coffee-cup.

Waythorn watched him in a kind of fascination. What was he thinking of—only the flavour of the coffee and the liqueur? Had the morning's meeting left no more trace in his thoughts than on his face? Had his wife so completely passed out of his life that even this odd encounter with her present husband, within a week after her remarriage, was no more than an incident in his day? And as Waythorn mused, another idea struck him: had Haskett ever met Varick as Varick and he had just met? The recollection of Haskett perturbed him, and he rose and left the restaurant, taking a circuitous way out to escape the placid irony of Varick's nod.

It was after seven when Waythorn reached home. He thought the footman who opened the door looked at him oddly.

"How is Miss Lily?" he asked in haste.

"Doing very well, sir. A gentleman—"

"Tell Barlow to put off dinner for half an hour," Waythorn cut him off, hurrying upstairs.

He went straight to his room and dressed without seeing his wife. When he reached the drawing-room she was there, fresh and radiant. Lily's day had been good; the doctor was not coming back that evening.

At dinner Waythorn told her of Sellers's illness and of the resulting complications. She listened sympathetically, adjuring him not to let himself be overworked, and asking vague feminine questions about the routine of the office. Then she gave him the chronicle of Lily's day; quoted the nurse and doctor, and told him who had called to inquire. He had never seen her more serene and unruffled. It struck him, with a curious pang, that she was very happy in being with him, so happy that she found a childish pleasure in rehearsing the trivial incidents of her day.

After dinner they went to the library, and the servant put the coffee and liqueurs on a low table before her and left the room. She looked singularly soft and girlish in her rosy pale dress, against the dark leather of one of his bachelor armchairs. A day earlier the contrast would have charmed him.

He turned away now, choosing a cigar with affected deliberation.

"Did Haskett come?" he asked, with his back to her.

"Oh, yes—he came."

"You didn't see him, of course?"

She hesitated a moment. "I let the nurse see him."

That was all. There was nothing more to ask. He swung round toward her, applying a match to his cigar. Well, the thing was over for a week, at any rate. He would try not to think of it. She looked up at him, a trifle rosier than usual, with a smile in her eyes.

"Ready for your coffee, dear?"

He leaned against the mantelpiece, watching her as she lifted the coffee-pot. The lamplight struck a gleam from her bracelets and tipped her soft hair with brightness. How light and slender she was, and how each gesture flowed into the next! She seemed a creature all compact of harmonies. As the thought of Haskett receded, Waythorn felt himself yielding again to the joy of possessorship. They were his, those white hands with their flitting motions, his the light haze of hair, the lips and eyes. . . .

She set down the coffee-pot, and reaching for the decanter of cognac, measured off a liqueur-glass and poured it into his cup.

Waythorn uttered a sudden exclamation.

"What is the matter?" she said, startled.

"Nothing; only—I don't take cognac in my coffee."

"Oh, how stupid of me," she cried.

Their eyes met, and she blushed a sudden agonised red.

III

Ten days later, Mr. Sellers, still house-bound, asked Waythorn to call on his way down town.

The senior partner, with his swaddled foot propped up by the fire, greeted his associate with an air of embarrassment.

"I'm sorry, my dear fellow; I've got to ask you to do an awkward thing for me."

Waythorn waited, and the other went on, after a pause apparently given to the arrangement of his phrases: "The fact is, when I was knocked out I had just gone into a rather complicated piece of business for—Gus Varick."

"Well?" said Waythorn, with an attempt to put him at his ease.

"Well—it's this way: Varick came to me the day before my attack. He had evidently had an inside tip from somebody, and had made about a hundred thousand. He came to me for advice, and I suggested his going in with Vanderlyn."

"Oh, the deuce!" Waythorn exclaimed. He saw in a flash what had happened. The investment was an alluring one, but required negotiation. He listened quietly while Sellers put the case before him, and, the statement ended, he said: "You think I ought to see Varick?"

"I'm afraid I can't as yet. The doctor is obdurate. And this thing can't wait. I hate to ask you, but no one else in the office knows the ins and outs of it."

Waythorn stood silent. He did not care a farthing for the success of Varick's venture, but the honour of the office was to be considered, and he could hardly refuse to oblige his partner.

"Very well," he said, "I'll do it."

That afternoon, apprised by telephone, Varick called at the

office. Waythorn, waiting in his private room, wondered what the others thought of it. The newspapers, at the time of Mrs. Waythorn's marriage, had acquainted their readers with every detail of her previous matrimonial ventures, and Waythorn could fancy the clerks smiling behind Varick's back as he was ushered in.

Varick bore himself admirably. He was easy without being undignified, and Waythorn was conscious of cutting a much less impressive figure. Varick had no experience of business, and the talk prolonged itself for nearly an hour while Waythorn set forth with scrupulous precision the details of the proposed transaction.

"I'm awfully obliged to you," Varick said as he rose. "The fact is I'm not used to having much money to look after, and I don't want to make an ass of myself—" He smiled, and Waythorn could not help noticing that there was something pleasant about his smile. "It feels uncommonly queer to have enough cash to pay one's bills. I'd have sold my soul for it a few years ago!"

Waythorn winced at the allusion. He had heard it rumoured that a lack of funds had been one of the determining causes of the Varick separation, but it did not occur to him that Varick's words were intentional. It seemed more likely that the desire to keep clear of embarrassing topics had fatally drawn him into one. Waythorn did not wish to be outdone in civility.

"We'll do the best we can for you," he said. "I think this is a good thing you're in."

"Oh, I'm sure it's immense. It's awfully good of you—" Varick broke off, embarrassed. "I suppose the thing's settled now—but if—"

"If anything happens before Sellers is about, I'll see you again," said Waythorn quietly. He was glad, in the end, to appear the more self-possessed of the two.

~

The course of Lily's illness ran smooth, and as the days passed Waythorn grew used to the idea of Haskett's weekly visit. The first time the day came round, he stayed out late, and questioned his wife as to the visit on his return. She replied at once that Haskett had merely seen the nurse downstairs, as the doctor did not wish any one in the child's sick-room till after the crisis.

The following week Waythorn was again conscious of the recurrence of the day, but had forgotten it by the time he came home to dinner. The crisis of the disease came a few days later, with a rapid decline of fever, and the little girl was pronounced out of danger. In the rejoicing which ensued the thought of Haskett passed out of Waythorn's mind, and one afternoon, letting himself into the house with a latchkey, he went straight to his library without noticing a shabby hat and umbrella in the hall.

In the library he found a small effaced-looking man with a thinnish gray beard sitting on the edge of a chair. The stranger might have been a piano-tuner, or one of those mysteriously efficient persons who are summoned in emergencies to adjust some detail of the domestic machinery. He blinked at Waythorn through a pair of gold-rimmed spectacles and said mildly: "Mr. Waythorn, I presume? I am Lily's father."

Waythorn flushed. "Oh—" he stammered uncomfortably. He broke off, disliking to appear rude. Inwardly he was trying to adjust the actual Haskett to the image of him projected by his wife's reminiscences. Waythorn had been allowed to infer that Alice's first husband was a brute.

"I am sorry to intrude," said Haskett, with his over-the-counter politeness.

"Don't mention it," returned Waythorn, collecting himself. "I suppose the nurse has been told?"

"I presume so. I can wait," said Haskett. He had a resigned way of speaking, as though life had worn down his natural powers of resistance.

Waythorn stood on the threshold, nervously pulling off his gloves.

"I'm sorry you've been detained. I will send for the nurse," he said; and as he opened the door he added with an effort: "I'm glad we can give you a good report of Lily." He winced as the *we* slipped out, but Haskett seemed not to notice it.

"Thank you, Mr. Waythorn. It's been an anxious time for me."

"Ah, well, that's past. Soon she'll be able to go to you." Waythorn nodded and passed out.

In his own room he flung himself down with a groan. He hated the womanish sensibility which made him suffer so acutely from the grotesque chances of life. He had known when he married that his wife's former husbands were both living, and that amid the multiplied contacts of modern existence there were a thousand chances to one that he would run against one or the other, yet he found himself as much disturbed by his brief encounter with Haskett as though the law had not obligingly removed all difficulties in the way of their meeting.

Waythorn sprang up and began to pace the room nervously. He had not suffered half as much from his two meetings with Varick. It was Haskett's presence in his own house that made the situation so intolerable. He stood still, hearing steps in the passage.

"This way, please," he heard the nurse say. Haskett was being taken upstairs, then: not a corner of the house but was open to him. Waythorn dropped into another chair, staring vaguely ahead of him. On his dressing-table stood a photograph of Alice, taken when he had first known her. She was Alice Varick then—how fine and exquisite he had thought her! Those were Varick's pearls about her neck. At Waythorn's insistance they had been returned before her marriage. Had Haskett ever given her any trinkets—and what had become of them, Waythorn wondered? He realised suddenly that he knew very little of Haskett's past or present situation; but from the man's appearance and manner of speech he could reconstruct with curious precision the surroundings of Alice's first marriage. And it startled him to think that she had, in the background of her life, a phase of existence so different from anything with which he had connected her. Varick, whatever his faults, was a gentleman, in the conventional, traditional sense of the term: the sense which at that moment seemed, oddly enough, to have most meaning to Waythorn. He and Varick had the same social habits, spoke the same language, understood the same allusions. But this other man . . . it was grotesquely uppermost in Waythorn's mind that Haskett had worn a made-up tie attached with an elastic. Why should that ridiculous detail symbolise the whole man? Waythorn was exasperated by his own paltriness, but the fact of the tie expanded, forced itself on him, became as it were the key to Alice's past. He could see her, as Mrs. Haskett, sitting in a "front parlour" furnished in plush, with a pianola, and a copy of "Ben Hur" on the centre-table. He could see her going to the theatre with Haskett—or perhaps even to a "Church Sociable" —she in a "picture hat" and Haskett in a black frock-coat, a little creased, with the made-up tie on an elastic. On the way home they would stop and look at the illuminated shop-windows, lingering over the photographs of New York actresses. On Sunday afternoons Haskett would take her for a walk, pushing Lily ahead of them in a white enamelled perambulator, and Waythorn had a vision of the people they would stop and talk to. He could fancy how pretty Alice must have looked, in a dress adroitly constructed from the hints of a New York fashion-paper, and how she must have looked down on the other women, chafing at her life, and secretly feeling that she belonged in a bigger place.

For the moment his foremost thought was one of wonder at the way in which she had shed the phase of existence which her marriage with Haskett implied. It was as if her whole aspect, every gesture, every inflection, every allusion, were a studied negation of that period of her life. If she had denied being married to Haskett she could hardly have stood more convicted of duplicity than in this obliteration of the self which had been his wife.

Waythorn started up, checking himself in the analysis of her motives. What right had he to create a fantastic effigy of her and then pass judgment on it? She had spoken vaguely of her first marriage as unhappy, had hinted, with becoming reticence, that Haskett had wrought havoc among her young illusions. . . It was a pity for Waythorn's peace of mind that Haskett's very inoffensiveness shed a new light on the nature of those illusions. A man would rather think that his wife has been brutalised by her first husband than that the process has been reversed.

IV

"Mr. Waythorn, I don't like that French governess of Lily's."

Haskett, subdued and apologetic, stood before Waythorn in the library, revolving his shabby hat in his hand.

Waythorn, surprised in his armchair over the evening paper, stared back perplexedly at his visitor.

"You'll excuse my asking to see you," Haskett continued. "But this is my last visit, and I thought if I could have a word with you it would be a better way than writing to Mrs. Waythorn's lawyer."

Waythorn rose uneasily. He did not like the French governess either; but that was irrelevant.

"I am not so sure of that," he returned stiffly; "but since you wish it I will give your message to—my wife." He always hesitated over the possessive pronoun in addressing Haskett.

The latter sighed. "I don't know as that will help much. She didn't like it when I spoke to her."

Waythorn turned red. "When did you see her?" he asked.

"Not since the first day I came to see Lily—right after she was taken sick. I remarked to her then that I didn't like the governess."

Waythorn made no answer. He remembered distinctly that, after that first visit, he had asked his wife if she had seen Haskett. She had lied to him then, but she had respected his wishes since; and the incident cast a curious light on her character. He was sure she would not have seen Haskett that first day if she had divined that Waythorn would object, and the fact that she did not divine it was almost as disagreeable to the latter as the discovery that she had lied to him.

"I don't like the woman," Haskett was repeating with mild persistency. "She ain't straight, Mr. Waythorn—she'll teach the child to be underhand. I've noticed a change in Lily—she's too anxious to please—and she don't always tell truth. She used to be the straightest child, Mr. Waythorn—" He broke off, his voice a little thick. "Not but what I want her to have a stylish education," he ended.

Waythorn was touched. "I'm sorry, Mr. Haskett; but frankly, I don't quite see what I can do."

Haskett hesitated. Then he laid his hat on the table, and advanced to the hearth-rug, on which Waythorn was standing. There was nothing aggressive in his manner, but he had the solemnity of a timid man resolved on a decisive measure.

"There's just one thing you can do, Mr. Waythorn," he said. "You can remind Mrs. Waythorn that, by the decree of the courts, I am entitled to have a voice in Lily's bringing up." He paused, and went on more deprecatingly: "I'm not the kind to talk about enforcing my rights, Mr. Waythorn. I don't know as I think a man is entitled to rights he hasn't known how to hold on to; but this business of the child is different. I've never let go there—and I never mean to."

The scene left Waythorn deeply shaken. Shamefacedly, in indirect ways, he had been finding out about Haskett; and all that he had learned was favourable. The little man, in order to be near his daughter, had sold out his share in a profitable business in Utica, and accepted a modest clerkship in a New York manufacturing house. He boarded in a shabby street and had few acquaintances. His passion for Lily filled his life. Waythorn felt that this exploration of Haskett was like groping about with a dark-lantern in his wife's past; but he saw now that there were recesses his lantern had not explored. He had never enquired into the exact circumstances of his wife's first matrimonial rupture. On the surface all had been fair. It was she who had obtained the divorce, and the court had given her the child. But Waythorn knew how many ambiguities such a verdict might cover. The mere fact that Haskett retained a right over his daughter implied an unsuspected compromise. Waythorn was an idealist. He always refused to recognise unpleasant contingencies till he found himself confronted with them, and then he saw them followed by a spectral train of consequences. His next days were thus haunted, and he determined to try to lay the ghosts by conjuring them up in his wife's presence.

When he repeated Haskett's request a flame of anger passed over her face; but she subdued it instantly and spoke with a slight quiver of outraged motherhood.

"It is very ungentlemanly of him," she said.

The word grated on Waythorn. "That is neither here nor there. It's a bare question of rights."

She murmured: "It's not as if he could ever be a help to Lily—"

Waythorn flushed. This was even less to his taste. "The question is," he repeated, "what authority has he over her?"

She looked downward, twisting herself a little in her seat. "I am willing to see him—I thought you objected," she faltered.

In a flash he understood that she knew the extent of Haskett's claims. Perhaps it was not the first time she had resisted them.

"My objecting has nothing to do with it," he said coldly; "if Haskett has a right to be consulted you must consult him."

She burst into tears, and he saw that she expected him to regard her as a victim.

Haskett did not abuse his rights. Waythorn had felt miserably sure that he would not. But the governess was dismissed, and from time to time the little man demanded an interview with Alice. After the first outburst she accepted the situation with her usual adaptability. Haskett had once reminded Waythorn of the piano-tuner, and Mrs. Waythorn, after a month or two, appeared to class him with that domestic familiar. Waythorn could not but respect the father's tenacity. At first he had tried to cultivate the suspicion that Haskett might be "up to" something, that he had an object in securing a foothold in the house. But in his heart Waythorn was sure of Haskett's single-mindedness; he even guessed in the latter a mild contempt for such advantages as his relation with the Waythorns might offer. Haskett's sincerity of purpose made him invulnerable, and his successor had to accept him as a lien on the property.

Mr. Sellers was sent to Europe to recover from his gout, and Varick's affairs hung on Waythorn's hands. The negotiations were prolonged and complicated; they necessitated frequent conferences between the two men, and the interests of the firm forbade Waythorn's suggesting that his client should transfer his business to another office.

Varick appeared well in the transaction. In moments of relaxation his coarse streak appeared, and Waythorn dreaded his geniality; but in the office he was concise and clear-headed, with a flattering deference to Waythorn's judgment. Their business relations being so affably established, it would have been absurd for the two men to ignore each other in society. The first time they met in a drawing-room, Varick took up their intercourse in the same easy key, and his hostess's grateful glance obliged Waythorn to respond to it. After that they ran across each other frequently, and one evening at a ball Waythorn, wandering through the remoter rooms, came upon Varick seated beside his wife. She coloured a little, and faltered in what she was saying; but Varick nodded to Waythorn without rising, and the latter strolled on.

In the carriage, on the way home, he broke out nervously: "I didn't know you spoke to Varick."

Her voice trembled a little. "It's the first time—he happened to be standing near me; I didn't know what to do. It's so awkward, meeting everywhere—and he said you had been very kind about some business."

"That's different," said Waythorn.

She paused a moment. "I'll do just as you wish," she returned pliantly. "I thought it would be less awkward to speak to him when we meet."

Her pliancy was beginning to sicken him. Had she really no will of her own—no theory about her relation to these men? She had accepted Haskett—did she mean to accept Varick? It was "less awkward," as she had said, and her instinct was to evade difficulties or to circumvent them. With sudden vividness Waythorn saw how the instinct had developed. She was "as easy as an old shoe"—a shoe that too many feet had worn. Her elasticity was the result of tension in too many different directions. Alice Haskett—Alice Varick—Alice Waythorn—she had been each in turn, and had left hanging to each name a little of her privacy, a little of her personality, a little of the inmost self where the unknown god abides.

"Yes—it's better to speak to Varick," said Waythorn wearily.

V

The winter wore on, and society took advantage of the Waythorns' acceptance of Varick. Harassed hostesses were grateful to them for bridging over a social difficulty, and Mrs. Waythorn was held up as a miracle of good taste. Some experimental spirits could not resist the diversion of throwing Varick and his former wife together, and there were those who thought he found a zest in the propinquity. But Mrs. Waythorn's conduct remained irreproachable. She neither avoided Varick nor sought him out. Even Waythorn could not but admit that she had discovered the solution of the newest social problem.

He had married her without giving much thought to that problem. He had fancied that a woman can shed her past like a man. But now he saw that Alice was bound to hers both by the circumstances which forced her into continued relation with it, and by the traces it had left on her nature. With grim irony Waythorn compared himself to a member of a syndicate. He held so many shares in his wife's personality and his predecessors were his partners in the business. If there had been any element of passion in the transaction he would have felt less deteriorated by it. The fact that Alice took her change of husbands like a change of weather reduced the situation to mediocrity. He could have forgiven her for blunders, for excesses; for resisting Haskett, for yielding to Varick; for anything but her acquiescence and her tact. She reminded him of a juggler tossing knives; but the knives were blunt and she knew they would never cut her.

And then, gradually, habit formed a protecting surface for his sensibilities. If he paid for each day's comfort with the small change of his illusions, he grew daily to value the comfort more and set less store upon the coin. He had drifted into a dulling propinquity with Haskett and Varick and he took refuge in the cheap revenge of satirising the situation. He even began to reckon up the advantages which accrued from it, to ask himself if it were not better to own a third of a wife who knew how to make a man happy than a whole one who had lacked opportunity to acquire the art. For it *was* an art, and made up, like all others, of concessions, eliminations and embellishments; of lights judiciously thrown and shadows skillfully softened. His wife knew exactly how to manage the lights, and he knew exactly to what training she owed her skill. He even tried to trace the source of his obligations, to discriminate between the influences which had combined to produce his domestic happiness: he perceived that Haskett's commonness had made Alice worship good breeding, while Varick's liberal construction of the marriage bond had taught her to value the conjugal virtues; so that he was directly indebted to his predecessors for the devotion which made his life easy if not inspiring.

From this phase he passed into that of complete acceptance. He ceased to satirise himself because time dulled the irony of the situation and the joke lost its humour with its sting. Even the sight of Haskett's hat on the hall table had ceased to touch the springs of epigram. The hat was often seen there now, for it had been decided that it was better for Lily's father to visit her than for the little girl to go to his boarding-house. Waythorn, having acquiesced in this arrangement, had been surprised to find how little difference it made. Haskett was never obtrusive, and the few visitors who met him on the stairs were unaware of his identity. Waythorn did not know how often he saw Alice, but with himself Haskett was seldom in contact.

One afternoon, however, he learned on entering that Lily's father was waiting to see him. In the library he found Haskett occupying a chair in his usual provisional way. Waythorn always felt grateful to him for not leaning back.

"I hope you'll excuse me, Mr. Waythorn," he said rising. "I wanted to see Mrs. Waythorn about Lily, and your man asked me to wait here till she came in."

"Of course," said Waythorn, remembering that a sudden leak had that morning given over the drawing-room to the plumbers.

He opened his cigar-case and held it out to his visitor, and Haskett's acceptance seemed to mark a fresh stage in their intercourse. The spring evening was chilly, and Waythorn invited his guest to draw up his chair to the fire. He meant to find an excuse to leave Haskett in a moment; but he was tired and cold, and after all the little man no longer jarred on him.

The two were enclosed in the intimacy of their blended cigar-smoke when the door opened and Varick walked into the room. Waythorn rose abruptly. It was the first time that Varick had come to the house, and the surprise of seeing him, combined with the singular inopportuneness of his arrival, gave a new edge to Waythorn's blunted sensibilities. He stared at his visitor without speaking.

Varick seemed too preoccupied to notice his host's embarrassment.

"My dear fellow," he exclaimed in his most expansive tone, "I must apologise for tumbling in on you in this way, but I was too late to catch you down town, and so I thought—"

He stopped short, catching sight of Haskett, and his sanguine colour deepened to a flush which spread vividly under his scant blond hair. But in a moment he recovered himself and nodded slightly. Haskett returned the bow in silence, and Waythorn was still groping for speech when the footman came in carrying a tea-table.

The intrusion offered a welcome vent to Waythorn's nerves. "What the deuce are you bringing this here for?" he said sharply.

"I beg your pardon, sir, but the plumbers are still in the drawing-room, and Mrs. Waythorn said she would have tea in the library." The footman's perfectly respectful tone implied a reflection on Waythorn's reasonableness.

"Oh, very well," said the latter resignedly, and the footman proceeded to open the folding tea-table and set out its complicated appointments. While this interminable process continued the three men stood motionless, watching it with a fascinated stare, till Waythorn, to break the silence, said to Varick: "Won't you have a cigar?"

He held out the case he had just tendered to Haskett, and Varick helped himself with a smile. Waythorn looked about for a match, and finding none, proffered a light from his own cigar. Haskett, in the background, held his ground mildly, examining his cigar-tip now and then, and stepping forward at the right moment to knock its ashes into the fire.

The footman at last withdrew, and Varick immediately began: "If I could just say half a word to you about this business—"

"Certainly," stammered Waythorn; "in the dining-room—"

But as he placed his hand on the door it opened from without, and his wife appeared on the threshold.

She came in fresh and smiling, in her street dress and hat, shedding a fragrance from the boa which she loosened in advancing.

"Shall we have tea in here, dear?" she began; and then she caught sight of Varick. Her smile deepened, veiling a slight tremor of surprise.

"Why, how do you do?" she said with a distinct note of pleasure.

As she shook hands with Varick she saw Haskett standing behind him. Her smile faded for a moment, but she recalled it quickly, with a scarcely perceptible side-glance at Waythorn.

"How do you do, Mr. Haskett?" she said, and shook hands with him a shade less cordially.

The three men stood awkwardly before her, till Varick, always the most self-possessed, dashed into an explanatory phrase.

"We—I had to see Waythorn a moment on business," he stammered, brick-red from chin to nape.

Haskett stepped forward with his air of mild obstinacy. "I am sorry to intrude; but you appointed five o'clock." He directed his resigned glance to the time-piece on the mantel.

She swept aside their embarrassment with a charming gesture of hospitality.

"I'm so sorry—I'm always late; but the afternoon was so lovely." She stood drawing off her gloves, propitiatory and graceful, diffusing about her a sense of ease and familiarity in which the situation lost its grotesqueness. "But before talking business," she added brightly, "I'm sure every one wants a cup of tea."

She dropped into her low chair by the tea-table, and the two visitors, as if drawn by her smile, advanced to receive the cups she held out.

She glanced about for Waythorn, and he took the third cup with a laugh.